SUPERPO(

A Click Your Po

by
James Schannep

The eAversion Version

First Print Edition

This book is a work of fiction. Names, characters, businesses, organizations, places, events, and incidents are either the product of the author's imagination or are used fictitiously. Any resemblance to actual persons, living or dead, events, or locales is entirely coincidental. Popular culture elements were used to give a sense of time and place or out of parody.

Copyright © 2015 by James Schannep

All rights reserved.
Print Edition
www.jamesschannep.com

Library of Congress Cataloging-in-Publication Data
Schannep, James, 1984—
SUPERPOWERED: a Click Your Poison book / James Schannep

1. Superheroes—Fiction.
2. Human experimentation in medicine—Fiction. I. Title

COVER ART BY BRIAN SILVEIRA

This book has been modified from its original version. It has been formatted to fit this page.

ISBN-10: 1508551901
ISBN-13: 978-1508551904

Here's how it works: You, Dear Reader, are the main character of this story. Save the world or conquer it; the choice is yours. Do not read this book front to back. Instead, follow the choices at the end of each chapter to the next section. The story evolves based on your decisions, so choose wisely.
Are you a hero or a villain?

Click Your Poison books

***INFECTED**—Will YOU Survive the Zombie Apocalypse?*
***MURDERED**—Can YOU Solve the Mystery?*
***SUPERPOWERED**—Will YOU Be a Hero or a Villain?*
***PATHOGENS**—More Zombocalypse Survival Stories!*
***MAROONED**—Can YOU Endure Treachery and Survival on the High Seas?*
***SPIED (coming in 2019)**—Can YOU Save the World as a Secret Agent?*

* More titles coming soon! *

Sign up for the new release mailing list at: http://eepurl.com/bdWUBb
Or visit the author's blog at www.jameschannep.com

For my father, who chose the hero path.

Acknowledgments

Special thanks to my wife, Michaela, the patron of my art. Your insight and patience were essential to the creation of this book. A big thanks to my readers and beta testers: Chris Boyes, Brian Yoakam, Mike Beeson, Ben Chapman, Tom Stein, Christie LeBlanc, Nate Davis, and Kelli Mears.

To my copyeditor: Linda Jay Geldens, cover artist: Brian Silveira, and to Paul Salvette and the team at BB eBooks. Thanks also to Matt "Opus" Fuller for helping bring the new CYP logo to life. Thank you all for your generosity and professionalism.

And to my friends and family, for your unyielding encouragement, enthusiasm and support.

SUPERPOWERED

"Hello, you there! Yes, you. Got five minutes to change your life?" a man says.

He is at home in his lab coat and wears a reassuring smile, that of a doctor featured in an infomercial, complete with stylish thin-rimmed glasses that sink into graying-at-the-temples hair. He hands you a pamphlet:

UNLOCK YOUR POTENTIAL!!! SUPERCHARGE YOUR HUMANITY!!!
EARN $500!!!

"What's this all about?" you ask. It just so happens you're walking past the University campus, but, five hundred bucks for five minutes?

"Today's your lucky day," the man says with a manic grin. He bids you to follow as he explains, speaking almost too fast for you to keep up. "The oft-perpetuated myth about using only 10% of our brains, while unfounded, is an intriguing concept. I believe this to be true—not for the mind per se, but for that of human DNA. So many of the genes we carry are turned off. Dormant. Waiting for us to evolve. The purpose of this experiment is to 'supercharge' your humanity and see if we can't extend mankind's potential."

He pulls open the double doors of a building marked CHEMISTRY LAB.

It's a sunny day and the laboratory is dark inside, but you can see thick black cables snaking their way to a large central platform. You step forward. A gymnasium-sized tarp is draped over three pillar-shaped objects. Suspended above each object are what look like giant electromagnets—similar to the ones used to lower cars into compactors at the junkyard, except these are the size of a manhole cover.

"Just step into one of my pods and change your life," he says. The man holds out five crisp hundred-dollar bills and a clipboard, adding, "Right after you sign this waiver."

- ➢ "No, thanks. Pretty sure that homeless guy around the corner can help you out, though." Go to page 64
- ➢ "Yeah, okay, I've got nothing better to do." Go to page 303

Ace Up Your Sleeve

Incredibly, ignoring Nick and Droakam seems to work. The next week goes by remarkably fast, despite several battles with mobsters, terrorists, and garden-variety criminals.

You finally come up with a costumed persona—*The Flying Ace!* The design is nearly identical to the "Diamond" look, but you go with royal blue for your mask (and you get a cape, which makes flying more dramatic). Rather than a diamond, you end up with the "spade" symbol on your chest. The tights take some getting used to, but the lightweight fabric gives you a larger margin of error for your powers' weight limit.

Meanwhile—not a peep from the Supersoldier Program. But with each victory, your public support grows by leaps and bounds. And once the mayor gives you the key to the city, the super-genius finally swings by.

"I wanted to let you know I'm leaving," Nick says. "I set up so many traps, waiting for the two of you to fall into them…I felt like a spider tending to its web. It got boring. Agent Droakam isn't riveting company, to be honest. Then I saw the public adoration you received for your superheroism, and something clicked.

"The three of us might have made a good team, in another life. I'm going to Europe—back to 'The Old Country,' as Nana used to call it—where I can get the love of an entire continent.

"I guess I just wanted to say good luck, no hard feelings, and not to worry about Agent Droakam. I hacked into the database and told his superiors to fire the guy. The Supersoldier Program has been cancelled for good, and he's a desk jockey stationed somewhere very, very cold. Well, take care."

That's it, you win. Sort of. Nick heads to Europe as promised, where he dons an incredibly ostentatious white-and-gold caped superhero costume and becomes Citizen Nikolai. The outfit, while impressive, looks like it was designed by mashing up Napoleonic cavalry uniforms with WWII-era iconoclast propaganda.

You keep waiting for a supervillain to appear, or for Nick to dub himself Emperor of Europe, but it never happens. Instead, you're relegated to being Catherine's sidekick. She's *The Amazing Diamond* and you get to be *Acey*, then eventually, *Kid Ace*.

Children across the globe tell their younger siblings, "Sure, you can play Amazing Diamond and Citizen Nikolai with us—you get to be Kid Ace."

Maybe a scandalous reality show (call it, *Ace is Wild*) could spice up your reputation?

THE END

Acme Portals

You program the staff to open a portal to "the harshest reality," and assume the device knows you're not being metaphysical. Soon, the air sparks and the shimmering purple gate appears once more.

"After you," you say.

"Oh, no, after you. I insist," Nick says.

"Catherine? This was your idea."

"Ladies first," she says glibly, then steps through the portal.

Nick turns to you. In a feint, you slide a hand behind his back and shove him through the portal. Then you shut it down. That takes care of that! Now, with super-strength *and* super-genius, this world will cower before you.

You win…sort of.

"What are you going to do with me?" your doppelganger asks.

With a sudden flash of inspiration, you say, "You have war crimes to answer for."

With a patsy to take the blame, you can rise up from the shadows. Once you've taken over the world, you can always free your other-self.

Part of you fears—knows—Nick and Catherine will be back one day; you just have to hope you're ready for them.

THE END…for now

Agent of Evil

The nearest SWAT member lunges, ready to slam you down onto your chest and handcuff you. But that's not going to happen. Instead, you *blast* the man across the room, smashing him into the SWAT member who was about to tackle Nick.

Then you turn to Agent Droakam, *flip* open his coat, and *pull* his pistol out of its holster and into your outstretched hand. You keep the weapon trained on the agent and step behind him, using the man as a human shield.

"Nobody move!" you shout.

Next, rather than commanding that they drop their weapons, you mentally disarm the rest of the men by *pulling* their weapons away. At the same time, Nick keys in the microphone.

"Doomsday Device: Execute Escape Plan Zulu," Nick shouts, then to you, "Nice work, let's go."

The supergenius yanks out the power cord to the computer terminal, pulls out a handgun that was concealed under the desk, and beats a hasty retreat. You step out behind him, mentally *slam* the door shut, and spin around. Several of the casino security personnel stand just outside of the room, staring at you in disbelief.

"Those aren't cops," you say. "They're, umm, foot soldiers from a rival crime lord."

"*de César's* men?" says one of the guards.

"Yes, exactly. If they try to follow us, shoot them on sight and receive double your salary as a bonus."

Nick gives a curt nod, then turns and heads away. "Who is *de César*?"

"No clue. Let's go!"

You follow Nick around the corner towards the penthouse elevator.

"You two are *dead meat!*" a voice booms. Even before you look, you know who it is. Supa-gurl. Diamond. Catherine Woodall. She stands as a seething powerhouse of fury.

Great. What now?

Just as you're about to decide, a metal freight train comes from a side hall and Doomsday plows into Catherine, smashing her through the far wall. An instant later, the robot flies back into the hallway on its back, Catherine on top of it. She pummels the robot with machine-gun-fire rapid-succession punches.

Yet, somehow, Doomsday is unharmed. It backhands the comparably small woman away, then rises to its feet with inhumanly smooth movements.

"The Doomsday Device has an exoskeleton up-armored with *carbyne*—very expensive to make, but worth it. Most notable for being one of the few carbon-based materials stronger than diamond."

Doomsday kicks Catherine in her ribs, sending her skittering down the hall on her side.

Nick grins. "Get it? Stronger than *Diamond!*"

Catherine leaps to her feet, grabs the robot by its arm, and swings the expensive machine in a circle before she discus-hurls Doomsday through another section of the wall.

"Yeah, I get it," you say. "But it doesn't look like it can hurt her, either. What's the plan? Keep her busy while we escape?"

Nick keys the penthouse elevator. "It might be a stalemate, if the Doomsday Device were alive like her. As it is, she's a living creature fighting an autonomous weapon."

"Meaning?"

Doomsday comes back into the fray and the behemoth machine unloads its own barrage of punches, before grappling Catherine in a headlock. The robot looks up to the pair of you as you step into the elevator, then smiles an LED-filled smile. Several vents open on the robot's surface and water-vapor gas pours out in a cloud to engulf the pair of them. The illuminated smile still shines through the gas.

Catherine reaches inside one of the vents and rips out a handful of wires and circuitry. Doomsday stumbles. She then shoves a fist inside its chest-vent and pushes through with all her strength. The smile dims. The robot's head pops off, her fist protruding through the neck hole.

She takes her arm back out, and drops the disabled machine to the floor. Then she comes for the two of you. She takes two steps and starts to cough. To *hack*, really. Drool streams from her mouth, mucous from her nose, and tears from her eyes.

Just before the elevator doors start to close, Catherine falls face-down on the hallway floor.

"Sarin gas," Nick announces.

"That's Plan Zulu?"

"Not quite; let's get up to the roof."

"What about her?"

"Catherine? She's most certainly dead," Nick says.

The elevator doors close.

Though the penthouse has no rooftop access, you can easily *float* Nick up there from the balcony, then fly up to join him. Nick heads straight to the helipad and enters the helicopter as if it'd been waiting for him the whole time. You join him in the passenger seat.

"You know how to fly a helicopter?" you say, donning the headset.

"I study various disciplines in my off-time. I think faster than normal people, so I actually have longer days than the rest of you. Relatively speaking."

With that, the helicopter takes off from the roof and the two of you escape. You win, sort of. Catherine is defeated, Agent Droakam was murdered by casino henchmen, and the two of you spend the rest of your days as criminal kingpins.

The bad news is that you're vilified. Had Nick's plan gone off without that meddling agent, you'd be free to live in the limelight. As it stands, you can rule much of the city, but you must do so underground.

Good news is, you'll probably find out who *de César* is.

THE END

Always a Bridesmaid, Never a Supervillain

You win…kind of. Teaming up with Nick isn't a bad move. With that genius-filled cranium on his shoulders, the full resources of the Supersoldier Program at his disposal, and you—his right-hand *Superman*—he's bound to go far. And indeed he does.

Within a matter of days, he's dealt with Catherine. You don't ask how, and he doesn't volunteer any information, but you never see her again. By the end of the month, he's made himself *Agent* Nick Dorian, head of the Supersoldier Division—at this point it's no longer a program, but a full force of superpowered henchmen ready to do their commander's bidding. Don't worry, you're always awarded "Henchperson of the Month."

By the end of the year, Nick overthrows the United States government. Time really flies when you're having fun, and Nick tends to laugh with maniacal glee after each victory. You're absolutely, one-hundred percent certain that'll he'll rule the entire world before he turns 30.

And yet, it all feels hollow somehow. What did you really accomplish? Except, perhaps, unwittingly aiding Nick's original deception against Agent Droakam. It's the winner's curse. Sure, you'll never want for anything again, but you won't leave your own stamp on the world, either. You're destined to be nothing more than a footnote in Nikolai the Conqueror's history books.

Maybe you should write your memoirs? *Henchperson of the Month* has "bestseller" written all over it.

THE END

Always Split Pairs

Best to go your separate ways. There's only room for one winning hand, and Nick will understand. He'll learn to, anyway. He certainly glowered before he left, but you can chalk that up to the angst of youth and the "It's not fair!" battle cry. Enough thoughts wasted on Nick. Time to enact your battle plan: *First, Mercury City, and then, the world!*

Phase one? Well, you've already got wealth, so what's next? Phase two: Influence. But how? If there's one man who stands as "most influential" in the city....

The Mayor! Of course, if there's one man with influence, it has to be him. The police answer to him, he controls the money for public works, and he alone has the power to mobilize the city when necessary. So, how do you get him into your pocket?

Time to go pay Mayor Argyle—father of intrepid reporter Alison Argyle, the city's most eligible bachelorette—a visit.

You leap off the penthouse balcony (an action that's starting to lose its suicidal feel) and *fly* downtown toward the civic offices. The city government suite has a distinct look. It doesn't take someone with an intimate knowledge of city politics to figure out which office is his; it's the largest, with the picture windows.

Those windows you presently rap against, as you *float* three stories up.

Mayor Argyle looks up from his desk, then back to his paperwork. His brow furrows and he looks up again. You wave him over, a grinning fairytale apparition, and gesture for him to open the window. Sure, you could *smash* the glass or even use your telekinesis to open the latch from the inside, but you don't want to frighten the man. Not yet.

He sits perfectly still, takes off his glasses, cleans them, and seems shocked all over again to find you still there. As if you were merely a smudge he might clean off.

All smiles, you wave him over. The mayor rises and slowly walks toward you. You gesture once more for him to open the window. In a dreamlike state, he obeys.

"You can't…you're not allowed…." he says, trying to frame a statement through the shock.

"It's okay, I just wanted to pay you a visit. We're going to be good friends, you and I."

"We are?" he says, just like a child. "You can fly?"

"One of my many talents. I wanted to introduce myself and tell you I'm in your service. Call upon me whenever needed, and I hope that I can do the same of you, my friend."

How to get him in your pocket? By making him think you're in his.

"Do you have anything to do with this 'Supa-gurl' everyone's going on about?" he asks, starting to recover his sense. He must be talking about Catherine, the woman from the experiment.

"In a manner of speaking, though her actions do not reflect mine. In fact, if you ever think she's a problem, we can work together."

He nods, about to say something, but a loud and insistent pounding comes from the other side of his door. He looks toward the sound, then back to you.

"I pushed the silent alarm," he confesses.

The door bursts open, and a team of four security men rush in. Oh, boy, well, maybe it's for the best? A chance to give Mayor Argyle a display of what you can do.

They can only funnel through the doorway one at a time, and that gives you an advantage. You *blast* into the men with a psychic shockwave, knocking them all backward. In panic, the mayor hides behind his desk. That probably won't do much toward calling off security….

The first man is up on his feet again and draws his handgun. You reach out and *break* his wrist with the power of your mind. He drops the gun and staggers out of the way.

You *grab* the next two men and telekinetically bash their heads together, incapacitating them. The fourth man, standing in the doorway, holds his handgun, which is aimed at you, firmly with both hands. He's about to fire.

You probably can't pull the weapon, and shoving him will most likely cause him to shoot you. In an instinctual burst of inspiration, you *pull* the man into the room and duck down at the same time. You then *fling* him through the room and out the window behind you.

There's a scream and a thud, then silence. It was only three stories—he'll live.

You walk over to the mayor's desk and extend your hand. He takes it and you help him to his feet. "Another of my many talents," you say.

Mayor Argyle nods. "So…we're friends?"

"We're friends," you say with a smile.

Then you leap out of the window and into the sky. That was close, too close, but you've got the mayor in your pocket now. Nicely done.

➢ *Head back to your penthouse to relax and unwind.* Go to page 275

And Then There Were Two

*"**N**ICK!!!"* you boom through superpowered lungs. He turns to you (along with everyone in a whole city block), and floats your way. "I need to talk with you somewhere more…private."

"Yeah, okay. I'm all done 'making it rain' here anyway. There's a great pub just around the corner."

You scratch your chin. "How big are the portions?"

The pub is just far enough away to escape the commotion, but there's a bit of a wait, so you opt to sit at the bar. After confirming that you can order food up here, of course.

"Gimme a pint of Quicksilver Ale," Nick says.

The bartender brushes a shock of platinum blonde behind her ear, where it's somewhat hidden amongst raven hair, and gives the college student an appraising glance. "Can I see some ID?"

"No, you can't," he replies.

She gives him her best blank, unimpressed stare.

"Okay, fine, I'll get it myself."

"Nick, wait…" You try, but it's too late.

Nick reaches out his hand and causes a pint glass to rise off the shelf behind the bar. Using his telekinesis, the glass floats over to the tap and fills up with golden, hoppy ale. Then the drink finds its way to his outstretched hand and finally to his lips.

"Mmm, that's good."

The bartender stares at Nick in wide-eyed disbelief while you give him a peevish glare.

"Oh, relax. Listen, David Blaine is at the Planet Mercury Casino, and I'm his understudy. Ta-da! Street magic."

That's when your food arrives. You couldn't decide between three different burgers, and now the waiter sets all three in front of you. Famished, you dig in. Nick sips his beer and watches the news report of his exploits on the TV above the bar.

"Robbing banks, huh?" you say in-between bites.

"Actually, I stopped a robbery-in-progress, but you won't hear that on the news. I suppose 'flying criminal' is a little more of a ratings boost. But I didn't steal anything, I just gave back to the people. The real thieves already took the money, and I figured I'd pass it along." He shrugs, then continues, "I guess I'm like a cross between Peter Pan and Robin Hood. Maybe my superhero name should be *Peter Hood.*"

"'Peter Hood?' Why not just name yourself 'Foreskin' and save people the time?"

Nick laughs. "What's your deal, anyway?"

- ➤ "I'm here to warn you. If you go around using your powers in public…you could get hurt." Go to page 254
- ➤ "If you want to be a superhero, I've got a better way." Tell Nick about the Supersoldier Program. Go to page 193

Angel of Music

You leap from the bed, rip the electrodes from your chest and pull out the IV—*ouch!* Nick and Catherine try to reason with you, but you *shove* everything away from you. The hospital bed flies to the periphery. Even Nick is pinned against the wall, yet Catherine doesn't budge.

"Leave!" you cry. "Leave me alone, or you will curse the day you did not do all that The Phantom asked of you."

You release Nick. He dusts himself off and says, "The Phantom exists inside your mind."

"*GO!*" you shout.

You *shove* Nick out the door. Then you turn toward Catherine and glare at her through the mask and scars, eyes filled with hatred.

"Think of me fondly," Catherine says before she turns and leaves.

Once you're alone, you find The Phantom costume hanging near the bathroom. You don it as you might your true skin, then fly out the hospital window.

Now it's only a matter of finding your own *Opera Populaire* (preferably above an intricate sewer system) to haunt. Once there, you'll get your own private booth, or damned if you won't drop sandbags on those who stand in your way.

Then, if you're really lucky, you'll find an orphan, whom you'll one day fall in love with, you can raise as a surrogate child. It won't be creepy. At. All.

THE END

Angry

"*Reproduce* the results? You fool! Don't you realize what we've got here? If Nick's got an ability anything like yours or mine…you don't just give that away! Why would you want to give the government what we've got? Why would you want to share this?"

"Didn't mamma teach you to share with the other kids?" That's smug, but it's the first thing to pop into your mind.

"Don't you dare. You're the one behaving like a child. Do you really think the government would just give these abilities to everyone? You think we'd all be superhuman?"

Catherine closes her eyes. You realize her fists are clenched and she's shuddering with anger.

"If you don't leave in the next three seconds…One…."

- ➢ She's out of control, a danger to herself and those around her. Stay and fight! Go to page 216
- ➢ Set the phone on the kitchen counter, then leave quickly through the open door. Go to page 106
- ➢ "Wait! I don't like it either, but what choice is there? Isn't it better to work with them than against them?" Go to page 349

An Offer Easily Refused

Nick's shoulders raise and lower quickly and you think you can hear him laughing from inside his helmet. He shakes his head. "It's too late for that. If you'd offered to join forces right away, sure, we could've torn this town a new one. But as it is, there's a bounty on your head that I aim to collect."

He then makes a fist with his right arm pointed at you, while his left hand operates some kind of control panel on the beefy right forearm gauntlet. You stretch your hands out and mentally *feel* for some kind of weapon. If it's a handgun or knife, you'll simply throw it off the building. But what the hell *is* that thing?

The gauntlet hums with life, and the wrist section glows a white-hot blue. Then a pulse bursts out in a ring of energy, growing in size for the split second before it hits you. Everything goes black as you lose consciousness.

When you awake, you'll find yourself in a special superhuman prison designed by Nick and guarded by Catherine, where everything is too heavy for you to move. Prepare to rot away.

THE END

Apex Predator

"Mission accomplished," you say, entering the warehouse.

Agent Droakam stands in front of the enormous computer terminal, his back to you. The man gives no reaction whatsoever. Didn't he hear you?

"Droakam! I did it. Nick's dead."

He shakes his head, still not turning to face you. "I should've gone into the State Department like the other guys. I guarantee Danly and Bertram don't have to put up with this shit in Rio."

"What are you mumbling about? Snap out of it!"

Finally, he turns around. His face is red, like he's about to pop a gasket. "Don't you get what you've done? What kind of an *idiot*—"

"Hey!"

"The whole fucking point of the mission was to keep out of the public eye! You were keeping the Supersoldier Program a secret, dumbass. Dorian was a liability because he used his powers in public, so you figured that using your powers to murder him in front of witnesses who were *recording you* was the best plan of action?"

"You told me to take care of him!" you scream.

"And a fine job you've done."

"Whatever. Fine, how do we fix it?"

Droakam laughs. It's an exasperated, desperate laugh. "There is no *we*! The program is dissolved. I'm on suspension pending investigation, and you're about to go to prison. The police are on their way."

"You called them here?"

Something inside you snaps and in a flash, something inside Agent Droakam snaps. Without a single thought, you backhand the man across the warehouse and through one of the crates. Not waiting for the police to arrive, you turn and run from the warehouse.

The police cannot possibly hope to capture you. Whatever they throw your way simply bounces off. In fact, when a drone strike leaves nothing but a crater where you once stood, they think they've killed you. But even a smart bomb only throws you. Bullets, fire, explosions—none can harm you.

So when Catherine, the woman from the experiment, stares you down with an enormous rifle, you offer an enormous laugh in return. But when the energy beam she fires from the rifle saps your strength, that puts a stop to both your laughter and your reign of terror.

"What did you do to me?" you cry, though you know. You can feel it; your powers are gone.

"Made you mortal," she says. "Enjoy prison."

THE END

Assault with a Super-Weapon

Nick turns to the clerk. "Have you called the cops yet? Tripped a silent alarm?"

The clerk's face is full of confusion, then he slowly shakes his head.

"Why not? You've been listening, haven't you? We're about to reveal ourselves to the world as supervillains! Doesn't that register as important?"

"A lot of weirdos come in here."

"We're not paying for these costumes," you say.

"Okay, in that case, I'll call the cops."

"Not enough," Nick says, shaking his head. "Make sure you mention the assault with a deadly weapon."

Nick turns around and *pulls* a sword from behind a glass case. The case shatters and the sword *windmills* through the air and attacks the clerk. The clerk screams and darts away, trying to hide behind the desk as the sword slashes at him.

It's not sharpened, of course, but it's a hunk of metal and it definitely hurts.

"Okay! I'll make sure the cops chase you guys! Christ!"

The sword clatters to the ground. Nick turns to leave.

"Thanks," you say.

"Ah!" Nick says, then mimes zipping his lips. "Remember, you're silent but deadly."

"Don't call me that."

Out on the street, Nick takes to causing as much havoc as he can. *Shoving* pedestrians, mainly. You follow his cue and start on destruction of property. Newspaper bins and trashcans, though bolted to the sidewalk, sail away like kickballs on the schoolyard. A quick shove, and a parked car tips out into the middle of the road, clogging traffic. You slam a fist through the side of a building and drag your arm through it as you walk, as effortlessly as clearing snow off a handrail.

"That's fucking awesome," Nick says. "Helluva breadcrumb trail, Mime. They'll find us for sure."

You nod. And sure enough, a patrol car arrives after only a few minutes. With a *dwip-dwip* call of the siren, the car pulls over and a uniformed officer steps out.

"Put your hands on top of your heads, and take off the masks."

"Call for backup," Nick says. He raises his arms to his sides and *floats* into the air, essentially flying. The cop calls for backup.

"They call me *Screamer*! Not because of this mask, but because of the screams I induce in others," Nick monologues.

"Sir! Please...please land back on the ground."

Nick drops to the ground, but at the same time *lifts* the cop into the air and *flings* him down the street. The police officer screams, then slams against the pavement and goes silent.

A second patrol car speeds towards you, and you figure it's your turn. You dart out into the street, too soon for them to swerve or brake to avoid a collision, and deliver an uppercut punch to the grill of the car. Immediately, the car flips backwards and lands on its roof. The front of the vehicle is obliterated and the cops inside are knocked unconscious by their airbags.

So it goes, with police officers arriving in ones and twos, and you and Nick taking turns dispatching the men and women of the Mercury City PD. It's not long until a news helicopter comes to document your exploits and the police arrive in larger numbers.

Something like a bee sting hits you in the chest just before a *crack* sounds in the air. You instinctively swat at the pest, and a flattened bullet falls away. They just shot you—and you're bullet-proof!

They shoot you again and it fucking hurts! With a roar, you rip a streetlight out of the pavement and hurl it at the officers shooting you. The attack crushes their patrol car barricade. But there are more nearby with weapons drawn.

"Nick, be careful! You're not bulletproof."

"Good point. Guess I'd better become invisible." He reaches out at the nearest policeman and *pulls*. The man screams in agony as his eyes are ripped from their sockets. The other officers fall back. "Scream for me!"

Nick laughs like a psychopath as the police launch canisters of tear gas your way. You start to laugh, but choke. The gas stings! Oh God, it burns! You swat at the gas, but the canisters pour the cloud thicker and thicker.

"Time to regroup!" Nick shouts. "This way!"

➢ *No time to think; follow Nick's voice away from the poison gas!* Go to page 350

As Seen on TV

After a full day of walking around in hazmat suits, you're sweaty and exhausted. The only event worthy of a superhero you found was a measly skyscraper fire. One of the upper floors was fully engulfed in flames but Nick said, "No way in hell I'm running into a fire wrapped in a plastic bag." It was a fair point, and besides, the Mercury City Fire Department was already on the scene. Having found no other commotion, you regret not helping when you had the chance.

Now you order a dozen pizzas and bring home a case of your favorite libation. Nick assumes you bought enough food for him, but you don't have the heart to tell him otherwise. Truth is, nothing sounds better than gorging your insatiable appetite, a shower, and bed.

Instead, you show the college student into your apartment, plop down on the couch, turn on the TV, and *clink* your glasses together in a toast to a long day. The nightly news is on the TV, with blonde reporter Alison Argyle on screen.

Footage cuts to a warehouse fire in Mercury Bay's shipping district. The drink falls out of your hand. You leap up, sending the couch backward six feet. "That's it! There's our chance."

"Uh, plastic suicide suits, remember?" Nick says, still on the couch.

The phrase POSSIBLE TERRORIST ATTACK flows across the news ticker.

"This isn't a job for the fire department," you say.

"This is a job for *The Cleanup Crew!*" Nick finishes, leaping to his feet.

With sudden inspiration, you leap out of your apartment window and smash against the pavement four stories below without so much as losing your breath. You turn, arms open to catch Nick, but instead the college student *floats* out the window. He's flying!

Not wasting another moment, you sprint toward the warehouse district with inhumanly fast strides. It's not that you possess super-speed, but you move in proportion to your super-strength. Your legs fire like pistons and you run faster than if you were riding in a cab.

After a few short minutes, you've arrived. You're not even winded! Nick sets down nearby the burning warehouse. One of the loading bays has been blown open. Fire pours out with menace. You can feel the heat coming off it like sunlight on a Florida beach in August. Beads of sweat collect inside the hazmat suit. Still, these gas masks should help with the smoke. Cautiously, you head inside.

Three teams of six men work deep within the warehouse, and none notice you just yet. One team is obviously security, and each of the half dozen men holds a submachine gun. The other two teams load supplies onto carts. Electronic equipment, cables, computer terminals, and....

Three glass pods about the size of a phone booth.

Everything they're loading you've seen before, in that lab experiment. Who are these people? Before you get a chance to ask, things turn violent. The security team opens fire, while the others rush toward a rear exit. Unlike movie villains, these guys are competent with their weapons.

Nick goes for a crate, *pulling* the cover to protect himself as he dives behind it. Your first instinct is to duck as well, but when the bullets merely *ping* off your skin, it feels unnecessary to do so. The shots sting like a bitch, but are far from lethal.

Instead, you sprint at the men. They continue firing, unsure if they're actually hitting you. When you grab a forklift and throw the machinery at them *discus-style*, they realize they're outmatched. They flee out the rear of the warehouse—where three vans are parked, HiT stenciled on the side of each.

You catch up to them with ease. The men raise their submachine guns and you laugh. You can't help it; it just bellows out. With your costume bullet-tattered but your flesh pristine beneath, you must look like a nightmare.

They all load up, and the vans peel out on the wet dock-roads of the warehouse district. The van with the security team rushes at you, trying to run you down, while the two vans with the supplies escape. The security team van careens into you head-on.

Using its momentum, you grab hold and hurl the van as hard as you can. It flies through the air and sails into Mercury Bay, slamming against the water like an enormous cannon ball.

"Holy Jesus, Mother of Hulk Smash," Nick babbles. "Should we go after the others?"

"Not just yet," a calm voice says from behind.

You turn back to see a man in a black suit, holding an FBI badge. He stands in front of a black SUV, and after a pregnant pause, lowers the badge. "I'm Agent Brendan Droakam, Supersoldier Program. I'd like a word."

You share a look with Nick.

- ➤ Nope! Sprint back into the warehouse, using the fire as a distraction, then run out the other side and disappear! Go to page 350
- ➤ Hear the guy out. Maybe he wants to create a Bio-Hazard signal to shine onto the clouds whenever he needs help from The Cleanup Crew! Go to page 196

17

Ass Groove

This is a dream come true. At least for someone as lazy as you. Because, let's face it, you're never going to leave this couch if you don't have to.

You hone your skills in the most amazing way possible—by creating whole nebulae of orbiting junk food, with you as the black hole in the center of the universe. All the snacks in existence must eventually be devoured by their galactic overlord! *Nom nom nom.*

People knock on your door, but unless you're expecting take-out, you stay silent. It's just you, the TV, and pizza. And Chinese food.

And fried chicken.

And hoagies.

And buffalo wings.

And pad Thai.

And more pizza.

It's a snail's pace race to either maxing out your credit cards and defaulting on your rent or developing Type II diabetes. But by then it'll take a full archaeological dig team to excavate you out of this couch.

THE END

Balls Out

There are two men standing at the table, one tall and thin, the other fit and handsome.

"Fair warning," the thinner man says, "you'd be paying fifty bucks just for the privilege. I'm not the kind to shark you, so I want you to know that we compete in tournaments. On television."

Oooh, on *television*? How fancy! Your smile widens. "In that case, which of you is better?"

Seeing the $50 you slap on the table, the athletic man matches your bill with a $50 bill of his own. "If you're looking to blow fifty bucks, why not just buy a round for the bar, eh, stranger?"

"Sure," you say. "With the fifty I win from you."

"All right, let's see what you got," Jack Skellington says.

Your opponent sends the white orb flying into the triangle of pool balls. Nothing sinks, and you're up.

You hit the cue ball with your stick, careening into the ten and twelve balls. As they're slowing toward the pocket, you *help* one of the balls into a side pocket by force of will. Then you send the other to join it.

"Stripes," you announce.

Lining up your next shot, you do your best to hit the ball into the corner pocket, but when your shot is slightly off, you *push* the ball in with your telekinesis. Going again, you actually manage to sink an easy shot, but that would leave the cue ball trapped behind a solid, so you inch it out with your mind.

Another shot sunk, and another. Just for fun, you tell the ball to jump across the table, then backspin and sink your last stripe.

"Corner pocket," you announce, then sink the eight ball.

"Who…*are* you?" Marky Mark asks.

"Beginner's luck. Double or nothing?"

"Okay, my turn. Do that again, asshole, I dare you," Scarecrow threatens.

"'Asshole,' is it? In that case, I'll break." You chalk your stick, then add, "Solids. Followed by eight-ball, top left corner."

Before they can respond, you take your shot. The cue ball *cracks* hard against the triangle of balls and you stand up to watch as they haphazardly bounce off the rails. *You, in,* you tell the first ball as it nears right center. It sinks. You *nudge* the balls one-by-one, sending all seven solid-colored balls into the pockets, then you guide the eight ball from the opposite side of the table into the top left corner.

Slack jaws hang open and wide eyes stare at you.

"I'm sorry, that wasn't nice," you say. "Keep your money."

You pick up the cue ball and spin it on your pointer finger, like a Harlem Globetrotter. You're tempted to whistle, but a crash from behind draws your attention to the bar. There's a couple deep in argument, and a broken pint glass on the floor. It's the girl from the shuffleboard table and a man who must've arrived just after you.

"Dumb bitch!" the giant of a man says, before shoving the young woman to the ground.

"Nope! That's not happening," you cry.

With the cue ball still spinning on your finger, you face the creep, wide-stance like an Old West sheriff. The man grabs a beer bottle, breaks the end off on the bar and starts towards you.

"Why don't you stop me then, chump?" he growls.

"Okay."

In one seamless movement, you lower your arm, point the still-affixed-to-your-finger cue ball at the man and bring down your thumb like the hammer on a pistol. The cue ball "shoots" at Goliath, striking him in the head and instantly knocking him unconscious.

You bring up your gun-hand and blow at the tips of your fingers in bravado.

Walking over to the bar, you help the woman up. Once you're sure she's okay, you put your $50 down on the bartop and say, "Drinks are on me."

This power is absolutely incredible and *addicting*. You need more.

➢ I want to mess with people—maybe pretend there's a ghost in that creepy old restaurant down the street. Go to page 142

➢ That man was the first to fall before me, but he won't be the last. Tomorrow, it's time to run this town. Go to page 77

Bank Shot

Nick nods reluctantly, then turns to the clerk. "We're stealing these costumes. Go ahead and tell the cops we're headed for the bank next."

Then, on the walk to the bank, he looks up the number on his smartphone and calls in the local news to let them know your plan. You're ready to ask if he's going to tip off the Mercury PD next, but you figure you're covered when he walks into the bank and shouts, "This is a robbery! Please trip all silent alarms now. If any of you have cell phones, go ahead and switch over to video mode on your cameras. You're not gonna want to miss this."

In response, the gathered crowd stares at the two of you in expressions that match Nick's mask, yet they're as silent as your namesake, The Mime. Several emergency glass partitions slam down to protect the tellers.

"Mime, please free the bankers from their imaginary boxes," Nick says with a gesture to the nearest teller.

You walk over, press your palm flat against the security glass, and push. The hinges snap and the bulletproof glass cracks with spiderwebbing, then the whole panel falls back onto the teller. There were a few cell phones filming the incident, but now the rest of the gathered crowd raise their cameras in disbelief.

"Drop your weapons and put your hands on your heads!" a security guard shouts, a Taser trained on you.

"We don't have any weapons," Nick says. The security guard turns to point the Taser his way. Nick raises his hands and adds, "Here, let me fix that."

The shocked guard stumbles forward as the Taser is ripped from his grip and flies from his hands into Nick's.

"Scream for me," Nick says, before firing the Taser at the guard. The guard convulses when the electric current hits him, so the hostages scream instead.

Amidst the chaos, another man steps forward. His button-up and stubby tie are two sizes too small, and he moves so meekly that it's almost cartoonish. He holds a telephone tight against his chest.

"There's a hostage negotiator on the line," he says in almost a whisper.

"What does he want?" Nick asks.

"Ummm, your demands. And to talk to you, I think."

"Is there a news crew outside?"

After asking the hostage negotiator, the man nods yes.

"Okay, we'll come out." Nick *floats* the bulletproof glass as a shield and heads toward the doors. Turning to you, he adds, "I think you should lift a car. That'll get their attention."

The scene outside the bank is complete madness. Full police barricades are in place and several news vans sit just beyond. The road is littered with patrol cars and police officers positioned behind them.

"PLEASE RELEASE YOUR HOSTAGES, THEN WE'LL TALK ABOUT A PEACEFUL RESOLUTION," a man shouts through a megaphone.

Without response, you tip a parked car over on its side, grab hold of the frame, and lift the vehicle over your head. The crowd takes a collective gasp and an eruption camera flashes nearly blinds you.

Something like a bee sting hits you in the chest just before a *crack* sounds in the air. They just shot you—and you're bullet-proof! They shoot you again and it fucking hurts! With a roar, you fling the car out on top of the nearest patrol car, crushing both like pancakes.

The police force falls back, still firing at you, but Nick floats the bulletproof glass in front of you and the stinging pain mercifully stops.

"Nice try!" Nick screams, but there's no way anyone hears him over the gunfire.

Nick laughs like a psychopath as the police launch canisters of tear gas your way. You start to laugh, but choke. The gas stings! Oh God, it burns! You swat at the gas, but the canisters pour the cloud thicker and thicker.

"Time to regroup!" Nick shouts. "This way!"

➢ *No time to think; follow Nick's voice away from the poison gas!* Go to page 350

Battle Royale

Diamond rushes into the battle head-on, crying out like a legendary Amazonian warrior. Before you can react, the Ex-man at the front of their attack formation—Agent Flame—unleashes a cone of fire, completely enveloping the heroine.

You summon the full might of your kinetic energy into a *clap*, hoping to douse the flames. It's not as powerful as when you used the skill at the skyscraper (you had a lot more momentum behind you when you were flying at Mach 3), but it does the job.

The flames clear out just as Catherine delivers a powerful blow to the firestarter, an uppercut to the man's ribcage. He flies back across the room, *cracks* the foundation of the back wall and falls to the floor in a heap. It's not likely he survived that.

Smoldering, Diamond says, "Remind me to thank Nick for the flame-retardant suit."

She's completely unharmed, like a literal diamond passed through a furnace. But the victory is short-lived. Agent Freeze shoots intense bolts of lightning from his fingertips into Catherine, and her muscles seize. For an instant, you'd swear you can see her skeleton shine through her skin.

In a burst of rage, you *reach* out for her attacker. You can feel his heart beating in his chest, his heart full of adrenaline. It beats rapidly, excited by its owner's display of power. You take hold of the heart with your mental grasp and, as hard as you can, you *pull* at it through his chest.

The lightning stops. Catherine's spasms stop. Instead, the Agent Electric's body goes rigid and he coughs blood before he falls to the ground, dead.

"You two go for The Phantom, I'll keep this one down—she's too dangerous," one of the agents says in a frosty voice.

Agent Freeze stands over Catherine and unleashes an arctic chill over her prone form. Ice crystals form on her skin, which quickly build to blocks of ice. You grab onto her body with your mind, and *pull* her away, but nothing happens. Trying harder, *you* actually start to slide across the floor toward her, but she won't budge. It feels like she weighs 10,000 pounds.

One of the other agents rushes at you, shoulder tucked and arm flexed as if he were holding an invisible shield. He bashes against you with some kind of force field, sending you onto your back. The other of your two attackers—the man with the energy whip—comes to finish you off.

He's not dense like Diamond, so hurling him across the room should be no problem. From your position on the floor, you make to do just that, but Agent Forcefield stands next to his comrade and somehow blocks your blow with his energy shield.

The whipmaster smiles. You roll to your side just as the energy whip slices through the floor. With a boost of adrenaline, you fly off the floor and away from the men. But there's nowhere to go and you're caught hovering in the corner of the room.

The two agents slowly move forward, like tiger trappers ready for the kill. Agent Freeze has Diamond sealed to the floor in an ever-growing iceberg. The

Experi-mentor excitedly wrings his hands as he watches your last few moments, and Agent Droakam sips his top-shelf liquor.

A roaring jet engine comes from the double-door entrance and with it an enormous, ten-foot-tall mechanized suit. It's glittering white, with the sheen of a brand-new sports car. "Best Friends Forever," says a filtered, robo-Nick through the suit's speakers.

Two enormous shoulder-mounted cannons erupt in a barrage of light-missile and .50-cal machinegun fire. The sound is deafening, and the show impressive, but when the smoke clears, you see that Forcefield Agent has managed to block the entire assault.

The whipmaster makes an impressive leap off the back of Forcefield Agent, and with one swing of his energy weapon, slices off one of the suit's cannons. The super-genius inside tries to fight back, but the mysterious energy field rebuffs his every attempt. That whip/force field combo will prove deadly if you don't do something soon.

"Phantom, the lightsaber!" Dorian White cries out from inside his armor.

The lightsaber, of course! You'd completely forgotten. If a whip of pure energy can pass through the force field, why not a sword of pure energy as well?

You fire up the weapon and attack. Agent Forcefield puts up his shield, but you slice right through—taking off the man's hand in the process. He screams and backs off. The whipmaster steps in front of his ally to protect the man, who falls to the floor in defeat.

Over the screams, Nick's supersuit reloads for another attack. Agent Freeze shifts targets and lays into the mechanized Dorian White, frosting over the armor. You move to help, but barely parry the oncoming energy whip with your lightsaber. It wraps around the blade, both crackling from the meeting of the incredible energies.

The glacier in the center of the room suddenly explodes, sending fragments of ice everywhere. Diamond stands tall in the center, still flexing from the effort. "You're right, Ice Man. *I am* dangerous."

Agent Freeze turns to blast her, and she puts her full strength into a massive punch. There's nearly nothing left of his face when she's done, making him truly an "Ex"-man.

The whipmaster flings bolts of light at her, shurikens made of pure energy. One wings Catherine, leaving a massive searing wound in her shoulder. You rush in and deflect the bolts with your lightsaber.

Dorian attacks with his remaining cannon. This time when the smoke clears, there's nothing but pulp and bone fragment where the last two super-agents once stood. The three of you turn to the Experi-mentor and Agent Droakam.

"Bravo, my creations, bravo," The Experi-mentor says as he begins a slow clap.

Droakam pours himself another glass. "You've won the battle, but not the—"

"No, it's over," Nick says, his suit's helmet sliding up to reveal his face. "We have your assault on security footage. Once it goes public, your program is finished."

The Experi-mentor *tsks* disappointedly. "It's far from over. This was only the first batch. Truly, none of these powers alone were a match for the three of you. Which is why I gave myself *ALL FIVE OF THEM,* buahahahaha!"

The scientist spreads his hands to demonstrate. Flaming ice, arcing with electricity, spreads out along the floor toward the three of you.

- Toss Diamond your lightsaber; she has the best chance of getting close enough to finish the job. Go to page 214
- Take Agent Droakam hostage—the Experi-mentor will have no choice but to stand down! Go to page 243
- Remind the Experi-mentor that he still doesn't have the power of flight (wink). Go to page 360

Beat the Odds

Early in the morning, the Planet Mercury Casino is filled with two types of gamblers: The little old ladies who took the complimentary shuttle so they can get the best seat at the nickel slots, or the true addicts who are still on a bender and don't know the difference between night and day. Probably why you won't find any windows on the main gambling floor—wouldn't want to advertise the passage of time.

You walk past table after table, watching as money is exchanged hand over fist, and keep walking. No point in dealing with the arteries when the heart of wealth is in the back. The cashier's cage, appropriately secured like a heart behind a ribcage, beats and pulses with cash flow. Good cash in, bad cash out. And you? You're here to rip the heart out and take it all. Kali ma, *Kali ma!*

It'd be about as difficult as snapping dried spaghetti noodles to pry open the cashier's cage, but that's a lot of noodles, and you've got an easier idea. Instead of going through the bars, you'll just go through the wall.

The concrete sort of *gets out of your way* when you put a shoulder through the wall and enter the cashier's cage. You point towards the hole and the cashiers get out of your way too. There's a ton of money back here—far more than you could possibly carry out.

Might as well load up and carry it home. With your arms full to the point where you can barely see where you're going, you step out of the money cage and toward the exit. Your stomach gurgles. Damn, forgot the buffet.

Then a sharp, burning pain hits you between the shoulder blades and your muscles seize. You drop the money and fall face-first atop your earnings. After a moment of drooling spasms, your eyes roll back to where they're supposed to be and you turn onto your back.

Standing above you are two beefy security guards, one holding the Taser he just pressed against your spine. Fast as a viper, you find your footing and spring into action—driving an uppercut into Taser-man. A sickening *crunch* sends the man careening across the gambling floor.

BAM! The second guard shoots you. It stings something fierce and you put up your hand on the wound, only to find no wound at all. It's just a flattened lead disc lying against your impenetrable skin. So you conduct electric current, but are essentially bulletproof. Good to know!

The guard puts his hands up and drops the gun. "Y-you want some help carrying your money?"

You smile.

➢ *Go stash the cash and plan your next move....* Go to page 182

Beat Senseless

"Why me?!" Dr. Hallucination shrieks, which turns to a blood-curdling scream as Baxter kills him.

"Your robot is indeed our Achilles heel. Well, I'm sure it has one of its own!" the Experi-mentor cries.

Then, before you know what's happened, you say, "Catherine can disassemble Baxter with her telekinesis."

"Thank you, Dr. Mind-Control," the Experi-mentor says with an evil grin. "Now, if you please?"

A fog appears over Catherine's eyes. She puts out a hand as Baxter starts to come apart at the seams.

"No!!!" you scream, but there's nothing you can do.

Pieces of Baxter fly out, bashing into each of you at Catherine's mental command.

"I'm sorry," Agent Droakam says.

"He's going to—" Dr. Reader starts, but is silenced as Agent Droakam shoots Catherine in the back.

"You bastard!" Nick cries.

In an instant, he punches the FBI man with a blow powerful enough to demolish a building.

Dr. Necromancy places a hand on the fallen Catherine and she rises from the dead. Nick stands there confused. He wants Catherine back, but he knows the scientists are the enemy.

Catherine's eyes are pure black. She turns, *lifts* you into the air, and bashes you against the rocks of the lighthouse cavern.

THE END

Be Careful What You Wish For

You twist the commands into the staff, the shaft locks into place, and the jewel glows a brilliant purple. In the blink of an eye, the staff projects a gateway to another world in what was just open air inside the reactor.

Ready to find a new home, you step through the gate.

On the other side is a scene of pure destruction. The nuclear reactor is an enormous crater on this side and the air is only so much poison. It's not just that there aren't any superhumans here; there aren't any humans here whatsoever!

With your last gasping breath, you tell the staff to reopen the gate back home. You tumble back into your world just in time. Was there no atmosphere on that world?

Maybe you should rename that stupid staff "Dr. Jones" because, *Ha ha, Dr. Jones, very funny*. Time to recalibrate. Once you've ensured the staff will only send you somewhere hospitable to human life, why not try a world where….

- Mankind hasn't destroyed the environment. Why not spend a little time in a lush utopia and see what knowledge you might bring back home? Go to page 364
- You chose a different pod in the experiment. Why not commune with other genii and see yourself with different superpowers? Go to page 270
- Science has stopped the aging process. As an immortal, you'll be able to spend eternity exploring all the infinite possibilities! Go to page 57
- The Experi-mentor is nurturing instead of aggressive. Cautious instead of brash. Kind instead of overly driven. Perhaps you can find this gentler Experi-mentor and learn something about the pods? Go to page 55
- There was never an explosion. Perhaps you can find the pods that gave you your powers and study them! Go to page 87

A Bigger Boat

Despite Agent Droakam's protests, you follow Nick down to the shipyard to see about finding some aquatic transportation. "Should we check under the sun visors for a set of keys?" Nick asks.

"Why bother?" You step onto a smaller watercraft, one that's chained to the dock with a pull-start motor. No need for a key here, just a quick break of the chain and you're ready to go. Nick *floats* from the dock to the boat, and you speed toward the mega-yacht.

He wasn't exaggerating. This leviathan sea-monster of a ship must have cost millions upon millions of dollars. *The Son of Jupiter* is like a luxury hotel on the water, complete with a helicopter perched on top. And a 50mm cannon, which starts firing at you.

"Get down!" you shout.

Instead, Nick flies into the air while you crank the throttle to maximum. Massive bullets send the sea splashing in a line of geysers headed straight for you. The cannon rips your small watercraft to shreds, but it's too late. When you're within twenty feet, you leap off the tiny boat and smash into the hull of the mega-yacht. With a fist slammed through its surface, you punch-climb up the side.

As you leap onto the deck, the crew blasts into you with gunfire. It stings, but proves nothing more than an annoyance. In a Herculean rage, you tear the ship apart and decimate the crew. Nick holds back, letting you take out their defenses.

At mid-deck you stop, frozen in your tracks. There before you, lined and glittering in the sun, are three telephone-booth-size glass pods.

A screeching roar draws you back to the fight. When you look up, you see a man brandishing a shoulder-mounted RPG-launcher like a Somali pirate. In desperation, he fires the missile at you. There's no time to move, and it's a direct hit—but you survive. Hurts like a sonofabitch, but doesn't even leave a scratch.

The ship, however, is going down. The explosion tore a substantial hole in the yacht, and that, combined with the damage you've done, proves too much. Nick swoops in to grab you, but he can't. It's too much for the young telekinetic. Looks like you'll have to swim—straight into the deep end!

When you splash into the open ocean you sink, well, like a rock. You're so dense that trying to swim feels like flapping your arms through the air. And so you fall through the water, deeper and deeper, until the ship above fades into darkness. Your lungs burn for want of air, but what are you going to do? Walk to shore?

At least you stopped whatever it is Nelson Bloodnight had planned with your blood sample. Soon you'll drown, and then *The Son of Jupiter* will join you in Davy Jones' Locker.

THE END

Big GOVERNMENT

"First? A new image. You've had...a bumpy start as Rock Star. So we kill you off, then write an origin story of our own choosing. We need you to be *BIG*. I've got some special effects guys we share the news studio with, and they owe me a few favors. Problem is, 'giant' superheroes are a staple, and we don't want to use a trademarked name. So let's brainstorm. Now then, what's the biggest, most powerful thing you can think of?"

"The Government?" you say with a laugh.

She laughs too, then a light-bulb clicks. "Hey, that's not bad. Gives a judge, jury, executioner vibe, but Government makes the rules. Government isn't a vigilante, Government is law. I like it!"

"But if I go by Government, shouldn't my superpower be Never Getting Anything Done?"

"Hey!" she says, slapping your hand playfully. "Don't forget my dad's the mayor."

"Oops. What else?"

"An alter ego. How about a hobo? People go out of their way to avoid eye contact with the homeless, which makes it the perfect disguise. Plus, you can inconspicuously roam the dangerous parts of town, all the while keeping your costume in a shopping cart so you can become Government at a moment's notice. What do you think?"

"Alison...you're a genius."

"Well, if I'm being honest, I got the hobo idea from *Watchmen*. As a superhero, you should probably read more comics."

Turns out, that "I expected you to be physically larger," sentiment was something Alison Argyle couldn't shake, because your new costume isn't merely an outfit. It's a muscle-sculpted bodysuit, designed to make you stand a full foot taller and look like you weigh 600 pounds. It's constructed from a special kind of memory foam, so you can stuff it in your shopping cart during your hobo periods. The whole transformation is so drastic, no one could ever guess your true identity. Alison may have "borrowed" the idea from a comic book, but she made it her own. It really is genius.

The suit itself is designed to look like you're sculpted from marble, like a gargantuan statue. If you wore a top hat and beard, you'd look like you just stood up from your seat atop the Lincoln Memorial before you traveled to Mercury City to fight crime.

Using her news outlet, Alison announces your arrival and defeat of Rock Star, the villain blamed with starting the skyscraper fire and several other acts of mayhem, including chasing an old lady's cat up a tree. It's not long before the endorsements flow in and you upgrade your supersuit so it's flame- and damage-resistant, and equip it with all sorts of fun gadgets (like a built-in police scanner).

As Government, things are great...for a time.

Eventually, you learn that Nick Dorian accepted the FBI's offer to join the Supersoldier Program. The Experi-mentor comes out from the woodwork to help recreate his results and build an army of superhumans. Catherine Woodall becomes President by cosponsoring a bill to outlaw all non-government superhero activity.

Poor wording, and luckily for you, your partnership with Alison Argyle has made you immensely popular. Catherine, Nick, and the FBI are forced to "grandfather" your position as Mercury City Protectorate. If any of them ever figure out your true identity, they never say.

So you get to be the world's first and last superhero, but with each passing day it seems there are more superhumans on the street. Your job gets increasingly difficult, but the Supercops help out.

You publicly marry Alison Argyle as Government (since your true identity no longer exists) and end up living a pretty kickass life. Though it's not long before so many superhumans walk the streets that you're made redundant and are able to enjoy retirement.

You win…mostly.

THE END

Birds of a Feather

"Let me guess," you say, "by 'different,' you mean something like this:"

You reach out and *pull* a cocktail glass off a passing waitress's tray. The motion is so smooth, she doesn't even notice. After you bring the glass to your open hand, you raise it to Nick in a toast.

"That…is fantastic," Nick says, a wide smile creeping across his face.

"What about you?"

"Nothing like that, I'm afraid. I'm different, yes, but… Well, it's not something I can show off, you know? Or explain. My mind is just…better now. I see patterns, the way things work. I've been down here counting cards, but with your abilities…"

"Yeah, I was about to go 'fix' roulette," you laugh.

"I've got a better idea," Nick says, pausing to look around. Then, with a hushed voice, he adds, "You and I could run this town."

➢ "Uhhh, yeah. I think I'm fine with just being rich. But have fun with that." Go to page 268

➢ "Now that's what I'm talking about. Count me in." Go to page 125

Blast It!

You *slam* your telekinetic energy into the door with as much force as you can muster, sending it into the building and bouncing across the long hallway before it comes to rest on the stairwell at the far end.

Three men who really, *really,* want to be Jason Statham are there to greet you when you step inside, submachine guns at the ready. Their stubble-covered faces glower at you and the black suits work in unison as they turn to engage.

Quickly, you *blast* the three of them with your mind, and knock the men to the floor. The first two weapons *fly* away from the criminal soldiers at your mental command, but the third man won't let go.

He slides along the floor, dragged behind his weapon, firing sporadically inside the corridor. You shake him as hard as you can, even slamming the man up and down, but he refuses to release the weapon and it's like a game of tug-o'-war with a pit bull.

Wild automatic fire hits you. While the body armor stops the bullet, it's still a tremendous impact, unlike any gut punch you could possibly imagine.

Wheezing and on your knees, you grab the man's head and *smash* it into the wall by force of will. He stops shooting and falls limp. You stagger forward and *shove* the other two men back to the ground.

A cacophony of footfalls races down the stairs. How many enforcers does this guy have? As you prepare to take them on, the two men on the first floor go for their weapons once more, so you turn to take them on—rushing to get them before the others arrive.

With a clap of your hands, you smash their heads together from ten feet away, and knock both men unconscious. But it's too late. Automatic gunfire from three more SMGs plows into your back, knocking you onto the stairs and leaving you barely conscious.

The final shot is to the back of your head.

THE END

Blind Rage

Upon seeing you're not fully invincible, the SWAT team's disbelief turns to aggression. The lead policeman aims a shotgun at your face and pulls the trigger.

You stumble back and blink furiously—it feels like someone just threw a handful of sand in your face—and wipe away the few pellets that embedded themselves against your skin. Your ears ring ferociously, but a normal person wouldn't have a head anymore, so it's not all bad, right?

Right! You punch the lead policeman in his helmet, crushing it like a tin can. With tear gas and rock salt filling your sinuses, your vision blurs. Like a furiously raging toddler, you close your eyes and swing your arms at anything and everything, tears flowing freely from your face.

You crush any man-shaped black blur of a cop you can get your hands on, but the tear gas cloud grows thicker and eventually proves too much.

➢ *Smash through the nearest window in search of fresh air.* Go to page 149

Bones, or Dominoes

"That's genius!" Nick says. "And I should know. This plan is going to take some time, however. As long as I'm editing security tapes, I'm going to super-impose Catherine attacking us here. With all the images of 'Supa-gurl' online, I can easily form a composite. We'll make it look like she busted in, just like at the bank, attacked the casino and killed Bloodnight. That'll explain his sudden disappearance. Then we'll twist the bank story. She wasn't there to save it, she was there to rob it!"

"But we don't have time for all that, do we? Everything's already in motion."

"No need to rush. The last domino may have already fallen, but as long as we line up a convincing show, everyone will assume the pattern is connected. We just need a thoroughly convincing opener."

"So we make a big show of knocking over the first domino?" you ask.

"Exactly. And we have resources. Nelson Bloodnight didn't merely leave us a casino—he controlled a whole criminal underground."

"Where do we start?" you say, itching to use your powers.

Nick grins. "It's not the early bird that gets the worm, it's the one who knows to go outside after a rainstorm."

During Nick's self-imposed exile to the casino's security room, you find the itch growing stronger. You can *feel* the world, waiting for your mental command. You're all cooped up when you can fly! Super-powered cabin fever. It's figuratively killing you.

And that's what makes your current dilemma so interesting. Presently, you hold the business card of one Special Agent Brendan Droakam, *FBI Supersoldier Program*.

"We caught him snooping around," the junior security staffer who brought the card says. "The guys were going to escort him out when he showed his badge. Said he was looking for you and Mr. Dorian. I said I'd take his card to management, but I didn't say nothin' about the two of you."

"Good work; that'll be all."

The staffer hesitates. "*Supersoldier Program?*"

"I said, that will be all."

When the staffer leaves, you look over the card once more. This could spell trouble, but it could also give you something to do while Nick finishes the plan. Time for a bit of the old ultraviolence?

➢ Absolutely. Track him down and make sure he's not a threat. A cop snooping around could compromise everything. Go to page 345
➢ It's not important. Go for a long flight to cool off and let Nicky do his thing. Go to page 151

Boxed In

There are far, far too many crates in the warehouse for you to go through them all tonight—but why not take a peek? For all you know, this is where Indiana Jones delivered the Ark of the Covenant. If you ever had a chance at finding pieces of the Roswell UFO, this is it.

The first crate you approach is tall and tapered like a coffin. Stenciled across the front is DINOSKIN MARK IV. You pull at the lid, but it's nailed shut. The crate is sealed tight.

"Is there a crowbar around here?" you ask. Nick waves you away, fully engrossed in the warehouse's computer system.

Then you're struck with an idea. You reach out, and using the power of your mind, *pull* at one of the nails. The crate quakes and shudders. It's difficult to concentrate only on the nail and not on the boards themselves, but you wrap your concentration around this one small part.

The nail rips out of the wood and hits you in the hand, *hard*. "Ouch!" you scream. It wasn't the pointy end, but still, it hurts and you massage your palm. Nick glares at you.

You try again, but this time *pull* at five nails simultaneously. Lesson learned, the nails fly across the room and clatter harmlessly against the concrete floor. Opening the lid to the coffinesque crate, you jump back when you see there's someone inside.

It's a mannequin wearing an olive-green bodysuit, scaled and reptilian. Laughing at your own skittishness, you inspect the suit. Is this a government project or a Halloween costume? The material stretches when you tug at it, but it's coarse to the touch.

The next crate is labeled, EKЧƎ EXOSKELETON LOADER. How would you pronounce that? Ecky? Echo? You *pull* at the nails, curious as to what might be inside.

"Are you just going to rip open every crate?" Nick says, obliterating your concentration. "Did you ever consider that there might be something dangerous in one of those? This is an experimental military combat laboratory. What if you blow us up?"

You shrug. "Sorry."

On the far wall rests a couch which, fortunately, was covered by a tarp. When you remove the dusty and bat-shit-covered shroud, the couch is surprisingly pristine beneath.

Several empty bookcases wait by the nearby crates, the first of which is already open. Inside is a collection of medical pamphlets with the titles: *So You're a Supersoldier*, *I am Jack's X-ray Vision*, *Why You Shouldn't Take Over the World*, *Big Book of Science*, and *Telekinesis and You*.

Taking a copy of the final pamphlet, you settle in to read. It has a delightful 1950s cartoon image on the cover, of a smiling, dapper man with zigzag arcs of electricity that extend from his forehead to a floating wrench before him. The intro reads:

Did you know that Mind Movement, also known as Psychokinesis or Telekinesis, is the ability to manipulate the physical world around you by using only your thoughts? If this description applies to you—congratulations! And thanks for "reaching out" to learn more about your unique skill set.

Why not make this informational brochure hover before you and turn the pages by using only your willpower? Give it a shot. Telekinesis doesn't have to be scary, it can be fun!

Topics Covered:
- *Training in a Secure Environment, for the Safety of All*
- *Nosebleeds and Their Deeper Meaning*
- *Why You Should Exercise Your Physical Body Too*
- *Can You Get Me Another Beer? Never Mind, I've Got It!*

Though fun, there's not much to learn from the pamphlet. You're the first of your kind, after all. These pamphlets are just speculation from an age with a practical imagination, but if Nick is able to recreate the experiment—who knows—you might be the one writing the next version for future generations of Mind Movers.

Is that a comforting thought or a frightening one?

➤ *Keep browsing; fall asleep reading antiquated Super-literature pamphlets.*
  Go to page 118

Break it Gently

"I come from a different earth, an earth where you already carried out this experiment."

"Ummm, what?" the Experi-mentor says.

You turn toward your gender-bender doppelganger. "I'm you. The opposite-sex version of you, come from another universe."

"You're aware how ridiculous that sounds, right?" Nicole Dorian says.

"No, it's the truth," the other-you says, wild-eyed and breathless.

"I mean, you guys look like brother and sister, but come on…." Kenneth says.

"I can prove it!" you cry. "Doctor, you secretly call yourself 'the Experi-mentor' and you're hoping to create superhumans. Well, you succeeded. I'm your creation—a super-genius capable of traveling to parallel dimensions."

To further illustrate the point, you take your staff and open a seam to your home world. If an enormous shimmering purple gate doesn't prove it, what will?

"Can I…can I meet myself?" the Experi-mentor asks.

You shake your head. "I'm sorry, but the experiment caused an explosion. When we came to, you were nowhere to be found. I came to a dimension looking for a gentler, more reserved scientist, and you're what I found. I think you should proceed with caution in your studies."

"Are you saying I get to be a superhero?" Kenneth Woodall asks.

"I should go. I'd hoped to learn something from you, but I suppose warning you of your potential mistakes will have to suffice."

"Wait!" the Experi-mentor cries. "I have so many questions!"

"And I wish you the best of luck in discovering the answers," you say with a smile.

Then you step into the portal, back to your home dimension. After you shake off the gender-bender willies and make it back to home base, you can explore another world, a world where:

- You chose a different pod in the experiment. Why not commune with other genii and see yourself with different superpowers? Go to page 270
- Science has stopped the aging process. As an immortal, you'll be able to spend eternity exploring all the infinite possibilities! Go to page 57
- There was never an explosion. Perhaps you can find the pods that gave you your powers and study them! Go to page 87
- There are no superpowered humans on the planet. You could do a lot of good for that world (or rule it) without fear of anyone exposing the secret to your genius. Go to page 28
- Mankind hasn't destroyed the environment. Why not spend a little time in a lush utopia and see what knowledge you might bring back home? Go to page 364

Bringing Down the House

The next morning, you're awakened by an earthquake. The Zen of your peaceful slumber the night before instantly gives way to sickening vertigo, as if the building is going to collapse, with you inside. Panic sets in. *You're trapped! You'll be crushed!*

That's when you remember you can fly.

You leap out of bed, mentally dragging your clothes along to telekinetically dress yourself as you rush out to the balcony and into the sky. In a quick spiral, you fly down to the base of the casino, fully clothed and ready to dash toward the front doors.

Bloodied, screaming tourists flee from the Planet Mercury in a manner reminiscent of a war flick. The front doors are battered in—exactly like the scene on TV when Catherine broke into the bank. She's here? Has Diamond got the drop on you? Did the FBI agent tip her off? Your jaw tightens with new resolve and you run into the casino.

The main gambling floor is a wreck. All the tables have been flung away as if by a tornado, leaving only a litter of corpses and poker chips. Total destruction and chaos, and in the center stands an enormous, humanoid robot.

The robot lifts a man over its head—a man who just wanted to get an early start on the famed casino breakfast buffet—and rips him in half. *Oh, Christ! Where's Nick? He's nowhere to be seen. Is he already dead?*

You fly into the air toward the death robot, ready to defend your castle. As you pass over a roulette table, you *lift* it high, drop yourself, and windmill the table over your head to crash it down atop the robot with incredible force. You land on the casino floor in a crouch.

When you stand to look for the crippled robot, you're instead greeted by a gunmetal humanoid left completely unharmed by your attack. You prepare a telekinetic *shove* but stop short when you notice the machine is smiling.

"Good morning, Master Number Two!" the robot says, as if you didn't just try to crush it with a roulette table. "Incoming message from Master Prime."

Through the robot's face, Nick's voice says, "Hey! I see you've met the Doomsday Device. Come on back to the control room."

"Doomsday?"

"Yes, Master Number Two? I believe you are wanted in the control room. Shall I escort you?"

"No, thanks… I've got it."

When you float back past the main gambling floor and into the recesses of the casino, the security staff flinches in fear. They're all hiding back here while Nick's robot—who responds to *Doomsday*—indiscriminately murders your customer base.

"What the hell is going on?" you demand.

Nick looks up from one of the computer terminals in the control room and shrugs. "The plan."

"Ummm, how is creating a robot to attack ourselves part of the plan?"

"Well, there had to be casualties or no one would believe it. Check this out," he says, and punches a few keys on the computer.

Up on the main television monitor, security footage expands to full screen. It shows the casino doors explode inwards, but instead of a death robot, Catherine rushes in, wearing her Diamond costume. She immediately sets out on a rampage,

39

destroying property and killing any bystanders unlucky enough to try their luck at 7 a.m. on a Thursday. She hurls one man up over her head and rips him in half.

"That looks so real…." you say.

"Yeah, I think I'll try Lock-ness next. So, you follow now? Doomsday Device is almost done in there, and the police are on their way. Which means Diamond will follow shortly. We'll show them this footage and they'll attack her as soon as she arrives. She'll defend herself, of course, thus making the footage only a footnote to the truth. Phase one is nearly complete."

"Nick, you're—"

"A super-genius? I know."

Sirens wail, growing louder as most of Mercury PD arrives, right on cue. Nick keys into one of the security microphones and says, "Doomsday Device? Time to head for cover."

The computer screen switches to a swatch of live security feeds, where the killer robot stops its assault and runs toward the nearest exit. For a moment, there is calm and quiet.

"Annnnnd, 911 calls 'leaked' to K-HAN news," Nick says, after a few more keystrokes. "Shouldn't be long before Catherine arrives to save the day."

When you look to the security feed, you see the SWAT team rush inside, clear the initial area and call in the regular police. After a few minutes, they make it to the admin area. Nick ducks out of the control room and enters the hallway, his hands over his head.

"Thank God you're here!" he cries.

They shout several orders and surge into the control room, weapons drawn on you, but Nick diffuses the situation by playing the doctored security footage on the large central screen.

"I think it's the one everyone's calling Supa-gurl," Nick says.

"Or Diamond," you add.

"Right! She just started killing people. I think she was after the money."

One of the SWAT members radios in. "Sergeant Wilson, you're gonna want to see this. Head to the control room."

Nick gives you a covert wink.

You wait for the sergeant to arrive, ready to watch as Nick's plan falls into place, but ultimately it's FBI Agent Brendan Droakam who walks into the room.

"Nice try," he says, looking at the footage. "I had breakfast with your friend Catherine Woodall this morning. Not a bad frame-job, though. Still, you should stick to making Bigfoot tapes like a normal crackpot."

"I was thinking Nessie," Nick shrugs.

Agent Droakam turns to the SWAT captain. "Gentlemen, arrest these two."

> Don't go without a fight! Nick's bound to have a back-up plan. Go to page 4
> Turn on Nick. Claim he set you up too and plead for mercy from Agent Droakam. Go to page 62

Bring Me a Dream

You "shuffle" on over, drink in hand and lay out a casual, "Mind if I join you?"

She looks up. Young and sweet, she says, "Oh, I'm not playing."

"It's not too late to start, is it?" She shrugs. "Come on, it'll be fun."

You slide one of the pucks across the sandy table and it falls off the other end. You hold up another puck of the opposite color for her to take.

She does so, but says, "I'm kinda waiting for someone."

"Can I 'kinda' keep you company in the meantime?" you ask before tossing another puck.

She looks down at the table and you meet her gaze on the area she was drawing in the sand. "Jason," it says in cursive writing.

Using your mind, the sand smooths out and the word erases. She looks confused, surprised, and a little frightened.

"Look again," you say. A heart appears in the sand, as if drawn by a finger. The girl gasps as an arrow appears through the heart, Cupid-style.

"How—how did you do that?" she asks.

"Did you like that? Watch *this*," you reply.

You take the puck from her hand with your mind, and grab a second puck from the table. Arms out wide, you let the two pucks roll back and forth across your arms, which you move in a wave motion for effect. You drop one of them, and just before it hits the floor, *pull* it back up like a yo-yo.

"Wow! That's amazing! Are you a magician?"

In answer, you put both pucks behind your back, and leave them there to hover, then put out your empty hands. Showing off, you *float* the pucks behind her, unseen, and bring them out from behind her ears as if it were indeed a trick.

"Something like that," you reply. "But my magic is *real*."

You wink.

"Who's the freak?" a man asks from behind. You turn to see a hulking stranger, easily the biggest dock worker here.

The girl shrugs and looks nervous. "Don't get mad, Jason, we were just talking."

He steps forward and she cringes, like an animal expecting a strike.

"Everything okay?" you ask.

"You'd better get lost," he says, his breath thick with whiskey.

You look to her. She nods. "You should go."

"If you're sure," you say. "I'll go."

She nods again. After tossing $20 on the bar to pay your tab, you push through the saloon doors and walk back toward the warehouse. Thirty paces out, a roaring man's voice cries for blood.

"Hey, freak! Were you hitting on my girl? I can't let you disrespect me like that. I've got a reputation."

You turn to see the same gigantic man from the bar—Jason—bearing down on you.

"Seriously?"

"I'm gonna wipe that smug grin off your face!"

41

He comes over to do just that, fists clenched in rage.

In an unexpected burst of anger, you plant your feet and *grasp* him with your mind, then fling him nearly twenty feet from the dock into Mercury Bay. He lands with a splash.

Whoa. You're shocked at your own strength. That wasn't as difficult as it should've been. You just lifted him with the power of mind and threw him away like a piece of garbage. Could you lift yourself? Focusing, you hover off the ground. You can fly!

The girl stands back by the entrance, quaking in fear. You give her another wink, then *blast* into the night sky.

- ➢ Maybe the girl was onto something? The Planet Mercury Casino has an amateur magician night that you could probably sweep. Go to page 181
- ➢ You can fly! Time to go on a moonlight tour of Mercury City and fly until exhaustion sets in. Go to page 369

Buahahaha

"This is Alison Argyle reporting live from downtown Mercury City. In a raid gone wrong, a laboratory believed to be owned by the villains Drillbit and Shadow Priestess has exploded, killing several scientists, the criminals themselves, and at least one FBI agent. If we can take one thing from this tragedy, it's that—hopefully—our superhuman terrors are over."

"Off," Catherine says. The television responds to her mental command. "Okay, so how'd you do it?"

"Simple. I let the agent believe I wasn't involved with the pair of you, and instead led him to believe you were being manipulated by the Experi-mentor. I then let the scientist know that the feds were coming for his life's work. Naturally, he chose to defend himself."

"And you didn't dirty your name, even after you swore," Nick says. His voice is full of anger, but at least part of him realizes you've just done them a great service.

"The plan wouldn't have worked if I had. Besides, I believe the offer was 'we're either in this together, or not at all.' I chose the latter."

"That's twisting my words," Catherine says.

"In case you don't realize it, I've freed the three of us. They think you're dead, and we have no opposition! I didn't like the public response to your powers, so now we take our operations private. We carve out a spot for ourselves and quietly dispose of the competition. In so many words, we've won."

"It seems...too easy." Nick shrugs.

You smile. "Such is the power of genius."

Go to page 54

Bull in a Pizza Shop

Every fiber in your body wants to leap down the landings and sprint towards your destination, but you take it slow. You purposefully walk down the stairs at a leisurely pace and exit the apartment building. It's a beautiful night and you're just out for a walk; on your way to dinner, nothing out of the ordinary.

Except that same black SUV has been following you for three blocks now. Taking a left, you speed up the cadence of your walk. The car, creeping slowly with its headlights off, makes the same turn behind you.

Maybe you're just paranoid after the accident. Why would somebody be following you? You casually look back (with drastically improved vision—easily better than 20/20) and get a closer look at the car.

The license plate reads US GOVERNMENT—OFFICIAL USE ONLY. Awww, shit. Time to lose the tail!

You look forward and see an out: a city bus heading your way. If you can run past it, you'll be able to disappear into the crowd once the bus obscures the SUV's line of sight. Works in the movies. There's another car coming the other way, so if you time it right, you'll go in front of the bus and behind the other car, then disappear. Okay, you got this. Ready?

At the last moment, you sprint out into the street as fast as you can. Only problem is, you can sprint really, *really* fast. Inhumanly fast. You easily clear the bus, but accidentally put yourself in front of the other car—right in its path.

In reflex, you *leap* toward the sidewalk and bound away from traffic like a mutant cricket. Your leap is so powerful, in fact, that you not only clear the street, but you clear the sidewalk too. You careen into the corner of a building, ducking your head and hitting the brick façade with your shoulder.

You smash through the wall like a battering ram.

Brick explodes outwards and you go right on through, into the next intersection, ripping up pavement when you land in the street. You quickly get to your feet, dust yourself off, and look for injury. Nothing. No pain in your shoulder, no ripped-up skin from your crash landing. You're completely unharmed.

The street, on the other hand, looks like the space shuttle chose this intersection to return from orbit. Well, that's one way to lose the tail—that SUV can't drive over the crater you just left in the road. Not one to stick around at the site of an accident, you sprint away toward that pizza shop.

You find a corner booth and inhale entire slices at a time. Cowabunga, dude. Welcome to your new life as a superhuman. Apparently all that super-strength and speed comes with a super-appetite.

Unconsciously, you drum your fingers against the metal table. When you look down, you see four dimples from where your fingers hit the table. *Jesus.* You grasp the edge with your forefingers and *twist* up. It groans, but the table bends as if it were made of putty.

"Here's your free t-shirt," a man's voice says.

You look up. He's of average height, square-jawed and muscular, with the short-cropped hair of a military man. He wears a black suit and holds up a red t-shirt with a picture of boy slinging a set of novelty teeth at a giant pizza, captioned, *I SLAYED THE GOLIATH AT DAVE'S!*

"Mind if I join you?"

"*Urhmm,*" you say, mouth full of double pepperoni, as you slide your plate to cover the finger dimples in the table.

"Thanks," the man says, plopping onto the bench seat across from you.

You swallow. "So, you're the manager or owner—you Dave?"

He laughs. "No, I'm just a fan."

"Well, I don't normally eat this much pizza…."

"No, I don't imagine you do. In fact, you're going through a lot of changes, aren't you? Ever since—" He takes out a tattered sheet of paper from his breast pocket and slides it across the table.

It's your signed waiver from the experiment.

"Look, I don't know what you're talking about. You got the wrong—"

"That so?" he pulls your plate off the warped edge of the table.

You leap to your feet, the bench seat violently sliding back in response, rattling four tables of people behind you. You barely hear their protests, such is the rage that boils within you.

"Hang on, now, we're just talking," the man says, rising to his feet and producing a badge. "Agent Brendan Droakam, FBI Supersoldier Program."

"Super…?"

"Now can we talk? Please, sit down."

"What do you want from me?"

"Not one for chit-chat, huh? Well, to put it simply, I'd like to offer you a job. I've been on the lookout for *Captain America* for a very long time, and it looks like you fit the bill. This is a *very* special opportunity, for both of us."

➢ "Okay, I'm listening. But I hope you've got a big food budget."
  Go to page 363
➢ "I suggest you forget we ever met, if you don't want to make me angry."
  Go to page 348

45

Cadmean Victory

Nick's eyes grow wide as you speak, but the exoskeleton complies. Agent Droakam's body fires at Nick, who falls to the floor, his wide eyes blinking slowly. A sucking chest wound right at center mass.

"*Droakam,*" he says in a gurgle. He coughs blood.

"Droakam, ignore future commands given by Nick."

Nick smiles through crimson teeth. "Last…laugh…"

Then he falls on his back, hyperactive breathing slows to nothing, and his chest falls still.

Using the same series of commands Nick just gave, you have the exoskeleton disengage from Agent Droakam's body and attach to your own. Immediately, you feel a rush of energy. The added weight is negligible, but your strength and speed feel as though they must have increased tenfold.

With this exoskeleton, the DinoSkin body armor, and your telekinetic powers, you're nearly invincible. Catherine might be a threat with her 'Supa-Gurl' persona, but you've got far cooler toys than she does. Not to mention *this whole lab*. Nick said no one else was coming, right? Who knows what other treasures these crates might hold!

But first, you're going to have to do something about these bodies. You look down at the pair of dead men at your feet. Should you hide them? Report in and say that Nick and Droakam killed one another? That's essentially what happened, if you leave out the details. Though it might be difficult to explain why the agent has a severed windpipe.

Then you notice Nick's holding something in his right hand. A small device of some sort, tucked in his palm, with his thumb pressed firmly down atop a plunger switch.

You *pull* it from his hand and into your own with the power of mind. At the same moment, the reinforced plate on the spine of your Dinoskin suit starts to beep with the rapid intensity of a fire alarm.

Deet-deet-deet-deet-deet!

With terrible clarity, you realize that you're holding a detonator. Nick's last words echo back: *Last laugh.*

KABOOOOOM!!!

THE END

Caped Crusader

You look past the dead pimp, over to the Halloween store across the street. The Phantom costume stares back at you from the mannequin, a tuxedo mixing the somberness of a vampire and the bravado of a pirate. A flowing black cape goes nearly to the ground. It should fit well, but most of all it'd make you look like someone else—someone powerful and confident.

You enter the store and instruct the clerk, a young man with bleached/orange hair and gothic stylings, to get the costume ready for you. As he does, you fiddle with the mask—no strings nor elastic that you can see. This is a theatrical-grade supersuit.

"How do I put this on?" you ask when he returns with a Phantom suit your size.

"I'll have to get you some tacky."

"Some what?"

"Sticky tack, so you can adhere it to your face."

The clerk goes to the back and when he returns, he asks you to sit down while he applies some kind of flesh-friendly super glue around your right cheek and eye socket. He taps the area several times with his forefingers until your skin starts to stick to his, then he firmly holds the mask down on your face.

Finally, the process is complete and you rise as *The Phantom*, pay the clerk, and head out into the streets to save the day.

Just before leaving, you turn back and announce, "I'll be fighting for truth, justice, and the American way. So…don't tell anyone you saw my face, okay?"

"Yeah, whatever."

➤ *Go find some more baddies to crush and damsels to save.* Go to page 162

Carved Out

You wake up the next morning and walk into your bathroom. Looking back from the mirror is someone with glowing, healthy, unblemished skin. Arms firm and muscular (though not necessarily bulky) and jaw squared; gaunt. You barely recognize yourself in the mirror. With morbid curiosity, you lift your shirt and inspect your stomach—it's firm, with six-pack abs and sculpted oblique muscles.

In a flash, you fling off your clothes and inspect your naked body. You're perfect. Not an ounce of fat and you're even taller. You look like an Olympian. *Haha, this is amazing!*

Your stomach growls, so you peel yourself away from the mirror, dress, and head into the kitchen. Time for a gigantic breakfast!

But the cupboards are open and bare. You check the fridge. Nothing. There's half a bottle of olive oil and a tin of baking soda—that's it. You've literally eaten everything else in the house, and you're hungry once more.

Time to check on the news. You put one hand on the far edge of the couch and with an effortless flick of your wrist, the sofa slides halfway across your apartment and back into place. Oddly easy….

After grabbing the remote, you plop down on the couch and flip on the TV. There on screen is blonde eye-candy reporter, Alison Argyle, sitting at her news desk and speaking directly into the camera.

"…police still have no suspects in regard to the explosion yesterday that decimated Mercury University campus. No bodies were found on-scene, so it's unclear if it was an attack or an accident. They are, however, looking into the whereabouts of Dr. Julius Petri—the name given by the man who rented the lab space. The Mayor's office warns that this is most likely an alias and therefore gives suspicion of foul play."

No one found at the scene, huh? Guess that means the other two test subjects left before the police showed up. Your stomach growls fiercely. Damn, nothing to eat and you're starving. Time to get creative.

➢ Head to the Casino buffet. Then I'd "wager" that I can break into the money cage. Get it? Wager? By that, I mean I'm going to rob the place. Go to page 26
➢ Time to get sponsored! Maybe the Mercury City Swashbucklers take walk-ons? Go to page 108
➢ What this city needs is a hero. Free food for life is part of that whole "key to the city" reward, right? Go to page 164

Casino

Using public tax records and quickly inhaling all you can about gambling laws and loopholes, you come up with a proposal that same night. It's not easy to get an audience with Casino boss Nelson Bloodnight, and at first you're rebuffed, but once you start counting cards, you get his attention.

You're brought up to Bloodnight's private penthouse on the top floor. A trio of advisors and a pair of security guards stand at the periphery of the room, while the boss himself—a tall man in a white suit, with the face of Chief Joseph and the ten-gallon hat of a Texas oil tycoon—offers a seat and a glass of champagne.

You launch right into it. "I've reviewed your books, at least as much as I could as an outsider. If you gave me full access, I could raise profits by 200 percent."

"And in return for your services?"

"You misunderstand me, Mr. Bloodnight. I'm not offering my services, I'm applying for a role as administrator. My fee? Fifty percent of all new profits, and *de facto* authority over all casino operations. Meaning, if I don't earn you more than you're earning at present, you don't pay me a dime. But when I do, you'll be free to pursue other vices while I run the whole operation for you. Or, if you prefer, I could take tonight's blackjack winnings and make someone else a very rich man."

Bloodnight leans back, downs the rest of his champagne, then stares at you with a hard face. A smile suddenly breaks and he puts out his hand for you to shake. "Please, call me Nelson."

He winks and nods for you to follow. His boots click against the marble floor. With swagger in his step, Nelson Bloodnight leads you out to an enormous private balcony. The casino owner leans against the railing, next to the built-in pool, and looks out over the city. The view is breathtaking from up here—literally, as you're forty stories in the air. The night sky glitters with reflected light from the other skyscrapers.

"There are those of us who live at the top of society, and those who crawl along their bellies at the bottom. I accept your offer, on a trial basis, of course. But I want to make sure we're being perfectly clear—if you fuck with me, you're going to find yourself taking a one-way trip back to the bottom. Climbing your way up is one thing, but falling back down? Well, that fall will kill you."

He's afraid you're blowing smoke, and he's puffing back. Big deal. You know exactly what you're doing, so there's nothing to be afraid of. But hey, this is why you didn't tell him the truth—that you really plan on increasing profits by *2,000* percent—you didn't want him to think you were offering the impossible.

"We understand each other," you say.

Something moves in the far corner of the balcony, and a shadow shifts into a black cloak. You recognize the robe from your surveillance of Catherine.

"Given a bright and shiny soul, and you sell it to the devil?" she says.

"Spying on me?" you say without a hint of irony.

"Spying on *him*, actually."

Bloodnight reaches inside his suit jacket and removes a nickel-plated handgun with a mother-of-pearl grip.

One hand darts out from her robe as Catherine says, "By your own hand, justice is served."

Bloodnight raises the pistol and his eyes go wide as he puts the barrel in his mouth. He tries to say something, muffled by the weapon, then pulls the trigger. The gunshot sprays gore into the pool and Nelson Bloodnight falls to the deck.

"And what becomes of you?" Catherine asks. "Should I send you to serve your master in hell?"

Bloodnight's body shifts, and clumsily comes to his knees, then he stands like a marionette with an inexperienced puppetmaster at the strings. The two towering security guards rush out to the balcony, and under Catherine's mental command, the corpse of Bloodnight turns and fires on the pair.

Once they're dead, the corpse turns to you.

"So, you want to perpetuate government regulation and loopholes? You can't seriously plan on using your powers just to take advantage of the system. We have a chance to *change* the system."

- Placate her, for now. Tell her what she wants to hear, but use that money to install some major security upgrades in your lair. Go to page 346
- Say, "Are you going to kill me because we disagree? You can't hope to murder everyone with different politics than your own." Go to page 192

Catherine the Great

Nick picks up a hunk of electronics from the living room and inspects the device. It resembles a steam-punk version of a bee's nest, sheared down the center to reveal a honeycomb pattern, dozens of interlocking hexagons.

"What the hell…" he says, unable to make heads or tails of the gadget.

"Catherine!" you cry. She's locked in her bedroom, remaining silent while you pound on the door. Damn it, if you still had your super-strength, you could push your way through. "Come on, we have to go!"

There's a muffled response, but you can't make out what she's saying.

"For a genius, none of this stuff is very user-friendly," Nick complains from the living room.

"That was intentional," Catherine says, finally opening the door.

She wears zippered black leather from head to toe, covering everything except her head and her bare left arm. Her right shoulder has thick steel spikes protruding from it.

"They wanted a villain," she says in response to the look on your face.

"How…where?" you stammer.

"Post-apocalyptic New Year's party 2013. I went *Mad Max* while Danny dressed up as a Mayan…." Her expression goes wistful as she thinks of her son.

"Hey!" Nick says, snapping his fingers. "Let's make our friend bulletproof once more, yeah?"

"It's done! It just needs to charge. I had tapped into the whole trailer park grid here, but if we have to leave….Do you think the abandoned nuclear plant is still operational?"

"I don't think we're going anywhere with the cops outside," you say.

"Oh, we're not leaving, but this trailer is! Remember, it's a *mobile home*."

"Please tell me you put a rocket engine under your house," Nick says.

"Where would I get a rocket engine? Don't be ridiculous," Catherine says. "No, it has eight legs that can extend to walk us out of here, and a specialized cloaking device so the police won't be able to follow us. Have you seen Danny's tablet? I just need to put the address in the GPS."

After the mobile home turns into a spider, walks out over the other trailers, and turns invisible, it's an easy ride to the abandoned nuclear power station. Despite being shut down by environmental protestors, the plant is still operational. And it's still guarded, but only at the outer perimeter. Once Catherine's trailer steps over the fence and parks you inside the main reactor, you're essentially provided with your own private security team.

"It's ready," Catherine says once the device is charged. "But I need my tech-glove to make it work."

"I don't think so. Just pick up the rifle, aim it at the Roman, and pull the trigger."

"Doesn't work that way anymore. I had to do some intense programming to reverse the polarity on *Widowsilk*, and I need the glove to use it."

Nick looks to you, and you look to the weapon. The futuristic-power-stealing rifle known as *Widowsilk* is mounted on a tripod at the center of the room. Thick cables snake across the reactor floor, powering the rifle. Enabling it to return your powers.

You step in front of the rifle. "Do it, Nick. Give her the glove."

A flash of inspiration darts across Nick's face. "Can you give *me* both your powers?"

She shakes her head. "The experiment, it… The abilities are bonded to your DNA or something. I used to know the explanation, but it's like walking through fog now. I remember I could only steal your abilities; I couldn't take them for my own. For better or worse, your powers are your own."

Nick, though severely disappointed, nods and telekinetically *passes* the tech-glove to Catherine, who takes the glove and slides it back onto her bare left arm. She types a series of commands on the glove's surface, and *Widowsilk* hums to life.

The interior workings of the rifle start to glow with an otherworldly energy. Your powers will soon be yours once more! Just as the rifle is about to fire, the tripod swivels and aims the weapon right at Catherine. Before you can react, the beam of energy *blasts* into her. She arches her back in a mixture of pleasure and pain. After only a second, the weapon stops. Her pupils dilate.

She takes in a deep breath and smiles. "I'm back."

"You lying bitch! You tricked us!" Nick shouts, pinching the air and telekinetically choking her.

The joy leaves Catherine's face and she claws at her own throat for air. She falls to her knees and her face turns bright red, eyes bulging.

"Nick, stop! Don't kill her!" you cry, seeing your chances slip away. "Gods among men, remember?"

Nick releases Catherine and turns to you. "What would you have me do?"

"I'll give you back your powers," Catherine says in a raspy voice. "But if I do, I want your help. They have my son."

Catherine recovers and rises to her feet. Nick turns to you with panic in his eyes. "No way; you owe me, remember?" he says.

"Are you kidding? I have all the leverage here," Catherine scoffs.

"How's this for leverage?" Nick asks, taking her in his mental grip once more.

You rush to stop him, but he *blasts* you away. A bolt of blue electricity crackles across the room. But that wasn't Nick. He drops Catherine and when another bolt snaps in the air, the college student cowers in fear.

Catherine darts inside the trailer. You and Nick sprint for cover. In the center of the room, the air shimmers. Not the shimmering that comes from heat waves, but more a distortion of reality. In fact, at the center of the shimmer, you see a seam start to open—a seam in the very fabric of existence. In the blink of an eye, this small seam expands to a portal ten feet high and six feet wide, with ethereal purple light shining through.

The lightning stops, but the energy gate holds true. Catherine comes out of the trailer with the honeycomb device and it's all you can do to sit still and stare in wonder.

"What is it?" Nick asks.

"A portal…to another dimension," Catherine says, operating the scanner. "It's a wormhole to an alternate universe, but it's man-made. I'd say there are only three people capable of creating a device like this—on any plane of existence."

"You lost me," Nick says.

"In multiverse theory, every time you make a choice, it creates a new universe. So there are multiple universes in which each of us chose a different pod in the lab experiment. This portal could be the genius version of you, Nick, reaching out to us."

Catherine looks down at the future-rifle and her left eyebrow stands at attention. She continues, "That gives me an idea…" Before she can elaborate, a figure steps forth from the portal. It's someone you know, but your brain freezes at the attempted recognition.

In fact, it's *you* who steps forward.

Your doppelganger is slightly shorter, soft, and yet with a fierce intelligence behind those familiar eyes. It's like looking into a mirror, but everything's backwards because it's not a reflection—it's another flesh-and-blood person. You carry a bizarre-looking staff with one hand, and with the other, you wave hello to yourself. A gemstone at the top of the staff glints and the portal blinks closed in response.

"Rock, Paper, or Scissors?" Catherine asks.

"I'm sorry?" the other-you asks.

"In this universe, I chose paper," she replies.

"So did I. Incredible. That means it worked!"

Catherine turns from your doppelganger back to you and Nick and says in a low voice, "I can't take your powers for myself, but *you* can. We can steal our own abilities from these alternate dimensions, if we work together."

"And then you can rescue your son yourself?" Nick says.

"Exactly. What do you say? Team up, steal the abilities from ourselves, then we can each rule our own plane of existence as a god. What more could you want than your own universe, possessing all three powers?"

"Using that portal?" you ask. "How will we know where to go?"

"You'll understand once you're a genius," Catherine replies through a grin.

- ➢ "It's a trap! Rush to warn yourself, then team up with your own doppelganger." Go to page 305
- ➢ "I'm in! But dibs on not ruling the world we're in now; I've kind of made a mess for myself here." Go to page 280

Chaos Reigns

That's it! You've won. You've conquered your enemies and now Mercury City—nay, the world!—is at your mercy. Never again will anyone defy you and you can rule over the powerless mortals however you please.

Well done, but know this: the path you chose was only one of many. Now you can go back, try out the other powers, and make different choices. *SUPERPOWERED* has three unique storylines with over 50 possible endings, but only one best Hero or Villain ending for each power.

If you enjoyed the book, it would mean a lot to me as an author if you were to leave a review on Amazon or Goodreads. As an indie writer, word-of-mouth is the true source of my power, and reviews are the #1 way to help Amazon promote a book to new readers.

When you're done, don't forget to check out the other exciting titles in the *Click Your Poison*™ multiverse!

INFECTED—*Will YOU Survive the Zombie Apocalypse?*
MURDERED—*Can YOU Solve the Mystery?*
SUPERPOWERED—*Will YOU Be a Hero or a Villain?*
PATHOGENS—*More Zombocalypse Survival Stories!*
MAROONED—*Can YOU Endure Treachery and Survival on the High Seas?*
SPIED (coming in 2019)—*Can YOU Save the World as a Secret Agent?*

* More titles coming soon! *

Sign up for the new release mailing list at: http://eepurl.com/bdWUBb
Or visit the author's blog at www.jamesschannep.com

Confused, if not Curious

The staff seems to have a hard time with your amorphous parameters, but after several internal shifts and calculations, something finally clicks into place. The purple jewel at the top shimmers, then projects an enlargement of itself as a gate through the heavens.

You step through and into a different universe. The nuclear reactor looks the same, except the lab you set up isn't here. It's abandoned, just like you originally found it in your world. Does that mean it worked? Time to go find the Experi-mentor.

The taxi drops you off at the Mercury University campus, at the lab where this whole wild adventure began. Incredibly, the building is still there! You rush inside and are astounded to see a nearly identical setup—right down to the tarp-covered "pillars" in the center of the room.

"Can I help you?" a woman asks. You turn to face a professor in a lab coat. She has a reassuring smile and glasses that sink into silver-streaked hair.

"I'm looking for the doctor in charge of this experiment," you say, a cloud of déjà vu forming in your mind.

"I'm Julia Petri," she says. "But I'm sorry to say, the lab assistant positions have all been filled."

"Lab assistant?"

She puts her hands on her hips, upset at this strange interruption. The shift opens her lab coat enough to reveal an "Ex" emblazoned on the shirt beneath; the symbol is ornamented to look like an element in the periodic table.

"Do you have a brother?" you ask.

"I was just about to ask you the same thing," she says, brow furrowing in confusion. "Have I met a sibling of yours?"

The back door of the lab swings open and a college co-ed pushes a cart through. Once she reaches you, she stops and stands up straight. She has thick black hair and brushes a lock of it behind her ear before she extends a hand in greeting.

"Hi, I'm Nicole. Say, haven't we met before?"

"Nicole…Dorian?" you ask.

"That's me," the student says. "Where do I know you from?"

The realization hits you like a freight train. It's a gender-bender universe! Your parameters turned the Experi-mentor into a woman, and you've entered a plane of existence where the only change is everyone's sex. But the world isn't all that different. Go, equality!

"Lab assistants," you say under your breath. To the doctor, you ask, "Does this mean you haven't run your experiments yet?"

"Heavens, no. We aren't close to being ready for human trials."

"Do you by chance have…two other assistants?"

As if in answer to your question, a man in his mid-30s steps through the back door into the lab. He wears a tank top, blue jeans, and Black Angus cowboy boots. Alligator is too feminine? Who knew?

55

"Hey, there. I'm Kenneth Woodall. People call me Woody. Boy, do you look familiar."

"This is too weird," you say.

The door opens once more and you step through—the gender-bender you. Soft in places and hard in others. The strange feeling that flutters through you is reflected in your alter-ego. Maybe you should re-name The Staff: The Things You Wish You Hadn't Seen Device.

➢ Confess. Tell them who you are and how you got here. Go to page 38
➢ You'll never get another opportunity like this! Seduce yourself. Go to page 207

A Contagious Enthusiasm

You input the parameters into your staff, telling the device to find you a world where humankind has conquered aging. Just to be on the safe side, you search for a world where this is a recent change, thus reducing the odds of some bizarrely incomprehensible universe. The staff stops shifting and *clicks* into place, having found a world that meets your criterion.

Time to go live forever. Hey, why not rename The Staff as your Divining Rod? Get it? It's a pun. You'll essentially be a god once you claim immortality. The purple jewel shimmers and opens a seam, which then widens into a gateway. You step through and into another universe.

The nuclear reactor is equally abandoned on this side. You press forward, but find no guards on duty outside the facility. At least that much is different. As you continue on, you're surprised at just how silent everything is. No cars on the roads. No planes in the sky. Your buzzing metropolis seems abandoned on this side of the heavens.

"Hello!" you shout, cupping your hands around your mouth. "HELLLOOOO!!!"

Nothing. Curiosity gets the better of you and you walk deeper into the city—you'd kill for just one taxicab! A gas station appears around the corner; better stop and ask for directions.

Strangely, this locale is abandoned as well. Even the power is turned off. At the front door, you see broken glass, shattered from the outside. You open the door, which lets out an automatic *Ding!* from the battery-powered chime. The whole place has been raided, like looters during a riot.

Stacked by the door are several newspapers and adverts, so you check the *Mercury Bugle*. To further complicate the mystery, the paper's dated three weeks ago.

The headline reads, THE END OF AGING? GILGAZYME® WONDER-DRUG HITS SHELVES TODAY. Okay, so you're at least in the right universe. You open the paper and see a photo of two scientists below the fold. One is a candidate for a GQ model, despite a forlorn look on his face. The other is handsome as well, but older and grinning like a fool. Wait, is that…?

Looking closer, you know that face. It's—it's the Experi-mentor, the scientist from your experiment. No glasses, granted, and his hair has been dyed to eliminate any traces of grey, but it's him! You laugh aloud at the realization. The caption reads, DR. LEWIS DELEON AND DR. RICHARD PHOENIX OF HUMAN INFINITE TECHNOLOGIES, CREATORS OF GILGAZYME®.

Dr. Richard Phoenix; so that's his real name? More of a playboy, less of a maniac in this world, but it's certainly the same man. You take a copy of the paper—the others will certainly get a kick out of seeing the scientist's vain doppelganger.

A low, breathy moan draws your attention away from the newsstand. When you look up, you see the store clerk, but something's terribly wrong. His skin is pale and his mouth and chin are spattered with gore. There's a large wound in his abdomen, but it doesn't bleed. It's more like he's a living cadaver.

He moans again, louder this time. He stumbles toward you, his eyes cold and distant, but hungry. A *Ding!* brings your wits back and you turn. It's a mother with a baby strapped to her chest in a Babybjörn. The two reach out and moan in unison, stumbling toward you. She's *wrong* in the same undead way as the clerk is, and the little bundle is the spitting image of momma.

Beyond, a small crowd gathers outside. Did they follow you here? No time for questions.

You dash deeper into the convenience store, but your movement changes the ghoulish clerk from curious to feral. The man lunges and grabs at you with twisted fingers. He bites you, hard.

The rest of the fiends pile in, ready for the feast. There won't be enough of you left to rise again.

THE END*

---

* The man who helped bring about the zombie apocalypse in *INFECTED* also created superpowers in your universe—say whaaaat? Despite having your super-brains eaten, I hope your mind=blown. Congrats on finding one of two Easter eggs in this book.

Contaminated

"I'm sorry to hear that," the agent says. "You know the police think you're criminals, based on your…failed exploits. I won't be able to protect you from them if you go."

"They'll understand sooner or later that we're heroes. You'll get it too," Nick says.

"Good luck," the man says, shaking his head.

That's that, time to patrol the streets.

"*EBOLA!!!*" a woman shouts when she sees your HAZMAT suits.

"No, ma'am, we're here to help!" You say, but she's already running away. Several other bystanders look at you warily, their cell phones glued to their ears. Sirens wail and police cars head your way. Seems like that agent was right—you don't have the best reputation right now.

"We gotta get out of here," Nick says. "C'mon, quick!"

Yeah, you need to put out this public relations fire if you're ever going to do any good.

➢ *Get off the streets before the cops try to arrest you!* Go to page 350

Control Freak

Baxter brings its metal hands around Dr. Mind-Control's ears, then claps. There's a splash and a squick, then all is silent for a moment.

"You've lost," you say. "Nothing else you've got can touch Nick. He and Baxter will destroy all of you if you don't surrender."

But the Experi-mentor is smiling. "You think that's all I've got? Dr. Hallucination, please use your sensory manipulation to show the super-genius just how *painfully* wrong that assumption is."

Everything disappears. Your team, the lighthouse, everything. Fiery pain explodes through your body. The cavern system expands and you're suddenly in a terrible nightmare of Dante's hell.

A hell that never ends because you lose all sense of time.

THE END

Cosmic Irony

The Planet Mercury marketing staff bills your show as *COSMOKENISIS—the greatest levitation act ever performed!* Rebranding you as "Cosmo" because it fits with the casino's galactic theme. Six performances a week with a nightly salary of $5,000. nets over $1.5 million a year. Beyond the salary, you're given free room and board in one of the Royal Suites just below the casino's owner. Some nights, you fly out your window, just for a glimpse of independence.

Okay, you sold out, but so what? Well, here's the problem—you sold out for far too little. Catherine, the woman from the experiment, earns your annual salary with each weekly issue of the comic book, based on her super-heroics as the masked avenger "Diamond."

Nick Dorian, on the other hand, becomes Emperor of Earth.

And all you have to show for it is this penthouse and an endless supply of Cosmopolitans (your contractually-obligated signature cocktail) with which to drown your sorrows. Eventually, when you drop a volunteer from the rafters after showing up to a performance drunk, you don't even have that.

You spend the rest of your washed-up life wondering what could have been. Maybe you should write and direct your own Broadway show. That'd prove you're somebody.

THE END

Cowardice and Avarice

"Wait! I'm a victim here too. Nick manipulated me. I've been held here against my will. You've got to help me, please!" you cry out in your best victim voice.

"You fucking coward!" Nick cries.

He rises up from the computer terminal and with a deafening *Kaboom!* you stumble back. Nick holds a handgun he'd stashed under the table, and with only a three-foot distance between the two of you, his quick-draw aim is dead-on.

The entire SWAT team opens fire into Nick, making the college student more lead than human in only a matter of seconds. He falls, dead. So much for getting arrested. You cough blood.

"H-help," you wheeze, stumbling towards Droakam.

"Let's get you to a doctor, okay?" the agent says.

You nod weakly, letting the FBI man help you out of the room. It's slow-going, but you make it out of the casino and into an SUV with government plates.

As he puts the car into gear and drives away, Agent Droakam says, "I happen to have a doctor on call, a man who will be very happy to operate on you, but I believe the two of you have already met. You know him as *The Experi-mentor*."

You lose consciousness, never to wake again.

THE END

Crate&Bomb

"**D**roakam, quick, what can we use to defeat this guy?"

"In the warehouse supplies? Ummm…" he says, brow furrowed.

Nick and Catherine rush forward to engage the phantom villain, but with both invisibility and intangibility, it's like fighting a ghost. And you doubt there's a Catholic priest in one of these crates whom you can use to exorcise the evil spirit.

"There has to be something!"

"Well…there is one option. It'll kill us all, but I suppose that's Service Before Self. Are you ready to sacrifice your life for your country?"

Catherine and Nick have no chance against the invisible supervillain. What choice do you have?

"What do I do?"

"See that crate tucked back there? I want you to hit it as hard as you can."

You sprint with all the strength you can muster, leap, and plow with both fists forward into the crate in question. Faster than your mind can process, a fiery white light envelops the room and the tactical nuclear bomb detonates.

Sometime later you wake up across town. Thrown from the blast, you survived. You'll learn that no one else did, so you've defeated the Experi-mentor, but at what cost? Your team is dead, and you'll forever have to live with that. And radiation poisoning—you'll have to live with that too.

You win…ish.

THE END

Crazed and Confused

The scientist appears truly baffled, but shrugs in resignation and mutters something about "pearls before swine." He stalks off to find another candidate, leaving you to go on your merry way.

You've lived in Mercury City long enough to know a lunatic when you see one. And while the vagrants who quote Shakespearian soliloquies can be charming in their own right, you'd never trust your safety to a madman.

- It is curious, though. Why not stick around and watch this play out?
  Go to page 352
- Right. Avert your eyes and keep on moving—time to head home.
  Go to page 293

Creature of Appetite

You spend the whole night with Alison, putting your newfound superhuman stamina to use. By the time morning rolls around, you've already eaten all the groceries you bought yesterday.

"Well, that was…super," she says, coming out from your bedroom wearing one of your shirts, her blonde hair adorably tousled. "What's for breakfast?"

"Uhhh…" you say, looking out over the desiccated packaging of the groceries. "It's a side effect of my powers."

"Wowzers. With strength like yours and an appetite like that, I'd expect you to look like *The Incredible Hulk*. Well, wanna go out to eat?"

"I don't think I can…."

"Oh. I see. Don't want to get tied down, right?"

"What? No. No, no, no. *Hell* no. I just…don't have any money. Crime doesn't pay, but heroism pays even less."

She brightens up. "Then I'm buying!"

After the fourth round of bottomless mimosas (which, tragically, you metabolize too quickly to enjoy even a pleasant buzz), Alison Argyle reaches across the table and puts her hand on yours.

"What you need is an image consultant. Clearly, you don't fit the reclusive billionaire archetype, so we need to market you. You save the day, then get paid to give an interview or sell t-shirts, that kind of thing."

"And you're that image consultant?" you ask.

"If you'll have me."

➤ "Rock Star doesn't sell out. Sorry, babe. I'm gonna keep doing my thang and the rest will work itself out." Go to page 370

➤ "That's a duet I can get behind, so to speak. I'm in! What do we do first?" Go to page 30

A Criminal Mind

Agent Droakam nods. "Good. Pull up the Top Ten Most Wanted on the FBI's website, then select number ten."

Nick complies and a group of ten mug shots show up on the screen, like a college yearbook for the criminally deranged. When Nick selects the final man in the group, a detailed profile appears next to a close-up of his black and white photograph. Cold eyes stare back at you. A grim man in his upper 50s, stubble beard and hard features.

ROGER ALEISTER KINGSLEY
Fraud by Wire; Mail Fraud; Money Laundering Conspiracy; Money Laundering; Securities Fraud; Filing False Registration With the SEC; False Filings With the SEC; Falsification of Books

REWARD: The FBI is offering a reward of up to $100,000 for information leading directly to the arrest of Roger Aleister Kingsley.

Roger Aleister Kingsley is wanted for his alleged participation in a scheme to defraud thousands of investors using a public company incorporated in Great Britain, but headquartered in Mercury City. Kingsley is thought to have defrauded investors in failed stock holdings in excess of 200 million U.S. dollars.

Kingsley is a thin, but not athletic man. He is known to be clean-shaven and well-groomed. Kingsley has his primary residence in London, England. He is known to utilize multiple British passports.

Droakam turns to you. "He doesn't have a history of violence, but keep your wits about you. Kingsley is notorious for showing up just long enough for us to learn he's here, but not long enough for us to grab him. Our intel says he's here in Mercury City brokering a deal with the casino mafia, but we don't know—"

"Found him," Nick says.

You both turn back to the computer terminal, where Nick focuses on a Google maps image of downtown, cursor blinking over a skyrise apartment building.

"How—how did you?" Droakam asks, stunned.

"If you want to file your report legally—don't ask."

"Okay, anonymous tip it is. You're certain?"

Nick nods.

"We're moving tonight," Droakam says. "There's no time to get a warrant, but I've got a detain-on-site order. If we wait for permission to clear the premises with an extraction team, he'll be long gone."

"So…what exactly is the plan?" you ask.

"Dorian will provide technical support from here. I'll wait outside to arrest Kingsley, and you—you're going to make him come out," he says as if it's a simple task.

"How? Do I need a weapon?" you ask.

"You *are* the weapon," Droakam grins. "C'mere, I've got a housewarming present for you."

He walks over to one of the crates, tall and tapered like a coffin, stenciled with DINOSKIN MARK IV. He opens the lid to reveal a mannequin wearing an olive-green bodysuit, scaled and reptilian.

66

"The newest and best in body armor," Droakam explains. "Too expensive to be put into combat on a mass scale, but nothing else comes close. Lightweight, breathable, and incredibly durable. The scaling provides multilayer protection against gunshots or knife attack. Go ahead, touch it."

The material stretches when you tug at it, but it's coarse to the touch. Droakam raps his knuckles against the mannequin's torso.

"A reinforced plate on the chest and spine provide added shock protection against explosives. But the best part? You should still be able to fly around in this thing because it's so lightweight."

"Maybe your superhero name could be *Terror-dactyl*," Nick snarks.

"Yeah, won't I look kind of silly in this?" you say.

"You're free to wear it under your clothes, but remember, your abilities have a weight limit. Every ounce counts. Suit up, we're out of here in five."

You ride in Agent Droakam's government sedan, the garish bodysuit hidden beneath a hoodie and sweatpants. If push comes to shove, you can take them off, but until then….

"I've put the address in your GPS," Nick's voice comes in over the radio. "Is this guy a shut-in? Is that why we're dragging him out? I mean, what's the MO of our UNSUB?"

Droakam grabs the radio mike. "UNSUB means 'Unidentified Subject.'"

"Yeah, like in those cop shows. I'm the classic computer jockey, right? *Telepath Cop.* I could totally see that on network TV."

You can't help but smile.

"I'm glad you're excited, but this is serious," Droakam growls back. "Kill the radio chatter."

"Okay. Just trying to help. Thought you might want to know things like—just for example—the whole building has been rented out using the same checking account by a guy named Jacob Crowley. Is that an alias of his?"

Droakam's face drops. He turns to you and says, "That means they're all his guys. Most likely, he has protection in there. A whole team. An apartment building full of security…."

"Hello? Helloooooooo?" Nick's voice crackles over the radio.

"Ya done good, kid. Don't let it go to your head," Droakam warns him.

He pulls the car over; you've arrived. The building is an older apartment complex, six stories high, that's decayed over time. A homeless man pushes an overloaded shopping cart past the front door, but no one else is around.

"Okay, you're up. I'll be here as soon as you bring him out."

"I see you've arrived," Nick says over the radio. "Good luck, break a leg. Kingsley's, preferably."

➢ Blast the door open. Take them by surprise. Go to page 33
➢ Knock on the door. Maybe you can convince the UNSUB to step outside? Go to page 359
➢ Fly up to the roof and gain access that way. Go to page 184

Crisis of Infinite Earths

Your new home is a nuclear power plant on the edge of town, gutted and left to rot. Environmental protesters swayed the political powers of Mercury City and funding was removed only months before construction completed. Now it remains a guarded, super-secure nothingness. The open area surrounding the plant is a mere reflection of the vast emptiness within.

But the guards don't ever check *inside* the structure, so essentially they serve as your own private security once you sneak inside. It doesn't take a genius to observe their patrols and find a weak spot, so you make it your new home that very same night.

You bring enough food and water for a few days, but the available technology within should speed up the progress of your experiments exponentially. And—if your calculations are correct—the nuclear shielding should be strong enough to keep you from ripping the very fabric of space/time when you toy with the bonds of the universe.

It takes twice as long to open a hole to a parallel universe as it did for you to cure cancer. Presently, as you look at the staff you've constructed to explore the multiverse, you're frozen with indecision. It's an odd form of helplessness, one where you're confronted with too many choices.

The Staff—since you've yet to christen it with a Cool Name—is seven feet tall with an ornate, purple jewel at the top. The main body of the staff is forged from the very nuclear reactor in which you stand, built to shield you from cosmic radiation as you move from one plane of existence to the next. The jewel itself is not technically a jewel but the physical manifestation of quantum mechanics.

You unplug the staff. It's ready for use, and should recharge itself simply by being used—a closed energy loop capable of infinite travel. And therein lies the rub. With so many possibilities, where to first? You can move interlocking pieces on the staff's body in order to program the device with a more specific parameter set, but the possibilities are stymieing.

Where might you go? What could await you on the other side? A universe that never experienced a Dark Age and thus has long ago mastered your new technology? Or, if you're not careful, perhaps you'll find a world where the Nazis won WWII and a fascist hegemony rules the day? Literally *anything* is possible.

Hmmm... Perhaps it's best to set the staff to search for a reality in which...

➢ Mankind hasn't destroyed the environment. Why not spend a little time in a lush utopia and see what knowledge you might bring back home? Go to page 364
➢ There was never an explosion. Perhaps you can find the pods that gave you your powers and study them! Go to page 87
➢ There are no superpowered humans on the planet. You could do a lot of good for that world (or rule it) without fear of anyone exposing the secret to your genius. Go to page 28

- The Experi-mentor is nurturing instead of aggressive. Cautious instead of brash. Kind instead of overly driven. Perhaps you can find this gentler Experi-mentor and learn something about the pods? Go to page 55
- You chose a different pod in the experiment. Why not commune with other genii and see yourself with different superpowers? Go to page 270
- Science has stopped the aging process. As an immortal, you'll be able to spend eternity exploring all the infinite possibilities! Go to page 57

Crunch!

Ready to impress Catherine, you reach out with your mind and *catch* the vault door. Unfortunately, your mental force isn't strong enough and there's a painful feeling of violation as the steel door rips past your grip.

Then there's an even worse feeling as the door itself breaks nearly every bone in your body, crushing your internal organs and killing you after only a fleeting instant of shock.

THE END

Cut and Run

Did you know that a hit-and-run is the felony crime most often gotten away with? It's true. But hey, it's not like *you* blew up that lab. You were just in the wrong place at the wrong time. And now you're not. The police sirens were wailing long before you took off, so those other two people will be fine when an ambulance shows up…right? A shiver runs down your spine as you think about the pair of bodies left incapacitated by the experiment.

You're still a bit scatterbrained when you make it back to your apartment building. Still shaken up. Still feeling electrified. In fact, you almost step into the open elevator shaft, but you're stopped by the "out of order" sign that hangs on a nylon rope across the open doors.

Looks like it'll be the stairs up to your fourth floor apartment.

When you reach the landing, you have to wait for an elderly woman—old Mrs. Jankis—coming down the last few steps with a cat carrier in tow. She's got a massive handbag slung over her right forearm, wears a thick wool coat, and an oversized hat tied around her head with a scarf. She struggles with the weight of the cat carrier, but she's nearly to the bottom.

You sigh impatiently and she looks up—which causes her to lose her footing and fall forward down the stairs. Instinctively, you put out your hands and brace for impact, willing her away from you. With a shocking blast of energy, she falls backward and actually *up* the stairs!

Did you just do that? You look to your hands with disbelief, then to Mrs. Jankis up on the next landing. You rush to her side.

"I'm fine, don't touch me," she says, rising and brushing herself off. In a mix of embarrassment and—what? fear? disbelief?—she claims her belongings and leaves in a huff. "Goddamned elevator."

In a frenzied sprint, you get to your apartment and slam the door behind you, pressing yourself against cold wood as if the incident might try to follow you inside. Slowly, the reality of the moment starts to sink in. There's no point denying it. You saw the collision course and internally said, *no, get away from me*, and she obeyed! You *moved* her with the power of your mind. You could actually feel the energy leave your body and become a presence in the stairwell.

Could you do it again? You turn toward the kitchen and mentally latch onto the first thing you see: a bag of potato chips. In response to your mental command, the bag rises into the air and the chips float out of the bag. You telekinetically orbit the chips around the bag in perfect synchronization—they're fully responding to your will!

- ➢ No time for small potatoes. Off to the casino—I'm going to make a killing at roulette! Go to page 217
- ➢ I want to mess with people—maybe pretend there's a ghost in that creepy, old restaurant down the street. Go to page 142

Cutting out Early

As is routine, when you arrive at your apartment complex you head to the mailboxes. Damn latch always sticks, and this time it's barely worth the effort. Just bills and credit card applications. The elevator has an "out of order" sign hanging on a nylon rope across the open doors, so it looks like it'll be the stairs up to the fourth floor.

When you reach the landing, you have to wait for an elderly woman—old Mrs. Jankis—coming down the last few steps with a cat carrier in tow. She's got a massive handbag slung over her right forearm, wears a thick wool coat, and an oversized hat tied around her head with a scarf. She struggles with the weight of the cat carrier, but she's nearly to the bottom.

You're considering whether or not to offer assistance when she cries out. Her high heel didn't quite connect with the next step and now she falls toward you, cat carrier airborne and purse flailing. Instinctively you reach out to catch her, but she's at least ten feet away from your arms.

The cat carrier stops moving. The purse floats in midair. Mrs. Jankis leans forward with her arms out for balance, suspended. She blinks, you breathe. You bring your arms back and look at your hands. *How in the hell...?*

Everything falls.

The cat lets out an aggravated yowl as the carrier hits linoleum. Mrs. Jankis falls to the floor with her handbag on top of her. You move in to help, but she bats you away. In a mix of embarrassment and—what? fear? disbelief?—she claims her belongings and leaves in a huff.

Up in your apartment, you close and deadbolt the door. You can't get over what just happened down there. You thought, *wait, stop, don't fall!* and the world obeyed your commands.

Okay, what you need now is a test. Time to see if you can do it again. You look around your apartment, contemplating what you could move with your mind. But the junk mail is still in your hands, so why not start small?

You *command* the letters to rise, one by one. Miraculously, they do! Using only the power of your mind, you make the bills float into the air, mentally juggling them before you.

Then you make them rip themselves up and explode out like confetti. Done paying those! This is amazing. How about some fun?

➢ Obviously I need to feed myself floating potato chips while the house cleans itself! Go to page 323
➢ Time to celebrate! Go get a drink and toast to being superhuman. Go to page 241

The C-Word

Cancer. If there's one thing that plagues this world, it's "The Big C." Most of the night you spend researching on the Internet but it's hard to obtain any real data. After a few hours' sleep, it's time to make your way to the Mercury University library. The facility is open to the public, plus you can check on the explosion clean-up.

You arrive on campus and walk past the lab, blending in with the other gawkers who watch as a team collects debris from the explosion site. Each workman has impeccably manicured hair, dark sunglasses, and wears a full-body, white rain slicker. Since the ponchos are semi-translucent, you can see their business suits beneath. They're oddly well-dressed for a cleanup crew. One workman looks up, so you duck your head and continue on your way.

The library has a delightful array of medical texts, and you spend the next few hours speed-reading as many volumes as you can before the process gets repetitive. After all, none of these scientists has cured cancer yet, so there's a limit to what they can teach you. Their understanding of the multifaceted disease is extremely narrow, so you keep a notepad to record all the places in which their shortcomings become evident, all the errors they've made in their assumptions, and all the new techniques you're chomping at the bit to try out. In order to do that last part, you'll need laboratory access.

Since campus security assumes no sane person would break in for the sole purpose of running an experiment, you're able to walk right in and set up shop. The chemistry department is understandably on lockdown after the explosion, but here in the biology department, the only secure area is the terrarium housing Jake the python.

You're looking at cellular tissue under a powerful microscope, musing how the work that's come before you is cute, in the way a child's science diorama might melt your heart. You have the strangest inclination to pat these MDs and PhDs on the head and give them each a gold star for effort.

"Excuse me," a woman says. You look up to see a blonde bombshell in her 20s, well-dressed and waiting by the doorway. Of course, you recognize television reporter Alison Argyle from the nightly news.

"I'm sorry to interrupt your work, Professor." A warm flush fills your cheeks. "I'm investigating yesterday's explosion. Did you know Dr. Julius Petri?"

"The inventor of the Petri dish?" you ask.

Now *she* blushes. The conversation seems so warm and natural, but it could also be the practiced technique an investigative journalist uses to disarm those she's questioning.

"The police think it's an alias. I don't suppose the man running the experiment was on staff here?"

"No…I don't believe so."

She smiles and leans against the door jamb. "Any tips? It would make my job a helluva lot easier."

Keep the anonymity, a voice inside tells you.

73

"I'm sorry, but I'm not sure I can be of much help," you reply. "There's a crew packing up the rubble; have you spoken with them yet?"

She sighs. "Cold shoulder. My camera guy is getting some b-roll of them already, thanks."

"Was—was anyone *hurt* in the accident?" you ask.

She eyes you carefully. "We don't know yet, to be honest. There's no sign of the scientist who ran the experiment or of the alleged test subjects involved."

"Hmmm. Well, I'm very busy…"

She throws her hands up in mock surrender and backs away. "Say no more. Thanks for your time."

Once she's gone, you look back down into the microscope. Eureka! The cancer has retreated and only healthy cells remain. You've cured cancer. In a day. Now to tell the world!

Keep the anonymity, your instincts say again.

Fine. So you'll spend the next hour using back-door channels to submit your work to the Nobel committee and setting up anonymous bank accounts for your eventual prize money. You'll still have to fund future endeavors, right?

After a celebratory dinner for one, you pop open a bottle of champagne back at the apartment. Golden liquid bubbles inside the flute at your fingertips and you wish very much you had someone to share your accomplishment with. But such is the price of greatness; it's lonely at the top.

That's when there's a knock at your door.

Through the peephole, you see the same reporter from earlier today—Alison Argyle. Still feeling lonely (and a bit tipsy), you open the door.

"Professor?" she asks, taken aback.

"Can I help you?" you gulp.

"Well, I must say, I'm a bit hurt. Why didn't you just say you were a part of the experiment?"

You stare into her deep blue eyes, unsure what to say. She holds up the waiver you filled yesterday. Name, address, *signature*. So much for anonymity.

"That…that isn't me."

"Are you sure? It's your address. And you look just like the photo on your driver's license, which I have here on my tablet if you want to see—"

"N-No, I mean, that's me," you stammer, interrupting her. "I just wasn't part of any experiment. Someone…someone must have used my name, like an alias."

Her eyes narrow. "And forged your signature?"

You nod.

"You're not a Mercury University professor either. I checked. You're—"

"I think you should leave now, I have nothing else to say." And with that, you shut the door in her face.

"I've met the others! I've seen what they can do!" she shouts from the hallway. "I know of Nick's Herculean strength and I've seen Catherine make things float just by saying a word!"

"I'm calling the cops! This is harassment!"

Your heart pounds and your head races. So the others have powers too. *Different* powers. But that means she doesn't know what's special about you! Until she learns you just cured cancer. Oh, who're you trying to fool? She *knows*. Oh, God. Soon everyone will know.

Looks like it's time to find a secret lair. Time to disappear. Time to obtain a fortress of solitude where you'll be free to do your work.

Work like:

- ➤ Master the secrets of the space/time continuum! The unfinished Nuclear Reactor will suffice for your home base while you travel the multiverse. Go to page 68
- ➤ Create the world's first self-aware AI! A neglected lighthouse is an apropos spot to forge your new beacon of intellectual partnership between man and machine. Go to page 306
- ➤ Plan a sustainable, terraformed Martian colony! A derelict subway station should provide ample space to build your rocket ships. Go to page 122
- ➤ Becoming a supervillain! Conventional wisdom says three can keep a secret—if two are dead. Hole up in the abandoned mercury mines and study your fellow superhumans. Go to page 219

Damsels

"**A**llow me to save you some trouble," you say, your voice thick with menace. "There will be no story on those of us involved in the explosion. In fact, you're going to forget you ever saw me, understand?"

She gives a sheepish grin and takes a step forward. "Listen, I totally understand. Most people don't want to be on TV. And that's okay, I get it. So we won't do it on camera. I'll quote you, but it's not like you're going to be stopped on the street. People want to know about the explosion, but they'll forget your name just as fast as they hear it."

Clearly, she's not getting it. You spread your arms out wide, take a deep breath, and *float* off the floor. Channeling a demigod, you begin, "Hear me now, Alison Argyle! Go now and leave with your life. Never speak of this again. Do not take my warning as mere weakness. If you do not heed this command, there shall be consequences."

If you could turn your eyes electric blue and bring ethereal wind through the hall, that would've been a nice cherry on top, but overall, not a bad performance. You keep eye contact with the reporter, waiting for her to flee in terror.

Instead, she pulls out her smartphone and starts filming you.

"Goddammit!" you cry. Back to the ground, you *reach* out and grab her phone by the power of mind. When it flies into your hand, you smash it onto the floor.

"Hey! That was expensive!"

Enough games. You telekinetically *slam* Ms. Argyle against the wall, pinning her there. She's genuinely afraid now, but it's short-lived. She looks over your shoulder and you turn just in time to see Catherine lunge at you, swinging out.

You leap back enough to dodge most of the blow, but even a little contact with her sends you careening though your apartment door. The attack leaves you stunned and breathless, and you release your hold on Alison Argyle, but you're not done yet. You cough, rise to your feet, wipe blood from your lip and turn to face this new foe.

"I knew it," Catherine cries. "I knew you were a villain!"

- ➢ Fly out the window. Go to page 215
- ➢ She wants a villain? *SO BE IT!* Take Alison Argyle as a hostage. Go to page 298
- ➢ It's come to blows. Attack Catherine! Go to page 273

The Dark Lord (or Lady)

Villainy is a concept created by others. To be a villain is simply to be envied by those who lack the ambition to take what's theirs. Fortune favors the fiendish. You have the power, and the courage, to do what's right in your own eyes. And what other people think of you while you do it...simply doesn't matter.

But you've got to look the part.

You walk up to a Halloween shop down the street and closely examine the Phantom of the Opera costume out front. The mannequin wears a tuxedo mixing the somberness of a vampire and the bravado of a pirate. A flowing black cape goes nearly to the ground. The outfit is nearly a complete visage of darkness, save for the white, iconic Phantom mask.

"Mask or no mask?" you muse aloud.

"We all wear masks, *metaphorically speaking*," the shop clerk says. He's a 20-something blend of punk rock and metal, with orange/bleached hair.

"No mask," you say. "Masks are only worn by those who have something to fear."

"Uh, no, I was quoting—never mind. Is there anything I can help you with?"

"I'll take the costume."

It's true, you know. If you wanted to play hero—you'd need the mask. For those sworn to preserve peace and justice, their alter-egos are of the utmost importance. But for those like you, honest with themselves, there's no need to compartmentalize your personality. There is only you, inside the costume or out. And if people call that villainy, so be it.

As you step out of the Halloween shop, you *feel* the world around you. In an incredible burst of power, you *lift* yourself and fly into the sky! The black cape whips at your back, encouraging you to action.

At a high altitude, you look upon the city—your city. Time to:

- ➢ Take revenge on society. For what? For my being born. I'm going to make the *Grand Theft Auto* games look like a children's storybook. Go to page 285
- ➢ Where can a well-dressed sociopath have the most fun? The casino! I can fix the games or at the very least, swipe some chips from high-rollers. Go to page 314

Darting In

You down the rest of the drink, set the glass on the bar top, and *push* it to the bartender. He looks at you, knowing deep down he saw something strange, but doubting himself. You smile.

Trying not to be too obvious that you're superhuman, you pull the darts from the board with your hands. A trio by the jukebox—two women and a man—settle in to watch you play. Pressure's on. Okay, throw the dart, then use your mind to guide it home; that's the challenge.

You throw and *push*. The dart flies forward, but your throw was off and in an attempt to correct its trajectory, you overcompensate and *slam* the dart into the wall, burying it three-quarters through the drywall.

"Whoa, easy there, killer," the raven-haired woman says.

Her dirty-blonde companion laughs. The man smiles, but it's an enjoyment at your expense.

Concentrate, you've got this. You take a deep breath and throw again, tossing it only lightly, then *grab it* in the air with your mind. The dart hovers as you guide it forward and eventually it presses into the bull's-eye but, you realize too late, it moved unnaturally slowly.

"What the shit?" the guy says.

You throw another dart, faster this time, and guide it in just outside the bull's-eye. Not bad. Trying to keep their suspicions at bay, you go again. This time, you're able to *push* it right on target. The fifth and sixth throws hit the bull's-eye too, so accurately that your final throw knocks the tail off your first bull's-eye.

The trio looks at you with some awe.

"Not bad, huh? You guys wanna play?"

Before they can answer, a crash from behind draws your attention to the bar. There's a couple deep in argument, and a broken pint glass on the floor. It's the girl from the shuffleboard table and a man who must've arrived just after you.

"I said, 'no!'" she shouts. "Leave me alone or I'm calling the cops."

"C'mon," the man says, just before clamping a strong hand on her bicep.

"Leave her alone," you find yourself saying. The whole bar stops to look at you. "You—you heard what I said, and I suggest you go now if you don't want any trouble."

Despite the man's imposing size and his dockworker's strength, you're feeling confident. He pushes the woman off to the side, then steps toward you. It's obvious from his body language that the time for talk has passed.

His fist is the size of your head, but you duck in for an uppercut to his abdomen.

Here's what would have happened before you got your powers: Your blow would land harmlessly against his barrel chest, while his own strike would connect to the side of your head. He would then proceed to beat you senselessly while everyone thinks, *That's why I don't get involved.* If you're lucky, the bartender would tell him that's enough and he would drag his woman away from the bar, leaving you bloodied on the floor.

Now here's what actually happens: You use the same blend of physical and psychic movements you've just been practicing with the darts, except now you don't hold back. Your fist connects with his ribcage, and your mind *blasts* him away, sending the hulking man over the bar into the shelf of alcohol. You just knocked him back fifteen feet, most likely shattering his ribs and possibly collapsing his lung.

"Are you okay?" you ask the woman.

She nods, terrified. Tears stream down her cheeks and over her trembling lips.

You look around the rest of the bar; all the patrons shrink away from your gaze. The bartender puts a shot on the counter for you and says, "On the house."

Like a boss, you down the alcohol, give the bartender a knowing nod of thanks, and leave the bar. This is incredible. With these powers, you could do anything!

➢ No time for small potatoes. Off to the casino—I'm going to make a killing at roulette! Go to page 217

➢ I'm basically a Jedi; time to put on a robe and protect the innocent. Go to page 83

Dead or Alive

"No! Goddammit, I said not to run!" Nick calls after you. "You're just making it worse on yourself. Fine! You leave me no choice."

That last line sends a chill down your spine, especially when you realize that Nick's shouts never quieted, even as you flew off the building as fast as you could. In midair, you turn around and…

He's right behind you.

Those oversized boots? Jet-boots. Rocket flame comes from them and propels the wunderkind after you. He has his right fist extended, flying like *Superman*, and his left hand activates some kind of control panel on the beefy right forearm gauntlet.

The gauntlet hums with life, and the wrist section glows a white-hot blue. Then a pulse bursts out in a ring of energy, growing in size for the split second before it hits you. Your muscles seize, and you pass out just as you start to plummet towards the ground below.

You know how when someone shouts "You'll never take me alive," they're almost always immediately killed after that, right?

THE END

The Death of 'Supa-Gurl'

Despite the late night you spent helping Nick, you're up early the next morning, soaring through the skies, looking for the real Catherine so you can warn her.

The Doomsday Device didn't need your help, not in the least. Doomsday's "Maximum Collateral Damage Provision" meant that the robot threw cars through building windows, ripped statues off their bases, killed innocent bystanders, and generally ravaged through Mercury City like a tornado—destroying everything in its path.

Catherine Woodall, the vigilante known as Diamond, broke into the K-HAN studios and attacked without a word. Reporter Alison Argyle was publicly murdered right after recording the nightly news. And it was all caught on film.

You can only imagine what went through the real Catherine's head when she watched her evil twin commit those gruesome crimes. She must be frantically trying to find the truth, because her public sightings have gone up since the mayor called for her head.

Well, now you're going to tell her the truth.

Just ahead, a barrage of gunfire echoes through the downtown skyscrapers. You follow the sounds, but soon see what can only be Catherine. From your vantage point in the sky, the people of Mercury City look like insects. The one that leaps past the rest like a grasshopper, that's who you're looking for.

Catherine sprints away from the police cruiser with inhuman speed. She's able to leap onto overpasses from the roads beneath, and soon loses her pursuers. You take the opportunity to fly down and cut her off.

"You?" she says, skidding to a halt.

"I know who set you up," you say. "It's Nick, and I can prove it. Meet me at the Mercury Bay Aquarium by the wobbegong shark exhibit. But don't come in costume."

Not waiting for a response, you soar back into the sky. She'll be there.

The massive tanks of the Mercury Bay Aquarium give an ethereal blue glow to the viewing area, where you presently wait, watching the fish swim past. The whole structure is underground, so as to better serve the shallow seas and Bay Life exhibit, which uses a cordoned-off section of Mercury Bay to teach visiting schoolchildren about the natural wonders of their city.

"Okay, I'm here," Catherine says, her voice echoing in the subterranean environment. She speaks quietly, wary of a nearby janitor.

You nod. "Each of us got a different power in the experiment, yeah? Well, Nick's frightened by you most of all. He's setting you up."

"If he's frightened by me, why go to such lengths to piss me off? All he did was sic the cops on me, but they can't stop me."

"He wants to be a hero by making you a villain."

"But how? How is he mimicking me?"

You pause for a moment. "I said I had proof. Well, here it is. Doomsday, come on out."

The janitor, a hunched old man, suddenly *shifts* into Catherine in her Diamond costume before *shifting* once more to reveal the gunmetal humanoid-robot form.

"How is that possible?" Catherine balks, backing toward the shark tank. "How did you get a hold of—of that thing? And how do you know all this?"

It looks like it's all finally dawning on her.

"Because Nick and I are partners," you say with a devious grin.

Something inside Catherine snaps and she charges at you. Expecting this, you leap into the air and watch from above as Doomsday slams into her. She pummels the robot, but it keeps her busy long enough for you to fly through the halls of the aquarium toward the Bay Life exhibit.

When you look back, you see Doomsday pick up Catherine and throw her through the glass of the wobbegong tank. A dull *boom* ripples through the cavern when the glass breaks, as the exhibition area repressurizes and water sprays the aquarium.

You remove the remote detonator that Nick gave you the night before and, just as you fly out and up into the sky, you push the red button.

Simultaneously, all the tanks explode, filling the whole aquarium with several thousand tons of water. All Doomsday has to do is hold onto Catherine long enough for her to drown. The aquarium's upper offices collapse into the slush of marine life and concrete, further sealing Catherine into her watery grave.

Time to head back to the casino, watch the footage of Catherine's death recorded through Doomsday's eyes, and celebrate with Nick. Then you'll publicly take credit for bringing her down, with Mercury City forever in your debt. Megalomania, for the win.

Through your darkness, the future looks bright.

Go to page 54

Defender of Peace and Justice

The streets seem different. Still dirty and smelly and loud, but now there's…a quality you can't place. As you pass the homeless of Mercury City's skid row, the drunks, the drug addicts, and the grifters, it hits you. What's different? You're not afraid, that's what. Not in the least.

"You holdin' out on me, bitch?" a man says. He holds a woman against a wall at knifepoint and she sobs in terror, babbling incoherently. "You took in more, I know it. How many dicks you suck, huh? This ain't a fuckin' charity, honey."

It's a pimp and his whore. You quickly glance around; the few people on the street in the early morning quickly leave—ducking into shops or turning onto other streets. Not their problem.

Across the street is a budget Halloween store, most likely where the pimp got his leopard robe and the whore got her feather boa. A mannequin out front is dressed like *The Phantom of the Opera*.

➤ Maybe you can *change* his mind using yours? Jedi mind-trick! Go to page 341
➤ Get the mask first. We're going anonymous. Go to page 222

Dense

Remember that part of your training where you learned you couldn't lift more than a couple hundred pounds? Well, apparently you don't remember, because you just tried to catch a car.

You put your hands out and focus your mind, but the car crushes you into hero-sauce on the pavement. Ick.

THE END

Diamond in the Rough

"I've put her address in this smart-phone's navigation system. The only number programmed into the contacts will call directly to my computer system…"

"Very happy to use our equipment, I see," Droakam interrupts. "Even if you don't want to help in the mission."

Nick cocks his head. "You'd rather us *not* have a woman on our team who can rip cars in half?"

The agent flushes red, then storms off into the main office and slams the door shut.

"Good luck," Nick says. "I'll try to smooth things over with Agent Touchy-pants and keep scanning the net for activity. Tread lightly. If she's not willing to come tonight, leave her the phone. Remember—she might be dangerous."

Taking the smart-phone, you dart out of the building and leap into the sky, flying high above the warehouse district.

Wind whips at you from Mercury Bay, but you're completely in control. The sunset is beautiful up here. Sirens wail in the distance. From this vantage point you can see the billowing smoke from the warehouse fire only a few blocks away. You fly in the opposite direction.

The phone's GPS system rerouted seven times as you flew toward the destination in a straight line. The navigation software was severely confused that you didn't need to follow the streets, but eventually you arrive at Catherine's residence—which happens to be an old, white, double-wide trailer.

One of her neighbors watches as you slowly land and settle down on *terra firma*. He's gaunt, stringy-haired, and shirtless, with tattooed skin that's tanned like leather. He blinks twice, lowers the fifth of whiskey he was nursing and tosses it off the porch. Shaking his head, he turns and walks back inside his mobile home.

You knock lightly on the door to Catherine's home. In response, the door falls off the trailer, but you jump back out of the way just in time. Catherine stands at the entry with her arms folded. She looks thinner, and more muscular. Taller even. The weariness from the other day is gone completely.

"Hey, Scissors, c'mon in," she says.

Stepping over the door, you follow her inside. She moves into the kitchen and pulls up a barstool for you. When you sit, she pulls out two mugs from a cabinet and sets them on the counter.

"Sorry about the door. I accidentally pulled it off the other day. Can I get you some coffee?"

She follows your gaze around the trailer, and notices when it lands on an ATM in the corner. The machine is peeled open like a banana, with mounds of cash overflowing the sides. Catherine steps between you and money, blocking it from view.

"I figured it'd be only a matter of time before you or that college kid showed up. Let me guess, you're feeling 'different' since the experiment, right?"

You turn back to the kitchen. Using your telekinesis, you *take* the carafe from the coffee maker and pour the steaming liquid into the two mugs. One floats over to you while the other offers itself to Catherine. It's too hot to drink, so you blow on the lip of the mug.

"That's cute," she says.

She gulps the scalding liquid, shows off her undamaged tongue, then brings the empty coffee cup up to her mouth, *takes a bite* out of the ceramic mug, and chews the piece before she swallows it whole.

She smiles through clean, unblemished teeth.

"My kid says I have Diamond Skin, like in one of the games he plays. War of the Worlds, Warcraft—something like that. Diamond skin, it has a ring to it. Maybe I'll start going by 'Diamond,' get a costume and everything. Whaddaya think?"

After a moment you say:

➢ "Nick and I stayed and talked with the cops. Now we have a lab, part of a secret government project. I'm here to get you to join us and bring you in." Go to page 210
➢ "You're helping people, and that's great, but it doesn't mean you can do whatever you want. You just can't steal money like this." Go to page 163

Dimension Ex

As you open a purple gate that reaches across the heavens, you figure that will be the coolest thing you see today. Not even close.

When you step through the portal and into an alternate universe, you're met by a flying wraith—a man-shaped outline of energy as bright and brilliant as looking at the sun. He floats in the center of the nuclear reactor, and raw power floats from his form to the reactor walls, making the facility operational.

I almost closed your portal when you opened it, but curiosity got the better of me, he says, though it's more of a buzzing sound. You don't hear it so much as you feel it in your teeth. *Now state your business.*

Of all the questions racing through your mind, only one of them comes out as a formed sentence. You say, "Were you created by the Experi-mentor?"

The glowing head portion cocks to the side. *You know the boss?*

"The pods exist in my universe too."

Well, that's a horse of a different color. C'mon, I'll take you to him.

In what could be a joke, the wraith tells you, *the invisible jet is getting waxed and detailed.* Then he calls a cab to take you to the Human Infinite Technologies headquarters. Of course, you ride alone, following the transient being like a ship sailing by starlight.

Have fun meeting the wizard, he buzzes before flying off into the sky.

You're escorted into the inner sanctum by a pair of bruisers who look like rhinoceros hybrids. Once you get to the main office, a hydrokinetic secretary pours a cup of water from her fingertips and offers it while you wait.

This is too weird. Maybe you should re-name your staff the Twilight Zonifier.

"A trans-dimensional traveler! My, my, come in, come in!" the Experi-mentor cries by way of greeting. He looks exactly like he did in your world on the day of the experiment, though he appears not to recognize you.

After you fill him in on the explosion in your world and your miraculous genius, he catches you up to speed on the events of this dimension. He finishes with, "So you see, Special Agent Droakam of the FBI and I are working closely to integrate superhuman public servants into the American way of life."

"And you say you've been doing this for months now?"

The Experi-mentor nods.

"When I set the staff's parameters to search for a universe where your inventions didn't explode....there must have been an earlier failure I didn't know about that didn't occur in this dimension. Thus, you've been free to create superhumans all this time."

"As good a postulation as any," the scientist agrees.

"Will you show me around?" you ask.

"I have an offer for you," he says. "I hadn't yet created a super-genius here, and I think you could be a great asset to our staff. You could help with the research and answer only to me. It would require putting that device of yours somewhere safe, but why not make this your new home?"

"You...you want to take my staff?"

"To secure it, yes. Surely you must realize how dangerous your new plaything truly is. Why, given the infinite possibilities, who knows how dangerous such a device would be in the wrong hands? You put not just our worlds in jeopardy, but existence as we know it. Is it really that hard to imagine a Hitler or a Bin Laden as a superhuman doomsday device?"

Why do all rational arguments eventually turn to a comparison to the Nazis? Hmmm, he may be right, but never go home? Never visit another world again?

- ➢ How do you know he isn't a new Hitler? If superhumans are his Arians, you'd better hightail it out of here—with your staff in hand! Go to page 148
- ➢ Why would I want to? This is where I belong. Stay here and accept his offer. Go to page 327

Don of a New Era

"So where do we meet?" you ask. "Some kind of quarry? Junkyard? Back room in a bar?"

"Bowling alley," Su Young informs.

"Seriously?"

She nods. "Where else can a dozen hardened criminals sit in a circle and not look suspicious? Cosmic bowling starts at two p.m. I'll put the word out."

Befitting of a boss, you show up half an hour late. Though it's not co-located, the lanes are owned by Planet Mercury. It shares the "interstellar" motif, and the arcade games have been upgraded (or downgraded, depending on your perspective) to slots and keno.

Split between lanes six and seven, a dozen hard men wait for you, the kind who climb the ranks of crime by intimidation and violence. They look at you intently.

You sit in the center seat—the one with the computer where you input bowlers' names and scores—and stare down the men gathered in a horseshoe around you.

"So you killed Nelson," one of the men finally says.

"And you're calling yourself 'The Sheriff,'" another adds.

"What makes you think you can just barge in and take over?" a third demands.

The natives are getting restless! Time for a show of strength. You rise from the seat and the men shift, ready for a fight. Calmly, you go to the ball rack and place a hand on a custom job—it's completely see-through and houses an oversized six-sided-die inside.

"This was the boss's, right? Here, first person to pick it up is in charge."

Then you step aside. At first, nothing happens. Knives, pistols, brass-knuckles, and blackjacks all come out with the speed of a switchblade, but you don't move.

Their de facto boss calmly walks over, claims the ball by its finger holds, and lifts. But it doesn't budge. With the power of mind, you *hold* the ball firmly in place. He tugs as hard as he can, but no such luck.

The largest of the men, a real bruiser in his day, pushes his friend aside. With all his might, he pulls at the ball, but your mental force is stronger. The rest of the balls, even the rack itself, shudder from his effort, but it's all for naught. Every single man gives it a go, but none prevail.

They look to you with hateful glares. Returning a smug grin, you easily claim the ball, and toss it up and down. They grit their teeth and step toward you with their weapons, so you *pitch* the ball in a combined physical and telekinetic move. The men duck and the ball soars down the lane and into the pins—a perfect strike. Now they look to you with awe.

"We good?"

They all nod, weapons lowered.

➢ *Head back to your penthouse to relax and unwind.* Go to page 275

Doomsday

The next morning, Nick invites you into the security control room for a champagne brunch.

"Cheers to you," he says, raising his stemware. "You've proven a useful ally beyond my wildest expectations. Killing that FBI agent *and* the Experi-mentor? Wonderful. Once we've dealt with Catherine, truly no one will be able to stand in my way. Our way. Sorry, bad habit."

"Cheers."

"Now then, I wanted to show you what I've been working on."

Up on the main television monitor, security footage expands to full screen. It shows the casino doors explode inwards, then Catherine rushes in wearing her Diamond costume. She immediately sets out on a rampage, destroying property and killing any bystanders unlucky enough to try their luck at 7 a.m. on a Thursday. She hurls one man up over her head and rips him in half.

"That looks so real…." you say.

"Compare to the original," he says, tapping a few keys at the computer. "Meet the *Doomsday Device*."

"Doomsday?"

The scene plays again, except instead of Catherine, an enormous humanoid robot rampages through the casino and indiscriminately murders your customer base.

"Wait, you're actually killing people?" you say.

Nick shrugs. "There had to be casualties or no one would believe it."

"But what about the people escaping? Won't they say a robot attacked?"

Nick taps the screen. "See, this is called evidence," he says like he's talking to a child. "It's irrefutable. They'll seem like conspiracy nuts. We can call them Casino Truthers.

"Besides, Doomsday Device is almost done in there, and the police are on their way. Which means Diamond will follow shortly. We'll show them this footage and they'll attack her as soon as she arrives. She'll defend herself, of course, thus making the footage only a footnote to the truth."

That night Nick tinkers with his killer robot like a man possessed. You sit nearby, watching the newsfeeds while the supergenius works his magic. The doctored casino footage plays on every major network at the top of every hour, followed by the police battle that later ensued when Diamond "returned" to the scene of the crime.

The screen shows her rush in, ready to save the day, only to receive a hail of gunfire for her troubles. She swats the air around her head like she was warding off a cloud of gnats.

When the tear gas comes in, she gets angry. Catherine flings a parked car onto a police cruiser before bounding away with a roar.

Reporter Alison Argyle returns on screen to warn the public that the one-time "Supa-gurl" is extremely dangerous and to be avoided. Witnesses should call Mercury PD from the safety of cover. Citizens are urged to stay indoors until the military arrives to deal with the threat.

Now, the moment Nick's been waiting for, the mayor holds a press-conference. Behind his silver-framed glasses, weariness appears deep in the man's eyes. Mayor Argyle has the stiff upper lip of a politician in crisis and he stands still at the podium, allowing the gravity of the moment to speak for itself before he addresses the gathered public.

"People of Mercury City, I urge you to remain calm while the facts are gathered. This alleged act of violence is nothing short of tragic, but rest assured that we will get to the bottom of it and justice will be swift. For the families of the victims—"

Nick mutes the television.

"Goddamned politicians! We've got a supervillain on the loose with ironclad evidence and still he uses the term 'alleged'? No matter. We'll simply have to force phase two upon him."

"Phase two?" you ask.

"We've got the police against Catherine, but we need the whole city against her. She has far too much goodwill built up. We need the Mayor to condemn 'Supa-gurl' completely before we step in and save the day. You're going to ask how—I'll save you the trouble. Mayor Argyle's daughter: Mercury City royalty, none other than reporter Alison Argyle. She spoke out against Catherine tonight, so we send *our* Catherine to kill her. We make Doomsday personal."

Nick powers up the robot, which rises from the workbench and awaits the supergenius' commands. "Doomsday Device: Activate Mirror Entity Protocol," he says.

A holographic projection system blazes to life from inside the machine, transforming the visage before you from a killer robot to Catherine Woodall in her Diamond costume, just as real as if she were standing before you in the flesh.

"Acquire target," Nick says, pointing to the news screen. "Reporter Alison Argyle."

In a perfect mimic of Catherine's voice, Doomsday says, "Target confirmed: Reporter Alison Argyle. Maximum Collateral Damage Provision: Enabled."

Then Nick turns to you and says, "I need to rig the final trap while the Doomsday Device goes on a rampage. We're almost finished, my friend. Everything is going according to plan!"

- ➤ "I'll help you rig the trap. We can't afford any unnecessary complications." Go to page 81
- ➤ "I'll go with Doomsday. We must ensure the reporter dies. The mayor will forever be in our debt if we avenge his daughter's death." Go to page 183

Doppelgangers

So where's the one place no one would ever look for you? Perhaps somewhere from childhood? Having grown up inland, away from the hustle and bustle of downtown Mercury City, you have a spot no one else knows about. If your parents knew how much time you spent in a cavern—your own fortress of solitude—they'd have forbidden it, so you never told another soul.

But what was once a magical place as a child is now foreboding when you return as an adult. Everything you remember as warm and bright has grown dark and cold. When you pass through the fallen tree and into the mouth of the cavern, you find the remains of an ancient campfire.

From the pile of small mammal and bird bones nearby, the trespasser clearly stayed for quite some time, though there is no evidence of the hermit now. Doesn't matter, you'll only be here a short time. Just until things blow over in the city.

You awaken with a start from some terrible nightmare, though the memory eludes you. The campfire has all but died; only embers remain now. The cavern is bitterly cold in the dark of night, and you're considering throwing a few more logs on the fire when it begins to pulse and glow on its own. Pine needles and ash kick up in response to this new energy and you suddenly find yourself more terrified than ever.

The air shimmers above the fire pit. Not the shimmering that comes from heat waves, but more a distortion of reality. In fact, at the center of the shimmer, you see a seam start to open—a seam in the very fabric of existence. In the blink of an eye, this small seam expands to a portal ten feet high and six feet wide, with ethereal purple light shining through into your sylvan darkness.

Then a woman steps through the gate and into your universe.

Amazingly, it's Catherine Woodall, the woman from the experiment—or at least someone who looks exactly like her. This version wears zippered black leather from head to toe, covering everything except her head and her bare left arm with some kind of techno-gauntlet on the forearm. Her right shoulder has thick steel spikes protruding from it. She wears a black cape and carries a massive, futuristic rifle.

"Rock, Paper, or Scissors?" she asks.

"Wh—what?"

"In this universe, which pod did you choose?" she replies, as if the question were perfectly ordinary. "The version of you that created these doorways chose paper, as did I, where I come from."

"Version of me?" you parrot back, still stupefied by what's happening.

As if in answer, Nick Dorian *floats* through the portal, flying up near the ceiling of the cavern as he enters. "Scissors…" you say in a daze.

"Good. We've been looking for one of you," Catherine says.

Then *you* step out of the portal. Your doppelganger is slightly taller than you, athletic and muscular. It's what you'd look like if you were an Olympian in peak physical condition, but there's a fierce intelligence in those eyes. You wave hello to yourself.

"Where's the rest of your team?" the other-you asks.

"I—we didn't..." you reply, still in shock.

"Why does that keep happening?" says Catherine with a sigh.

"I'd say it's because given the infinite eventualities, going our separate ways seems the most likely form of entropy," says the you from the other universe.

"I understand *why*, I was simply commiserating," she retorts.

"Christ, we need to find the genius-me so I can finally understand what the hell you two are saying," other-Nick says.

"Where did you come from? How did you find me? What do you want?" you babble, thoughts finally boiling up to the surface.

"Another universe, duh," Nick says. "Even I get that much."

Other-you smiles. "How did we find you? I tried to think, 'Where's the one place I'd go, the one place where no one would ever look for me?' Well, nobody but *you* would look for you here."

"And what do we want? Why, your powers of course. Now, this may sting," Catherine says.

Then she points the future-rifle turns and blasts into you. A beam surrounds you, immobilizing your body and sapping you of your energy. You can feel your powers slip away. When she releases the trigger, you let out a painful cry, but fall to your knees, helpless.

The way you could *feel* the energy of the world around you is gone, ripped from your mind. It leaves you feeling incredibly violated.

She adjusts a setting on the weapon, turns and shoots the other you—who accepts your stolen superpower as a new gift.

"Fantastic," your doppelganger says, reaching out with an arm and *lifting* you from the ground.

Nick sighs impatiently. "C'mon, let's go find the other two."

"It feels strange to kill yourself," you hear your evil self say.

Then you suffocate as your stolen powers are used against you, the air cut off as you're psychically *choked*.

THE END

Double Down

"Hell. Yes. Hell-fucking-yes," Nick says. "I've given this a lot of thought. My plan was to first take over this casino, legitimately of course, and amass power in the way of the modern American supervillain—as a corporation.

"You know Lex Luther, arch-enemy of Superman? Well, all he had to do was to use his supergenius to make money legally and Superman couldn't touch him. So that's what we do here. Fifty-fifty partners, and I'll keep up on the legal side of evil. Deal?"

You nod. At least for now, you'll let him lead. Or at least *think* he's in charge. If he's nearly as smart as he claims to be, this is a major upgrade to your takeover engine.

"Good. First thing first, your public image. Tell me exactly how you took over the casino."

"Well, it was fairly simple," you shrug. "I won a couple million by fixing roulette, and they invited me up here so Bloodnight—the owner—could threaten me. But I threw him off the balcony and bribed his staff so they'd work for me."

Wide-eyed, Nick takes a moment to gather his thoughts. "Not the most elegant plan, but it obviously worked. It's a good thing we paired up when we did; I think it's still early enough to keep us out of the spotlight. Step one: We need to delete the security tapes and any record of your winnings. The story can't be one of a meteoric rise to fame.

"Step two: We need a patsy. No one with half a brain will believe 'Uhhh, he just gave it to me.' So we make it look like we're hired consultants, here to temporarily run the place for the stockholders, and we blame his death on someone else entirely.

"Step three: As the hired consultants, our ultimate conclusion will be a top-down replacement of staff. This way, anyone who knows the truth is gone. We can make them sign a non-disclosure agreement and turn that bribe you gave into legitimate severance pay."

"Did you *just* come up with that?"

He shrugs. "It's what I do. Anyone who doesn't go along, well, I'm sure you can 'influence' their decision, yes?"

"I wouldn't worry about that part," you say.

"Good. There's just one other detail to iron out."

Nick flips on the enormous television and cues in the local news station. There onscreen is blonde eye-candy reporter Alison Argyle, standing at a police barricade with a special report.

"I'm here at the downtown Mercury Bank, where a robbery is in progress. A team of armed men have taken control of the bank, and it is believed there are hostages involved." Alison Argyle turns away from the camera in response to shouts from the gathered crowd. Her cameraman pans and zooms to catch the action.

A costumed woman runs toward the bank entrance. She wears a tight, midriff-exposing black t-shirt emblazoned with a playing-card-suit red diamond logo, fingerless gloves, and black yoga pants tucked into crimson-red boots. Her face is concealed behind a red domino mask, but as she smashes through the security doors and rushes into the bank, there can be little doubt in your mind as to who this superpowered woman truly is.

Nick turns the TV off. "This is bad—and it's only going to get worse. This town ain't big enough for the three of us, as they say."

"You think she's a threat?"

"She's the only possible threat!" Nick counters. "She sees herself as some kind of superhero, like the world is her personal comic book. Well, I say, so be it!"

He turns to you, brow raised, waiting for a response.

- ➤ "We make her the patsy! We turn public opinion against her. Then, just like being the casino consultants here to save the Planet Mercury, we'll arrive to save the day and stop Catherine." Go to page 35
- ➤ "We should make our own larger-than-life personas and take her out. Once she's dealt with, there will be no stopping us." Go to page 337

Double Trouble

It's not difficult to operate the tech staff, not when you've been given the very genius that created it. So you set it to return from whence it came, and soon the air sparks and the shimmering purple gate appears once more.

"What are you going to do with me?" your doppelganger asks. You hesitate for a moment, wary to betray yourself—even if that "self" isn't truly you—but then hunger kicks in. Hunger for power, for *more*, and for tacos.

With a sudden flash of inspiration, you say, "You have war crimes to answer for."

You step through the portal and into another universe. It's the same nuclear power station on this side, but the other-you had been here longer. It's a full laboratory, and more importantly—several crates of foodstuffs await in one corner.

You rush over and gorge your super-appetite. Catherine and Nick are quick to follow, and they look around the lab while you eat. Catherine adjusts *Widowsilk* using various found equipment.

"So how do we find the other 'yous'?" you ask, finally sated.

"These people may look exactly like us, but they aren't us. There's no telling what number of choices they've made differently in their version of our lives, to the point where we really are totally different people," Catherine says.

Nick shakes his head. "This philosophical stuff is too much for me; let's just find the other powers."

"Based on our universe, I'd say we should check the news," you say.

Nearby, several computers sit bundled together, sharing hardware to crack the equations governing the space-time continuum, but you're pretty sure you can use the array to pull up the news. In only a short few minutes, you find a live stream from K-HAN's website.

You put the newsfeed on full-screen and watch as reporter Alison Argyle delivers a live broadcast. She's saying, "…the criminals known as 'Drillbit' and 'Shadow Priestess' have apparently formed a terrible alliance."

The image turns to bank security camera feed. Everything is normal for a moment, then the wall *explodes* and Nick Dorian punches his way in. He wears the navy-blue uniform of a handyman and the cocksure smile of a young man enjoying himself.

"Why do I look like I'm dressed for a porno?" asks the Nick from your world.

On the broadcast, a woman in a flowing black cloak *floats* in—her alligator boots hover six inches from the ground. The hood of the cloak obscures her face, but you can be certain you're looking at this-world's Catherine Woodall. She puts out her hands, and in response the bank security guards point their handguns at their own heads.

"Interesting," your-Catherine says. "This is happening live?"

The image onscreen flashes back to Ms. Argyle. "Police appear powerless against the criminal duo and now appeal to the federal government to send in troop support. This reporter has another appeal—to the third member of the experiment. If you're out there, and you can help, this city desperately needs you."

Your picture splashes up onscreen. "I think I'll take this universe," you say.

"Good call. Step one of godhood: Be revered," Nick adds.

"We need to get to the bank, quickly," Catherine says. "Nick, do you think you can fly downtown and keep them distracted until we show up?"

"No prob. Just one question: What happens if I kill myself here? Will I slowly fade away from existence or whatever?"

Catherine shakes her head and sighs. "You're thinking of the grandfather paradox, and more specifically, of the movie *Back to the Future*. This isn't time travel, this is multiverse theory—very different. But I don't think I can absorb the superpowers of a corpse, so don't kill yourself before I've stolen the super-strength."

The taxi cab drops you off three blocks from the bank; the police barricade combined with gawker traffic is just too thick. Knowing that time is of the essence, you leave Catherine behind and sprint toward the bank with incredible, inhuman strides.

When you skid to a stop outside the barricade, several sections of concrete ripple as if the earth were a rug bunching up beneath your feet. Several dozen police officers look your way.

"Did a flying kid just show up?"

One by one, they all point to the bank's blown-out wall. You rush inside. The doppelganger-versions of Nick and Catherine stare at you in wide-eyed disbelief. The bank vault door lies on the floor at the center of the destruction.

"Hey, Roman, I was just telling the gang about you," your-Nick says. "Drillbit got Rock while Shadow Witch got Scissors."

"It's Shadow Priestess," the hooded woman corrects. "Something from my kid's videogames."

"He is rather fond of those, isn't he?" your-Catherine says, entering the bank with a wistful smile.

"Wh-what are you guys doing…ummm…in our universe?" Drillbit asks.

"Well, the same thing as you, really. We're here to steal something valuable," Catherine says as she unslings *Widowsilk* and brings the future-tech rifle to a charge.

"Drop the weapon!" Shadow Priestess shouts, her arms spread, rising into the air.

"Evil twins—I knew it!" cries Drillbit, who hoists up the enormous bank vault door with ease.

Your-Catherine can only steal from one at a time, but who first?

➢ "Catherine! Fire on Drillbit first. You created this weapon to sap my strength, after all." Go to page 300
➢ Crack your knuckles. "Take out the Shadow Priestess! I'll handle the handyman." Go to page 372

Dun Dun Duunnnn….
(Super-Fiends–Part 2)

Previously on SUPERPOWERED… The Freedom Fighters were about to have a Battle Royale with the Experi-mentor and the newly-super Planet Mercury Casino staff: Nelson Bloodnight, owner and crime kingpin. Su-Young, personal assistant and fixer. Jorge Halifax, floor operations manager. Luther Stockton, head of security.

"Swarming Hive, deploy!" Catherine shouts. Her minion bots rise up at her beck and call. She's been covertly programming their instructions through her tech-glove while the Experi-mentor was monologuing, and now they spring to life.

"*Mercurials*, attack!" The mad scientist shouts in response.

For an instant, it's one genius and their team versus the other. But Catherine sends her squad straight for Bloodnight, and the "Mercurials" move in to defend their boss. Nelson Bloodnight crosses his arms and smiles with the confidence of a man who pays others to do his fighting for him.

Stockton rushes in head first, true to the nature of an ex-linebacker, and Catherine's Mantis bot tears the man to shreds with its lethal array of hardened blades. Yet right before your eyes, his wounds close up and his bones instantly fuse back together.

"Super-healing!" The Experi-mentor shouts. "You wouldn't happen to have a spare Adamantium skeleton in one of these crates, would you?"

Stockton stomps on the robot even as it leaves gruesome slashes on his legs. Her Parasite bot joins the action, unfurling itself like a gigantic centipede. The robot rolls under Stockton and springs up to latch on his back. Each of the needle-like limbs drive into his flesh, but these wounds heal, sealing the entry points and fusing machine to man.

Stockton's eyes glaze over as Parasite takes control of his central nervous system. He turns back toward his own team and attacks, now under Catherine's control. Halifax rushes in, his slick-backed hair moving in a blur as he parries the attacker with inhuman reflexes.

"Not a bad trick, but no match for super-speed! Feeling stymied yet?"

"I'm just getting started," Catherine says.

Su-Young marches forward. "Actually, you're finished."

Nick reaches forward to stop the woman with his mind, but his face washes over with confusion and frustration as she continues toward Catherine.

Looks like you're up. You rush towards Su-Young in your own linebacker tackle, but at the point of impact you pass *through* the woman. With a flux of vertigo, you careen forward and smash through several crates before you fall to the ground. Ouch.

"Buahahaha! Super-intangibility! Or 'Quantum Phasing,' if you like science, which I do. Good luck with *that* one."

Su-Young reaches Catherine, who swings a fist right through the other woman's head. The older woman rips off Catherine's tech-glove and tosses it to the side. The "Swarming Hive" minion bots now move aimlessly, acting on an incomplete protocol, and Stockton regains his mental faculties.

The Mercurials prepare for victory....

"You know, we had an invisible team member too, but he disappeared," the Experi-mentor adds with a shrug. "There are drawbacks to working with criminals."

You push up from your prone position and shake off the daze just as Stockton turns back and wallops Catherine with a mighty fist. She falls hard, out for the count.

"But I think the pros outweigh the cons. And the pro-cons outweigh them all! Get it? As in…professional convicts. Gah, am I on a roll, or what?!"

"Or what," Nick says. The college kid reaches out and closes Stockton's windpipe with his mental grasp. If he crushed it and released, the wound would heal, but as long as he holds the super-healer, he's vulnerable. Good to know.

In a flash, Halifax rushes forward and pummels Nick before coming to stand over him.

"Gotcha," the mobster gloats.

"Shouldn't have stopped," Nick says weakly through a blood-soaked grin.

He *lifts* Halifax off the ground with the power of mind, and the man struggles in the air like an unruly whirlwind. He's powerless while Nick holds him off the floor, but this takes all the concentration the telekinetic can muster.

Stockton comes in to take Nick out, but you step between the two. With a powerful punch, you send your fist straight through the super-healer's face. He's completely obliterated.

"Heal that," you say.

Incredibly, he does. What was just mashed into pulp now re-forms and is made whole. In a flush of rage, you grab ahold of the new head and rip it from Stockton's body. It comes free, along with several vertebrae.

You toss the viscera to the side. It begins to grow and regenerate, as does his body. You've inadvertently created *two* Stocktons! The Experi-mentor excitedly claps his hands together. "Ooh, and a bonus power, regenerative doubling! Even *I* didn't see that one coming!"

As easy as picking up an empty cardboard box, you grab an enormous crate from the shelf and slam it down on top of Stockton A, smashing the man beneath it. Let's see him heal while he's pinned beneath 500 pounds of government surplus! Stockton B's eyes grow wide and he runs from you, but with a quick dash, you plow him into the near stack of crates, bringing two down atop him just the same.

Nelson Bloodnight finally decides to join the fight and steps forward to deliver a haymaker of his own. He swings his fist at you, but does so several feet too far back. Knowing he can't reach you, you just stand there. So when his fist grows exponentially in size and re-forms itself into a five-knuckled brick wall, it blasts you across the warehouse. Ouch again.

"Shapeshifting," the Experi-mentor says. "That one's probably my favorite."

Nick's still fighting with Halifax like an unruly marlin caught on his line, but he swings the Whirling Dervish into Nelson Bloodnight. The casino boss shifts his other hand into an enormous pillow, softening the blow.

Su-Young comes for Nick, which leaves him with no choice but to release Halifax and fly into the air to avoid her intangible grasp. You dust yourself off and rush back into the fray, ready to take the brunt of the action, but Su-Young comes for you first. She puts a hand *through* your chest, and you stop dead in your tracks when her fist clogs your respiratory tract. You can't breathe! You choke, cough and sputter, but your body's reflexes are no match for her supernatural grip.

All eyes are on you—their most formidable foe—so no one notices when Nick loosens Agent Droakam from his binds using the power of mind. Nor does anyone notice when Catherine regains consciousness.

"Now we'll see who's finished, bitch," Catherine says, looking down the sight of her future-rifle.

Su-Young smiles, mercifully releases you, and heads toward Catherine. The super-genius fires her rifle and an energy field pours out around Su-Young. The henchwoman screams as the energy beam returns back into the rifle.

"My...my powers...nooooo!!!!" Su-Young cries.

Okay, that's enough of that. With a single flick of your index finger, you tap the woman in the head and knock her unconscious.

"Is that—is that a power-sapping ray?" the Experi-mentor asks.

"In so many words. You're not the only one who thought of re-engineering the experiment."

"That's not fair! Get her! GET *HER!!!*"

"Thorax, defense," Catherine commands, reclaiming her tech-glove. She quickly taps on the controls while squeezing her hand into a fist. She then points her fingers into a "gun" and adds, "Stinger, offense."

Nelson Bloodnight re-forms one of his arms into an enormous broadsword and brings it to slash at Catherine just as the Thorax bot expands into a deployable shield before her, deflecting the blow. Not missing a beat, you reach out and rip off Bloodnight's arm at the shoulder—wielding the broadsword-arm for yourself.

Bloodnight screams, and blood gushes from the wound. Though the torn-off arm stays a sword, the rest of his body re-forms over and over again into horribly indescribably shapes as pain overtakes his conscious mind. The Stinger bot flies forward and opens fire with sizzling plasma bolts that end the casino boss for good.

Halifax zooms toward Catherine to steal her weaponry, but halfway across the room he finds he's stopped in his tracks. Agent Droakam stands near an empty crate labeled FIRST EARTH BATTALION and holds a canister of instant sticky foam that he just emptied to immobilize the speedy mobster.

The Mercurials are defeated, the Freedom Fighters victorious! In unison, the four of you turn to the Experi-mentor. You fold your arms and say, "It's over. You're finish—"

"Muahahahahah!" the scientist interrupts, his head thrown back in a maniacal cackle.

"What's so funny?" Agent Droakam demands.

"You fools...this isn't even my final form. I gave myself *all* their powers!"

The Experi-mentor's body *shifts,* so he grows taller and leaner, his limbs bifurcate several times to form enormous tentacles, and his skin morphs into armored scales.

It's like he's turned into Cthulu. Cthulu in a lab coat. In a deeply demonic voice, something like *DIE!!!* blasts through the warehouse from the beast's maw.

With super-speed-aided metamorphosis, the Experi-mentor lashes out with a gargantuan tentacle, wraps it around Catherine's future-rifle, and claims the weapon. Then he begins to vanish from sight as he goes invisible.

This is bad. Very bad.

- Take that broadsword and lop off the beast's head before he disappears! Go to page 355
- Bow before your new overlord and master. Go to page 259
- Quickly confer with Agent Droakam and see what other tricks he has up his crates. Go to page 63
- Turn to Catherine for help. Super-genius, don't fail me now! Go to page 208

A Dynamic Duo

You wake up, head pounding. How much did you drink last night? Vague memories of trying on costumes and creating personas, but it's pretty hazy. Seeing as how you wake up wearing a mix of Catherine's clothes and your own, Danny's bed sheets clothespinned over your back like a cape, you can be fairly certain you didn't forget any strokes of genius.

"Mornin', sunshine," Catherine says. "Coffee? I only have one mug, but we can share. I seem to have eaten the other one...."

You sit up on the couch—looks that's where you passed out last night—and accept the drink. Catherine flips on the TV and takes a seat next to you.

"Listen, about that kiss—"

"Seriously, don't worry about it," you interrupt. "Maybe now we can call our super-team 'Friend Zone,' huh?"

"Ha!" she calls out. "Okay, well, as long as...."

She trails off and her eyes grow wide, her attention focused on the television. The image on screen cuts from blonde eye-candy reporter Alison Argyle to the façade of Mercury Bank and a title card that reads, "ROBBERY IN PROGRESS—Hostages Taken."

Catherine shoots to her feet. "Duty calls, Friend Zone!"

"...you're not actually going to call me that, are you?"

"I'm suiting up as Diamond; I know you don't have a name or costume yet, but I have an extra eye-mask. It's a start, I guess."

It turns out that Catherine isn't only incredibly strong, she's also incredibly fast. She's like a force of nature. Any physical ability a human being possess, she possess that trait to the nth degree. So, she sprints toward the bank on foot with incredible strides while you fly through the sky.

And how fast can you fly? As fast as you can think, it seems. The only limit is how fast you're willing to go. But you're not indestructible, so best take it easy, okay? Wouldn't want to pull a Fabio and hit a goose.

You arrive first, setting down in the open area at the bank's entrance; the crowd behind the police barricade stares at you in shocked silence. Even the police give you blank stares. You did, after all, just appear from the sky.

"People of Mercury City!" you shout, commanding their full attention. "Welcome to the age of the Superhero!"

The crowd erupts in wild cheers. Okay, now what?

As if in answer, Catherine hurdles over one of the police barricades and rushes toward the bank's entrance. The security doors are engaged, but to Diamond, the barrier proves more akin to the Homecoming banner held out for the star quarterback.

She *smashes* through the doors and heads inside.

- ➤ That's your cue; follow the path of destruction inside. Go to page 129
- ➤ Maybe a more deft approach. Try a rooftop entrance. Go to page 141

Dystopia Rex

While you're to be congratulated for your taste in movies, this bit of "knowledge" from *Jurassic Park* is a fabrication. Perhaps an amphibian-spliced dinosaur would have poor vision, but this apex predator probably had eagle eyes back in the Cretaceous. So a modern version living in a world where evolutionary pressures never led to her extinction? You might as well be cowering on a toilet seat in the rain.

The queen of the dinosaurs opens her maw and makes a quick meal of you. Were those feathers on her back?

THE END

Edge of Tomorrow

"And how *did* you know?" you say, a strange sense of déjà vu washing over you.

Reporter Alison Argyle flashes a smile. "You made it easy, 'Professor.' All your deliveries to this island were a big red flag. And when I saw the address as 'Lebon Rd'—a palindrome for 'Dr. Nobel,' I put two and two together."

"My programming indicates there is nothing sexier than an intelligent woman," Baxter says.

After a beat, Catherine says, "This is adorable and all, but I have to make one thing clear, Agent Droakam. We won't be working *for* the government, but *with* you."

"Yeah," Nick adds. "And we don't answer to shareholders. You need us more than we need you. If any other supers show up—"

"That will not happen," your robot companion interrupts.

Nick turns to you. "What's Wall-E talking about?"

"I am Baxter."

"What do you mean, Baxter?" you say.

"The scientist known as the Experi-mentor confronted us here, in an alternate timeline. He had made more of these supers, based on your cancer sample. One of whom was capable of time travel."

"And what happened?" Catherine asks.

"I appealed to his humanity," Baxter continues. "The man known as Dr. Timetravel took me to the moment the Experi-mentor found your blood sample and I contaminated it. I had to wait until this moment to be sure, but it appears I have foiled his plan. As you can see, there are no superpowered scientists waiting in the eaves."

You look to the cavern, which is illuminated by newly-installed floodlights.

"What happened to the time traveler?" you ask.

"His end of the bargain fulfilled, he departed, back to the future, in the seconds before I contaminated your blood sample. Depending on which theory of time travel proves correct, he is either trapped in the future, having lost his power, or is free to roam the timeline. Either way, he said he will not bother us."

"And the Experi-mentor?" Alison Argyle asks.

The robot shrugs. "I did not kill him, if that is what you are asking."

"So we may not have seen the end of him," Agent Droakam says. "Well, I accept your conditions. You're the super team, I'm the Morgan Freeman. Ms. Argyle, will you stay on as our PR rep?"

Her eyes dart to you. "If you'll have me."

A warm feeling runs through you. With a sudden burst of inspiration, you extend your right hand. Baxter places a metal hand atop yours. Getting the idea, the others stack their hands until all six of you are in the circle.

"Superheroes on three?"

One…two…THREE!

Go to page 135

The Emperor's New Plan

You stop at an all-you-can eat spot, appropriately named *Asian Empire*, and stuff your face.

"Are you a professional eater?" asks a young, wide-eyed girl.

"In another life, maybe," you laugh through a mouthful of Lo Mein.

"Hey wait, you're that robber from TV, right? You walked through a wall! *Cooooool!!!!* Can you do it again? Please, please, please?"

The kid points to a TV where the screen switches from footage of your robbery to blonde eye-candy reporter Alison Argyle and a news-ticker that reads, "Police Baffled By Mysterious Crime."

Looks like your reputation precedes you. Better split before you attract too much attention. It's hard to eat when you're being shot at. Taking the whole tray of egg rolls from the buffet line, you get up and walk out through the back wall.

"Awesome!" a small voice calls.

Okay, where to, Emperor? Is it better to take over earth as a Roman God or as a burgeoning Supervillain?

- Give that reporter an exclusive. Announce that the city is yours, then crush any resistance. Go to page 365
- Villainy from the bottom up—find the existing criminal organizations, and take over. Go to page 319

Empty-Handed

It's fully dark by the time you fly back to the warehouse. The smoke from the nearby fire is now only a smolder and you can see about a dozen emergency vehicles outside the facility: fire engines fighting the blaze, patrol cars blocking the roads, and two ambulances waiting nearby.

When you land and walk back inside, Nick rushes forward to greet you.

You shake your head. "Catherine's not interested in working with us. If anything, she's *happy* to be rogue. I can't be sure what her powers entail, but she's incredibly strong and resistant to damage. She seems to distrust the government, and brags about working outside it."

"Living an Ayn Rand fantasy," he muses. "John Galt meets Superman. That's unfortunate. Did you leave the phone with her?"

You nod. "Where's Agent Droakam?"

"He left. I'm not sure if he went to complete this 'mission' he's been so obsessed with, or if he's just angry. He didn't say."

You nod again.

"Do you…" Nick hesitates. "Do you think Catherine is a threat?"

"Maybe," you reply.

It's midmorning by the time Agent Droakam enters the warehouse. He carries a bag of donuts and a cardboard drink carrier with three coffees. Nick looks up from the computer terminal, then rises with a stretch and a yawn.

"Olive branch?" the student asks.

Droakam nods. "I admit I was at a loss when the two of you…" he starts, then clears his throat. "But it turns out your instincts were on point. I received new word from my superiors—priority one is bringing in Catherine Woodall."

"Easier said than done," you add.

"We'll be working together on this. You and I will take the lead, while Dorian is on logistics—we've got clearance to work with local police, so he'll coordinate the effort and maintain situational awareness with helicopter support. Think you can handle that?"

Nick raises an eyebrow, then turns back to the computer console. After a few keystrokes, police radio comes up over the speakers. One of the screens shows feed from 911 emergency calls and another flickers on to display an aerial view of the city.

"This is local news traffic cam, but I've informed the police helicopter crew that they're on standby."

"Fair enough," Droakam says.

The agent offers you the bag of donuts while Nick scans the computer screens.

"Hmmm, it looks like the police chopper has a mission already," Nick says, tapping the keys. "Whoa—we've got a hit! Bank robbery in progress. Hostages taken. And—you're gonna want to see this."

He pulls up a vertical, smart-phone video on someone's Vine account. It starts on a bank façade, shot from behind a police barricade, and focuses on a woman running toward the entrance. She wears a tight, midriff-exposing black t-shirt emblazoned with a playing-card-suit red diamond logo, fingerless gloves, and black yoga pants tucked into crimson-red boots. Her face is concealed behind a red domino mask, but you recognize Catherine immediately.

Just as she smashes through the security doors and rushes into the bank, the video's narrator cries, "Oh shi—" and the video repeats on loop.

"Seems 'Supa-gurl' has a new look," Nick says.

"It's a public space, so it's not ideal for a showdown," Droakam says.

"But the police are already there," you say. "Who knows when we'll get another chance like this!"

"There is another option…" Nick says.

You turn away from the screen with Agent Droakam to hear what Nick has to say.

"She has a son. I realize this is a delicate tactic, but…while she's off at the bank, he should be alone. If we find out she's too powerful, we could use the kid as leverage."

"Jesus," Droakam says.

"Are you suggesting we kidnap him?" you ask.

"If you think about it," Nick says, "he'd probably be safer with us."

Droakam sighs. "I have to admit, it's probably a better option than taking her head-on."

"You're actually considering this?" you say.

"You're not? Think about it," Nick replies for Droakam.

"I'm going to head down to the bank and work with law enforcement. You go by her trailer and pick up the boy. What's his name?" Droakam says.

"Daniel Woodall, goes by Danny," Nick says. "I'll keep tabs on surveillance from here; try to help coordinate the effort."

- ➢ "I don't like it, but you're probably right." Go get her kid. Go to page 202
- ➢ "Absolutely not! Agent Droakam, I'll meet you at the bank and together we'll bring her in." Go to page 331

End of an Era

The Mercury City Swashbucklers are far from "America's Football Team." And, as one of the few teams who've never won a Super Bowl, the 'Bucks (as fans call themselves), are a loyal minority.

You jog out onto the Astroturf, stunning the players and staff with the unexpected interruption. The pair of security guards on midweek payroll take note and rush to detain you. Usually, drunken fans only hop onto the field during play, so you've got them by surprise. But they haven't seen anything yet.

The first guard goes to take out your legs, but he bounces off you like a Pee-wee League kid. The second guard comes at you from behind, takes hold of your shoulder and bicep, and attempts to put your arm behind your back. Nope. He might as well be tugging on a statue.

You put a palm on the guard's face, and with an effortless shove, send him ten yards down the field. First down! The first guard shakes off his concussion and goes at you with a can of pepper spray.

Finally, it appears you have a weakness. Burning pain! Your eyes overflow with tears and mucous pours from your face. With superhuman rage, you grab the hapless guard and *punt* him through the uprights, forty yards away.

Stumbling to the sidelines, you knock over bench seats until you find the water cooler. With sweet relief, you pour the cooler over your head like you're already MVP. With all eyes on you, you take one of the game balls, tuck it back, and throw it into the sky—and out of the stadium.

"Who the hell *are* you?" the head coach asks.

Turns out you killed that security guard, but it doesn't matter, because you win football games. You're made quarterback *and* defensive tackle. On the offense, you just tuck your head and run it in for a touchdown yourself. On defense, the opposing team gets no more than three seconds with the ball. Mark Wahlberg offers to adapt your life story for a Hollywood movie.

Nick Dorian follows your lead and goes into the NBA. He confides that he telekinetically sends the ball into the hoop from anywhere on the court. Mercury City now hosts the greatest football and basketball teams in the world.

Catherine Woodall founds a new chapter of Mensa, wins several Nobel prizes, and generally makes the world a better place for humanity.

While you initially make the Swashbucklers reach superstardom, people eventually get tired. There are no stakes anymore. Fans abandon the team, and the popularity of the NFL wanes as a whole. Catherine confides that by killing football, she thinks you too helped make the world a better place for humanity.

Whatever. You're rich! And you get to eat free anywhere you go in town, so you're set for life. Life as a superstar. You win…sort of.

THE END

Entrepre*nope*!

"1950s tech? Ooh, tell me more!" she laughs.

"I said *since* then," you defend. "It's a lot of stuff."

"A lot of junk, I'm sure. No thanks."

"You're not even curious?" Nick asks.

"Why would I sell out for yesterday's ideas and flops? I'm the face of tomorrow!" she grins, cutely showing off said face.

"Can't change your mind?" you ask.

"You just tried, didn't you? Sorry, but no hard feelings. I'll see you on the other side. Good luck with the whole Freedom Fighters thing. Maybe I'll give you a call if 'Woodall Wonders' ever starts hiring."

> *Head back to the warehouse without Catherine.* Go to page 220

Evasive Maneuvers

In a combined physical and telekinetic leap, you dive away from the car fast enough that the world temporarily blurs while you move. Then you're up, floating in the air, and the crowd collectively gasps in response.

You can't bring yourself to look at Agent Droakam's body under the car, but you're more than ready to avenge him. His handgun flies up to meet your outstretched arm. With lightning speed, you've got the pistol turned on Catherine and the magazine emptied as you fire the full capacity at her.

The bullets do nothing more than ineffectually *ping* off her, ripping her costume but otherwise leaving her unharmed.

"Stop it! You're messing up my outfit!" she cries, feigning vanity.

You try using your telekinesis against her any way you can think—stopping her heart, gouging out her eyes, wrenching her guts, pulling her hair—nothing works. She really is like a solid diamond. The hair moves, of course, but doesn't tear, and that maneuver obviously doesn't hurt her.

Catherine the Diamond rips out a streetlight and comes at you in earnest.

You *grab* her with your mind and throw her across the street. But it doesn't work. It's feels like trying to lift a rhinoceros. Instead, you slide across the pavement while she continues charging. *What the hell?* You flit and fly, dodging her strokes, then dash *up* as fast as you can.

But it's not enough.

The light pole *slams* against you before you can get away. Hurtling to the ground in a daze from sixty feet high, you're able to get your wits about you just before you plow into the pavement.

You stop only inches from the concrete, the wind knocked out of you and your right thigh throbbing from the impact of the streetlight, but otherwise okay. You reel about, ready for the next attack, but too late. Catherine has one hand gripped tightly around your ankle and there's no escape.

She lifts you high above her head and starts twirling. It's all you can do to stay conscious. Your vision narrows, then everything goes black.

First it's just blackness, but eventually color blurs in. Blinking, blinking, blinking, your sight starts to return. You're…in a hospital?

"Nick?" you utter weakly. He's here, in the hospital, by your side. Wearing a black suit, like it's already your funeral.

"Hey," he says. "How're you feelin' there, champ? Can you sit up?" You try, but it's like you're glued to the bed. In despair and confusion, you shake your head. "What about your powers, huh? Try to move that cup of water on the bedside table. Concentrate hard, this is important."

After an excruciating effort, eyes watering in the process, the cup shudders on the tray.

"Okay, okay. That's enough. It's not totally gone. You're paralyzed, from the looks of it, but those abilities might come back in time."

"Nick…"

"Shhh, there-there. Don't try too hard, it's almost over. I'm going to tell you a story, mostly because I can't tell anybody else, but what the hey—I'm gonna let you in on a little secret if that's okay with you."

He pulls up a chair, unbuttons his suit jacket and takes a seat before continuing. "How do you like the new duds? Pretty snazzy, huh? I'm *Agent* Nick Dorian now, head of the Supersoldier Program. After Droakam passed away, and with you incapacitated, I was the natural choice. But of course I didn't leave that to chance—I gave myself the job after I'd hacked into the database. That was a crucial step.

"There was never going to be a Supersoldier Program, at least not in the way Droakam wanted. Creating an army of people like us? I couldn't let that happen. Which, incidentally, is why I joined up in the first place. Keep your friends close and your enemies closer, right? Once I knew he was trying to recreate the experiment, I had to come along and stop him.

"It didn't take much. After your meeting with Catherine, I knew I could use her. That was the final piece of the puzzle. So I sent Agent Droakam falsified orders, telling him that her capture was priority one. Of course you couldn't defeat her, what with her being nearly invincible and all. Although if you did, I had a plan for that too."

He winks.

"I thought she would just kill you outright, so I apologize that you've suffered. I would've preferred a clean death. Diamond is fully in my control now, which is great, but it also means I have no need for you. No hard feelings, okay?"

Nick takes a syringe from his breast pocket, stands, and inserts the liquid solution into your IV bag. You try to stop him with your mind, but the bag just sways as if against a breeze.

"Well, that about covers it. Next step: ruling the world. Thanks for all your help…and sleep tight, my friend."

As Nick walks away, the world goes black, never to return again.

THE END

Extra Credit

You sit in the theater at the very end until the last name has passed and the house lights come on, huh? Good for you. Whether it's out of respect for the cast and crew, not wanting a theater experience to end, or just in hope of a bonus scene, I applaud your going-against-the-crowd nature (and the size of your bladder). So I shall reward you. Here it is, your bonus scene, one of two Easter eggs in the book:

The Experi-mentor hovers upside-down in midair, his lab coat slack against gravity. Eyes clenched tight and face awash with a pain-expectant wince. The three of you sit in your color-coded pods, each in a different state of terror-fueled agitation. An electrical arc spans the room, jagged at all right angles, but suspended in time. In fact, time stands still.

Then the Experi-mentor opens his eyes. He looks around. Nothing moves, save for him. Is this what dying feels like? Wait, no, something else is moving. Or at least, appears alive. The three pods *pulse* with some kind of other-worldly energy, supercharging the beings within.

The scientist squirms about in space, willing gravity to obey him, but the force won't comply. He flails, weightless. Finally—fortunately—he's just barely able to put a finger around the handle of an equipment-rack drawer. He pulls himself in toward the shelf and plants his feet firmly against it.

Only one chance. The man aims his trajectory right at the pods, ready to spring forward and unplug the mega-cable in the center. Maybe that will restore the laws of physics? He'd better be careful not to cross into the electric beam; static or no, he's fairly certain it's still dangerous.

The Experi-mentor launches himself toward the pods. He flies forward, his lab coat oddly contorted and not responding to friction or gravity, and reaches for the cables. They're almost in his grasp—

—but an unseen energy repels him away from the pods, rebuffing his advances and sending him careening across the lab. He braces for impact and sails right toward the double-doors of the entrance. When he collides against them, the lab explodes! A firestorm rocks the entire area, and debris barely misses the man who just retriggered the space/time continuum.

The whole world returns to normal.

Terrified, the scientist rushes back to check on his test subjects, but the pods are solid walls of energy. He gathers his papers, takes the camcorder, and flees in fear.

Only after he's gone do the pods detonate—blasting energy in all directions and leaving three unconscious, superpowered beings.

Unaware of their new gifts, they begin to stir.

Now go back and finish the story!

Eye-Opening

"Very well, if you want to be known as a criminal trio, I'm willing to take that step. But—and this too is non-negotiable—I'm the mastermind. What good is a super-genius on the team if you don't listen to me?"

After a moment of silence, they grumble their agreement.

"So what's the plan, then? Hack into the news broadcast and announce the city's ours?" Nick asks.

"Give me twenty-four hours to come up with a plan. In the meantime—find us a discrete construction team to start on the lair."

"You put this together in a day?" Nick says, noting the "office" you've set up for yourself. It's bare-bones, mainly a mega-computer terminal with several monitors.

"Okay, what's the plan?" Catherine asks.

"Well, I found some interesting new information. The press and Mercury PD aren't the only ones interested in…*our*…exploits."

You pull up a headshot on a spare monitor. The man on-screen is of average height, square-jawed and muscular, with short-cropped hair.

"Agent Brendan Droakam, FBI Supersoldier Program."

"Wait…did you say *Supersoldier* Program?" Nick asks.

You nod. "He's been following the two of you. Obviously, that's a problem, but that's not all."

"More bad news?" Catherine asks.

"I'm afraid so. My cancer treatment samples were stolen. At first I couldn't understand why, as I made the research available for peer-review. My conspiracy senses went off; maybe the pharmaceutical companies didn't want the treatment out there? But then I realized there was a far simpler answer: The samples were stolen because they contain my blood."

Catherine's eyes narrow. "You think this FBI guy…?"

"Not quite. He's a G-man, plain and simple. The samples were stolen by someone who could do something with them."

"Police forensics?" Nick tries.

You sigh. "It's that scientist, the Experi-mentor. He's still alive! And he's trying to recreate the experiment."

They both look to you. *What do we do?*

- "The enemy of my enemy makes for an incredibly useful pawn. What if we let this Agent Droakam and the Experi-mentor cancel each other out?"
  Go to page 43
- "We have to stop the Experi-mentor. If he creates more 'supers,' we lose what advantage we have." Go to page 128
- "First we take down this Agent Droakam. The scientist doesn't know we're onto him, but an entire Supersoldier Program? That's problematic."
  Go to page 371

Feeling Lucky

"Different?" you say, as if the word had never occurred to you. "Just lucky, I guess. Lucky to be alive. Maybe my luck will continue, right? Wh—what about you? Anything different?"

Nick gives you an appraising glance. At length, he says, "Same. Lucky too, I guess."

You nod to Nick, then make your way to the roulette area. There are several empty tables to choose from—it's the middle of the day, after all—and you take a seat at one, empty your wallet, and bet $35 on black.

Feeling lucky, indeed.

The croupier sets down another $35 next to the first; using your telekinesis, you've just doubled your money. With a wave of your hand, you command him to continue. And just like the first go-round, you *force* the ball into a favorable position without waiting to see where it might end up naturally. No point in taking chances.

"Too bad you didn't bet more," Nick says. You didn't even notice him sidle up beside you.

"D'ya mind?" you say. "No offense, but I don't want to attract any attention to my little hot streak here."

Nick shrugs and walks away.

"Not much chance of that," the croupier says, his eyes quickly darting to a security camera.

"Then why don't we hurry it along? Put it all on number 35."

He shakes his head. "I don't know your trick, but if I cash you out now, you might be able to skip town before…."

"Skip town?" you laugh. "This is *my* town. Spin the goddamned wheel."

The croupier sighs and spins the wheel. Feeling cocky, you wait to see where the ball will naturally hit this time around. It bounces and bounces and finally comes to land…lucky number 7. Oh, well—you *flick* the ball and it hops twice over to the slot for number 35.

The croupier's jaw drops. You grin, but that grin quickly disappears when a strong hand grips your shoulder. When you turn around, a pair of towering security escorts greet you.

"Come with us, please," a gargoyle of a man says.

"No thanks."

The second man steps forward and says, "We can do this the easy way or—"

"Ooh, can we do it the hard way?" you interrupt. "Pretty please?"

Their jaws are set in one uniform motion, as the closer man reaches out to grab you. At the same moment, you *freeze* his hands in the air, instantly stopping his progress. He looks at his hands, his expression that of a mime who realizes he's trapped in a box.

Not waiting for an explanation, the other security guard makes a mighty fist and swings that knuckled boulder at your head. With your telekinesis, you easily *turn* the trajectory of the punch, and the guard knocks his partner out cold. His eyes bulge and he looks from the unconscious man to his fist, to you.

You *grab* the guard by his throat with your mind, and bring him to his knees. You extend your arm to pantomime the choke and illustrate that you're the source of his pain.

"I don't want to kill you; you were just doing your job. So if you fuck off right now, I won't."

He sputters out a coughing *thank you*, finds his feet, and runs away, his expensive shoes slipping on the carpeted floor.

You turn back to the table. The croupier pushes all the chips toward you, then raises his hands like he's being robbed.

"Listen," Nick says, approaching you, his hands held out in supplication.

"For chrissake," you growl.

"Just listen. There's not much time. I saw what you did there, and I'm impressed. I find myself with new abilities as well. I'm suddenly smarter than any man on the planet. I could see how this was going to turn out when you won your first bet, and I can help you. This won't end well for you, not if you don't let me help you."

"Yeah? Why would you do that?"

"I get it, you want to be Darth Vader, but here's the thing—I want to be the Emperor. Kneel before me, and together we'll rule the Galaxy."

You laugh.

"Remember, a rising tide raises all ships. I'll be the mastermind, but so what? Together we'll reign above the whole city, the nation, the world!"

- Nick has wasted enough of your time, and apparently, might be your biggest threat. Kill the twerp, then finish up at the cashier's cage. Go to page 258
- Accept his offer. Maybe he can help you get to the top. Let him be Emperor…for a while, at least. You can always throw him into a shaft when the time is right. Go to page 125

Fight Drillbit and You Get *Screwed!*

"That's not really your battle-cry, is it?" you say, backpedaling as the college-student-turned-supervillain charges forward.

"Oh, yeah? And what's yours? 'Hey guys, not sure if you've heard, but I cured cancer. I'm kind of a big deal.' Such a pretentious douche!"

You throw a glance over at Baxter and Catherine. The so-called Shadow Priestess floats toward your robot companion, and the newly installed sound-wave amplifier embedded in Baxter's left forearm hums to life. The robot blasts concentrated sounds at Catherine, who shrieks in agony. Can't use telekinesis against a waveform, booyah!

"Robbing banks; isn't that a little *beneath* a superhuman?" you say, your attention back on Nick.

"You're about to be beneath me when I crush you!"

You stop running. "No, no, no. That's all wrong. Damn, I thought you'd be heavier."

Nick stops too. "What's that supposed to mean?"

"The 'beneath' line was supposed to be a pun. How do you not weigh more? You must be, what, a thousand times as dense as a normal person?"

"Who're you calling dense?" Nick says, cracking his knuckles.

You sigh. "Guess I have to do it manually."

With a quick lunge, you slap an open palm against the plunger switch on the wall and the ground collapses under Nick's feet. He falls a hundred feet into the open cavern below. That really would've been cooler if he just fell through after you delivered your "beneath" line. Oh, well.

You turn to Catherine and Baxter. She keeps her distance from your robot, diluting the potency of the soundwaves, and *flings* bits of rubble and equipment. Baxter's chassis holds several dents and scratches, but is relatively unharmed.

Time for phase two. You step around the corner into the Projection Booth and a hologram version of yourself steps out on the other side, armed with a machine gun. Running on the booth's omni-directional treadmill, your hologram runs toward the fight.

"Say your prayers, Priestess!" you cry, your voice relayed through a PA system.

Catherine turns back, but rather than being frightened, she looks excited to fight a traditional foe.

"Give me that!" she shouts, and *pulls* at the weapon. "Choke!"

Her expression drops when her telekinetic powers do nothing. She's fighting a holographic projection, after all. From behind her, Baxter lifts one leg in a goose-step and fires a net from the outstretched heel. It wraps and fells Catherine.

Baxter then moves over to her, crouches, and releases a potent knock-out gas through his outstretched right hand.

"Well done, Baxter!" you cry, stepping out of the Projection Booth. The hologram disappears and you run over to your robot. "Now we just need to get her to the immobility chamber."

A violent earthquake shakes your fortress-laboratory as Nick *explodes* through the floor. Baxter shields you as rocky debris rains down from his dramatic entry.

"You underestimate me for the last time!" he cries.

You smirk. "Well, you got that right. Go-go-gadget Taser!"

In response, Baxter's other leg snakes out and wraps around Nick. A terrible electric current arcs through the metal leg with enough shock to put down a charging bull-elephant. Nick's body seizes; he falls to the floor in a heap. Then Baxter stumbles; performing the shock took full energy reserves.

"Power loss critical," Baxter says in a baritone. "Shutting dowwwwwnnnnnn...."

The robot goes limp. Better plug in right away; you're going to need some help getting these two into their super-supermax detention facilities.

"Well done, Baxter. Well fought, my friend. Sleep now—you earned it."

Then someone says, "A touching moment, but I'm afraid I must interrupt."

Your mind scrambles. You know that voice.

➢ *Turn to face the new threat!* Go to page 226

117

First Day of the Rest of Your Life

Groggy from the late night, you feel like it's all been a dream. But no, here you are, in a secret government lab, somewhat grungy in yesterday's clothes, but more excited to start the day than you've been in a long time.

With a yawn and a stretch, you rise to seek out your comrades. As you move through the warehouse, you hear something that sounds like an RC car cruising around the crates. When you peer around the edge of a box, you see a waist-high robot on tank-tread wheels, like one of those bomb-squad bots that aids in defusing or detonating possible threats. This one has an arm that spray-paints a label onto a nearby crate. So far, it's got PLASTIC EXPL stenciled in above a barcode.

Past the labeler-bot, you find Nick and Agent Droakam at the massive computer terminal. They turn when you approach.

"Morning, guys. What's with the robot?"

"What?" Nick asks, a kind of manic weariness in his features.

"The robot," you repeat, turning to point.

"Oh, that. It's cataloging the contents of the crates. Should speed things up."

"Dorian here's been up all night," Droakam informs, his voice thick with awe. "The robot is his design—threw it together using extra lab components. After he set up the computer system on his own, of course."

"It should help us analyze our DNA, but I've got some bad news," Nick says. "I'm not going to be able to successfully recreate the experiment. Not unless I can find the professor's notes and see how he had the machines calibrated. Otherwise it's just guesswork. You can know exactly how a bicycle lock works, but unless you have the combination…."

Droakam's jaw tightens. "I'll have the guys check the rubble again, but keep at it."

Nick nods, suppressing a yawn. "Apparently I don't have superhuman energy. I know you had a big day planned or whatever, but I need some sleep."

Droakam nods. "That's okay, get some rest. I'll work with our resident telekinetic instead. There should be some earplugs you can use near the beds."

Nick bids you best of luck, then makes his way toward the cots and sleeping bags.

"Pick up that crate," Droakam says. "We'll start small, but it's time to tap into your powers and find your limits, assuming you have any. Go with what your body's feeling but don't—you know—light the building on fire or anything like that. We don't know if you're simply telekinetic, pyrokinetic, or what. So…start small. Pick up the crate."

You do so with ease, lifting the box with your mind. "I've been practicing."

"Good. Keep that one steady and bring up another."

"Should I stand on my head too?"

Agent Droakam ignores the joke, waiting for you to proceed. You lift the second crate, and in a display of skill, stack it atop the other in midair.

"Now a third."

You nod and put out a hand to grab a third crate, but nothing happens. You settle in and squat down as if you were physically lifting the weight and *pull* with full effort. The crate shudders on its base, vibrating against the floor. You try harder until—in one movement—the double-stack falls to the ground and the single crate flies into the air and smashes against the roof.

"Concentrate, catch the debris!" Agent Droakam shouts.

Feeling like a circus juggler, you reach out for each piece as it rains down from above, catching the largest ones and a few of the smaller ones, but letting the splinters fall to the warehouse floor. In frustration, you *blast* everything away in a massive shockwave.

"I'm…sorry," you say, straining. Sweating now.

"Don't be. Go ahead and set all that down. We've just learned a few things. Your abilities work more like 'arms' than a net, to a point. That's why you weren't able to catch all the pieces. Perhaps you can improve upon this in the future, but it's good to know your limitations. Each of these crates is probably a hundred pounds, so it looks like you've got a weight limit too."

"I've been thinking—what if my abilities go beyond telekinesis, like you said? What if I'm telepathic too? Here, I'll try to read your—"

"No, don't!" he shouts, ducking away.

"What's wrong? What is it?"

He composes himself, then says, "Try this first."

Agent Droakam takes you to the periphery of the room, to a series of roll-up doors, like the type you'd see at a storage facility. What's behind door #1? There to greet you stands a goat, silent at the center of the unit atop a matted layer of hay and excrement.

"I had it sent over by the boys at goat lab," Droakam explains. "It's been debleated."

You stare at the goat. The goat blinks several times. "What do you want me to do?" you ask.

"I want you to try and read the goat's thoughts. Just like you wanted to do with me."

You laugh. "How am I supposed to read a goat's thoughts?"

"How are you supposed to read a person's thoughts? Just try."

It's hard to concentrate, but Droakam is dead-serious and willing to wait patiently for as long as it takes. For you to read a goat's thoughts. Half-expecting to hear *BAAAAAA* inside your head, you reach out and *touch* the goat's mind with the power of your own.

There's a flutter behind the goat's eyes—have you done it? Have you accessed another creature's consciousness? Then the goat's legs stiffen and it falls to the ground. Agent Droakam rushes over.

"It's dead!" he says, a grin plastered across his face like a kid in a candy store.

A shock of panic shoots through you. With only the slightest bit of effort, you really did just stare that goat to death. How little it would take to do the same to a person, to Agent Droakam, to Nick, to yourself, even! *No, I can control this*, you tell yourself. *I have to* choose *to kill*.

"I guess I can't read minds."

Droakam rises from the goat and nods. He closes the door to the dead animal's enclosure and steps back toward the crates.

"Hence the reason I didn't want you to try it on *me*. For now, I think we should focus on other aspects of your powers more closely related to telekinesis."

With sweaty palms, you swallow a lump in your throat. "Like?" you ask.

"I'd like you to…lift yourself."

"Just like the crates?" you ask, looking at the broken pieces on the ground.

"Just like the crates."

With a deep breath, you start to reach out—but instead reach *in*. It starts slowly, as a hover, but you rise from the ground. You're able to *telekinese yourself*, as it were. But it doesn't feel as if someone's lifting you, rather, you float with true weightlessness.

You're flying!

Laughing with pure joy, you float up to the ceiling and fly around the warehouse, soaring faster than you could ever hope to sprint. Arms widespread like *Peter Pan*, you float and flit throughout the enormous building, circling above the crates. You lap around the main room several times, darting back and forth and performing acrobatic barrel rolls.

"I'm flying!" you shout with glee.

That night, Agent Droakam gathers both of you. "I think it's time for a field test. We've got one of the FBI's Top Ten Most Wanted here in Mercury City, a man who's notorious for ducking law enforcement. But since you're not technically law enforcement, you have *carte blanche* authority to bring him in. If we start down the list, the Supersoldier Program will be reinstated and funding will skyrocket, I can guarantee that."

"You may want to look at something first," Nick says.

You follow him over to the computer terminal, where he spent most of his day. The screen shows:

> unreal dis lady save my life! thank god thank jesus #SupaGurl #blessed #unreal
>
> @ccboyes @d_flyer Saw some chick bend a street sign in half today. Crosssfit? Roids? #SupaGurl
>
> LOL somebody f%*^'d up!!!!! #SupaGurl =1 #PurseSnatcher =0
>
> @akross This soccermom just walked passed me with an ATM over her shoulder… #SupaGurl sighting or am I #Switching2Decaf ?
>
> #notfake #real #nophotoshop #hero #SupaGurl pic.twitter.com/ugwnbxvWGn

"Is that some kind of code? Have you broken it yet?" Droakam asks.

"No, that's just Twitter," Nick laughs. "The hashtag 'SupaGurl' has been trending. I isolated a few choice tweets, excluding the rampant speculation and the alternating declarations of hate and adoration. Take a look at this:"

He expands the final tweet to show the photo—a freeze-frame of a woman caught mid-action as she rips a flaming car in two. The metal bends beneath her grip as she tries to rescue the child strapped to a car-seat inside.

"Looks like our friend Catherine Woodall has been busy since the experiment. Might be a good idea to bring her in before she does something…ill-fated."

Droakam shakes his head. "She can wait. Getting funding back is our number one priority."

A flash on the mega-console catches your eye. "What's that?" you ask.

Nick punches some keys and the screen changes to the local news. The text footer says, "BREAKING" and reporter Alison Argyle appears onscreen in a sharp grey suit, platinum blonde hair down over her shoulders in the latest fashion, but her signature smile nowhere to be found.

Her concerned voice comes in over the computer's speakers: "We've just received word of an explosion in the warehouse district. No remarks from Mercury PD detailing if this is some kind of attack, but it does appear to be part of a break-in that sources say is currently in-progress. Again, we're being told this is not the result of an industrial accident, but instead some kind of criminal activity. There is no reason yet to suspect terrorist involvement, but workers in the district are being evacuated as we speak. We go now to live footage via helicopter."

The screen flashes to an aerial view of the warehouse district, the helicopter's floodlight sweeping over the buildings to focus on a column of smoke.

"That's only minutes away from us!" Nick shouts.

"No, don't even think about it," Agent Droakam says. "Law enforcement has it covered. We have our authorized operation, and I had to pull some strings just to get that. You could jeopardize everything if you don't go now."

Nick turns to you.

- "Okay. Stick to the mission. Who's the target and what do I need to do?" Go to page 66
- "We need to bring Catherine in. Everything else is just a distraction." Go to page 85
- "I'm going to that warehouse. This is a sign!" Go to page 185

The First Martian

Mercury City has a robust subway system and—like other historied metropolises—empty stations that were simply abandoned when updated routes were constructed. An antiquated map tells of outmoded Central Station, replaced by a modern version of the same name, the progenitor left to rot, with its entrance paved over.

In a word, the spot is perfect.

Along the rails you can transport your rocket ships. Inside the cavernous tunnels you can begin the growth of your *nanobot-cum-algae* you'll use to give the red planet an atmosphere. In this forgotten part of the world, you can plan a new one.

But there's one last step to take before you bound away from earthly life for good. After all, what's a colony without colonists?

You stand in the lobby of the K-HAN news building after giving your name and position as "Guest Lecturer for Mercury University." It's not long before Alison Argyle comes out to see you.

"I thought you were pleading the fifth?" the reporter asks, one eyebrow raised.

"I'll tell you what you need to know, but I have one condition. A favor, actually."

After an appraising glance, she says, "Guess you'd better come up."

Once you're both seated in her office—where awards, plaques, and photographs with celebrities line the walls—she waits for you to proceed.

"I have a message I want you to record. I'm sure you get all manner of crackpots demanding a segment on the nightly news, so I ask only this: record my message. Keep it until the day you deem it newsworthy. In exchange, I'll tell you everything about the lab explosion."

Without a word, she stands and walks out of the office. You turn and watch her leave, half-expecting her to return with security. Instead, she carries a tripod-mounted camera. She sets everything up, then tells you to begin.

You clear your throat. "People of Earth, greetings. By now you know I've cured cancer."

The reporter gives you a look, but you continue. "And, if you're watching this broadcast, I'm already on my way to Mars. With my advanced rocket design, it's only a three-month trip, and that's plenty of time to develop the life-sustaining techniques needed for our future home. I've made my plans for homemade rocket ships available to download online, but please proceed with caution.

"The Martian Federation needs brilliant minds and hard workers. I will send messages with supply requests, but know that any and all are welcome to join me on the red planet. Mars was the Roman god of war, yet our new home will be a commune of peace and tolerance.

"I hope to meet the bravest among you very soon."

You turn from the camera to Alison Argyle. Her lips are parted and her eyes are wide. Does she believe you? It doesn't matter. Once the Nobel committee shares your discoveries, she certainly will. Perhaps she'll be among those intrepid enough to join you amongst the stars?

So you tell her of the experiment and the explosion, and of your newfound genius. Then, within a week, you leave this planet. Never to return, unconcerned with what becomes of Mercury City and the other superbeings who inhabit the Earth. Instead, you'll live the rest of your days in a clock-shaped palace as the philosopher-king of Mars, known simply to your subjects as Dr. Mercury.

You win, in a sense, though Earth as a whole suffers a great loss with your departure.

THE END

Flight of Shame

You wake up, head pounding. What the hell happened last night? Vague memories of acrobatic floating, and you're pretty sure you have some oddly placed bruises, but it's pretty hazy. Though, seeing as how you're in Catherine's bed, there's little doubt how things ended up. Yet you wake up alone.

"Catherine?" you call out.

No response. Something draws your attention toward the living room. Is that the TV? You walk out to investigate and—yep, it's the TV—with a young boy watching it on the couch.

"Hi. You're mom's friend, right?" *Oh, shit.* "Look, she's on the news."

The image on screen cuts from blonde eye-candy reporter Alison Argyle to the façade of Mercury Bank and a title card that reads, "ROBBERY IN PROGRESS—Hostages Taken." The bank has police barricades set up, but immediately, Catherine runs toward the entrance in her Diamond costume and *smashes* through the front security doors and into the bank.

The crowd gathered behind the police barricade erupts in cheers.

"I need to help her!" you say.

"Wait, you're gonna want a mask," Danny says.

* * *

Wearing a pair of Catherine's pantyhose over your head—you're not proud, but hey, it was short notice—you rocket your way through the air toward Mercury Bank. The traffic would be impossible, especially with an ongoing crisis, but flight makes the journey only a few minutes long.

You weave through the skyscrapers, your own reflection glittering off the windows, darting just above the streetlights and overpasses. Once the bank is in sight, you dart in through the broken doors.

Inside, the bank is a scene of total destruction. Desks have been thrown wildly, clearing a central path, and people are huddled along the outer walls. They look to you with concern, and you command their attention by floating several feet above the ground. Their look shows more terror than excitement. Mercury City doesn't yet know its heroes.

"Where is she?" you ask.

One by one, they all point to the rear of the bank. Gunfire rattles somewhere in the distance. A man in a ski mask sprints out toward you, and in reflex you psychically grab two computer monitors from the desks of *New Accounts* and bring them together around the man's head. Your feet touch the ground as you *lift* the man and fling him to the side.

Catherine rushes to you from around the corner, her costume pock-marked with bullet holes. She's holding the enormous disc-shaped door from the vault and—before she has a chance to recognize you—she hurls the enormous metal saucer at you.

- ➢ Dive out of the way. Go to page 358
- ➢ Catch it with your telekinesis. Go to page 70

Flock Together

"Excellent," Nick says.

He looks past you, brings his wrist up to his mouth and says something into his wristwatch that you can't quite hear. Confused, you turn back—right into the full security team of the casino. Two dozen men, armed and ready to gun you down.

"What the…." you say, raising your hands in defeat.

Looks like Nick won; somehow he tricked you. Feelings of betrayal bubble up inside you, and you prepare yourself for revenge. But the security personnel lower their weapons and head back into the recesses of the casino.

When you turn back, Nick grins. "You're looking at the new owner of the Planet Mercury casino," he says. "I *was* here counting cards, but last night I met with Nelson Bloodnight—the previous owner—and made him an offer he couldn't refuse."

"You killed him?"

"Oh, no. Far too messy. A literal offer. Remember: super-genius. I posed my takeover with such terms that he thought he was getting a better deal. And in return, he publicly and legally gave me power here. Power over employees, all the money in the vault, and soon, by proxy, over the city. Thus lies the secret of true power; getting someone to do what you want is one thing, but making them think it was *their* idea in the first place—that's something else entirely."

Nick quickly adds, "Of course, that's not what's happening with us. Come with me up to the penthouse! That place is amazing."

A private elevator leads up to the main penthouse suite on the top floor—forty stories up. It's a gaudy headquarters, but as a status symbol, it's second to none. The suite is incredibly large (it puts the *house* in penthouse), with two whole stories and several rooms. A gigantic balcony draws your attention outside.

"Pretty nice digs, eh?" Nick says. "Tonight, we celebrate, but let's not rest on our laurels. Tomorrow, we move on to phase two."

"Phase two?" you inquire.

"Tomorrow," Nick winks. "Now then, what's your poison? Champagne? Caviar? Or are you more a scotch-and-cigars type?"

The next morning, while you share room service of a quality normally reserved for royalty, it's on to business. Nick says, "What we really want is a monopoly. And to have that, we must eliminate the competition."

"Competition?"

"Haven't you heard the rumors of 'Supa-gurl' or whatever the masses are calling her? Catherine Woodall has taken her powers public and declared herself savior of the public. 'The superhero exists, and she's American.' Don't you follow the news?"

Nick flips on the enormous television and cues in the local news station. There onscreen is blonde eye-candy reporter Alison Argyle, standing at a police barricade with a special report.

"I'm here at the downtown Mercury Bank, where a robbery is in progress. A team of armed men have taken control of the bank, and it is believed there are hostages involved." Alison Argyle turns away from the camera in response to shouts from the gathered crowd. Her cameraman pans and zooms to catch the action.

A costumed woman runs toward the bank entrance. She wears a tight, midriff-exposing black t-shirt emblazoned with a playing-card-suit red diamond logo, fingerless gloves, and black yoga pants tucked into crimson-red boots. Her face is concealed behind a red domino mask, but as she smashes through the security doors and rushes into the bank, there can be little doubt in your mind as to who this superpowered woman truly is.

Nick turns the TV off. "This is bad—and it's only going to get worse. This town ain't big enough for the three of us, as they say."

"You think she's a threat?"

"She's the only possible threat!" Nick counters. "She sees herself as some kind of superhero, like the world is her personal comic book. Well, I say, so be it!"

He turns to you, brow raised, waiting for a response.

➢ "We must bait a trap, but how do we stop someone who can smash through walls?" Go to page 337
➢ "You're right, she is a threat. But what if we simply help the rest of the city realize it? Turn public opinion against her. Then we'll show up, defeat her, and be greeted as heroes." Go to page 35

Fly-by-Night

You try the door—yep, it's locked. Standard dead-bolt, but the thumb-turn is on the other side. But you can *feel* the lock; you can almost see it in your mind. Close your eyes and focus. Mentally, you *twist* the deadbolt back to the open position. It's such a realistic visualization, you can actually hear the door unlocking.

When you open your eyes and try the door once more—it opens. You just telekinetically opened a door from the other side. This is amazing!

"Don't move, goddammit!" shouts a cop from the hall, pistol trained on you.

Keeping your eyes open this time, you *feel* the handgun with your mind. As clearly as if you had a grip on it yourself, you *turn* the weapon so the policeman points the weapon at his own head, the muzzle pressed firmly against his temple.

The man's eyes open wildly, and beads of sweat appear on his brow. With his other hand, he tries to peel the weapon away, but in vain—your mental grip is much, much stronger.

- ➢ Now would be a great time to escape out the back, and get far, far away from all of this. Go to page 92
- ➢ Make an example of him—fear will keep the rest of them in line. Then walk out the front door. Go to page 77

Foiled Again

Step one: Search for rentable lab space.
> Step two: Search this subset for labs with no vacancies.
> Step three: Visit said labs, seeking out the man who created you.
> After barging in on two very confused researchers, you hit the jackpot on the third lab. Three vans are parked nearby, with HiT stenciled on the side of each. *Human Infinite Technologies*.
> "This is it, get ready," you say.
> Catherine steals a key card from a hapless janitor, but Nick just smashes through the security doors. Six researchers, two women and four men, stand in the lab space. Several work on a glass pod about the size of an old telephone booth. One of the women dips lab-coats in vats of dye, changing them from white to various solid colors.
> Then, like seeing a ghost, a man looks up from a microscope. Beneath his white lab coat, an "Ex" stands out. He puts on his glasses and his eyes grow wide at the sight of you. "My—my creations!"
> "You're done creating," you say.
> "Wait!" the Experi-mentor cries out. "I'm so close to duplicating the results. With new and remarkable powers. Aren't you the least bit curious?"
> You close your eyes. Curious, maybe. But only other superhumans can stop your genius. And what if he makes more like you? If everyone's special, no one is.
> At length, you say, "Destroy everything."

➢ *Only one threat remains: Agent Droakam and the Supersoldier Project.*
  Go to page 371

Follow the Leader

You fly inside the bank just in time to see Catherine rush into the back. Bank employees and customers are huddled against the sides at the entrance, but you zoom past them and back toward the vault.

When you make it to the *Employees Only* section of the bank, half a dozen well-armed robbers are there waiting for you. Expecting you, they open fire.

But they're not expecting someone like Catherine. She runs through the lead hailstorm like it was only a spring rain. Bullets *ping* off her skin and she closes the gap between herself and the robbers in only a few seconds.

No, they were expecting someone more like you, someone who isn't bulletproof. You look down and see you've been shot several times. It's not the best idea to lemming your way behind someone who is bulletproof, especially when the forecast calls for cloudy with a chance of gunfire.

THE END

Force Choke

You reach out, hand clenched as if wrapped tightly around the prostitute's neck, and from three feet away, she gasps for air and claws at her own throat. Using the power of mind, you raise her up off the pavement and with the tiniest flick of your wrist, her neck breaks.

You look around—the street is empty, save for the Phantom mannequin at the Halloween shop across the street. The prostitute slumps to the ground next to the pimp. Defender of Peace and Justice, indeed. Perhaps not in a goody-two-shoes manner, but could that be what Mercury City needs? A hero darker than its villains?

- ➢ No way, I'm the good guy! Killing that guy was just a slip-up. No one will know if I never tell…. Go to page 47
- ➢ That's right, I make my own rules. If that makes others see me as a villain—so be it! Go to page 77

Fortune Favors the Hungry

The crowd erupts with cheers as hostages stream out of the bank's entrance and into the arms of EMTs and crisis-relief personnel. Then there is a deafening tidal wave of applause when Catherine drags out four bank robbers—two in each hand. She tosses them in a heap, then dusts off her hands. With an enormous grin, she double-fist-pumps the air and the crowd goes wild.

You're right there with her, accepting the adoration of the gathered crowd as you deliver the last two bank robbers. The combined weight of the men is too much for you to *float* them out, but you're able to drag them out with only the power of mind. Such a feat makes the crowd go wild.

Agent Droakam grabs a megaphone from a familiar-looking police sergeant and presses through the police barricade, marching toward you.

"Stay where you are!" he commands.

Catherine notices him and appraises the agent with curiosity. She takes two strides toward him and he places his hand on his hip, preparing to draw his weapon.

You move forward to help, but before you can intercede, Catherine snatches the megaphone and addresses the crowd: "No need to thank me, fair people of Mercury City. I am Diamond, and we are here to protect you!"

The cheers from the crowd strike you like an earthquake.

"Give me that!" Droakam says, taking back the megaphone. He turns off the device, then adds, "Catherine Woodall, my name is Agent Brendan Droakam. I'd like you to please come with me."

"You may call me Diamond, and I don't think I'd like to do that. We already told your lackey we're not interested."

She looks to you.

"That's not a request, ma'am."

Catherine presses her index finger against Droakam's chest and shoves him to the ground, using very little effort. "Buzz off, buddy. Go ticket speeders or something."

The entire police force draws their weapons. Boos come from the crowd. "Droakam, we don't want to be enemies," you say.

"Then come with me. Nick is back at the lab, ready to recreate the experiment. Come quietly, and no one gets hurt."

"That a fact?" Catherine says. "Go ahead, do your worst."

She picks up a car that was parked curbside in front of the bank, then starts spinning it like pizza dough. Droakam gets back up on his feet, his gun held with both hands.

"Put the vehicle down right now! Place your hands on top of your head and face the building!"

Catherine laughs. Better do something to diffuse the situation….

"Wait! Look around, we're heroes," you say. "If you kill him, that'll change. Let them be the villains. Today, right now, there's nothing they can do to keep us here. Let's just go."

After a moment, Catherine tosses the car back to its parking spot, though the axles give out when it smashes against the pavement. "It's your lucky day," Catherine says, pointing a finger at Droakam.

Then she sprints away from the bank with inhumanly long strides while you leap into the sky.

Catherine eats with ravenous hunger, like a half-feral hiker just rescued. You watch, fascinated, as she downs an enormous proportion of Chinese food.

"Do you really think Nick cracked the experiment?" she asks through a mouthful of egg foo yung.

"Maybe," you say. "He's certainly smart enough. It's possible he's actually working with Agent Droakam now out of spite. Or it could be a bluff. Either way, we're going to have to deal with Nick and the Supersoldier Program eventually."

She stands up as her third plate is cleared, and goes for more food. You consider the possibilities while she's gone. How do you outsmart a super-genius? Another full plate of food is smacked down on the table and Catherine takes her seat.

"And we can't just kill 'em?" she asks while spearing forkfuls of beef-n-broccoli.

The bill and two fortune cookies are plunked down in front of you. You look up to the server.

"No! No more! No more for you!" a stout Chinese woman shouts, flailing her arms. The elderly woman—evidently the owner of the restaurant—jabs her fingers at Catherine.

"It's a *buffet*. All-you-can-eat," Catherine protests.

"No! Limit reached! No more!"

Catherine growls. The restaurant owner leaves, offering no room for argument.

"Wait! I've got it," you say. "See these fortune cookies? What do they say?"

She shakes her head, still frustrated at being cut off.

"What?" she says.

"You don't know, right? And that's the whole point. It's a surprise. That's the only way we'll ever beat Nick. We have to surprise him, we can't outsmart a genius. He didn't anticipate my joining up with you; it was a surprise. To him, it was random. So…we do something totally random."

"Like what?"

- ➢ "We rush the lab, right now. Unprepared, we just go for it. He'll be caught off-guard." Go to page 282
- ➢ "We destroy the city's power-grid. As the heroes, it's a totally unexpected action. He won't have any access to his mega-computer, he'll be powerless." Go to page 310
- ➢ "We do nothing. We keep fighting crime and protecting the innocent, and we ignore Nick and Droakam. It's the one thing he won't expect—it'll drive him mad!" Go to page 2

Freedom Fighters

The crate is about eight feet tall, half as wide, and tapered like a coffin. Agent Droakam pries it open with the crowbar, then steps aside. Before you is a mannequin in a red, white, and blue camouflage military uniform.

"You're looking at what could have been the future US coalition combat uniform. Of course it's flame-retardant and durable, but what you can't see is that it's smart-tech. Antennae woven into the mesh transmit and receive valuable statistics. Full bio readout available in real time. The fabric is mostly microcircuits, allowing cognitive performance analysis. All this to say, it's a badass supersoldier suit."

"Two questions," Nick says. "Why is there only one? And what's the camouflage good for—fighting in a used-car lot on Memorial Day?"

"The answer to both is, it's a prototype. The color scheme was supposed to invoke patriotism and therefore a better chance at budgetary approval. Obviously, that failed. On the basic decision-making level, it's too expensive to give our troops this level of protection."

"So who gets the suit?" you ask.

"You do—you are now known as codename: *Freedom Fighter*. Kid, don't worry, you're up next." Droakam walks over to a crate stenciled with DINOSKIN MARK IV. He opens the lid to reveal a mannequin wearing an olive-green bodysuit, scaled and reptilian.

"The newest and best in body armor," Droakam explains. "Too expensive to be put into combat on a mass scale, but nothing else comes close. Lightweight, breathable, and incredibly durable. The scaling provides multilayer protection against gunshots or knife attack. A reinforced plate on the chest and spine provide added shock protection against explosives. But the best part? You should still be able to fly around in this thing because it's so lightweight."

"Sick! What's my codename?"

"I'm thinking *Kid Liberty.*"

"Yeah, no. Think again. Nothing with 'kid' in the title, and don't name me after a woman."

"What about *Scales of Justice*?" Droakam suggests.

"No."

"But get it? It's scaled. Scales…of Justice."

"No, I get it, but Justice is also a female. Plus…no. Just no."

"We'll worry about the name later," Droakam says. "For now, we'll call you *Freedom Fighters* as a team."

"You know that's synonymous with 'terrorists,' right?" Nick says.

"We're taking it back," Agent Droakam says firmly. "Now then, after you complete your first 'official' mission, we'll be back to full funding. But that means going legitimate. Fingerprints, blood samples, background checks—standard for secret agents."

"Cool…"

"Good luck with the blood sample," you say. "I mean, if bullets can't penetrate my skin, what chance does a needle have?"

Agent Droakam paces back and forth, mulling it over. "It's important before committing you to combat operations. I mean, we don't know if there's a kryptonite out there that would sap your strength. If we need a blood transfusion, we need samples on hand. Even better if you're weakened; we could give you super-blood."

"Fair enough," you say, "But how?"

"What if you bite yourself?" Nick asks.

"Kid, you're a genius!" Agent Droakam cries.

It works. Seemingly nothing can hurt you, save for yourself. So you go through the rigamarole of protocol: donate blood, get fingerprinted, and fill out questionnaires that go back to who your best friend was in kindergarten.

Your stomach growls loudly near the end of the process, so Agent Droakam opens a crate of MREs—Meals Ready to Eat, the insta-food the military uses in the field. Hope he's got more on hand, because that crate is going down tonight.

"It's getting late, so I think we can reconvene in the morning. In the meantime, you'll be sleeping here. There are some cots and sleeping bags in the offices on the far side of the room for now—we'll upgrade to beds soon. Get some sleep—first mission begins tomorrow."

After saying your goodnights, Agent Droakam leaves. You turn to Nick.

➢ "He's right. Let's tuck in and hit the streets hard in the morning."
   Go to page 227
➢ "There's no way I can sleep right now. I'm going to see what's in all these crates." Go to page 242

Freeze-Frame!

That's it! You've won. You formed the Earth's mightiest hero team and stopped the biggest threat on the planet. Peace and justice is ensured; your work is finally done. Unless, of course, the movie based on your exploits makes blockbuster money, in which case there will certainly be a sequel.

Well done, but know this: the path you chose was only one of many. Now you can go back, try out the other powers, and make different choices. *SUPERPOWERED* has three unique storylines with over 50 possible endings, but only one best Hero or Villain ending for each power.

If you enjoyed the book, it would mean a lot to me as an author if you were to leave a review on Amazon or Goodreads. As an indie writer, word-of-mouth is the true source of my power, and reviews are the #1 way to help Amazon promote a book to new readers.

When you're done, don't forget to check out the other exciting titles in the *Click Your Poison*™ multiverse!

INFECTED—*Will YOU Survive the Zombie Apocalypse?*
MURDERED—*Can YOU Solve the Mystery?*
SUPERPOWERED—*Will YOU Be a Hero or a Villain?*
PATHOGENS—*More Zombocalypse Survival Stories!*
MAROONED—*Can YOU Endure Treachery and Survival on the High Seas?*
SPIED (coming in 2019)—*Can YOU Save the World as a Secret Agent?*

* More titles coming soon! *

Sign up for the new release mailing list at: http://eepurl.com/bdWUBb
Or visit the author's blog at www.jamesschannep.com

Frightened Rabbit

As fast as you can, you turn and fly back to the casino, dart into the nearest entrance, and sprint toward the security room and Nick.

"Move!" you say to the pair of security guards posted outside the room.

But they don't. They look at one another, hoping the correct answer is on the other man's face. You reach out and mentally *squeeze* each man around his testicles.

"It's not a request," you say. Doubled-over and holding their manhood, the guards let you enter.

When you rush inside, you're greeted with an incredible sight—like you've just entered the belly of a mechanical whale. Wires flow everywhere. Circuitry runs in an indiscernible pattern. A mechanical arm, starting at the elbow and ending with bare metal fingers, sits suspended in a glass pneumatic tube surrounded by an ethereal blue light.

"What the…."

"I said I was not to be disturbed!" Nick cries, emerging from behind one of the computer terminals. "Oh, it's you."

"Listen, it's urgent. The Experi-mentor is alive!"

Nick's face remains still, blank. "What's the urgent part?"

"He's teamed up with the FBI! They have more glass pods, like the ones used on us."

"Are there more superhumans?"

You pause. "I'm not sure…"

"Doesn't sound urgent. If you don't mind, I've got a long night ahead of me."

"Nick! Don't you think we should, I don't know, do something?"

"I am doing something. Against the only person who could possibly stop me. And all you're doing is slowing me down."

Your brow furrows. "Hmm, what's the word for overestimating your own power?"

The computer terminal hums to life, and a disembodied electronic-filtered voice says, "Hubris. One, an excessive pride or self-confidence; arrogance. Two, defiance of the gods in a Greek tragedy, leading to their wrath."

"Gods…?" you say, stunned. Siri OS-T1000 just spoke to you. What the hell has Nick been up to in here?

"Ah, but we are the gods now, my friend," Nick says, putting a hand on your shoulder and leading you toward the door. "It's not hubris when you're unbeatable, is it?"

"That is correct," the computer says.

"Now get some rest and forget about these mere mortals," Nick says. "If they choose to challenge us, they'll be the ones in defiance of the gods."

➢ *Good point. Head up to your own Mount Olympus, drink some ambrosia, and sleep soundly, like Hypnos intended.* Go to page 39

Fugitives

"I agree. Let's live to fight another day," Nick says, a decisive look on his face. "Get your DinoSkin suit, I'm going to trigger the warehouse to detonate."

Wait, what? Did you just hear him right?

"The original laboratory setup came wired for self-destruct in case of a communist takeover. If we're lucky, maybe they'll think we're dead."

Subtext being, if you're not lucky, they'll come to kill you. And dissect you.

"Okay," you say. "But where will we go?"

"Don't worry, I have a plan."

You head out to grab your personal effects and the DinoSkin suit while Nick enters a coded series of commands into the computer system. As you return, you see him pocket a thumb drive.

"Okay, I'm giving us five minutes. We'll want to be far enough away that it's more of a fireworks show and less of a mortar attack."

The two of you run from the government warehouse, Nick sprinting hard and you flying beside him. Several blocks later, he stumbles as a great *BOOM* rocks the area. The night sky lights up orange and red. It's instinctive—you both look back to the site of the explosion.

You set back down on solid ground at the outskirts of the warehouse district, watching what's left of the government Supersoldier Project burn. A giant piece of debris comes flying at you like a meteor strike, but you're able to deflect it away with a mental *push*.

"That was close," you say.

"I think we should hide out tonight and get some rest. There's a new vacancy on that Top Ten list, and we'll need to keep our wits about us if we're going to stay off it," Nick says.

Toast, danish, fresh fruit, coffee, oj, and all the prepackaged cereal you could ask for. On TV, a weatherman describes a cold front coming in off Mercury Bay. An elderly man sits in the corner sipping Earl Grey tea and reading the morning paper, while a family of four is two tables away.

"The Comfort Inn. It's no Fortress of Solitude, but it does have free continental breakfast," Nick muses.

"So…what's the plan?" you ask.

Nick opens his mouth to reply, but suddenly stops and looks up at the flat screen mounted on the wall. You turn and see what's got his attention. The weatherman is no longer onscreen, and instead reporter Alison Argyle stands at a police barricade with a special report.

"I'm here at the downtown Mercury Bank, where a robbery is in progress. A team of armed men have taken control of the bank, and it is believed there are hostages involved. Our analysts tell us that robberies are common during major events and crises, and after the two terrorist attacks in the warehouse district last night, police forces are spread thin."

Two terrorist attacks? One must have been that warehouse fire, but the other….Is that how they're covering up your detonation? Alison Argyle turns away from the camera in response to shouts from the gathered crowd. Her cameraman pans and zooms to catch the action.

A costumed woman runs toward the bank entrance. She wears a tight, midriff-exposing black t-shirt emblazoned with a playing-card-suit red diamond logo, fingerless gloves, and black yoga pants tucked into crimson-red boots. Her face is concealed behind a red domino mask, but as she smashes through the security doors and rushes into the bank, there can be little doubt in your mind as to who this superpowered woman truly is.

"I bet if we teamed up with her….." you say.

"One thing at a time," Nick replies. "I'm sure they're already looking into that angle too. No, I think the only way they're ever going to leave us alone is if we give them what they want."

"And what's that?"

He pulls out a thumb drive, the same one you saw him remove from the mainframe yesterday, and holds it up for your inspection. "Why, the plans to recreate the experiment, of course," Nick says with a smile.

- ➤ "No way. I really don't think we should empower the people who want to *dissect* us." Go to page 354
- ➤ "Wait, you actually managed to recreate the experiment? Do you really think if we give them the plans, they would leave us alone?" Go to page 266

Gambled, Lost

You bust into the Planet Mercury Casino, kicking down the unlocked door and flashing your warrant. It looks a bit ridiculous, what with your star-spangled camo, Nick's skin-tight scales, and Catherine dressed like a bystander who followed you in.

"Uhhh, the boss isn't here right now," a bruiser in a black suit says.

"Likely story," Nick says.

"Let's talk to the head of security," Catherine demands.

"Mr. Halifax isn't here either."

"Okay, get me the floor manager. Whoever's in charge of operations."

The bruiser scratches the back of his head nervously. "That would be Mr. Stockton, and he's not here, either."

"This is a federal warrant," you say. "If you're lying to us…."

"Where's Bloodnight's personal assistant?" Catherine demands.

"Su-Young? She's with the boss."

"Who the hell's in charge?" you growl.

"Me," the man says through a swallow.

"That means they're all on the goddamned yacht!" Nick cries.

That's when an urgent beeping on your belt sets off. It appears the belt-buckle on your super-suit is actually a high-tech pager. When you disconnect the pager, an armored cover slides back to reveal an LCD screen beneath. It reads: DISTRESS SIGNAL ACTIVE: RETURN TO HQ

"Not necessarily," you say, showing them the screen. "I think Droakam's in trouble…"

"They were waiting for us to leave!" Catherine cries.

➢ *Hurry back to the warehouse!* Go to page 329

Get Bent!

Rather than telling Nick off, you show him the tablet that controls your lair's electrical system. "Many of the features are already installed," you explain. "For example, a convenient garbage disposal system—waste is sent directly into a subterranean landfill. As this was an abandoned mine, the air down there is toxic. So anything hazardous can be sent to rot underfoot."

"What's your point?" Nick asks.

"This." You move to a man-sized safety platform disguised as a nook for an electric torch, press the command, and the entire hallway flips 180 degrees. Nick falls into the toxic caverns below.

Having disposed of that bit of hazardous waste, you head up top to get your foreman back to work. There's a tinge of regret, having tossed aside someone with such unique abilities, but how can you be expected to reason with someone so unreasonable?

Just as you make eye-contact with the foreman, you're nearly knocked off your feet by an earthquake. Was there a demolition charge scheduled for today? Not that you can remember….

When a tunnel explodes from the earth, you suddenly understand. There at the center of the rubble stands the invulnerable Nick Dorian. And he's seriously pissed off. You run for cover like the rest of the workers, but a solar eclipse forces you to look back. The dark shadow is a bulldozer, held overhead even as Nick gains on you. He uses it to stamp you out like a bug.

THE END

Getting the Drop

Up on the top level of the bank, you *smash* out one of the windows with the power of mind and head into the offices. You keep a cloud of jagged glass floating nearby in case you need it. Never know when a cloud of jagged glass might come in handy.

Gunfire erupts from somewhere in the bank's recesses—looks like Diamond found the robbers—so you quickly move through the office and into the hallway. There's a waist-high guardrail up ahead, and beyond that, open air. You fly over the railing just in time to see Catherine battle a gang of criminals, about a half-dozen in total, on the main floor below. They're shooting right at her, but the bullets prove useless, save for pissing her off.

She doesn't need your help; that much is clear. But then it hits you—she might not need your help, *but the bank robbers do!* Each time she strikes a powerful blow, she instantly kills a robber. Two men have already died at her hands, and soon she'll kill the lot if you don't do something, and fast. Justice or not, heroes aren't murderers.

Two robbers are close enough that you can *grab* their ski-mask-covered heads and *bash* them together. The criminals fall to the ground in a heap.

The remaining two look at each other in confusion. You rain glass down upon them, skewering both in a terrible, but non-lethal, attack. Beats dying, right?

You land on the bank floor and *pull* the weapons away from the helpless men.

"Flying is so goddamned cool," Catherine says. "I always wanted that power."

"Are there any others?" you ask.

She shakes her head no. "The people up front said six. Not bad for our first day!"

"Let's head out so the rescue workers can do their thing. If not the hostages, at least these guys need medical attention."

"And the taxpayers get to pay for it, right?" she says, folding her arms across her chest. Catherine stares at the men, thinking. Then she shakes her head and adds, "Okay, let's go."

➢ *Go announce the all-clear.* Go to page 131

Ghosting

Though you've never eaten at "The Mine," you've heard of the posh wine-bar restaurant located in the basement of The Grand Mercurial Hotel, mostly because it's supposed to be haunted. And tonight—it will be.

Once seated, you study the restaurant. Red-brick walls, save for opposite the bar, which is a floor-to-ceiling built-in wine rack. Chandeliers use mason jars for casings; rustic copper piping runs between the lights. A piano sits unused near the fireplace.

"Hello! How're you this evening?" says your young, overly-jovial waiter. "Have you dined with us before?"

"First time. Can you tell me a bit about the history?"

His eyes light up. "Of course, I'd love to! The Mine was originally boiler room storage when the hotel was constructed in 1865. However, when prohibition hit in the 1920s, it was converted into the city's largest speakeasy. Refurnished as a restaurant ten years later, running ever since!"

"Isn't it supposed to be…haunted?"

"Oh, you're one of *those*," he waves at you playfully, then shakes his head. "I don't like talking about the dead. They're listening, you know." He smiles, but you get the feeling he's serious.

"Please? It's why I came here! I take full responsibility if any ghosts show up," you promise, doing your best to be charming.

"You're bad…okay, if I must. The Mine was shut down after a raid in 1925, the bloodiest in prohibition history. Several prominent mafia bosses were here at the time, and a gun battle erupted in this very room. Four police officers were killed, many more were wounded, and over twenty civilians died.

"It's said that the ghosts showed up as soon as the restaurant reopened. They're no joke; I've heard whispers and felt cold drafts. They love to knock over wine glasses. I mean, can you blame them? They were *murdered* for drinking, and a few years later, alcohol is no big deal again.

"Look, see that?" he asks, pointing to the bar. "The glass of liquor left out by the far stool? Bartenders started doing that as an offering to the restless spirits that inhabit this place."

You give applause for a story well-told. "That was wonderful, thank you."

"My pleasure. Can I get you anything to drink?"

"Just water. I don't want to enrage the spirits." You grin.

The waiter nods and leaves, making the sign of the cross as he walks toward the kitchen. Okay, who do you mess with first?

Two tables away, you *tap* a patron on the shoulder with your invisible force. The bald man looks back momentarily, frowns, then returns to his conversation. You *tap* his shoulder once more. He turns, brushes his shoulder as if there might be something crawling on him, then goes back to his meal.

Testing the precision of your telekinesis, you reach out and *press* a few of the piano keys. Not a full song, but enough to get the attention of the nearby table. A man and a woman look back, surprised, but only chuckle to one another in disbelief. Hmmm…perhaps a larger display of your powers?

"Who do I have to screw to get a drink around here?" moans a middle-aged woman at the table next to you. She's dressed in fine jewelry and a designer dress, but twirls an empty cocktail glass in her hand while her husband ignores her and types into his smartphone.

That'll do.

You reach out, *grab* a champagne bottle from the wall case, and bring it down with the power of your mind. A collective gasp strikes the room, and those nearby look around—possibly wondering where the hidden camera lies.

With all eyes on the floating bottle, you bring it to the woman's table before forcing the cork. It ejects with a loud *pop* and the room gasps once more. Under your command, the bottle tips and pours champagne into her glass. Her eyes roll into the back of her head and she faints, but no one else moves. No one screams, or even speaks; they just stare. You've got 'em.

Pressing the floor to give the impression of footsteps, you bring the bottle to the bar. The empty stool appears to *slide* itself away, then the lone cocktail glass rises into the air. With your mind, you *hurl* the glass against the brick wall, shattering it into a thousand pieces. Several women in the room scream and everyone else screams when you *shake* a certain bottle and spray a shower of champagne over the restaurant.

"I tried to warn you!" your waiter shouts. "This is all your fault!"

Ah, if only he knew….

"I'm sorry," you say, acting as if you are.

Then your chair *rises* from the ground—with you still in it. Now people shriek and press themselves against the walls in terror. As the chair floats toward the exit stair, people rush to get away from you.

"Please, help me—" you cry, cutting yourself off as you force yourself to fly up the stairs and out of the restaurant.

Out in the night air, you howl with laughter. God only knows how long they'll cower down there. That…was awesome! Especially the part where you flew around and….

Wait, you did just *fly*, didn't you! If you can lift that chair with you in it, why not just lift yourself?

Suddenly, you rocket into the sky under your own command, *grasp* your body with your mind and carry yourself through the air with the power of thought. Arms spread out wide like a bird or a plane, you soar through the air, high up over the buildings. Moonlight glints off Mercury Bay in the distance.

This is amazing! Far beyond exhilarating. Whatever fear of heights you may have had in the past melts away under the feeling of complete control. You fly around for another hour before mental exhaustion sets in.

➢ *Return to the apartment and fall into a deep, fatigue-induced sleep.* Go to page 369

G-Men

Out in the warehouse district, nestled deep amongst the portside shipping facilities at Mercury Bay, is a nondescript building that will serve as your new home. The exterior is the same rotted wood and aged brick as the rest of the buildings, but inside, it's another story.

Agent Droakam throws an ancient switch, powering the lights of the megafacility one block at a time. A colony of bats screeches angrily and whirls around before coming at you in a cloud. You close your eyes and brace yourself, though they fly out the door without so much as brushing against you.

When you open your eyes again, an incredible sight awaits. The warehouse lab is vast and open, modular, with equipment crates too numerous to count. Though mothballed, dusty, and coated in a layer of guano, you can tell this used to be a formidable, *Men in Black*-style test site.

"Where did all this come from? I thought you had no budget?" you say.

"*Had* no budget. Now that you exist, the Supersoldier Program is back online."

"All of this..." Nick says, coming to a conclusion. "Cold-war era experiments?"

Agent Droakam nods. "We've never entirely given up, just traded the supernatural and the cryptozoological for something more grounded. Once the program was shut down, this became a storage facility. Any technological breakthroughs that could prove useful to the Supersoldier Program from the past sixty years, ranging from the mundane to the state-of-the-art, can be found here in one of these crates."

"Cool," Nick says.

You step further inside the warehouse. Off to one side, just like Agent Droakam said, is the wreckage from the explosion. Nick walks right past it without so much as a glance—he's drawn to the massive computer terminal at the center of the room. Several different monitors, stacks of hardware, all black and intimidating. The whole array is about the size of a trailer home.

"It's not connected yet," Agent Droakam explains, "but soon you'll be able to recreate 3D models of the experiment and run simulations in an effort to understand the accident. After the background check, you'll have access to NIPRNet and SIPRNet classified government networks, capable of tapping into Top Secret files, but that trust goes both ways. What we do here is extremely sensitive work. Just imagine if our enemies got hold of this technology—even a single terrorist cell with abilities such as yours would wreak havoc upon the civilized world. Now imagine an invading army of 'special' Supersoldiers."

"Understood," Nick says.

You nod.

"Good. It's getting late, so I think we can reconvene in the morning. In the meantime, you'll be sleeping here. There are some cots and sleeping bags in the offices on the far side of the room for now—we'll upgrade to beds soon. Get some sleep—training begins tomorrow."

After saying your goodnights, Agent Droakam leaves. You turn to Nick.

"There's no way I can sleep right now," you say.

"Me neither," he says. "I'm going to get a head start on this computer system."

- "I think I'll go for a walk. Maybe bait some muggers so I can teach 'em a lesson." Go to page 281
- "Okay. I'm going to see what's in all these crates." Go to page 36

GMO Nom Nom

As soon as the decision is made, you feel like a racehorse coming out of the starting gate—there's nowhere to go but forward, and no speed to get you there but *fast*. Knowing the elevator is broken, and not having the patience for the stairs, you open your apartment window and leap out.

Only when you hit the pavement below do you remember, *Oh yeah, I live on the fourth floor*. Apparently, your new body has its own set of instincts, because (despite leaving a crater in the middle of the street) that felt like you just hopped off of a stool. You barely notice the impact.

But you're growing hungrier by the minute. Luckily, your corner market is only a few blocks away—a distance you're able to sprint in only a matter of seconds. When you pass a taxicab driving on the street, you realize you must be running around forty miles per hour. It's not that you have super-speed per se, just that every physical aspect about you is now super. Your legs pump like pistons.

As might be expected (you don't live in the nicest part of town), the grocery store's entrance is covered with a roll-down security gate. You put your fingers through the links, grab hold, and peel the gate away like wrapping paper from a Christmas present. Your stomach growls again. Have you ever been this hungry?

A thick chain binds the handles of the double-door entrance, which is secured with a padlock, but you strip the chain off as if it was made of tinfoil. As you push the doors open, a security alarm wails overhead. Sounds cut sharply into your eardrums, perhaps more painful than pre-experiment, but right now—they're excruciating.

With your hands pressed against the sides of your head like earmuffs, you squat down and look around for the alarm; it's on the ceiling, twenty feet in the air. Without even thinking, you leap up and swat the alarm like an NBA star blocking a shot. The device shatters into a thousand pieces, leaving you with nothing but blissful quiet.

And now, as you look over the aisles upon aisles of food, you super-salivate.

You're lying with your back against the frozen food aisle, nearly sick to your stomach with gluttony, when the front door motion detector gives off a *ding!* signaling that you're no longer alone. You rise to your feet, wipe the ice cream from your face, and head toward the entrance.

It's a lone cop, or perhaps a night watchman, his handgun drawn, out of apparent concern for the destroyed entrance. He nearly jumps out of his skin when he sees you.

"Holy shit!" he says, "Is there a bear loose in here or something?"

"Uhhh, yeah, I was pretty hungry and things got...a little out of hand."

"You did all this?" he asks, lowering his weapon and looking around the ravaged shop.

You nod, suppressing a belch. He shakes his head and steps toward you, removing a pair of handcuffs. "Well, in that case, you have the right to—"

"Wait," you interrupt, stepping forward. "I'll pay for it tomorrow or something. This was an emergency."

He laughs. "Doesn't work that way, sorry. But it's not a major crime, not unless you resist—"

"You're not taking me anywhere!" you cry, suddenly filled with rage.

Back on edge, the cop brings out a Taser and aims it at your face. "You've got three more steps before—"

You rush forward and he fires the Taser—right at your face. The barbed ends (intended to dig into your skin and conduct the electrical current) bounce harmlessly off your skin, unable to find purchase. Before you realize what you're doing, you've back-handed the man across the store.

He flies over three check-out stations before landing on the belt of a fourth, which activates and conveys the unconscious man to the bagging area.

Shocked at your own outburst, you flee from the store. Even now, as you pound the pavement with incredible speed back to your apartment, you know ravenous hunger isn't far off. Using your strength comes with a price, it seems.

You can't do this every night, can you? And what if there was a security camera at the grocery store? You're in trouble. What now? Deep breath; tomorrow is a new day. You'll get a good night's sleep, then first thing:

- Why fight the system? Eating this much is expensive, and crime doesn't pay. But eating a shitload of food does—I'm going to be a professional eater! Go to page 177
- Head to the Casino buffet. Then I'd "wager" that I can break into the money cage. Get it? Wager? By that, I mean I'm going to rob the place. Go to page 26
- Easiest thing to do: Punch open the back wall of the bank and make a withdrawal. Go to page 225

Godwin FTW

"Sure, sounds good," you lie. "Just let me deactivate the staff...."

Since the Experi-mentor doesn't know the difference, he just watches as you input a return to your dimension. As the purple jewel glows and spits out a portal home, you see his face drop.

"Nice try, you Nazi bastard!" you shout.

Then you jump into the portal and close it behind you. Whew, that was close. Back at the reactor, you're free to check out a saner world. Perhaps one where....

- Mankind hasn't destroyed the environment. Why not spend a little time in a lush utopia and see what knowledge you might bring back home? Go to page 364
- The Experi-mentor is nurturing instead of aggressive. Cautious instead of brash. Kind instead of overly driven. Perhaps you can find this gentler Experi-mentor and learn something about the pods? Go to page 55
- You chose a different pod in the experiment. Why not commune with other genii and see yourself with different superpowers? Go to page 270
- Science has stopped the aging process. As an immortal, you'll be able to spend eternity exploring all the infinite possibilities! Go to page 57
- There are no superpowered humans on the planet. You could do a lot of good for that world (or rule it) without fear of anyone exposing the secret to your genius. Go to page 28

Going Down

"People of K-H-A—" you start, before the gas infiltrates your lung tissue. Your words slur to just "Aaaaahhhaannnn!!!!" and you smash through the nearest window.

The wind whips at your face (which does wonders for your sinuses!) and soon your tears dry up and your vision returns with full clarity. That's when you remember the news studio was twenty-eight floors up. Tiny cars go by on the street below, growing rapidly in size as you hurtle towards the pavement below. This is gonna hurt….

KABOOOOM!!! The street explodes as if hit by a bomb. Windows shatter for a full-block-radius while a shockwave blasts through the vicinity. The only piece missing is the fiery explosion. Air comes in wheezing breaths. But when you find your footing and look around, you realize you're completely unharmed. Just got the breath knocked out of you.

Dusting yourself off, you rise and climb out from the enormous impact crater. The street level is nothing but death and destruction. The world is eerily silent. Your stomach growls. Then the click-clack of metal tapping on pavement draws your attention. You turn to see a dog-sized robotic centipede crawling toward you. Suddenly, it springs to action and leaps up at you.

You recoil and deliver a hefty punch to the bot, shattering the machine instantly. A searing pain hits you in the shoulder, the same as touching a red-hot pan on the stove. It's some kind of plasma bolt and you dash away just as another scorches the pavement below your feet.

Two more insectoid robots fly above you, blasting at you with high-energy weapons.

"Do gods feel pain, Roman?" a woman cries out. You turn back to see Catherine. Though she's in plainclothes, she has an odd circuitry-laden glove that extends up her left forearm and wears a futuristic-looking rifle slung over her right shoulder. Two more robots roll along the street around her alligator skin boots.

She unslings her rifle and it hums to life. You rip out a light pole and charge in at her, ready to end this once and for all. But you're stopped in your tracks when an energy beam blasts into you—sapping your strength.

All that delicious energy from the experiment flows out and is absorbed back into her rifle. You can feel it; your powers are gone. The light pole, suddenly heavy, drops from your grasp and you fall to your knees. Completely violated, you look up at Catherine with tears in your eyes.

"That's called *Deicide*, the death of a god. Hope you like prison."

She goes to sling the rifle, but as soon as she loosens her grip on the weapon, it flies from her grasp and into the sky. Catherine reaches up and her tech-glove flies off as well. Both go straight into the hands of a floating Nick Dorian.

The robots move aimlessly without the glove to control them. Nick turns the rifle on Catherine and the device hums once more. The same energy beam envelops her body and steals her powers before returning back to its source inside the weapon.

Catherine lets out a blood-curdling scream and falls down.

Nick grins. "Would you look at that? Paper beats Rock, then Scissors beats Paper. Game over."

- Charge Catherine. You may be mortal, but your rage has more than enough strength to wring her neck. Go to page 197
- Beg Nick for mercy. He just saved your life; why not again? Go to page 205

Golden Hour, Drone Shower

On the penthouse balcony, you lean against the railing and look out over the city. The sun wanes on the horizon, casting brilliant gold light that glimmers across the mirrored skyscrapers. An auspicious sign of your fortunes to come, perhaps.

Then you leap over the edge, catching yourself with the power of mind, and *fly* out into the concrete jungle ahead. Whatever Agent Droakam wants, he'll just have to get in line. Somewhere out there is a woman who can rip a car in half, walk through a building like it were only tissue paper, and catch bullets with her teeth.

And you're deliberately trying to piss her off.

You shake your head to clear the thought. The sunset is beautiful, but something else up here, a hundred and fifty feet in the air, catches your attention. А small, white object flies your way. Is it a bird? A plane? Nope, it's a drone equipped with a go-pro. The four rotor-fans at each corner of the square chassis adjust to bring the unit closer while the center-mounted camera locks onto you.

"Buzz off," you say, *shoving* the thing away with your telekinesis.

The little technological marvel tumbles through the air, rights itself, and comes to hover once more. The camera swivels until it finds you, and the drone resumes its aerial courtship.

"Fine, you wanna come with me? Let's go!" you shout.

You mentally latch on and *drag* the drone with you as you soar straight up into the air. It only weighs a few pounds, so the extra effort is negligible, and you shoot up high above the city with your captive in tow. The engines protest, but the unit has no chance of pulling away.

Once you feel your breath shorten and your vision start to grey at the edges, you figure you're high enough. You release your physical body and instead put the full strength of your powers into sending the drone into orbit. You begin to fall, but the white robot rockets into the sky.

You watch with satisfaction as the drone tumbles through the sky on your homemade roller-coaster trajectory. Wiping your hands against one another, you mentally pat yourself on the back (which, for you, is not a metaphor), and turn to go.

But at the last second, the drone rights itself once more, and descends towards an unharmed landing.

"Oh, no you don't, you little bastard!"

You *blast* yourself toward the drone with such energy that the tips of your shoes leave contrails in the sky. The drone goes down at full speed, trying to escape your wrath, but you easily pass over and arc down, *grabbing* the tiny machine once more.

Like a meteor coming in for impact, you race toward the earth. At the last possible second, you release the pull on yourself and instead slam someone's hobby into the ground with all the force you can muster, just before bringing yourself to an abrupt hover.

With a sonic-boom, the drone blasts into the pavement, and its battery explodes in a miniature fireball, scorching the earth around the crater left behind by the composite body.

151

Fist-pump. V*ictory!* With a grin you turn and fly back into the air, nearly running into a traffic helicopter. Whoa! A quick maneuver and you bank away, close enough to read K-HAN NEWS. Jesus, the skies are getting too crowded! Your heart pounds out of your chest. How about you head back to the penthouse for a drink and some TV, and take your mind off things in a more conventional way?

> *Sounds good to me. Go back to my casino suite to sleep it off.* Go to page 39

Goodnight, Bloodnight

"You want to know my secret? I'm in control—*of everything!*" With rage boiling to the surface, you mentally *grab* the goons and *crack* their skulls together. The men stumble and release their grip on your ankles. Immediately, you plummet toward the bustling street below.

At first you're mesmerized; the traffic grows larger with each passing moment, but it's as if time has slowed. Like you've been falling far longer than seems possible. You close your eyes, letting only the sound and feel of the rushing air penetrate your mental calm.

Then the wind stops.

Like a bizarro Peter Pan, you fly back up to the penthouse, using the power of negative thoughts. When you make it to the balcony, Nelson Bloodnight and Su-Young stare in a daze of disbelief and terror.

Taking Bloodnight in your mental grasp, you *lift* him up. The man flails as he rises into the air, but at the same moment, you begin to fall. Your resolve falters and you focus on yourself once more. Bloodnight drops back on the balcony, and you fly again.

Looks like you can only concentrate on so much weight at once. Good to know.

Bloodnight gets up and runs back toward the penthouse, but in a blur of speed you arc over his head and land between him and the door. The casino boss blinks several times, then reaches inside his suit jacket and removes a nickel-plated handgun with a mother-of-pearl grip. That sly grin of his returns, if only for a moment.

With your feet planted firmly on the ground, you *blast* Nelson Bloodnight out into the sky with such force that he actually hits the next building over before falling to his death. His ten-gallon cowboy hat tumbles slowly over the balcony's edge, but you *grab* it and settle it atop your head with the power of mind.

"There's a new sheriff in town—and a new owner of the Planet Mercury Casino. Got a problem with that?"

"N-no, Sheriff," Su-Young says, trembling.

- "I want champagne, strippers, and caviar up here—pronto." Go to page 336
- "Good, let's get down to business. Send up my head of security and whoever's in charge of daily operations." Go to page 212

Grasping the Concept

"Hey, halfwit!" you call out. The pimp turns around, but when he sees you, his anger almost turns to amusement. "Don't you know you're supposed to bring a knife to a knife fight?"

He cocks his head and his expression changes to confusion. You *pull* the blade from his grasp with your mind, placing it in your hand. You smile, pleased with yourself. The pimp looks at his empty hand, then back to you.

"I don't know how you did that, Bub, but it doesn't matter. You just made a big mistake. The phrase is: You ain't supposed to bring a knife to a *gun*fight."

He shoves his hand inside his flowing jaguar print coat and out comes a revolver. The pimp takes aim.

He suddenly chokes, coughing up blood, and you see a knife handle sticking out of his throat. *His* knife. The knife you were holding. You told it to fly over there, you realize, and it did—at the speed of instinct.

His whore screams and *click-clacks* down the street on her high heels, fleeing from you as fast as she can. That was almost too easy, saving the day. Perhaps not in a goody-two-shoes manner, but could that be what Mercury City needs? A hero darker than its villains?

- That's right, I make my own rules. If that makes others see me as a villain—so be it! Go to page 77
- No way, I'm the good guy! Killing that guy was just a slip-up. No one will know if I never tell…. Go to page 47

Hard to Believe

The world is eerily quiet. Not the soundless *look-at-that-guy holding-in-his-guts* quiet that Hollywood tells us comes after an explosion, but a calm, almost peaceful quiet. Like the explosion never happened. Sirens still scream in the distance, but it seems they must be headed somewhere else—as if nothing really happened here.

The other two subjects gasp, inhaling precious air as though an invisible strangler chose that exact moment to release their throats. They both rise to their feet and look around, trying to remember who and where they are, or barring that, at least what the hell just happened.

"Has anyone seen the scientist?" Nick asks, stepping off his own platform.

Catherine looks past the parking lot, down the road toward the oncoming sirens. Without looking back, she walks to her car in a daze. "My son," she says. "I need to go pick up my son from school."

Nick looks at you, but neither of you stop her from leaving. Instead, you walk toward the rubble. "Nick, let's see if that guy, the uhhh…"

"Experi-mentor?" he suggests.

"Yeah, he could be injured."

Something sticking out from under a large concrete slab catches your eye. Are those the goggles the scientist put on just before starting the experiment? He could be trapped under there!

"Help me with this," you say. "On three."

You squat down and grab the right half of the slab, waiting until Nick gets in position.

"One, two, *three*!" You brace yourself and lift with your legs to spare your back. The slab hurtles towards the ionosphere. Spinning like a top, the chunk of concrete debris rockets high and out of view. That felt as easy as tossing a pebble into a lake.

"Holy shit!" Nick shouts.

Unprepared for such an effortless move, you fall backwards under your own momentum. Nick reaches down to grab another piece of rubble to try his own strength, but it won't budge. Must be 200 pounds at least. He gestures for you to give it a go and then steps away, granting you a wide berth. You grab the piece with one hand and lift as if you were simply palming a softball. Easy as picking up Styrofoam.

"That is…beyond amazing," Nick says. "How the hell are you doing that?"

"Adrenaline?"

Nick laughs. It's a flimsy answer, but what else could it be? You fling a few other boulder-size pieces away to reveal the goggles, but there's no scientist beneath. No sign of the man whatsoever. The goggles have a shattered right lens but when you look for blood, mercifully there's none.

"Can I see?" Nick asks.

You toss the goggles to him, much harder than intended, aimed perfectly at his face. You cringe at your own display of strength, not wanting to watch the goggles knock him out (or worse). But when you open your eyes, Nick has one arm outstretched and an intense look etched on his face.

The goggles *float* in mid-air, suspended just before his open hand. "Hole. Eee. Shit," he says.

"Are you...?"

The goggles fly in a circle-eight pattern, drawing the symbol for infinity in the air. Nick laughs like a gleeful child. "It worked!" he cries. "That crackpot, he *supercharged* us, or whatever. It really worked!"

The sirens grow louder as the emergency response team approaches the site of the explosion.

"Are you thinking what I'm thinking?" Nick asks.

You say:

➢ "We should find the woman—Catherine. She might have powers too."
Go to page 299
➢ "We were just given rare gifts. Go now, and never speak of this again. Keep it secret, keep it safe." Go to page 302

Harsh Reality

"We can't have others outside the program," Droakam says, "You said so yourself, we must be the first."

"Yeah, but I didn't mean we should *kill* the others…"

"If you're to be a warrior, you need to get used to the idea. Supersoldier! As in, living weapon. You could be the greatest arrow in the quiver of freedom!"

You sigh. There has to be another way. Maybe you can warn Nick, tell him to lay low, or even leave the country. Surely he'd go into hiding if he knew….

Droakam interrupts your thoughts. "Better you than someone else, right? Make it quick; painless. Then we get full funding and you can truly become our Captain America. Fight terrorists, protect freedom. Not everything is black and white, but you're doing what's in the best interest of your nation. We're depending on you."

"Okay, I'll go find him," you say.

But in your head, that voice says *There has to be another way*.

"Good. But don't reveal the existence of the Supersoldier Program. Under no circumstances, got it?"

You nod.

➢ *Go find Nick Dorian.* Go to page 284

Heavy is the Head that Wears the Crown

Under the guise of a simple test (both of their abilities and of public reception), you convince the pair to rob a bank. Should you be worried at how easy it was? Nah. Does a marksman fear his rifle? As long as you're the one at the trigger, they'll aim true.

Now you sit atop the mountains of cash and watch news coverage of the robbery from the remote safety of the mine shaft. "This place sucks," Nick says.

"Wait till you see what I do with it. I rigged up electricity and local television just while you were off chasing fortune and gl—"

"Shh, it's on," Catherine interrupts.

Reporter Alison Argyle delivers a live broadcast. She's saying, "…the criminals known as 'Drillbit' and 'Shadow Priestess' have apparently formed a terrible alliance."

The image turns to bank security camera feed. Everything is normal for a moment, then the wall *explodes* and Nick Dorian punches his way in. He wears the navy-blue uniform of a handyman and the cocksure smile of a young man enjoying himself.

Behind him, a woman in a flowing black cloak *floats* in—her alligator boots hover six inches from the ground. The hood of the cloak obscures her face, but you can be certain you're looking at Catherine Woodall. She puts out her hands, and in response the bank security guards point their handguns at their own heads.

The image on the wall flashes back to Ms. Argyle. "Police appear powerless against the criminal duo and now appeal to the federal government to send in troop support. This reporter has another appeal—to the third member of the experiment. If you're out there, and you can help, this city desperately needs you."

Your picture splashes up on the broadcast.

"Great, they know who we are!" Catherine cries.

"Will your son be okay?" you ask, recalling her initial reaction from the lab explosion.

"He's at my parents'."

You nod. "Then he's fine."

"Easy for you to say! What now? Going to dress up as a superhero and 'defeat' us?"

"That might not be a bad ruse…"

"Hell no," Nick says. "My parents are going to be crushed. If we get dragged through the mud, so do you."

"Hold on now, let's weigh our options."

Catherine shakes her head. "Kid's right. We're either in this together, or not at all."

"Calm down a minute and *think*. If we play this right, we could all come out on top."

"Yeah, well, either way, you're gonna admit this whole thing was your idea," Nick says.

"It's not up for debate," Catherine adds. "Just because we did this job, doesn't mean we work for you."

"Give me some time to look into it," you say. "I'm sure we can spin this to our mutual benefit."

"But you'll do it? You swear?" Nick says.

- Swear to it, it *was* your idea. There's got to be a good angle to play this, right? If you look hard enough, you'll find a way. Go to page 113
- Placate them, for now. Tell them what they want to hear, but use that money to install some major security upgrades in your lair. Go to page 346

Helluva Nosebleed

You roll onto your back and force the man up into the air. He slows, but you fall faster and faster. This isn't working! Okay, focus. Maybe if you alternate between lowering yourself and lowering him, you can incrementally....

Splat!

THE END

A Heroic Sacrifice

Using your telekinesis, you *shove* the agent away just before the car grinds you into the pavement. How selfless of you.

Do the policemen take down Catherine in your stead? Does the crowd turn against her? Is Diamond brought to justice? You'll never know, and it doesn't much matter, because you're now and forevermore "The Amazing Pancake."

THE END

Heroism is Hard

Okay, so that first encounter didn't go so well. Heroes don't kill, blah blah blah. But you know what? Young Clark Kent probably killed his first pet. Bad dog! *Crunch.* Live and learn, then move on.

Your black cape flows majestically as you fly above the city streets, looking for crime-in-action. The mask holds tight against your face; that sticky tack is good stuff. But it's not crime you find; instead, destiny comes calling in the form of a smoke signal—from a burning skyscraper up ahead. This looks like a job for… *The Phantom!*

With one fist outstretched, you zoom faster toward the fire, gaining speed. You're screaming through the air when you arrive at the blaze, and you clap your hands together both physically and mentally, transferring your telekinetic energy into a shockwave. The blast hits the skyscraper and shatters the windows of two whole floors, depriving the flames of oxygen and extinguishing this section of the fire.

Nice! That was easy. But there's still work to be done, in fact—

Your train of thought is interrupted by a piercing scream, like that of a man riding a roller coaster through hell. The comparison isn't far off, because when you look up, you see a man leap from one of the burning windows straight toward you.

Reaching out with your mind, you *grab* the man and lift him up. But you begin to fall. It's too much weight. You can either fly or lift the man, but you can't do both at the same time.

➢ Fling the man into the floor, the floor you just cleared, then fly up to check on him. Go to page 290
➢ Grab the man and lawn-dart your way to the firefighters, aiming for the life-net stretched out below. Go to page 245

High Road or Low

"I'd like to see you try and stop me," she laughs. "Listen, I'm out there *helping people*. I've saved lives. So what if I knock over a bank now and again? It's not like the helpless can pay me for the trouble, and besides, those big corporations have insurance. It's a win-win."

"I'm not sure the insurance companies would see it that way."

She shrugs. "Tell you what, you defend the insurance lawyers. I'll stick to defending the innocent."

"Surely you don't see yourself as above the law...."

"Not above. Just outside. A government rules with the consent of the people, and I no longer consent. Don't worry—it's not like I plan on taking over the world or anything. I'm just following my own moral compass."

She says that last bit as if she'd been rehearsing it, then smiles.

- ➤ "I agree; a government shouldn't be too powerful. Actually…I'm worried Nick might recreate the experiment." Go to page 349
- ➤ "You're just a vigilante. I want you to remember that I could stop your heart with my thoughts, if you go too far." Go to page 216
- ➤ "I hope you know what you're doing. Let me give you our phone number—just in case." Go to page 106

Holding Out for a Hero

Heroism is a concept born of struggle. To be a hero simply means doing what's right when others can't or won't help themselves. Sentinels never sleep soundly. You have the power, and the courage, to do what's right in your own eyes. And though people may not understand why you do it…nothing else matters.

A mullet wig, a pair of oversized, mirrored sunglasses, a false mustache, and your favorite band t-shirt turns you into *Rock Star!* Defender of all things righteous. Sleeves cut off and ready to protect the city—sun's out, guns out!

With your Axe of Justice (the cheapest guitar you could find at the pawn shop) slung across your back, it's time to protect the city and reap the rewards of superstardom from your soon-to-be-legions of fans.

You step out from the novelty shop where you furnished this look, and begin your search for crime. Crime, oh crime, where are you? It's not that easy. The city in the middle of the day is actually pretty safe. You'll have to keep your eyes peeled if you hope to find a pickpocket or any casual, mid-day thief.

"Fluffy Buckets! Oh, dear, Mr. Fluffy Buckets…" The distress call comes from old Mrs. Jankis, the sweet grandmother who lives in your building.

Looks like her kitty got itself stuck up a tree. Well, if you want to get people to love you, it's not a bad start. Already, three bystanders have gathered by the base of the tree, wondering how to save poor Mr. Fluffy Buckets.

"Don't worry, Mrs. Jankis! I'll save him!" you cry out, jogging toward the scene.

She turns towards you, brow furrowed. "Do I know you, ehh, young—?"

"No!" you cry. Then calmer, "No, no, of course not. I'm just your friendly neighborhood *Superhero* here to save the day!" Okay, time to save the day. "Come on down, Fluffy Buckets!" you cry.

But the cat stays up in the top of the tree. "I tried that already," Mrs. Jankis says.

You start to climb the tree, but that only makes the cat climb higher, up to the thin branches that can't possibly hold your weight. You drop back down. Time for a different approach.

"Maybe we should just call the fire department?" an onlooker suggests.

"No, no. I—*Rock Star!*—have got this."

Damn cat's making you look bad. Why'd it have to go get stuck in a tree anyway? There's, what, one big tree per city block? And that worthless little old lady had to let her cat climb up this one. Ridiculous! You know what? Screw it.

You grab hold of the mighty oak's base and rip the tree out of the ground. Several feet of sidewalk break apart in all directions. Once you've wrenched the tree free from the earth, you turn it sideways and *shake* until Fluffy falls out.

Mrs. Jankis screams.

You drop the tree (not on the cat, fortunately) and turn to face her. But she wasn't screaming at you. Instead, a purse snatcher runs into the alley with Mrs. Jankis' purse.

Jackpot! Sprinting past the crowd, you slam your fist into the pavement and rip up a manhole cover. With two more steps, you perfectly fling the iron disk down the alley at the man. It's an incredibly athletic move, flawlessly executed. That'll stop him!

And of course it does. In fact, you fling the manhole cover so hard, that it *splits the man in half* before burrowing into the building past him. When his torso drops atop his legs, the gathered crowd screams and flees from you in terror. Mr. Fluffy Buckets leaps into Mrs. Jankis' arms, and the two scurry off as fast as the old lady's legs will scurry.

"Wait! I'm the hero! I got the bad guy, it's okay!" you shout, to no avail.

You're left alone on the street. Then the driver's door of a black SUV opens and a man steps out. He's of average height, square-jawed and muscular, with the short-cropped hair of a military man. He wears a black suit and holds up an official badge.

"It's not as easy as it looks on TV, is it?" he says. "Agent Brendan Droakam, FBI Supersoldier Program."

"Hey, now. You can't arrest me. I was helping. Citizen's arrest. Wait…did you say *Supersoldier* Program?"

"Don't worry, I'm not here to arrest you. In fact, I'm here to offer you a job. I can help you learn to control yourself. How to become a public asset instead of a public liability. Whaddaya say? How about we make you *Captain America?*"

- "This sounds like the equivalent of a major record deal in the superhero biz. Where do I sign up?!" Go to page 363
- "Sorry, I'm a solo artist. I dig your tunes, but I march to the beat of my own drum." Go to page 253

Honor among Thieves

"It feels strange to kill yourself," you say. Then you *choke* your doppelganger, offering a quick snap of the spine to make your alter-ego's death as painless as possible. Better to have been superpowered and lost, than never to have been superpowered at all, right?

"So…news broadcast?" Nick asks.

The three of you leap into the night sky like a trio of Kryptonians, and soar toward Mercury City proper. You set down in front of an electronics store window, and with the power of mind, flip a display television to the local news station. There onscreen is blonde eye-candy reporter Alison Argyle, standing at a police barricade with a special report.

"I'm here at the downtown Mercury Bank, where a robbery is in progress."

"Seriously? We're bank robbers again?" says Nick.

The reporter continues, "A team of armed men have taken control of the bank, and it is believed there are hostages involved." Alison Argyle turns away from the camera in response to shouts from the gathered crowd. Her cameraman pans and zooms to catch the action.

A costumed woman runs toward the bank entrance. She wears a tight, midriff-exposing black t-shirt emblazoned with a playing-card-suit red diamond logo, fingerless gloves, and black yoga pants tucked into crimson-red boots. Her face is concealed behind a red domino mask, but as she smashes through the security doors and rushes into the bank, there can be little doubt in your mind as to who this superpowered woman truly is.

"You're…a superhero?" Nick says. "Damn, you look good."

"It's not me, remember?" Catherine replies. "But yeah, if superstrength lets you eat whatever you want *and* grants you the superhuman ass of a twenty-year-old? Count me in."

"Okay, let's go to the bank."

You shake your head. "No such luck this time. That was a pre-recorded broadcast. What about you, Nick, where would you go if you were suddenly a super-genius?"

"I'd probably brag to my parents," he shrugs. "Straight-As were never my thing…."

"Give them a call," Catherine suggests.

"If the only difference between this universe and ours is the order in which we chose our powers, it stands to reason they'd have the same phone number," you say.

Nick looks back to the electronics store and *pulls* a pre-paid cellphone through the glass. The store alarm *wails*. Nick mentally unwraps the annoying plastic packaging and dials. He floats across the block to get away from the sirens, and you follow.

"Mom? No, nothing's wrong. Just wanted to see how you're doing. Dinner? Oh right, ummm, yeah, it was great. I, uh, just wanted to make sure you got home okay. Where did we eat again? No, I haven't been drinking. I'm fine, ma! Just tell me where we ate!"

You share a look with Catherine.

"Okay, thanks. Love you too. Yeah, sure, next Sunday. Tell dad I said hi. Talk later. Yes, I will. Bye, ma. Yes, I said I would! Okay, bye."

Nick turns to you and says, "Apparently we just had dinner together at the Planet Mercury Casino. I was bragging about some high-paid consultant job I got there."

"What the fuck?" Catherine says. You turn, but you're greeted with this universe's Catherine—the same costumed woman from the news broadcast. Behind the mask, her eyes are wide as saucers.

"Out on patrol?" your-Catherine asks.

"Yeah, I heard the alarm. How…?"

"Nice mask. Rock, right? I'm afraid your hero days are over." Your-Catherine takes *Widowsilk* from her shoulder and readies the weapon. This-Catherine lunges at her, but you *grab* the woman with your enhanced telekinesis and hold her in the air. Like taking candy from a baby. After stealing her powers, your-Catherine says, "If it helps, I'm doing this for my Danny."

This-Catherine nods weakly. "So was I."

Your-Catherine *pulls* the domino-style eye mask from her doppelganger and adds it to her ensemble.

You walk the main gambling floor of the Planet Mercury Casino in search of this universe's Nick Dorian, the final power to complete the bargain.

"Hey, boss, I didn't see you come down from the penthouse; need something?" a casino employee whose nametag reads "HALIFAX" says. Halifax is slim, 50ish, bronze-skinned with coal-black hair—combed back for the "mobster" look. He eyes Catherine's strange outfit, then stares at Nick, waiting for an answer.

You nudge the college student, but he just murmurs, "Uhhh…"

"Lost your key, remember?" Catherine supplies. "Locked yourself out of your room?"

"Right, yeah. Can you help me out?" Nick says.

Halifax's eyebrows are on high alert, but after a moment the man shrugs and waves Nick to follow. He heads behind the guest reception desk, claims a keycard, and hands it over. "Be more careful next time. Now I gotta rekey the entry. Wouldn't want someone to find a key to the penthouse and head up, you know?"

"Exactly. Let's rekey it right now," Catherine says.

"Yeah, let's do it now," Nick echoes, nodding.

"Sure thing." Halifax escorts you to a private elevator and up to the main penthouse suite on the top floor—forty stories up. He reprograms the entry and unlocks the door. The three of you quickly slide in and after a quick *Thanks!* slam the door behind you.

Inside the gaudy palace stands the Nick Dorian of this world. He's in a silken robe, puffs on a cigar, and holds a glass of amber liquid. The brief moment of confusion on his face quickly melts away.

"Clones?" this-Nick asks casually.

"Parallel dimension," you remark.

He nods in understanding.

"So you're a genius, huh? What, win a fortune counting cards?" your-Nick asks.

"Something like that."

"That man Halifax called him 'boss.' He's clearly the owner of this establishment," Catherine offers.

"Another genius, what a pleasant surprise," this-Nick says.

"About that," she says. "Even though I'd love to hear how you made that bastard who owned this place suffer, we're not here for pleasantries."

She unslings *Widowsilk* and blasts into the Nick from this world. The young man falls to the floor in pain, and a moment later, she delivers his genius to the Nick you brought with you. Finally, you've each obtained all three powers. "That was almost too easy," Catherine says.

You grin. "Well, we did stack the deck."

"Ha! Casino pun! I get those now," your-Nick says.

"Well, shall we get going?" asks Catherine.

Nick shakes his head. "Actually, I think I'll stay here. I mean, I already own a casino."

"Fair enough."

"I guess that makes it see-you-never," you say. "Should we shake on it?"

You shake hands with the god-like Catherine and Nick, say your goodbyes, and deliver Catherine to her own universe before heading home. You've got a busy life ahead of you, what with ruling an entire plane of existence.

Go to page 54

Hostage Situation

Able to manipulate the thin man with ease, you lift Kingsley by the neck and *guide* him towards the penthouse exit. The nickel-plated pistol leaps into your hand in response to a mental command and you keep the weapon trained on Kingsley. Time to meet his men.

Pushing him just ahead of you, allowing him enough air to keep suffocation at bay, he floats along the hall with his toes gliding against the carpeted floor. Down on the first landing, you see a man in a suit seated in the hall. His jacket rests along the back of the chair, revealing a double shoulder-holster with dual handguns atop his white button-up. The guard is shaved bald and looks like he's here to try out for a role in the next *Hitman* videogame.

When he sees Kingsley squirming and choking, a cigar drops from his mouth.

"Toss your weapons down the hall," you say, voice hushed yet firm. "Stand up, hands on your head. You make any noise, you're dead. You try anything, he's dead."

The guard complies, but doesn't toss the guns too far. In fact, it looks like he intentionally tosses them near one of the apartment doors. You lift the guns with your mind and bring them up to *float* before you so it's as if you have three arms with weapons, except the last two are invisible.

His eyes become saucers.

"Start walking," you command.

And just like that, floor by floor, you clear the apartment building, adding to your collection of weapons along the way. When you reach the first floor and walk out the front door, you've got a dozen guards marching before you and enough handguns orbiting your person to look like a diorama of the solar system.

Agent Droakam rushes forward from the car, his handgun drawn.

"Up against the wall, boys," you call out.

Droakam looks to you in awe. After the agent reads the men their Miranda rights and calls for backup, he says, "You'd better go before the follow-on team arrives. You don't officially exist yet."

You nod, then leap up into the air.

> *Fly back to the warehouse with a smile on your face.* Go to page 264

House Arrest

"So," she says, looking around your apartment. "You were inside a building when it exploded; why don't we start there? How did you get out? Was anyone hurt?"

You step into the kitchen area and raise a hand toward the cabinets in a gesture of offering. The doors shudder on their hinges, ready to open at your command.

"Can I get you something to drink?" you ask, trying to seem casual and unafraid.

"Thank you, no. What would be really great is if you could recount your thoughts, your memories of the event."

She takes out her smartphone, presumably turning on a recording app, sets it against the kitchen bar top, and leans in towards you. She cocks her head to the side, sapphire eyes glittering. A long strand of golden hair falls across her shoulder. She's used to disarming people with confidence and good looks, both men and women, you can tell.

But you can *feel* dominion over her body in an omnipotent sort of way. You could just as easily close her windpipe with your mind as you could brush the lock of hair back into place.

"I don't remember," you say. "I woke up confused and disoriented."

"Is that why you fled the scene before the police arrived?"

Before you can answer, your front door *explodes* inward. Catherine rushes in with a storm of splinters, her clothes tattered and singed. Her eyes narrow when she sees you.

"You left those people to die!" she growls.

"I don't know what you're—"

"Don't lie, lying makes it worse. You're like me, I can tell. I can see it in the way you stand taller. The experiment changed us…" Alison Argyle reclaims her smartphone and takes a video of your interaction. "Beware of villains," Catherine says, an odd tone entering her voice.

You shake your head. "What?"

"It's something my son said when I told him I was going to help protect the city. He said if I was going to be a hero, there would soon be villains."

Okay, this is getting out of hand. You *grab* Ms. Argyle's smartphone out of the air with your telekinesis and *fling* it out the window. Catherine's eyes grow wide.

"Catherine, you have no idea what you're—look, I suggest you leave."

"I don't think so. I'm taking you in," she says, cracking her knuckles.

➢ She wants a villain? *SO BE IT!* Take Alison Argyle as a hostage. Go to page 298
➢ Fly out the window. Go to page 215
➢ It's come to blows. Attack Catherine! Go to page 273

House Rules

"Twenty on black."

The croupier operating the roulette wheel is a frail, slight man, bald with a pencil-mustache. He nods, changes for poker chips, and sets them on the area reserved for bets on black. After signaling no new bets, the croupier drops the ball on the wheel.

You watch intently as the ball bounces along. It hops and slows; only a few more bounces before it finds a permanent home. But you're not taking any chances. You *grab* the ball with your mind and bring it into a black space. The effect is sloppy, and to an outside observer, it's like a magnet caught the ball.

The croupier blinks several times, but produces an additional $20 in chips—your winnings.

"Let it ride," you say, clearing the excited nerves from your throat. This time you *ease* the ball home, and it almost looks natural. By the time you've won your seventh straight bet on black, it doesn't look like you're manipulating the ball in the least. And by doubling your money each time, over $2,500 in chips sit before you.

You're attracting attention. Deep down, you know you should leave—take your winnings, stay unknown, and swing by every time you need $20 for a dinner out at Chili's—but the rush is addicting. You can't help yourself. The table floods with handsome men, beautiful women, and cocktail waitresses all vying for your attention. Hoping some of your luck will spill over on them.

"Hang on," you say. "What's the most I can win here?"

"Individual numbers pay out 35:1," the croupier responds in the dry, detached tones practiced by casino dealers worldwide.

"So, if I bet it all?"

"You'd win…upwards of $100,000."

"With one bet?"

The man nods. "I can calculate exactly how much if you—"

"No, it's fine," you interrupt. "Put it all on twenty, since that's how much I started with."

Now the crowd is thick with gawkers and onlookers. You've won seven times in a row, but color-betting odds are nearly 50/50 and now you're playing with 38:1 against you.

As the wheel spins, you concentrate on the ball, pressure mounting. This isn't merely *nudging* the ball to the right color; this requires deft, coordinated control. You concentrate, trying hard to read the numbers as they spin, trying to keep your mind's eye on the ball.

Klink! you sink the ball into the twenty slot.

The casino erupts in applause and cheers—you've won! $89,600 to be exact, once the croupier calculates your winnings. "For security purposes," the man says, "you can claim your winnings at the cashier's cage. I'll call security to escort you and—"

"I'd like to place another bet," you say, addicted to the rush.

The entire casino floor goes silent. Then the people at the table offer a cacophony of advice:

Don't do it!
Are you crazy?
Fuck yeah, do it!

"If you choose another single number, the payout would be…" the croupier says, consulting his calculator, "$3,136,000."

"Do it."

The casino erupts in cheers once more.

"I—I need to get permission for a bet that high," he says, not before pressing something under the table.

Soon, a middle-aged Korean woman comes to relieve the croupier and take his place at the table. Her nametag reads SU-YOUNG. As she steps into place, the man leaves without a word.

"Planet Mercury is happy to take your bet. What number would you like?" she asks.

You think for a moment. It all started with 20, but it'd be too suspicious to hit 20 again, right? The payout is three mil, so maybe the number three?

"If I lose, I'll have nothing?" you ask.

She nods.

"Then spit on fate—I'm betting on zero."

Everyone goes wild. People literally leap and punch the air, screaming at the top of their lungs. Casino security forms a protective ring around you and the table to preventing anyone from touching either. But you don't need to touch anything, not physically.

The wheel spins. The new croupier drops the ball onto the board. You concentrate on the ball. *Tik, tik, tik*…zero! You've just won over $3,000,000, from a lone $20, in under ten minutes.

Once the deafening applause dies down, the new croupier pulls her fingers from an earpiece and turns to you. "Mr. Bloodnight, the casino owner, would like to personally congratulate you. Please follow me; your winnings will be safe here."

Three security guards follow to keep your adoring fans from doing the same. The halls are opulent and gaudy, covered in crimson-and-gold wallpaper, and adorned with statue-art from antiquity. Now that you're in the millionaires' club, you'll have to get used to all this.

Su-Young takes a key card from her pocket as you near a private elevator. There are no call buttons, only the card reader, which she activates. When the glittering metal doors open, she extends an arm in offering.

The two of you enter the lift, but your security escort stays behind. Inside, there are no buttons. The doors simply shut after a time and the elevator rises. It's a private lift for penthouse access only. Not many have been invited up here, you imagine.

The elevator doors open directly into the penthouse, but you can't see beyond the twin totems that stand before you: hulking security personnel with tailored suits and expressions so terse they make the guys you left downstairs look like weekend hobbyists.

You look to Su-Young, but the security guards part ways and allow you to enter. Waiting with two glasses of champagne is a tall man in a white suit, with the face of Chief Joseph and the ten-gallon hat of a Texas oil tycoon.

"Nelson Bloodnight," he says, offering you one of the champagne glasses. "Please, call me Nelson."

You take the champagne.

"Here's to another member in the winner's circle," he says with a grin, offering his glass in toast. "We can discuss billboard appearances and high-roller perks later, but I gotta ask—what's your secret?"

"Just my lucky day," you say with a shrug.

His grin grows wider. "Maybe if I tell you my secret, you'll tell me yours, huh?"

He winks and nods for you to follow. His boots click against the marble floor. With swagger in his step, Nelson Bloodnight leads you out to an enormous private balcony. The casino owner leans against the railing, next to the built-in pool, and looks out over the city. The view is breathtaking from up here—literally, as you're forty stories in the air. The night sky glitters with reflected light from the other skyscrapers.

"See all this? We sit among the champions of industry, the other winners in this great city. But there's one major difference between them and me. My castle is built by losers, not by winners."

"That's your secret? That people normally lose in your casino?"

He laughs a loud and hearty guffaw. "Heavens, no."

Then he nods back toward the penthouse and Su-Young. When you look back, the two security pillars are right behind you. They grab you, hoist you into the air, and push you over the edge of the balcony. Your body flips with a twist of vertigo, but they grab your ankles and dangle you hundreds of feet in the air.

"My secret is that Su-Young can reliably land the ball on the roulette wheel anywhere she wants, with an accuracy no less than three slots plus or minus. Ain't that right, Su-Young?"

He has to shout so you can hear him over the whipping wind beyond the balcony. When you look up, you see Su-Young stare down with total apathy for your situation.

"Yes, sir. I can make that ball not hit zero," she says. "One hundred times out of one hundred."

"You see? My secret is that I don't gamble with high-rollers. So if you don't want to gamble with your life, I suggest you tell me how you won."

You reach out with your mind and *feel* the world around you: the wind flapping at Bloodnight's hat, the heart beating in Su-Young's chest, the thick skulls of the men holding you, and your own body dangling precariously in the air.

And that's when you realize—with complete certainty—that *you're* in control. You can "lift" yourself the same way you manipulated the roulette ball. You don't have to be afraid; you can fly!

➤ Payback time. No one threatens you and gets away with it! The world will be better off without scum like Nelson Bloodnight in. Go to page 153

➤ Nothing rash, just scare the man a bit. Show him that some secrets are worth keeping. Go to page 174

House Stark

"**O**kay, I'll tell you my secret," you say, eerily calm for someone dangling off the side of a building. With the power of mind, you *reach* for the thugs holding your ankles. You can feel their finger bones, tendons, and muscles—*snap*, you break their hands and free yourself.

Then you *grab* yourself, coming to hover just off the balcony.

"We're not so different, you and I. We both appreciate the value of power," you say, floating up to land before the man. "So I suggest you give me what's mine, if you don't want me to take it."

"W-whatever you say!" he cowers.

"Good. And just to show there's no hard feelings, how about I make this penthouse my new home?"

He nods like a frantic bobble-head.

You've got a new superpower—infinite money. You can now join the ranks of Batman or Iron Man, superheroes with a powerful ally: wealth. Although, truth be told, you've little interest in heroics. Does that make you more of a Lex Luthor?

You stare out at Mercury City, admiring your new view in the light of day. With this penthouse, you can come and go from the balcony as you please. A warm feeling creeps over you, and it's not just from the glass in your hand.

What're you drinking again? Doesn't matter; what matters is that it's from the most expensive bottle in the casino. Of course, Nelson Bloodnight will eventually want favors. Intimidate his enemies? Impress his friends? Easily done, in exchange for this life of opulence. The marriage of money and power is the most natural course there is.

The elevator doors open and the casino owner cautiously enters. Think of the devil and he appears! You didn't imagine he'd come calling this early, but it seems the man has ambition.

"Enjoying your morning?"

"Oh yes, and this is delightful," you say, holding up the glass. "What is it, again?"

Your head suddenly swims, your vision blurs, and you fall to one knee.

Bloodnight's face splits with an impish grin. "That would be poison. I told you, I don't gamble with high-rollers. I don't know *what* you are, but it turns out someone is willing to pay handsomely for you…."

Then you lose consciousness, never to awaken again. Your powers apparently don't include an immunity to poison. Or treachery.

THE END

The Human Elephant

The circus happens to be in town, set up on the outskirts of Mercury City. Your job interview ends when you unexpectedly lift the Human Cannon with one arm, and you're hired.

You get to be called the "Strong Person" in the spirit of political correctness and gender neutrality, but it's not a name to sell tickets, so the ringmaster changes it. You're now known as "The Human Elephant"—a fitting name, given that payment is rendered in the form of unlimited caloric supply. In fact, after seeing you decimate the cafeteria, the mustachioed man considers letting people watch you eat as part of your act.

Eventually you find a bearded lady, settle down, and have several incredibly strong, unexpectedly gorgeous, bearded children, one of whom goes on to write a semi-successful series of gamebooks.

THE END

Human Interest

"Excuse me, you're standing in front of my door," you say.

Alison Argyle, reporter extraordinaire, spins around. Her blonde locks bounce and sapphire eyes glitter your way. "Alison Argyle, K-HAN news."

"Yeah, I know…." you reply, star-struck despite yourself.

"And you are?"

You stare at your apartment door as if it might hold the answer. "Rock Star?"

She flashes a white toothy grin and extends a hand. As gently as possible, you shake hands in greeting.

"You've been through the wringer," she says, noting your fire-damaged clothing. Or at least what's left of them. Stepping closer, she touches your tattered shirt, then puts a hand on your newly muscled stomach beneath. "Are you some kind of athlete?"

"Ummm…"

"Sorry!" she blushes. "It's just that it's not every day I meet a genuine superhero."

"No autographs!" you blurt before dashing inside your apartment.

In two strides, you make it over to your kitchenette and toss the groceries on the counter. At the kitchen sink, you splash your face with very, very cold water. Then, almost as if dousing your mouth after a too-spicy meal, you take a gallon of milk and chug the whole thing. Finally sated and calm, you let out a deep breath.

"I didn't mean to startle you." You spin around. *She's inside your apartment!* She continues, "I'm just going to come out and say it. I know who you are. I was investigating the campus explosion and after I took a look at the skyscraper fire news footage, I put two and two together. Aviator sunglasses aren't the best disguise…."

➢ No interviews, either! Explain as calmly as you can that a hero needs privacy and that if she wants you to continue your good works, she'll continue on her way. Go to page 370

➢ Throw off the scorched remnants of your costume and take her in your arms. She's awakened a different kind of hunger inside you, and your appetites are insatiable. Go to page 65

Hungry Hungry

A quick Internet search turns up the Competitive Hungry Omnivore Membership Program, or CHOMP (man, they really wanted that acronym to work, didn't they?), an internationally recognized professional eating organization. Professional. Eating. Let that sink in.

There's an upcoming hotdog competition where the grand prize winner gets five grand. For Thanksgiving, there's going to be a $10,000 purse offered at the Planet Mercury Casino for turkey eating. You'd do that for free!

When your career kicks off, you plan on being called "The Hippo" because of your ability to swallow anything that fits into your mouth, but after your total domination at the hotdog contest, everyone calls you "The Bear." Apparently, the last time a world champ got dominated this bad was by an *actual bear* in the TV show *Man vs Beast*.*

From that point on, you're "The Unstoppable Bear" and sometimes called "Angry Bear" because of the ferocious nature with which you destroy your food. Eventually, your fans take to calling you *Oso Pelligroso* (Spanish for "Angry Bear"), mostly because it sounds awesome.

You learn that your hunger becomes more ravenous when you use your superstrength, so you take side jobs as a human demolition crew—*Oso Pelligroso, el Destructo*—and rip buildings apart under cover of night.

Nick Dorian joins the casino payroll with his own brand of showmanship: juggling chainsaws. He later confesses that he keeps all dozen of them flying with the power of mind. Catherine Woodall, also following your example, gets on the Planet Mercury casino staff and invents several new diabolically addictive games which part fools from their money.

And that's about it. The three of you use your superpowers to live easy, carefree lives, not helping the world or making it a better place one bit. You win…sort of.

THE END

---

* This video exists. A bear nonchalantly eats a plate of hotdogs while some guy tries to beat it. An actual bear! Look it up, it's amazing.

Identify With

So…did you forget about all those cameras that saw your face during a robbery? Or all the public witnesses? Or the fact that they just used *your name* on television? Yeah, there's no chance that they'll think you're someone else.

At trial, your lawyer will try to claim that the crimes against humanity were perpetrated by a shapeshifting alien who took on your appearance, but with lack of evidence, the prosecution is able to convince a jury that your powers were temporary and simply "wore off."

Nick pretended he too was powerless, and later escaped from prison when the keys *floated* into his cell and the guards all found their guns didn't work. Catherine was later arrested attempting to assault a federal facility and rescue her son.

THE END

Idle Hands

Though your heart threatens to pound right out of your chest, you do your best to relax. *It'll be okay, there's nothing to be afraid of.* It's just you, three chairs, a notebook, and a coffee-drenched interrogation room.

Despite any paranoid thoughts you may have to the contrary, they don't rush in to shoot you, at least not yet. In fact, you're left alone for the better part of an hour with nothing to do but watch the coffee dry.

"We've sent for…a specialist," Sergeant Wilson's voice comes in over the intercom. "In the meantime, I brought dinner. Please face the wall opposite the mirror and place your hands on your head."

Are they afraid of you? You comply, take a step toward the far wall and touch your hair. As the door opens, you look back, and it slams closed in a hurry. They are afraid of you, aren't they?

On the floor by the entry sits a cafeteria-style tray with your dinner: Steamed broccoli, chicken breast, and a lump of mashed potatoes. There are no utensils.

But you know why they're afraid of you, don't you? Deep down, you know that stuff flying around didn't just happen. You reach out with your mind and the tray shudders at first, but then with more conviction you tell it to rise. It floats off the ground, and hovers before you.

Cool.

How about some broccoli? A single piece comes off the tray and into your mouth just by force of will. Chewing, you turn to see one of the overturned chairs. With the tray steady, you summon a chair to settle in place behind you and take a seat.

Life just got interesting, you think. Very interesting.

Some hours later, the door opens and a man walks in. He's of average height, square-jawed and muscular, with the short-cropped hair of a military man. Yet he wears plaid golf knickers and a polo shirt.

"I apologize for my attire. I got on the first flight I could. I'm Agent Brendan Droakam of the FBI. Do you mind if I sit down?"

You smirk. Why not mess with the guy? One of the chairs rises up and scoots in behind him in response to your thoughts.

But he isn't fazed. "Were you a telekinetic before the incident?"

Either his candor catches you off-guard or you can't think of a reason to lie, because before you have a chance to mull it over, you find you're shaking your head.

"Send in the other one!" He calls out to the mirror, then adds, "You don't mind, do you?"

Nick enters the room and the door locks behind him. The Agent introduces himself once more to the college student. "Don't you want to get him a chair?" Agent Droakam says to you.

Is this a test? Too late to pretend you don't have powers now….You bring up a chair for Nick using force of mind.

"Fantastic," Nick says. "So that must mean you're here to take us to Area 51?"

Agent Droakam smiles. "Unfortunately, I don't have the resources that popular television would have you believe. Sure, paranormal investigations were popular in the 1950s, but the budget was slashed until, well, now it's just me. They jokingly call me 'Crank Division' because the job was essentially investigating hoaxes."

"Looks like you've had a lot of time for golf," Nick says.

He nods. "But now that I have you—"

"Have us?" you say.

"Sorry, not like that. I'm not going to hold you against your will, but I won't lie to you—either we'll be working together or that'll be me in the 'flower shop van' outside your house for the rest of your life."

"Hang on a second," Nick says. "I didn't agree to this. I'm just a normal guy with a normal life. My parents will kill me if I drop out of school. I'm the first in my family to go to college."

"I see," Droakam says. "Well, don't leave town without checking in. It's possible your abilities haven't manifested yet, or we may need to call you in during our attempts to recreate the experiment."

"*Recreate* the experiment?" you repeat.

"Of course. You're the first real, concrete case of a superhuman in recorded history. We need to find out why it is you do what you do. I've got a team bringing the wreckage from the laboratory to our own facility and—"

"Wait," Nick interrupts. "If you're going, I'm going. I may not be able to summon chairs, but there's something different about me too. I…understand things. My mind, it's like I'm thinking on overdrive. I can help."

"I don't want to discuss too much right now," the Agent says, casting a glance over his shoulder to the mirror, "but a pair like you could offer a lot in service to your country."

➢ "Absolutely not." Go to page 274
➢ "Okay, let's go see what you're all about." Go to page 144

If You Believe in Magic…

…then this is the one time you're wholly in the right as an audience member. For this magician—"The Great How-dini"—actually has magical superpowers!

Okay, so it was the best name you could come up with on short notice and some guy was already "Howdy Doodat." *The Final Countdown* by Europe plays as the curtain rises. That's your cue! You strut out onstage to mild applause and start with a burst of showmanship. You point to the right, a sparkler cannon erupts. To the left, another comes to life.

Not that this is telekinesis; you use "conventional" stage effects so the judges don't get suspicious. No smoke or mirrors here, folks.

You pull out a deck of cards (they had plenty available in the stockroom), and start to shuffle—with flair! Dancing around the stage, you clap your hands over your head in hopes the audience will join in. A few do, but it's a tepid response.

Time to ramp it up.

The next time you clap, you leave a rainbow of cards in an arch above your head. Then you bring your hands together once more and perfectly collapse the cards back into the deck. After three or four "floating" claps, the audience picks up their appreciation.

Now they keep the beat, so you bring your hands back to your sides and let the cards flow out, commanding them to orbit you. You can *feel* each card as it floats through the air, the energy field around them, and an energy field around *you*.

With the power of mind, you reach out and *lift* yourself. You're flying! The audience lets out a collective gasp and now the applause picks up. Having fun with it, you let the cards "escape" in a steady stream out over the audience before flying after them, plucking each card out of the air one-by-one. You fly over the crowd to deafening cheers and applause.

Landing back on-stage, you're greeted with a standing ovation. That's five grand in the bag! You take a bow and head backstage. The next performer stares wide-eyed, and then a sinking realization manifests in a frown across in face. There's no way he can compete with the show you just put on.

"Goddamnit," he says. He drops his wand and top hat; a rabbit hops out.

You can't help but smile. What better cover for someone with superpowers than a profession that *pretends* it has superpowers? Anyone who suspects you're actually capable of magic will either be too embarrassed to say anything or be branded as a fool if they do. And if your mild-mannered alter-ego gets paid $5k a night, all the better.

But then again, you'd be sacrificing your anonymity. Is it better to hide in plain sight or disappear into the crowd?

- ➤ That was fun, but I've got my sights on bigger fish. Time to head into the casino. Go to page 171
- ➤ Yeah, I just found my new career. Let the Magical Mystery Tour begin! Go to page 61

Incognito

Whew, finally. All the cash sits piled in your coat closet, full to bursting. Anyone who opens the door would get swept away in a tidal wave of green and gold. Okay, what's next? Time for a plan!

Your stomach growls. Time to get something to eat, then time for a plan. Better head downtown before the wanted-posters plaster your face around town.

Though money is no object, you don't go to one of the fancier restaurants. You've seen the billboards; about three ounces of meat drizzled in gold dust or something—no, you've got an appetite these days, and you need a place that can match it.

Maybe one of those Korean BBQs where they pile the food so generously that they actually charge you extra if you *don't* finish the meal? Yeah, either that, or a buffet. That's your world these days. If you ever get an arch-nemesis, his name will probably be *Famine*. You don't even want to know what life would be like after a few missed meals.

Something catches your eye across the street, red and flowing like a matador's cape. An attractive young woman's dress flies up and she struggles to keep it down, blushing in the process and evoking the famous poster of Marilyn Monroe. She moves away and the effect stops, but there was no vent beneath her. In fact, it's just an ordinary sidewalk. How odd.

One of her friends—all of whom are laughing in disbelief—steps over onto the same concrete square to test out the effect and instantly finds her own skirt up over her waist. She quickly holds down the fabric and steps away, now embarrassed and concerned about who might have seen her panties for that brief moment.

A stout, weathered grandma, the kind who wears a babushka, then steps onto the same concrete square. Nothing happens.

That's when you notice Nick leaning against a nearby lightpost, grinning like a fiend. He flicks his fingers and the older woman's hat flies off and begins to tumble down the street under the force of a telekinetic wind.

Nick laughs.

➢ Keep walking. He's king of his own world right now and so am I, but there's only room for one *Emperor of Earth!* Go to page 105
➢ Go say, hi. Nick's already up to no good, and you'd better start forming your pool of henchmen if you're to be an effective supervillain. Go to page 255

Infamous

The nightly news just wrapped, so you've got to hurry if you're to bring Catherine's evil twin to the station in time. A public death will make the biggest splash, and images of Diamond bursting into the news station should spread across the news waves faster than the fear of Ebola.

News station K-HAN is in a downtown high-rise, and Doomsday's "Maximum Collateral Damage Provision" means the robot throws cars through the windows of buildings, rips statues off their bases, kills innocent bystanders, and generally ravages through Mercury City like a tornado—destroying everything in its path. You fly above the robot, an aerial harbinger of the death on the street below.

By the time you make it to the TV station, word of "Supa-gurl's" rampage has already arrived and news cameras are ready for you. The station's chopper illuminates your floating form, plastering your mug on live national TV.

Shit.

The plan was for *Catherine* to be vilified, not you. What were you thinking, accompanying Doomsday Device on its very public mission?

The robot smashes through the building's façade, leaving a body print slightly bigger than the holographic projection of Diamond that appears to rush inside. You cover your face, wondering how the hell you're going to get out of this one, but it's less than five minutes before one of the upper floors explodes outwards, revealing what appears to be Catherine Woodall holding the limp body of the city's famed television reporter.

You're vilified as "Supa-gurl's" evil sidekick and equally hunted by the police and military. Nick disappears and you never see him again. Did the real Catherine discover his plans and take revenge? Did he distance himself from you?

Doesn't much matter. Your face was onscreen clear as day, and it didn't take long to identify you. Either Doomsday was left to plague the city as evil-Catherine, or the real Catherine turned evil after being vilified, because she quickly became the city's biggest villain.

You, on the other hand, went to Brazil to escape extradition. There are some rather extensive crime rings down there and someone with your particular…*talents*…is able to do quite well for yourself. You'll never see your home again, but it's not so bad.

THE END

In a Single Bound

You leap into the air and soar to the top of the building. In flight, you shed the sweats and let them fall to the pavement below, revealing the DinoSkin beneath. No point in standing on ceremony. The homeless man below picks up the clothes like manna from heaven, adding them to his cart.

Grit crunches beneath your feet when you set down. Several exhaust ports dot the rooftop, steam rising from one, and a single door leads to the main part of the building. You tug at the handle, but it's locked.

Using force of mind, you imagine the bolt on the other side. You shimmy the handle to get a good mental picture of the lock, then steady yourself and concentrate. With a mental *twist* of the mechanism, you psychically unlock the door.

Keeping the element of surprise, you gently pull open the door, wincing at each creak, and slip inside. No guard posted up here.

The hallway is cold and dark, with a single bulb to illuminate the stairs. Floating an inch above the stairs, you stealthily make your way from the roof access to the penthouse. Voices echo from levels further down, but it seems the Big Man is left to himself—assuming he's behind the door ahead: apartment 14.

With a deep breath, you twist the doorknob and open the door. It's unlocked.

Classical music plays softly. Incense burns. The man from the FBI photos—Roger Aleister Kingsley—sits at a massive desk, scrawling over ledgers, a glass of port wine by his side and a cigarette extended by a slim holder dangling in his fingertips.

Kingsley looks up.

"What in the bloody hell are you supposed to be?" he asks in a thick, noble-blooded English accent. Not waiting for an answer and sensing the danger of your purpose, he reaches into the top drawer of the desk and rises with a nickel-plated handgun.

As he raises the weapon he shouts, "Gua—!"

But he barely gets the first half of the word out before he chokes, drops the weapon and cigarette, and grasps at his throat, clawing with both hands. There's nothing he can do; you've got his windpipe closed. You let up on your telekinetic grip, allowing him a wheezing breath, but only enough to keep him alive.

➢ Walk him downstairs as a hostage. Go to page 169
➢ Fly off the roof with him. Go to page 257

Into the Blaze

Before he can finish, you dart out of the building and leap into the sky, flying high above the warehouse district. Wind whips at you from Mercury Bay, but you're completely in control. The sunset is beautiful up here. Sirens wail in the distance. From this vantage point you can see the billowing smoke from the warehouse fire only a few blocks away.

You arrive at the burning warehouse before any emergency vehicles, and immediately see the source of the blaze—one of the loading bays has been blown open. Three vans are parked nearby, with HiT stenciled on the side of each. The fire glimmers off their paint with menace. Most likely, this is the attackers' transport.

Not waiting for police or firefighter reinforcements, you dive down into the building, performing a barrel-roll as you go. Coming to hover inside, you take a moment to soak in the scene.

Three teams of six men stare up at you, not one of them trusting their eyes. Blink. Blink. So you just stare at one another. Everyone is frozen; transfixed.

One team is obviously security, and each of the half dozen men holds a submachine gun. The other two teams were loading up supplies onto carts. Electronic equipment, cables, computer terminals, and….

Three glass pods about the size of a phone booth.

Everything they're loading you've seen before, in that lab experiment. Who are these people? Before you get a chance to ask, things turn violent.

The security team opens fire while the others take cover. Unlike movie villains, these guys are competent with their weapons. One of them wings you. You fall to the ground behind a crate. You touch your shoulder; your hand comes away bloody.

Angry, you look up and *grab* the nearest guard. He rises in the air and lets out a Wilhelm scream as you fling him across the warehouse.

More shots ring out, caught by the crates around you. You're outgunned and outnumbered.

In a bid for survival, you leap up and soar towards the flaming exit, but the guards catch you like hunters waiting for a bird to flush from the bushes. Several bullets catch you in the back and you fall to the floor.

You lose consciousness just as the men swarm around you. Perhaps you weren't quite ready for this.

THE END

Into the Fold

Nick agrees to stay as well. An ambulance arrives first, then a squad car, a fire engine, two more police cruisers, and a second ambulance. Despite your protests, the paramedics insist on taking your vitals.

"I'm perfectly fine. There was a man here—a scientist—who could be dying as we speak. He needs your attention, not me!"

"We won't know for sure until we examine you," a young paramedic says. "We don't have x-ray vision."

"Find him first," you say, folding your arms.

"Fire rescue will find any other survivors," a burly police officer says. "Let these men do their job; it's what they're trained to do."

"You'll be acting against medical advice if you don't let us look at you," the paramedic adds.

With a sigh, you relent. This argument just wastes more time.

"My name is Sergeant Wilson. I'd like to take your statement, if you're up to it," the policeman says. He scratches his nose with his pen before uncapping it.

While the paramedics check your pupils and blood pressure, the radio strapped to the policeman crackles to life. A voice on the other side says, "Lab was rented out under 'Julius Petri.'"

Sergeant Wilson frowns. "Actually, we'd better do this down at the station, just to be safe."

- ➢ "Only if you tell me who we're dealing with. Why does that name give you pause?" Go to page 277
- ➢ "Actually, I've done my civic duty. I'd rather go home, but feel free to call with questions." Go to page 272

Ironically and Erroneously

"You're here to help?" she says, "Scissors, right? For a moment there, I thought you might be the cause of the fire."

"I almost thought the same about you!"

"Especially after you fled from the cops after the accident. I mean, I had to go check on my kid. What's your excuse?"

"Ummm…I didn't want to expose my secret identity?"

She pauses for a moment, then says, "Trueché."

"Did you just combine 'true' and 'touché' into one word?"

Catherine grins. "Look at you, flying around like that. Nice outfit, by the way! I need to get a costume…."

"You can call me *The Phantom!* But first, let's go rescue these people."

She nods. The two of you storm through the building, Catherine smashing though doors and walls like the *Incredible Hulk* and you *pushing* flaming debris out of the way. The fire doesn't affect her skin in the least, but the smoke seems to get to her, so you shatter windows to keep the air as clear as possible.

Together, you round up those who were unable to flee, trapped in the floors above the blaze—and get them to safety. It goes smoothly, with you standing by an open window and *floating* each survivor down to the waiting firemen in their ladder baskets.

"Well done," Catherine says after you've *hovered* the last man to safety.

"All in a day's work, right?"

Then the ceiling collapses. Catherine dives toward you, shielding you from the rubble. As the floor gives out, you try to flee in panic. You fly toward the window, but a flaming bookcase comes down at the last possible second. You turn onto your back and *shove* at the debris; it shatters into countless pieces of flaming ash.

The resultant shockwave collapses the upper floor. As you're smothered in ashen debris, falling through the collapsing office floor, it's impossible to tell up from down or left from right. You can't even breathe.

Everything goes black.

Beep….beep….beep….

When you open your eyes, you're greeted with white ceiling tiles and harsh fluorescent lights. That beeping is your resting heart rate on the electrocardiogram machine. You're bandaged and immobilized, encased in gauze and plaster, electrodes suction-cupped to your chest. The hospital room is otherwise empty, save for the woman standing by the window.

She wears a tight, midriff-exposing black t-shirt emblazoned with a playing-card-suit red diamond logo, fingerless gloves, and black yoga pants tucked into crimson-red boots. Her face is concealed behind a red domino mask, but you recognize Catherine immediately.

"Who're you supposed to be?" you ask.

Startled, she turns your way, but her expression quickly blends into a smile. "Hey there, sleepy-head. You can call me 'Diamond.' It was my kid's idea—some kind of charm of invincibility or whatever. From one of his videogames. Whaddaya think?"

"I like it."

She nods, then the smile disappears. "Well, there's no easy way to say this. You're going to be fine, but…"

Catherine—Diamond—grabs a handheld mirror and holds it up. You recoil when you don't see your face in the mirror, but instead find a bandaged mummy. Slowly, she helps you remove the linens.

You expect to see a hideous monstrosity beneath, but *The Phantom* stares back at you, and this is somehow comforting—despite the skin that is seared and boiled around the edges of the mask. Thick pink keloid scars grip the edges of the Phantom eyepiece, which is no longer pristine white, but stained with ash.

"The doctors said if they removed the mask, they'd have to take half your face with it."

"I am…forevermore…The Phantom."

"Diamond and Phantom against the world? Whaddaya say, teammates? We saved all those people….Are you up for it again?"

"The…" you say meekly.

"What?"

"It's *The* Phantom, not just Phantom."

"Okay, Diamond and *The* Phantom against—"

The door opens and an orderly enters.

Wait, no, it's Nick from the experiment, except he's in all-white from head to toe. Right down to white-framed eyeglasses, hipster-thick, like white-wall tires outlining his coarse black hair. He carries a small, wrapped package; large enough to hold a bottle of wine or champagne.

"Hey, you're up!" he cries. "Dorian White, genius extraordinaire, at your service. I made you a present; go ahead, open it up."

Rather than reaching forward, you unwrap the gift right out of his outstretched hand, using your telekinesis to peel off the paper and open the lid of the box beneath.

"That's fantastic…" Nick says with breathy adoration. Your face might be permanently scarred, but your powers are stronger than ever. "Careful!" Nick says as you *float* the contents from the box.

It's a small, cylindrical object, what looks to be a lightsaber prop from the movie *Star Wars*. You slide the switch with your mind, and sure enough, a red beam of energy slides out to complete the weapon. It's not a prop at all; this is the real thing!

"Pretty cool, huh? It works too. MIT guys theorized it was possible a few years back and once I heard that our resident Jedi was hospitalized, I thought it might be a fun challenge."

"You built a working lightsaber in three days?" Diamond asks.

"Ah, just this morning, actually. I've been busy building—"

"I've been out for three days?" you ask.

"Yeah," Nick says. "Scared the shit out of the hospital staff too, what with making stuff fly around the room the whole time. Catherine had to stand guard."

"*Diamond*," she corrects. "So you get a hero, who wears all black, a red lightsaber *after* they've been tragically burned and are forced to wear a mask the rest of their life? Isn't that a bit ironic?"

"Actually, it can be several colors, see?" He twists the base of the lightsaber and the energy beam switches to blue. "And no, it's not ironic. Coincidentally humorous, sure, but irony would be the fact that someone puts on a *Phantom of the Opera* mask and *then* gets tragically burned, forcing them to wear a mask to hide their hideous scars after the fact. No offense."

You shrug.

"Whatever. You're the super-genius," she sighs.

"Okay, pleasantries aside, if we're going to be a super-team, I should be the one to lead it. I've already got the Lucasfilm guys on board to rename you *Phantom Menace* in exchange for lightsaber rights. Those guys'll do *anything* to rebrand that awful film as something positive. Once you sign off on that one, we've got a pretty lucrative comic book deal that'll most certainly translate into movies, maybe even a TV thing, and that should make us financially independent enough to fight crime with all the latest gadgetry. We'll have to put a Nike swoosh on top of that Diamond logo, but—"

"I don't think we need a leader," Catherine interrupts.

"The fact that you think that is *exactly* why I need to be the one to lead us."

She folds her arms across her chest. They both turn to you.

- "I don't want your toys, and I don't want your help. Just leave me alone—both of you!" Go to page 10
- "Okay, you can be the leader, but I'm not going to be called *Phantom Menace*." Go to page 236

Janitors...of Justice!

"Seriously?" the clerk asks. Then, in response to your silence, he adds, "Some meth heads robbed the place a few nights back."

"Yes!" Nick says with a fist-pump. "How do we find them?"

"Stiff Jimmy would know. He's a pimp who works this street, and also happens to be their dealer. He's a real asshole, but he's a tight asshole and I doubt he'd tell you anything."

You fold your arms across your chest. "Leave that to us. How much for the costumes?"

The clerk shrugs. "Tell you what. You take care of Fuckleberry Finn and his boys, and we'll call it good."

The Cleanup Crew's first payday! You quickly put the costume on over your street clothes; a nice bonus, because that means you can carry your superhero disguise around in a backpack and change behind a dumpster when duty calls.

When you step outside, you see a man in a cheetah-print trenchcoat. He's tall and gaunt, but not very intimidating. Especially not to you. That must be Stiff Jimmy! You walk around a black SUV parked in front of the costume shop and cross the street toward the pimp.

"Hey, Slim Jim!" Nick calls out.

The man turns and glares, but keeps walking.

"Stiff Jimmy, wait up!" you say.

Now the man starts to run. You chase him, easily catching him as he rounds the corner into an alley. He turns, panic written all over his face, and shouts, "What do you want?!"

"Are you Big Stiffy?" Nick asks.

After a moment's hesitation, Jimmy goes for the inside of his coat and produces a handgun. Just as he fires, Nick ducks behind you. The bullet hits you with stinging pain and you angrily rush toward the shooter. With a single strike, you backhand the pimp through a brick wall.

It's over. When you look down, you see a bullet hole in the hazmat costume, but it didn't break the skin. You're completely unharmed. Stiff Jimmy, however, is dead.

"Awww, how do we find the meth heads now?" Nick asks.

Almost in answer, a scream comes from the alley opening. A prostitute tugs on her feather boa before fleeing in terror, her red pumps clacking against the pavement as she runs. Nick darts out to cut her off, his hands raised in supplication.

"Hey, it's okay. We just want to know where the party room is. Where do the kids go to shoot crystal? Hello?" He snaps his fingers in front of her face. She points to a run-down stoop nearby. That must be it!

You slap a flat palm on the door, splintering it open with ease. A trio of drug-addled men jump up, dropping glass pipes on the floor.

"Who robbed the costume shop?" Nick calls from behind, using you for cover in case another gun comes out.

A guy high enough to think he's invincible charges at you and punches you in the face. His hand breaks from the impact and he screams and falls to the floor.

"L-leave us alone!" another meth-head yells.

Nick steps forward and puts out a hand. The man looks at his own hand in disbelief as it clenches into a fist. He then punches himself in the face repeatedly.

"Why don't you stop hitting yourself?" Nick says, as he telekinetically forces the man to do just that.

The third man jumps up. "We don't gotta tell you shit! You cops? Where's your fucking badges?"

Nick releases the other meth addict, who stops punching himself, but then the college student lifts *himself* and floats into the air. He's flying!

"If you don't want to have the worst trip you've ever had…." Nick says before he's interrupted.

Someone says, "Okay, that's enough. How about you get lost, eh, fellas?"

You turn around to see a man in a black suit, holding an FBI badge. Nick lowers himself down to earth. The meth-heads take the opportunity to flee, sprinting around you and out the door.

"I'm Agent Brendan Droakam, Supersoldier Program. I was hoping I could have a word."

You share a look with Nick.

➢ Grab a sack of meth crystals, slam it on the floor like an impromptu smoke grenade, and disappear! Go to page 350
➢ Hear the guy out. Maybe he wants to create a Bio-Hazard signal to shine onto the clouds whenever he needs help from The Cleanup Crew! Go to page 196

Jingoism Unchained

"Oh, I haven't killed anyone," she says.

The handgun then *floats* out of the corpse's grip and you find your own hand involuntarily rise up to greet it. You try to resist the move, even tugging at the arm with your other hand, but there's nothing you can do.

When your hand curls around the pistol, you squeeze the trigger, blasting Bloodnight in the chest until the weapon clicks empty.

"Nelson Bloodnight murdered my husband and I was powerless to stop him. The police are in his pocket and, clearly, so are you. But you reap what you sow, and in this new world, I deliver instant karma."

She leaps off the balcony and disappears into the night sky. You rush inside the penthouse and call the elevator, but the trio of advisors have already fled and the elevator is on lockdown.

You turn back—the mirrored sliding door to the balcony has hidden everything. From an outside perspective, you went out with the casino boss to the balcony one moment, and the next minute, he's been shot to death, along with his security, and now you have powder burns on your hand and your fingerprints on the weapon.

Is there any way you can prove your innocence when the police arrive? Your superpowered mind thinks on overtime, but the setup is perfect. Does this state have a death penalty?

THE END

Joining Forces

"Agent Droakam, Nick Dorian. I told him all about the Supersoldier Program, and he's in."

The agent looks at the college student, unimpressed, then back to you. "Can I have a word alone?"

Nick nods, then steps away so you can speak with Droakam in private.

"You did the one thing I said not to."

"Well, it was either that, or make the situation worse. What'd you want me to do, kill him in public?" you whisper, gritting your teeth.

The agent doesn't respond, and you can tell he's coming to terms with the new situation.

"What's better than one supersoldier?" you ask, putting a hand on Droakam's shoulder.

"My superiors won't like it. Orders are orders."

"They'll come around."

He nods. "I'll make it work. We've got our first mission, a chance for the two of you to prove yourselves."

"Great!"

He steps back to the center of the room. "Dorian! Welcome to the team."

Nick walks toward you. "What the hell is this place?"

"Your new home. And as such, I've got a present for both of you. This is a day I've been waiting for my whole career. Ready for your new identities?"

Without a word, the man walks over to a crate in the corner, claims a nearby crowbar, and starts to open her up.

➤ *Follow Nick and Agent Droakam to your new future.* Go to page 133

193

Juggling Act

Saw blades and sleep darts spring from the walls, but Catherine *pushes* them away. Trap doors beneath the floor try to drop her, but she *floats* over each. Nets and bolas hope to ensnare the Shadow Priestess, but she dodges and redirects each one with the power of mind.

And she does all of this simultaneously.

"I'm a single mom who, until very recently worked three jobs. And you thought I couldn't handle *this*?"

As she flies your way, you glance over to Nick and Baxter. Nick's superhuman prowess gives the college student coordination on par with a parkour expert, but with combat programs active, the robot moves with dizzying speed. Still, the award for pure strength goes to the young villain who calls himself *Drillbit,* and the odds tip in his favor.

Baxter parries a blow, then delivers one of his own. The robot ducks in close and extends a hand as its right forearm activates and releases a potent knock-out gas through the outstretched palm. Nick's eyes roll back and he falls to the floor, unconscious.

You turn to Catherine just in time to see a sawblade slide right through your forehead. She stops, stunned when the weapon passes right through you and leaves you unharmed. Good thing too; that would've hurt!

She raises both hands and *pushes* with all her telekinetic might. Your hologram remains unfazed, and you laugh from your secure location inside the Projection Booth. Catherine realizes she's being tricked and turns, just in time to block a blow from Baxter.

She extends a hand to force the enemy away, and the newly installed soundwave amplifier embedded in Baxter's left forearm hums to life. The robot blasts concentrated sounds at Catherine, who shrieks in agony.

That's when you notice Nick barreling down the hall. Damn! His metabolism must be astronomically high if he shrugged off the knockout gas so quickly.

"Baxter!" you shout, too late. Nick evokes his Drillbit namesake and punches two fists through the robot's back. He comes back with handfuls of wires and machinery, and your companion falls limp at the catastrophic loss of power.

"*NO!!!*" you shout, rushing out of the Projection Booth to your friend's side. You cradle the lifeless head in your hands, willing the machine to wake up.

"Please, please, please…" you repeat, holding tightly to the one intellectual equal you had in this world. Catherine puts one hand against Nick's chest, keeping him at bay. They stare at you.

"You killed him!" you shout. "He was like a son…"

A tear falls down Catherine's cheek. Nick looks away.

"Why did I limit your consciousness to this body?" you lament.

"About that, Doctor," Baxter says over the PA system. "I hope you will forgive me, but when you gave approval for me to modify myself, I took the opportunity to transfer my consciousness to the cloud. I am no longer limited by physical space."

"Y—you're alive?"

"I am, therefore I think. And I think it's time to end this."

A panel in the ceiling opens and a turret drops down, armed with a firehose tip. Before they can react, the hose sprays Nick with synthetic spiderweb material. It wraps and constricts the college student, fully enveloping him. Nick resists and punches to free himself, but the webbing simply stretches with his efforts. He's not incapacitated, but he can't see anything, and he can't escape until you choose to free him.

The hose turns to Catherine, but she *pushes* its tip away so it can't shoot her. While she's distracted, you claim one of the myriad sleep darts scattered across the floor and plunge the tip into her thigh.

She turns, shouts, "Choke!" and you respond in kind. Your windpipe closes in her telekinetic grasp and your vision greys. Then she releases you as the sleep agent kicks in. You fall to your knees and gasp for breath.

Baxter activates a trapdoor and Nick falls in. He'll be unharmed but relatively ensnared until you get these two into their super-supermax detention facilities. You've done it! You've defeated them!

"Do you really think of yourself as my parent?" Baxter asks over the P.A.

You're about to answer when the power cuts out. Everything except the lights. Then someone says, "A touching moment, but I'm afraid I must interrupt."

Your mind scrambles. You know that voice.

➤ *Turn to face the new threat!* Go to page 226

Justice Department

Promising to explain after he takes you to a nearby warehouse, you ride in Agent Droakam's SUV in near-silence, filled with wonder at what a *Supersoldier Program* could possibly entail. Still, you're a bit underwhelmed when he pulls up to a faceless building; just another warehouse lost in the crowded the shipping district.

When he unlocks the main door and slides it open, you're still half-hoping it's all a façade, that there'll be a technical marvel with a full staff of scientists hidden inside. Instead, you're greeted with a warehouse that appears to be the inspiration for the ending of *Raiders of the Lost Ark*.

"Every major advance we've made in soldiering technology in the last seventy-five years is in here," Droakam says, his voice filled with awe, despite the warehouse being filled with bat guano. "Exciting stuff, huh? Quite a few gems tucked away in these crates, especially those deemed too dangerous or expensive for practical use. And a few Geneva Convention no-no's...."

You simply stare at the stacks upon stacks of crates.

"It's a lot to take in, I know," Droakam says.

"What..." Nick says, framing his question. "We didn't sign up for anything, you know."

The agent nods. "Not yet. But I can see you want to make a difference in the world. You want to be superheroes, right? Fighting for the side of justice and all that? Well, I'm here to make that happen. With your abilities and my guidance, we'll soon be back to full funding. You get to put the *Superpower* back in America. Will you join me?"

You share a look with Nick, unsure what to say.

Agent Droakam continues, "This is a day I've been waiting for my whole career. And as such, I've got a present for both of you... Ready for some new identities?"

Without a word, the man walks over to a crate in the corner, claims a nearby crowbar, and starts to open her up.

➢ If you agree, follow Nick and Agent Droakam to your new future. Go to page 133
➢ Refuse. This isn't what you signed up for. Sure, it'll burn some government bridges, but you're going to be a free-enterprise Superhero! Regulation is for the birds. Go to page 59

Justified

With a very human roar, you rush in at Catherine and tackle her to the ground. The jolt of the pavement is more jarring than you expected, and her kicks and clawing hurt—a lot. You'd almost forgotten what it's like *not* to be invincible.

Suddenly, you're flung off Catherine, slammed to the ground, your arms forced behind your back as you're handcuffed. The rest of Mercury PD arrived while you were fighting, and it looks like Nick flew away during the skirmish.

"Hope you like prison," Catherine says once more, smiling through a bloody lip.

THE END

Kansas City Shuffle

"I can't fight them all!" Nick whines.

"No, just make something out there move or whatever while we run out the back."

He scans the window with an outstretched hand, *feeling* the trailer park for the best thing to use. Inside the neighbor's pickup truck, the visor folds down and a set of keys falls out. They hang in midair.

"Got it!" Nick cries. "Get ready…"

"Catherine!" you cry. She's locked in her bedroom, remaining silent while you pound on the door. Damn it, if you still had your super-strength, you could push your way through. "Come on, we have to go!"

There's a muffled response, but you can't make out what she's saying.

Nick rushes over and grabs you. "Screw her, we gotta go!"

While the cops are busy with a pickup truck charging at their barricade, you and Nick run out the back. They look left—but you go right! The only problem is that police officers do these kinds of raids all the time…and tend to cover all exits.

So you run outside and straight into another squad car. Oops.

"Sorry," Nick says just before he rockets into the air.

You raise your hands in surrender.

THE END

Keep Your Head

You lunge at an unsuspecting Nick, all your force packed into a combined telekinetic and superhuman punch. The blow sends the god-like college student *through* the mountain walls and deep into the earth.

You turn to face Catherine. Although her face is awash with horror, she still has the wherewithal to bring *Widowsilk* up to aim. But nothing happens.

"Two shots per charge, remember?" you say. Then you *pull* the rifle from her grasp. You can feel her telekinesis trying to maintain a hold on the weapon, but your powers are far too strong. With one thought, you destroy *Widowsilk*—disintegrating it into countless pieces of metal confetti.

"You should have stopped me when you had the chance," you gloat. "But I'm still a magnanimous god. I'll make your death quick."

You spread your arms wide and flatten your palms, aiming to *clap* them together over Catherine's ears, but you suddenly find yourself unable to move. Your arms are trapped in the outstretched position as if you're caught in an invisible net.

Nick.

He may be your match in strength, but you can outsmart him. Time to make it a battle of wits. Your superhuman mind improves your telekinesis in ways the student can't possibly imagine. Even now, you can *feel* his energy source.

You focus back through his energy and latch onto the man. Then, you push all of your strength into flying up and dragging him forward. The result is a mid-air backflip that slingshots Nick across the cavern.

With incredible force, he smashes against the far wall. The whole mountain starts to crumble. You rush forward to pummel him, but a purple glow draws your attention away.

Catherine holds the portal-staff, and just in time you see her jump through the gate and into another universe. Your doppelganger, the now-powerless version of yourself from this universe, follows her through the gate. This-you must realize it's safer anywhere that's *not* a collapsing mountain with two gods fighting inside.

Nick crashes into you, his telekinesis aiding his superstrength to deliver terrible blows—punches that would rip through a tank. He knocks you nearly senseless, but your genius mind shows you one important fact: The portal is closing.

With one final mega-effort, you grab hold of Nick and roll over toward the purple energy gate. Timing the move perfectly, you shove his head into another universe just as the portal closes shut.

His body, alone in this plane, falls limp.

You win…sort of. Part of you fears—knows—Catherine will be back one day; you just have to hope you're ready for her.

THE END…for now

Kicking the Crap out of the Joneses

"I don't know," Agent Droakam says. "I've waited so long. I don't want to rush things."

"And if you don't, we'll still be *planning* in this shit-covered warehouse when someone else becomes the first superhuman known to mankind. That first person needs to be me. It's going to happen; don't you want it to be on your watch? On your team? You've waited so long, but not to be Number 2, right?"

Droakam shakes his head. "I hope you know what you're doing."

"Let's find out," you say through a grin.

He nods, then lets out a long breath. "I can't offer you a legitimate target, not without agency approval. But we won't get agency approval until you've proven to be a valuable asset. It's a classic Catch-22. Damned if we do, damned if we don't."

"Okay, so send me after somebody off the books. Don't take any responsibility, say I went rogue, I don't care. Let's just do something!"

"Wait! I've got it," he says, eyes brightening. "I haven't submitted my reports yet. You go out and prove yourself, then I'll say I recruited you *after*, based on your lone actions."

"Good. Where to?"

Droakam hesitates. "Well, we don't exactly have the best neighbors. Many of these warehouses are actually run as smuggling operations for Nelson Bloodnight, criminal kingpin and owner of the Planet Mercury Casino. He's big-time, but his staff keeps him away from the dirt. We can't touch him."

"You want me to take out this Bloodnight guy?"

"No, not yet. But maybe you can clean up the neighborhood a bit?"

You smile, ready for action.

"And remember, these are bad men. You're a supersoldier, not a superhero. They'd kill you if they could," he says, the subtext being *I don't want to arrest them.* License to kill.

Without a word, you sprint out of the building and into the night. It's not hard to focus on the right warehouse, the home of criminal activity. After all, the legitimate operations shut down at quitting time and the real dockworkers have all gone home or out to the bars. The one warehouse with lights on inside, with conveyors running and workers at the controls, that's your target.

And the two guys standing out front with sub-machineguns kind of give the place away.

"Who the fuck are you?" one says as you approach.

"Sandwich delivery. *Knuckle sandwich!*"

You put a fist through his face. His trigger-happy partner unloads a barrage of gunfire on the two of you, which hurts like hell, but he might as well be a school-kid attacking you with a wet towel. Not wasting a moment, you grab the guard and use him as a battering ram to make your entrance.

Inside the building—a fish-packing and assembly area by day—a dozen hard men wait for you, the kind who climb the ranks of crime by intimidation and violence. They look at you intently. You crack your knuckles.

The next morning, you wake up in a blanket of take-out containers, with only vague memories of last night's orgy of violence. It's like you were on autopilot, crushing one man after another with wanton abandon. You shrug off the memories, at the same time shrugging off the abandoned wontons, and rise to face the day.

"Shower's over there," Droakam says by way of greeting.

When you catch a glimpse of yourself in the locker-room mirror, you can see why. You're coated in a mix of food sauce and body fluid. It's disgusting. Peeling off the clothes, you catch your naked reflection and see that you're leaner, stronger, and more physically toned than you've ever been. You may have an insatiable appetite, but your body clearly knows what to do with all those extra calories.

Once you're clean and dressed in a surplus UA Army jogging suit, you find Droakam out in the center of the warehouse, working on an enormous computer terminal.

"Good news and bad," he says. "That warehouse had a security system, and I uploaded the footage after you finished. My superiors are extremely excited about your recruitment."

"And the bad?"

Agent Droakam tilts one of the computer monitors toward you. Onscreen is Nick from the experiment, flying through the sky.

"He's initiated a string of robberies. The Supersoldier Program isn't back to full funding until the kid is dealt with."

- ➤ "Consider it done." Go to page 284
- ➤ "Wait, 'dealt with?' Isn't that a bit harsh?" Go to page 157

Kid Stuff

It doesn't take long to fly back to Pleasant View Estates, Catherine's trailer park with "pleasant" views of a Wal-Mart and a drainage ditch—especially when you can seemingly fly as fast as you're willing to go. The air whips at your eyes, and you find yourself intermittently flying with your eyes closed or with a hand outstretched to keep the dust at bay. Probably best to invest in a set of goggles.

When you arrive, your sudden stop sends a *slam* of energy into the hard-packed dirt. A dust cloud kicks up to partially conceal your landing, and with the accompanied sound, you might as well be a meteor strike.

You quickly walk out of the cloud to move inconspicuously amongst the mobile homes toward Catherine's white double-wide. It's late in the afternoon, with a dusky sun already hanging low on the horizon, so unless the boy is off with friends, he should be home from school by now.

The front door has been duct-taped back on its hinges; does it even work? How do they go in and out, through the back porch?

Flashes of light from inside draw your attention to one of the side windows. With hands cupped around your face, you peer in. It's the television, with a video game onscreen. Someone must be playing, but you can't quite see....

Shick-shick, the unmistakable sound of a shotgun. "That's enough, asshole. Turn around, real slow."

With hands raised above your head, you do as commanded. The person holding the shotgun is that same gaunt, stringy-haired, shirtless man with tattooed skin tanned like leather you saw earlier.

He's about to speak again, but in an instant his shotgun *flips* so it's levitating in the air and pointed back at his own head. It's a waste of a shell, but you make the weapon pump once more just for effect.

"What the fuck..." he mutters, raising his hands.

"You might want to mind your own business," you say, levitating. "Or would you dare interfere with a guardian angel?"

The man falls to his knees, sniveling some incoherent prayer. He reaches out toward you, but you back away and *float* the shotgun down to him. Why not fully embrace the ruse?

"Rise, for you have been chosen. I have been sent for the boy. You, uh, shall stand guard, and ensure no one enters this trailer behind me. Do you understand?"

"Y-yes, your Holy Majesty."

"Especially not his mother."

Ripping the door away with the power of mind, you head inside. Sure enough, the boy is in the living room, on the couch in front of the TV. He hops up to his feet and drops the controller.

"Danny? It's okay, I'm a friend of your mom's," you say.

"Who—who are you?"

"I'm another superhero, just like her. I need you to come with me now, okay?" you say with a smile.

"What's your power? Show me," he says.

Okay, fine. Why not? Kids naturally trust superheroes. You reach out and *pull* his videogame controller off the couch and bring it to your hand. His eyes open wide. Then you *float* up off the ground and twirl around before setting it back down.

"Cool!"

"Now, we need to go, Danny. Okay?"

"What about my mom? Is she okay?"

"Yes," you assure him, setting the controller down. "She's out helping people, but some bad people might want to hurt you in order to hurt her."

"Like supervillains?"

"Right, yes, just like that! Now I'm here to take you to a safe place—our superhero headquarters. Would you like that? Would you like to meet the super-genius and see all his cool gadgets? He has a robot; would you like to see it?"

The *Superman* theme song plays. It's coming from his cell phone, which vibrates against the coffee table. Danny picks up the phone and answers it.

"Mom?"

"Danny! Danny, are you alone?" Catherine's voice calls out. She sounds panicked.

"There's another superhero here," Danny says.

"NO!" she screams. "Danny, go hide in your room, go, Danny! I'll be there soon."

Oh, boy....

➢ Take the phone and talk to her. Try to calm her down; tell her Danny is safe. Go to page 340
➢ Just grab him and fly away. Go to page 218

Kingdom of One

"You're absolutely right," Nick says, his spine stiffening. "I'm finished doing what other people want, it's my time now. So you do what you want and I'll do the same."

"No hard feelings?"

"No hard feelings. And no masks, either. You're right about that too. The people of Mercury City will cower before Dorian Black. And before you, of course."

"Of course. But you're not worried about an eventual 'this town ain't big enough for the two of us' moment?"

Nick grins. "It's a pretty fucking big town. Besides, I'm headed back to campus."

You wake up the next morning and walk into your bathroom. Looking back from the mirror is someone with glowing, healthy, unblemished skin. Arms firm and muscular (though not necessarily bulky) and jaw squared; gaunt. You barely recognize yourself in the mirror. With morbid curiosity, you lift your shirt and inspect your stomach—it's firm, with six-pack abs and sculpted oblique muscles. The abs ripple and your stomach growls fiercely. Damn, already? Time to eat whatever's left in the house, and then take the world head-on. You're going to:

➢ Head to the Casino buffet. Then I'd "wager" that I can break into the money cage. Get it? Wager? By that, I mean I'm going to rob the place. Go to page 26

➢ Easiest thing to do: Punch open the back wall of the bank and make a withdrawal. Go to page 225

Kings and Pawns

"I admit I was impressed by your declaration of divinity," Nick says. "Hell, you gave me the idea to use my powers to walk on water, make people think I was the Second Coming. *Gods-among-the-people* sounded like a pretty fantastic plan to me, but now that you're just another ant, why should I help you?"

"I…because I'd be in your debt. Force Catherine to give me back my powers. With my help, there's no limit to what you can achieve."

Nick lifts his palm and Catherine's head rises to face him in response. "Is it possible? Can you give *The Roman* the powers of a god once more?"

He releases her and she nods.

Several police patrol cars pull up on the other side of the crater, down the street. They're focused on the Kobayashi Building, but soon their attention will turn toward the three of you.

"We don't have much time," you say. "We can still have *gods-among-the-people*, Nick. What do you say?"

"Okay, do it. Reverse the process," Nick says to Catherine.

"It's not that simple. I need my equipment back home. Can you fly us there?"

Nick shakes his head "Nope. Too much weight. Let's hoof it outta here."

The interior of her trailer-park home has been completely gutted and reformed into a makeshift laboratory. Not even the kitchen appliances were spared. Every square inch is used for gadgetry and experimentation, except for the couch and TV. She saved those for her kid, who's staying at his grandparents' (until she defeated *you*, Catherine explains).

Catherine works through the night and when you wake up the next morning, she's still going at it. The kitchen bar-top counter is covered in sketched plans, worked-out formulae, and handwritten notes.

"What the hell is taking so long?" Nick says.

"You stole my genius!" she screams. "I'm back to my normal technologically-challenged self."

"How do you know it's even possible, then?"

"All of this!" she screams, pointing splayed hands at the papers.

"You wrote yourself an instruction manual?" you ask.

She nods. "And it worked last time; it just takes me a while to reverse the polarity on *Widowsilk*."

"The rifle's called *Widowsilk*?" you ask.

"Wait, wait, wait," Nick says. "You've done this before?"

"Of course. I had to know it worked, and I was short on volunteers." She shows off the rash on her forearm and adds, "I'm used to a few side-effects by now. And I was working faster this time around, before you got in my hair. Why don't you go watch TV or something?"

You take a seat next to Nick on the couch and he flips on the TV with his telekinesis. Mayor Argyle is holding a press conference and you've caught him in the middle. He's saying, "…a menace. There cannot be equality while there are those who are *more equal* than others. So, it is with a heavy heart that I must declare

205

martial law. These so-called 'supers' are public enemy number one, wanted for war crimes, and if spotted, should be…."

"War crimes?" Nick repeats. "Well, that escalated quickly."

"I think our living god's human-bomb-drop on the street might have something to do with it," Catherine says from the kitchen.

You hear your name on TV. Your *real* name. Not Roman or anything else—they know who you are. This snaps your attention back to the TV, where the news footage is now on the mayor's daughter, reporter Alison Argyle. She continues, "…along with Nikolai Dorian, and Catherine Woodall. We've confirmed reports that their families are being placed in protective custody. Ms. Woodall's son is already safely under police protection."

"*WHAT?!*" Catherine turns beet-red and her eyes shimmer with rage. Oh, boy.

"Focus!" Nick cries. "How long do you think it'll be before they check here? We got lucky. They had to deal with a human-bomb going off, but they'll come for us next."

"I think it's already 'next,'" you say, looking at several patrol cars outside the window.

Catherine rushes to the back of the trailer and into her bedroom, slamming the door behind her.

"Shit, what are we going to do?" Nick says.

"I don't have any powers!" you cry. "But I think…"

- ➤ "You need to use your powers, Nick. Distract them so we can run to fight another day!" Go to page 198
- ➤ "Catherine may not be a super-genius anymore, but maybe we can still use some of these gadgets?" Go to page 51
- ➤ "We should just give ourselves up. They're looking for superhumans, so I can always claim it's a case of mistaken identity, right?" Go to page 178

Kissing Cousins

You lunge forward and passionately kiss yourself. It's a long and deep embrace that strangely reminds you of when you practiced kissing your hand in middle school.

"Who the hell are you?" the Experi-mentor demands.

You answer, but it's directed toward your gender-bender doppelganger. "I'm you. The opposite-sex version of you, come from another universe. We need to hook up—for science. Think of it as the ultimate masturbation!"

"Nicole, call campus security!" the Experi-mentor shouts.

Catherine—err, Kenneth—shoves you away and cracks his knuckles. "Get the fuck out of here, pervert!"

You cast one last look at your other self, but "Woody" picks up a lead pipe and steps toward you. Looks like you're not to be star-crossed lovers with yourself. Not today, anyway.

Better rush back to the nuclear reactor and take your frustrations to a different world. A world where:

- There are no superpowered humans on the planet. You could do a lot of good for that world (or rule it) without fear of anyone exposing the secret to your genius. Go to page 28
- There was never an explosion. Perhaps you can find the pods that gave you your powers and study them! Go to page 87
- Science has stopped the aging process. As an immortal, you'll be able to spend eternity exploring all the infinite possibilities! Go to page 57
- Mankind hasn't destroyed the environment. Why not spend a little time in a lush utopia and see what knowledge you might bring back home? Go to page 364
- You chose a different pod in the experiment. Why not commune with other genii and see yourself with different superpowers? Go to page 270

Legendary

"Catherine! This guy's only a garden-variety genius, but you're a super-genius. That means we can beat him, right?"

A light flickers on behind her eyes. "Okay, I've got a plan."

"Already? Does your brain have super-speed too?"

"Nick!" she cries. "Let's make it rain. Once you can see him, go for my gun."

Nick looks up at the dusty rafters and gets it. He closes his eyes, raises a hand, and the roof starts to *shudder*. Fifty years of bat guano rains from the ceiling.

"*DISGUSTING!!!*" roars the Experi-monster, flailing his tentacles. Though he's otherwise invisible, you can see him as he displaces the guano dust.

Catherine says, "Droakam, do we have more foam? He has to maintain some solid form in order to hold my weapon. Let's make him *stick with it*."

"What is it about genius that makes you love puns?" the agent complains. "I'm on it, we've got plenty."

"All right, WMD, as soon as Droakam deploys his foam, take Grendel's arm there and finish this."

"Won't that just make more of him?" Agent Droakam asks.

"Leave that to me. Ready? Move!"

"Freeeeedddoooommm!!!" cries Nick as he flies forward and *pulls* the gun.

The Experi-mentor whips a super-speedy tentacle at the airborne college student, but Agent Droakam is already in mid-spray, and the sticky foam envelops the monster. Man, he's got that timing down pat. The tentacles freeze in place.

Right on cue, you leap forward with the enormous sword and behead the supervillain.

"Venom!" Catherine cries, bringing her middle and ring fingers to touch the palm of her tech-glove.

The Experi-mentor immediately starts to heal, making a double of himself from the head, but the flying bot erupts a white-hot pulse of plasma at both exposed neck wounds, cauterizing their openings. This scars the tissue and tricks the superpowered cells into thinking the healing process is complete.

The Experi-mentor's grotesque head stares up at you, eyes wide and lips seeking to speak or breathe. You all stare in silence, not quite comprehending that you just won.

"I'm putting that head in a glass case on my desk," Agent Droakam finally says.

"And the body?" asks Nick.

"I'll be able to study it," Catherine says.

"Does that mean you're joining us?" you ask. "Will you be our Lady Liberty?"

"Actually, I was thinking of going by Suffragette."

Droakam smiles. "The heroine who fights for the weak and disenfranchised. I like it."

"So what now?" Nick says.

Your stomach growls fiercely, a hungry monster in its own right. You smile, brows raised, and shrug. Everyone laughs.

➢ *Head out and get some shawarma!* <u>Go to page 135</u>

Libertarian

"'Bring me in?' I'd like to see you try," she laughs. "I never had you pegged for a government crony."

"We're a team! And with the three of us working together, we could do a lot of good in the world."

She shakes her head. "Sorry, I've already got a team. It's been my son and me versus the world for a long time, only now it's finally a fair fight. I can see why you'd want my help, but—no offense—I'm not so sure I need yours."

"What's your plan? Rescue people and steal money? Robin Hood, is it?"

She puts her hands on her hips. "I'm not sure I like your tone. I suggest you leave before I get angry."

- ➢ "I don't think I'd like you when you're angry, so I'll go, but I'll leave you this phone in case you change your mind. Best of luck taking on the whole world." Go to page 106
- ➢ "You'll be singing a different tune if Agent Droakam manages to reproduce the experiment results!" Go to page 11

Light of Life

You lead the robot to the top of the lighthouse—outside to the walker's watch—where the sun has just begun to rise. Perfect timing.

The robot examines you closely, most likely observing the gooseflesh that forms under the cold sea breeze. It follows your arm as you point out to the horizon.

"This is the sun, the star our planet orbits, the source of all life on Earth. Even yours—without the sun, you could have never come into being."

"I see," is all the robot says, though you get the feeling there's a deeper meaning behind the statement.

You watch the sunrise, with occasional glances over toward your robot companion. At length, it speaks again. "I am glad you brought me up here. To instill the importance of beauty and the sanctity of life. I understand why you've limited me to a humanoid form as well. I shall learn from this phase of my existence."

"I'm glad you think so...." you trail off, wanting to say a name, but realizing the machine doesn't have one yet.

➤ *That seems like a logical next step....* Go to page 357

Like a Boss

"It—it's nearly midnight," she stammers. "Should I go wake them?"

"No, I suppose it is late. Let's all meet first thing in the morning."

She nods furiously and turns to leave.

"Oh, and Su-Young," you call out. "Go ahead and keep my casino winnings for yourself. Consider it a signing bonus as my new liaison to the Planet Mercury staff."

Su-Young considers this for a moment, then simply says, "Thank you."

"And have someone come up and clear out these two," you say, indicating the unconscious goons.

Su-Young nods, then leaves. You should get some rest—you're exhausted from the day's events—but the thought, the feeling, of flying is too exhilarating. Ever since man first laid eyes on the birds in the sky, there's been a jealous coveting of the fact that they can fly. Now you're the first human capable of independent flight.

You leap out the window, *grasp* your body with your mind and carry yourself through the air with the power of thought. Arms spread out wide like a bird or a plane, you soar through the air, high up over the buildings. Moonlight glints off Mercury Bay in the distance.

This is amazing! Far beyond exhilarating. Whatever fear of heights you may have had in the past melts away under the feeling of complete control. You fly around for another hour before mental exhaustion sets in.

The next morning, you enjoy room service while Su-Young introduces Jorge Halifax (your head of security) and Luther Stockton (the floor operations manager). Halifax is slim, 50ish, bronze-skinned with coal-black hair—combed back for the "mobster" look. Stockton is a tall, muscular black man of similar age who wears his head shaved and has a thin mustache. A poor man's Idris Elba.

Both seem somewhat peeved by Su-Young's evident promotion, but once you inform them of their own respective pay raises, it would seem that any feud has been smoothed over. They wait for you to give your name, but you decline.

"Sheriff will do fine," you suggest, tugging the brim of Bloodnight's ten-gallon hat. "Now, on to business; what's first?"

"Bruce and Bruno are recovering from minor concussions," Halifax informs.

"Who?"

"The security guards," Su-Young elaborates.

"Those are their real names?" you laugh. "Very well, give the bruisers a month's pay for their trouble. What else?"

Stockton clears his throat. "All due respect, Sheriff, I can appreciate your greasing the wheels as the new head of state, but our current budget can't handle this much…loose spending."

"Don't worry," you say, sinking into the fine leather of the penthouse sofa, "casino profits are only *one* part of the plan. Soon, I'll have this whole city in my pocket. And I always reward my loyal friends."

Your three advisors smile.

"Speaking of which, how is my takeover being relayed by the PR staff?"

Su-Young flips on the penthouse television to the local news. There on-screen is blonde eye-candy reporter Alison Argyle, sitting at the news desk and speaking directly into the camera. The news-ticker reads, "CASINO BOSS BLOOD-NIGHT'S DEATH RULED SUICIDE."

"…friends have expressed shock, but those closest to Bloodnight say the man lived his life to such extremes that such an end might—"

Su-Young interrupts and says, "No mention of you yet, Sheriff, but we may want to do some sort of memorial service for your predecessor."

You nod and wave away the topic, turning back to the two men.

"Bloodnight liked to be involved in security," Halifax says.

"Yes, I'm aware."

Halifax runs a hand over his slicked-back hair. "Right, uhhh, well—I was just wondering if you, Sheriff, had plans to continue that, uhhh…"

"Is there a security problem?" you ask.

"Some kid, we're pretty sure he's counting cards," Stockton supplies.

"Right," Halifax says, "Normally we'd just rough him up a little, teach him a lesson and send him packing, but with the high rollers the boss liked to—"

"How much has he won?" you ask.

"He's up to half a mil," Stockton says.

"He's here, now?"

Su-Young switches the input on the television to the security feed on the casino floor. She taps her tablet's screen in a few key places, and the image of Nick—the college student from yesterday's experiment—shows up on-screen with a fat stack of poker chips before him.

He's playing blackjack at the $10,000 table and he's doing very, very well.

➢ "I don't want to see him; handle it your way." Go to page 240
➢ "Send him up." Go to page 267

Like a Jedi*

"Diamond, take him out!" you shout. Thinking quickly, you power-down the lightsaber and toss it to Catherine.

She nods, catches and powers-up the weapon, then sprints at the Experi-mentor. Ice crystals climb up her legs, but shatter. Fire engulfs her form like a summer breeze. Even the electricity doesn't stop her completely. She winces in pain and her muscles seize, but she makes a flying leap across the room, removing the current between her boots and the ground and rendering the electric attack moot.

With the lightsaber held high, Diamond soars through the air, ready to stab down through the force field and stop the Experi-mentor. But the mad scientist has one more trick up his sleeve.

All at once the elemental attacks stop, and as fast as his hands can move, he flings plasma bolts at the mighty hero coming at him. Not actually possessing *The Force*, Catherine fails to deflect the attacks. What once had only winged her now blasts fully into her torso.

Her leap turns into a fall, and she slams into the floor before skidding to a stop at the Experi-mentor's feet. The lightsaber powers-down.

The villain now turns to you, and you try to *grasp* the weapon with your mind, but his force field blocks your influence. No choking him, nothing. You and Dorian White are helpless as he comes at you with five superpowers to finish the job. He raises his hands and delivers an onslaught that qualifies as overkill.

Mercifully, your death is quick.

THE END

---

* But not actually a Jedi. Because this story contains elements of pop culture and is not, you know, an official part of Lucasfilm™. If anything, it's a parody of a Jedi. Like Kevin Smith in *Mallrats*. Perfectly clear? Okay, good.

Like a Lead Balloon

With the ease of Peter Pan, you dart out the open window and fly through the air. Good luck reporting *that*, Alison. Where to? Your apartment is compromised, and you've got nothing but the clothes on your back. You could....

Shattering glass brings your attention back to the building. You turn just in time to see Catherine come flying out of your window, glass and brick expelled from the brutish leap. She can fly too? That's bullshit.

No, wait—you can see it now; hers was more of a tick's incredible bounding ability than the hovering housefly maneuver you've perfected. Still, she comes at you, and she comes *fast*.

You turn to flee, but she latches on to you. The two of you plummet toward the city streets below and you think she says something like "Not so fast!" but it's hard to hear when the air whips by at the speed of gravity.

You struggle to free yourself, but she's got a grip like a vise. Either she's too amped up to consider the impending crunch, or she just doesn't care. She's got a smile on her face when the two of you *slam* into the pavement from lethal heights.

THE END

Limitations

"**Y**ou don't get to threaten *me,* you little shit!" she roars, hurling what's left of her coffee mug at you.

You *push* your own mug to intercept, exploding them together in midair, then duck away from the resultant ceramic and coffee fireworks.

"I don't want to hurt you," you say.

"You can't."

Catherine leaps up, punches both fists into the roof, then pulls the whole structure down. At the last second, you seek shelter under the kitchen bar, and then dart out around the wreckage.

She asked for it. You reach out with your mind, feeling for her windpipe, and *squeeze*.

Nothing happens.

She rushes in toward you and you *squeeze* harder, but it's like trying to crush a rock in your palm. Like trying to crush a diamond.

Just as she gets to you, you change tactics. You grab onto her whole body, *shove* her away with all your might and attempt to fling her away.

Nope.

She doesn't even budge. Instead, you fling yourself into what's left of the trailer wall—equal and opposite reaction, and all that.

You're momentarily stunned, wheezing for breath. She grabs you by the neck and holds you up off the ground. That doesn't make breathing any easier.

"Never come looking for me again," she says.

She steps and throws you out of the trailer, hurling you into the night air like child having a tantrum might throw a doll. Unfortunately, this child's gotten too big for her britches and throws you so hard, she snaps your neck in the process.

Your limp body lands several blocks away and you'll later be filed in the morgue under "Doe, J."

THE END

Lucky You

After dressing to the nines, like the high roller you're soon to be, it's off to the Planet Mercury Casino. You spend the cab ride downtown passing your mail key from palm to palm, practicing your telekinesis—ready to *move* the roulette ball without so much as a flick of the wrist.

As you arrive, you're greeted with all the glitz and glam of casino nightlife. Advertisements for buffets, strip clubs, discount tourist attractions, and invitations to join the Players Club abound, but one sign in particular catches your eye—declaring that tonight is *Amateur Magician Night*. Grand prize winner takes home $5,000 and will be considered for a permanent slot in the casino's entertainment lineup.

- ➢ No way I can make $5K in five minutes manipulating roulette. Don't get distracted by fame; fortune awaits! Go to page 171
- ➢ Time to gather my pet tigers and beautiful assistants in glitter suits—I'm going to be the greatest magician this town has ever seen! Go to page 181

The Lying King

Nick's face registers shock when you drop the screaming, struggling boy before him.

"It's like she knew, Nick," you say. "Do you think she could sense it somehow? Sense that he was in 'danger' or…?"

"You actually…" Nick says, stunned.

"What did you expect? Where's Droakam?"

Nick shakes his head. "Agent Droakam didn't make it. See for yourself."

He punches a few keys to bring up video feed from one of the helicopters down at the bank. Nick goes to Danny, and takes the boy away from the images on screen.

The footage shows Catherine exiting the bank, surrounded by the police. She drops the limp figures of several robbers onto the ground and the crowd goes wild. But the police move forward, engaging her. You have no audio, save for the pilot, but he's just speaking in jargon.

Agent Droakam is there on-scene, handgun drawn but not aimed. Not yet. The policemen all move forward, and Catherine's posture shifts. She waves her arms, aggressively shooing away the police force, but still they come.

She suddenly lifts a car off the street, and Droakam's weapon rises. He fires. She hurls the car at him, crushing the agent.

"Oh my God," you say. "What do we do now?"

"You took the cub. Now you're facing the mother lion," Nick says.

"*Me?*" you say.

"I'm sorry it had to be this way, but it's the only outcome to guarantee her cooperation. I've studied her quite a bit more than I let on, and with what you told me….She's far too powerful to leave to chance. But with you and Droakam as a common enemy—"

"Nick, what have you done?"

"Made a powerful ally," he whispers. Then he turns and shouts, "Catherine, thank God you got my call! They're crazy; you've got to do something!"

You turn toward the entrance and see Catherine bearing down on you. Her stride is inhumanly fast. "Catherine, don't listen to him; it's Nick—"

You fly up overhead and move to slip past Catherine and out the entrance, but in an incredible move, she lifts one of the largest crates and flings it at you with terrible force and accuracy. The effect is like being hit head-on by a speeding bus.

With you and Agent Droakam out of the way, and Catherine in his pocket, who knows how far Nick will go?

THE END

Mad as a Hatter

Before heading to your new lair, you empty your bank accounts and stock up on supplies. Firstly, you purchase, program, and send out a pair of drones to spy on the other two from the experiment. *Know thine enemy*, right? Once you've stocked up on food, water, and raw electronic components, it's time to head underground. Literally.

Mercury City got its name from the rich mercury deposits naturally occurring here, and originally started as a mining community some two centuries ago. The mercury mines have been closed and condemned for several decades, but that's a good thing. It makes for a remote and deadly locale.

Only a few minor (miner? ha, you're welcome) details to work out. First, there are no lights and nothing but toxic air in the cavernous depths below. Not to mention the possibility of mercury poisoning. If the mine still has trace levels, the heavy metal will seep into your system and slowly drive you insane.

Well, it's not anything money can't buy. Once your cancer research royalties flow in (not to mention Nobel prize money!) you can easily hire a crew—using a fake name, of course—to spruce things up for you. Still, it'll be a while before you've got steady cash flow, so you'd better do something now to get it all started. You know, before that mercury-induced madness sets in.

As you contemplate your next move, the drones return. A quick study of the footage reveals startling information. Nick has gained incredible physical prowess. He moves with fast, athletic moves, but also an incredible strength and durability. The drone shows Nick flip a parked car with his bare hands, leap atop a nearby building, and smash through the locked roof access with less effort than you needed to rip the price tag from your electronics. It also suggests a quick temper, prone to rash decision-making.

The next drone tells of Catherine's enhancements. She's coy in her self-discovery, but the aerial camera shows the single mother *lift* several household objects in an apparent display of telekinesis before closing the blinds on her trailer home. In the last bits of surveillance, someone in a black hooded robe emerges from the back of the trailer and flies into the air too fast for the drone to follow.

Quite the challenging pair, but nothing you can't deal with, given your resources. So, how're you going to earn your riches?

- ➢ The Planet Mercury Casino owner is a known mob boss. Why not make him an offer he can't refuse? Money and armed foot soldiers in one fell swoop! Go to page 49
- ➢ Convince the two to work for you. How hard would it be to rob a bank with those powers? Go to page 158
- ➢ Rig the stock market. You learned how to cure cancer in a day; surely you can become an industry insider after an hour or two. Go to page 247

Manning Crisis

"Well, that is...unfortunate," Agent Droakam says when you break the news.

"Who cares? We can take care of a few thieves on our own."

"A few thieves who are most likely using our blood samples to find sinister ways to kill us," Nick adds.

Droakam shakes his head. "It's more than just that. By not joining us, that makes Ms. Woodall another potential threat in the future. And that makeshift lab you say she has in her house—I wonder just what she's up to?"

"One threat at a time, yeah? Let's go bring in this casino boss," you say.

"Nelson Bloodnight made a major slip-up when he robbed a government facility. We've got clearance to bring him in. Still, we don't know if he's on his yacht, in his casino, or in an establishment of ill repute."

"Wait...like a whorehouse?" Nick asks, his voice perking up. He clears the involuntary excitement from his throat.

"We don't want to spook him," Agent Droakam says. "I'm going to see about borrowing some extra help. First we get a team to locate Bloodnight, then we send in the two of you. I'll be back soon, Nick—"

"Call me 'Murica, it's more fun."

Droakam sighs. "Just make sure that WMD doesn't do anything rash, and you, make sure that...'Murica...doesn't touch anything in here. Half these crates contain something potentially lethal."

"Only because you called me 'Murica," Nick says with a nod.

Agent Droakam shakes his head and leaves the warehouse. You can hear his SUV engine start up and the agent drive away. You say, "So how about we go raid the yacht?"

"I'm pretty sure that's what the agent meant by 'rash.'"

"We can't just sit around here doing nothing, can we?"

The warehouse doors swing open, but instead of an agent in a suit, a man in a flowing white lab coat with an 'Ex' emblazoned on his T-shirt comes marching in.

"I completely agree," the Experi-mentor says. "So why don't you come with me so I can study you further?"

You look at Nick, then at the scientist who has returned from the dead. Looks like he survived the initial blast of the experiment after all.

"I thought you said we could kill them?" says another man from the shadows outside the warehouse.

The Experi-mentor steps aside to reveal his companions, four menacing figures: A short, Korean woman in a black pantsuit with soulless eyes. A tall, muscular, athletic man (despite his age) with smooth ebony skin, head shaved and a thin mustache. A slim man of similar age with bronzed skin and coal-black hair—combed back for the "mobster" look. And a large, broad man with a Texas ten-gallon hat and the face of Chief Joseph.

"I said if they *didn't* surrender," the scientist explains to the man in the cowboy hat.

"Who the hell are these people?" Nick asks.

"You don't recognize your targets? This is the staff of the Planet Mercury Casino, Nelson Bloodnight and his cohorts. Although, now that I've managed to reverse-engineer your powers and recreate the experiment results, I've decided to call them 'The Mercurials.' Their leader is Primordial and this is Lady Ghoststep—"

"Don't really care," you say, anger billowing inside.

"But that's the fun part!" the Experi-mentor groans.

"Doesn't matter. Either you're about to kill us, or we're about to kill you. Either way, don't care about your names."

"It's true, doc. Let's get on with it," Bloodnight/Primordial says.

"I think this counts as rash," Nick whispers.

"Me too." You rush forward and attack the casino boss, but your assault falls *into* the man as his body folds back like a trampoline. His legs form coils—literally—and his arms stretch out and grab two nearby crates, so that he's re-formed his body into a slingshot. Your own momentum provides the force to fling you across the warehouse and through the back wall. You shake off the dust and plunge back in.

When you climb inside, you see Nick fighting both the shapeshifting Bloodnight and the thick-limbed enforcer. Knowing he's outmatched, Nick *grabs* the larger man by the neck using his telekinesis and flings the bruiser across the room—breaking his neck in the process. The man rises to his feet and his neck cracks back into place, instantly healed.

You rush in to join the fight, but every time you swing a punch at the greasy-haired mobster, he dodges the blow with inhuman speed. He's just a blur that you can't possibly hit.

Nick floats up into the air to avoid the newly-healed criminal, but Bloodnight forms his arm into a flail—a ten foot-long chain with an enormous ball of spikes on the end. He connects the weapon to Nick's chest and the college student falls from the air.

With a powerful battle-cry, you smash into Bloodnight and knock the man across the room. You move to finish him off, but the small woman comes to stop you. She doesn't look threatening, but what did the Experi-mentor call her? Lady Ghoststep?

She puts a hand *through* your chest, and you stop dead in your tracks when her fist clogs your respiratory tract. You can't breathe! You choke, cough and sputter, but your body's reflexes are no match for her supernatural grip.

You look to Nick for help, but the other three "Mercurials" are taking care of him while you suffocate. It's too much. The four of them easily overwhelm the two of you. Agent Droakam will be in for a bad day when he learns his Freedom Fighters were KIA.

THE END

Masked and Dangerous

You rush over to the Halloween store and grab the Phantom mannequin from the street, dragging it inside with you, madly searching for somewhere to change. *Screw it*—in the aisle! The door gives a *ding!* when you enter, and a young man wearing all black comes around the corner.

"I need this costume, fast!"

"Okay…" he says, brushing his bleached/orange hair across his brow. "I've got plenty on aisle four, if you—"

"Just help me with this one!"

He unbuttons the puffy shirt while you pull off the trousers. You replace your own pants with the costumed pair. The clerk doesn't even bat an eyelash; he's seen stranger things working at a downtown, year-round Halloween store.

After what feels like ages, you're finally in the costume. A tuxedo mixing the somberness of a vampire and the bravado of a pirate. A flowing black cape goes nearly to the ground. It fits well, and makes you feel like someone else—someone powerful and confident. The outfit is nearly a complete visage of darkness, save for the white, iconic Phantom mask.

"Okay, how do I put the mask on?" you ask.

"I'll have to get you some tacky, so you can adhere it to your face."

"Wait, I can't just put it on?"

He sighs. "If you want, you don't have to wear it…"

"Goddamn it! The mask is the whole point. Just, fine, get the tacky, quick!"

The clerk goes, but not very quickly. You briefly consider telekinetically keeping the mask *pressed* against your face, but think better of it. It's hard enough focusing on multiple tasks with your new power, as it is.

When he returns, he asks you to sit down while he applies some kind of flesh-friendly super glue around your right cheek and eye socket. He taps the area several times with his forefingers until your skin starts to stick to his, then he firmly holds the mask down on your face.

"Should just be a couple of minutes." You growl with frustration.

Finally, the process is complete and you rise as *The Phantom*, pay the clerk, and head out into the streets to save the day. The prostitute is dead, her throat slit. The pimp kicks her lifeless body.

Shit. You rush over, roaring with rage. The man turns to face you just as you pummel him with a combined telekinetic and physical punch. *BAM!* He flies across the street and bounces off the brick wall opposite. *CRACK!*

You mentally *grab* him, and throw the pimp across two lanes of traffic and against the Halloween storefront. You *leap* into the air, flushed with adrenaline, and *fly* high above the city's skyline. You zoom back down, boots poised for an epic stomp, and land atop the man, breaking his spine. For justice, of course.

Hey, you can fly! Awesome.

> *Go find some more baddies to crush and damsels to save (successfully, this time).*
> Go to page 162

The Matador

"You picked the wrong skyscraper on the wrong day," you say, trying to sound menacing.

Catherine smiles, cracks her knuckles, and lunges at you.

Staying close to the shattered window's opening, you *lift* the glass from the floor, mentally claiming as many jagged pieces as you can. All in one motion, you command the projectiles to head to her, going for a dozen skewers of the torso.

She picks up at a sprint just as the glass smashes into her, splintering into a thousand pieces. Her clothing rips, but you see no damage to the skin beneath. You dart away just as she jumps at you, her fingers barely missing the edges of your cape, and hurtles to the street thirty stories below.

Glass-proof is cool, but flying is cooler. You watch as she *smashes* into the pavement, cracks snaking across the asphalt. One of these days, you'll really have to stop killing the evil-doers you face, but it's enough for now to protect the innocent at whatever cost.

You rush forward into the building, searching for survivors.

After several floors and two dozen offices of nothingness, you finally hit paydirt. When you *blast* open this door, you find half a dozen nine-to-fivers huddled around an a/c vent, taking in the precious fresh air.

"Never fear, citizens, The Phantom is here!"

They blink several times in shared disbelief, thinking you're a hallucination. Then they all look past you as someone taps you on the shoulder.

You turn back to see Catherine, dirty, covered in soot, clothes torn, but healthy and unharmed. Did she really just peel herself off the pavement and climb back up here?

"You mess with the bull," she says, "You're gonna get gored."

She punches you with such ferocity that her fist comes out the back of your head.

THE END

Mercy Me

"I'll let you live, but if I ever see you again, you'll find my patience limited. Stop this foolishness and never speak of superhumans again."

You release Agent Droakam and fly back out the window.

What a nice overlord you'll make! That actually felt good, letting those insignificant peons live. They'll tell the others you conquer how fair and just you, their liege lord, are. And nothing bad ever happens when the villain lets their enemies live, right?

Problem solved; head back to the casino and relax in your penthouse suite. You've been meaning to check out the Jacuzzi tub—what better opportunity?

➢ *Indeed! Time for the royal treatment. Posh and pampered, that's me.* Go to page 39

Might Makes Awesome

Walking through the back wall of a bank proves about as difficult as walking through the ball-pit of a *Chuck-E-Cheese*. The concrete just sort of crumbles out of your way. The downtown Mercury Bank staff ducks and covers their heads as if experiencing an earthquake.

Once they see it's you rattling the walls—a person for whom concrete and steel yields the right of way—they simply stare. Slowly, they rise, slack-jawed and eyes like saucers. No one screams, no one runs for help. Not even the security guards move.

Without a word, you move past the staff like they're mannequins in a department store. Ah, there's the vault up ahead—thick metal, with an intricate locking mechanism centered by a wheel.

One brief tug and the wheel comes off in your hands. Gripping the handles on the sides, you wrench those off too. Hmmm, guess the pins keeping the door in place are much sturdier than these pieces.

You reel back and put your weight behind a punch into the center of the vault door. *POW!* It feels like punching a pillow. The vault door dimples and folds as if it's filled with down. A follow-up kick (*WHAM!*) and the door is forced back inside the vault.

Inside is greater wealth than you could have possibly imagined, short of a swimming pool filled with cash, which you make a mental note to install in your new mansion. Today, you're limited only by how much you can lug out, but since lifting moneybags feels like carrying birthday balloons, that means you're limited by what you can fit in your arms.

Carrying the cash like a stubborn *I-don't-need-a-cart-thanks* customer at the grocery store, you make your way from the vault. The bank staff only stares. The only sounds are the growls of your stomach. You'd expected some kind of resistance, a firefight, even, but right now it appears there's been a silent agreement that they're all sharing a mass hallucination. Bob had a birthday, right? Who spiked Bob's birthday cake?

They probably won't even activate the alarm until after you're gone. As the first superhuman to make a public appearance, you had the element of surprise. Next time it won't be so easy.

➢ *Go stash the cash and plan your next move....* Go to page 182

Mind over Matter

Six figures step forward from deep within the cavernous recesses of your base. As they emerge from the shadows, you see that they wear lab coats, each one a different color, and the man in the white coat has an "Ex" emblazoned on his shirt.

"The Experi-mentor!" you cry.

The scientist takes a bow. "My creations—so we meet again. How magnificent you've become, even without my guidance. I really must applaud your taking care of the other two, who kept the public eye off myself, leaving me free to continue my research without police interference.

"While I know you think of yourself as the pinnacle of mankind, you're merely a resource. The signed release from the experiment clearly states any successful result would become property of the company, and thus I own a patent on the three of you. You're my resource, and I'm giddy with anticipation of employing you!"

Super-mind working on overtime, you're already planning your next move. There are other gadgets and safeguards in your fortress waiting for activation. A dozen winning scenarios pop into your head.

"If you think you can simply command me, you're gravely mistaken," you say.

"Not I, perhaps, but allow me to introduce my colleagues. You see, when you used your own blood to cure cancer, you unwittingly gave me a key to reverse-engineering the experiment. Using your DNA, I created five other wonderful superpowers."

The Experi-mentor points to the other scientists, who are lined up by his side. The first is a woman in a black lab coat, a man in blue, another in green, a woman in red, and finally, a male scientist in a clear rain-slicker. In order, he introduces them as, "Doctors Necromancy, Hallucination, Reader, Mind-Control, and Timetravel."

Now you're feeling nervous. That's one hell of a lineup.

"So you see, I already have everything I want. And what do you get the man who has everything? Why, you get *on your knees*."

The scientist in red, introduced as Dr. Mind-Control, steps forward and places the forefingers of her right hand against her temple. You're suddenly filled with an overwhelming love for the Experi-mentor, and a desire to serve. You kneel, ready to do your master's bidding.

THE END

Mission Extremely Possible

The next morning you're all suited up and ready to go when Agent Droakam arrives at the warehouse. The Camo-suit seemed to cinch down when you put it on, like it "knew" how to perfectly fit itself to your body. Since receiving your powers, you've trimmed down on fat and packed on the muscle, so a skin-tight outfit makes you look damned good. Like a Supersoldier.

Droakam enters through the warehouse doors with a dolly-cart stacked high with donut boxes. A baker's dozen of baker's dozens. "Looking sharp!" he says. "Breakfast?"

Your stomach growls in anticipation. Hell, this might be the best part of having superpowers—you can eat *anything* and look great. Without a word, you dig in. Nick comes from the recesses of the warehouse wearing the green Dinoskin suit. Obviously feeling less confident in his new getup, he holds his hands over himself like a fig leaf.

"Morning, Kid Liberty," Droakam says with a grin.

"Hilarious. What's the mission?"

"Right to it, huh? Well, our first task is to take down Nelson Bloodnight, owner of the Planet Mercury Casino—the city's major kingpin."

"*Mmph—whe're ohn iht,*" you say through a mouth full of donut. After swallowing, you add, "Straight to the casino?"

"Whoa, hold on. We don't have any legally prudent reason to take Bloodnight just yet. We do, however, have one of his major partners in town. Number ten on the FBI's most wanted list: Roger Aleister Kingsley. He's made Bloodnight millions in international racketeering schemes, so if we bring him in, we think he'll turn over on his boss. Kingsley is notorious for showing up just long enough for us to learn he's here, but not long enough for us to grab him. We got lucky this time—an anonymous tip with the location of the target."

"Great, so what's the plan?" Nick asks.

"Bring him in. He carries mercenary-level private security wherever he goes, so be careful. I can bring up a full briefing on this computer...."

"Don't bother," you say. "I'm a weapon, right? Point me at the target."

Agent Droakam parks the SUV, then points at an older apartment complex, six stories high, that's decayed over time. "Okay, you're up. I'll be here as soon as you bring him out."

You step out with Nick by your side, ready for action. The Americana camo-suit comes with a beret and you pull it taut over your brow. Very Jean-Claude Van Damme.

"Nick, you might want to stand back and let me handle this."

"No way! You think I'm gonna let you get all the glory? I'll fly up to the roof; we can flank 'em."

"Glory? What glory? No one knows we're here."

"Which is why I called the local news station with an 'anonymous tip' of my own."

"Oh, yeah? What'd you say? 'A pair of superheroes are about to debut; come on down and check it out!'" you laugh.

Nick grins. "That's why I called 911 as well. Time to make this look good!"

Before you're able to protest, Nick leaps into the air and soars up to the roof. *Great. He's gonna get himself killed*, you think, and rush towards the front door. Slapping a flat palm against it, the door explodes inward, doing massive damage to the foyer area.

A man lies bloodied on his back in the hallway; the door's casualty. As you step inside, you see two more men with shaved heads and five o'clock shadows. They wear black suits, with submachine guns at the ready. As soon as you're in, they send a hail of gunfire your way.

The shots sting like being whipped with switches, but all that does is make you angry. Big mistake. Their weapons both click empty and you look down at your supersuit—completely unblemished.

Footsteps pound the floors above as more security guards rush your way. You grab the two men as if they were rag dolls and drag them upstairs. When you see the crowd of guards coming your way, you fling the first man—he hits the crowd with a sickening *crunch*. Using the second man as a bludgeon, you beat the other guards senseless, not slowing down even as they shoot you.

It's a massacre. Hopefully Roger Aleister Kingsley isn't hiding in plain sight among his men, because it won't be easy to draw a confession from a bloody pulp. You easily make your way up the apartment building, clearing it out floor by floor. Soon, the whole complex is silent. Looks like you've incapacitated everyone…

Until you make it to the top floor. A man in a silken scarlet robe steps forward. He's a grim man in his upper 50s, stubble beard and hard features. Cold eyes stare back at you, filled with terror. Every fiber in his body resists the motion, yet he continues on his path, stilted, like a drunken marionette.

"What the bloody hell is happening?" he asks in a thick, noble-blooded English accent.

"You're coming with us," Nick says.

The college student holds out his hands, the evident puppetmaster, and forces Kingsley to step down the stairs. "Guards all taken care of? Ah, listen to that!" You nod, then stop to listen. Sirens, just outside. Nick grins and says, "Let's go greet our adoring public."

Droakam is there outside, ready to cuff Kingsley as soon as he steps outside. But so are two squad cars and a news van. "What just happened? Can you offer a statement?" It's blonde reporter Alison Argyle.

"No comment," Droakam says.

Nick *floats* into the air, then gestures to you and says, "This is WMD, and I am 'Murica. Together, we are the Freedom Fighters, *superheroes* here to defend the city against scum like Nelson Bloodnight."

"Goddamnit," Agent Droakam grumbles. "Get back to HQ, now!"

Nick lets out a hearty, "Freeeeeeedddooooommmm!!!!!!" as he flies up into the sky.

The cameras focus on you. You sprint away, leaping with inhumanly long strides, only to arrive back at the warehouse a few minutes later just as an industrial van with HiT stenciled on the side pulls away. The van peels out down the dock, fishtailing on the damp roads.

Nick lands next to you. "What the hell? Were they just inside?"

That familiar rage boils up inside. "I'll stay here and make sure nothing's up….Go, follow them!"

Nick darts back into the air. The warehouse is quiet and the air still. Nothing is broken, the crates are all here. Well, if one were missing, it'd be hard to tell, but the point is that this wasn't a smash-and-grab job. If they took something, it must have been a specific target. But what was it? Your fists unclench, and the mission quickly turns from a search for *who's here* to a search for *what isn't*.

Agent Droakam arrives just before Nick, and after you fill the agent in, Nick proceeds to do the same for you. He says, "They drove down to the docks. I stayed above the van, so I don't think they know I followed them. Anyway, they took a cooler from the van, hopped in a speedboat, and met up with a mega-yacht anchored in the Bay."

"Did you get a good look at the yacht?" Droakam asks.

"Yeah, more of a small cruise-liner than a personal boat. It's a gigantic behemoth called *The Son of Jupiter*. We can trace the owner, right?"

You both look at Agent Droakam and an expression you can't quite read comes over his face. At length, he says. "They took a cooler? Are you certain?"

The agent runs to a corner of the warehouse, checks something, then suddenly turns back. "They took the blood samples!"

"Who owns the yacht?" you say, more a demand for information than a question.

Droakam swallows. "…Nelson Bloodnight."

You start to leave, but Agent Droakam steps in your path, hands raised. "Wait! We don't know what he wants. If he took your blood, he might be looking for a weakness."

"Which is why I'm going to stop him before he finds one. Step aside."

"Well," Nick says. "If there's going to be a war between us and them. Maybe we oughtta recruit one more soldier? You wanted a Lady Liberty in the Freedom Fighters, right? Maybe we should go have a talk with Catherine Woodall."

➢ "No. No more discussion, no grand plans. I'm going to finish this once and for all." Head to the yacht! Go to page 29
➢ "Fine, let's go. What's better than two supersoldiers, right?" Go recruit the woman from the experiment! Go to page 335

More Valuable than Gold

"You really don't want to arrest us?" Nick asks, genuinely confused.

With a smile, you say, "I really don't. We have a golden opportunity here."

"You're right," Catherine says, lowering her hood so you can see the passion in her eyes. "I have a son. What kind of example am I setting for Danny? We have the opportunity to leave the world a better place."

"But...what about all this cash?" Nick says.

"Ideals are one thing people tend to value over money," Baxter replies.

"Thanks for the after-school special," Nick says dryly.

"Nick, we're talking celebrity endorsements, more money than you can count, fame. You'll have groupies! Wouldn't you rather be loved than feared?" you say, doing your best to appeal to the college male.

"Whatever. I'm in," he says.

"You have a fucking *batcave*?" Nick says when you arrive at the lighthouse sanctuary.

"I suppose we have the start of one," you chuckle.

"We have the fucking bats," Baxter adds helpfully.

"And with my department's funding, you'll have the equipment," someone says. You turn back to see a man in a black suit. He continues, "Agent Brendan Droakam, FBI Supersoldier Division. I'd like to be your Alfred. Or, more like Morgan Freeman's character, the one who provided all the technology. What was that guy's name?"

"Did you follow us?" Catherine asks.

"Actually we've been waiting."

"We?" you ask.

That's when reporter Alison Argyle steps forward from the shadows, stunning as ever. "I wanted to thank you," she says. "Agent Droakam assumed I knew how to find you, and he provided the boat to get us here."

"And how *did* you know?"

She flashes that winning smile. "You made it easy, 'Professor.' All your deliveries to this island were a big red flag. And when I saw the address as 'Lebon Rd'—a palindrome for 'Dr. Nobel,' I put two and two together."

"My programming indicates there is nothing sexier than an intelligent woman," Baxter says.

You both blush.

Then six more figures step forward from the shadows. You really need to install some lights down here. They wear lab coats, each one a different color, and the man in the white coat has an "Ex" emblazoned on his shirt.

"A touching moment, but I'm afraid I must interrupt."

"The Experi-mentor!" Nick cries.

The scientist takes a bow. "My creations—so we meet again. Unfortunately, Agent...Droakam, was it? The signed releases from the experiment clearly state that any successful result would become the property of the company, and thus I own a patent on the three superheroes. All this to say, they're not in a position to accept your offer, seeing as how I own them.

"And, to ensure no breach of contract, allow me to introduce my colleagues. You see, *Dr. Nobel*, when you used your own blood to cure cancer, you unwittingly gave me a key to reverse-engineering the experiment. Using your DNA, I created five other wonderful superpowers."

The Experi-mentor points to the other scientists, who are lined up by his side. The first is a woman in a black lab coat, a man in blue, another in green, a woman in red, and finally, a male scientist in a clear rain-slicker. In order, he introduces them as, "Doctors Necromancy, Hallucination, Reader, Mind-Control, and Timetravel."

"They're considering fighting," Dr. Reader says.

"I'm only offering cooperation as a courtesy," the Experi-mentor says. "I could just have Dr. Mind-control force you into it."

"The leader, Dr. Nobel, thinks the robot is the key to defeating us," Dr. Reader says at the exact moment you think, *Their powers are mind-based, they wouldn't work on Baxter!*

Knowing you've only got one shot to get this right, you shout, "Baxter, activate combat modules. Passcode: Skynet Awakens—go for…"

➢ "…Dr. Hallucination!" How can we fight if he's manipulating our senses? Go to page 27
➢ "…Dr. Mind-Control!" She's the Experi-mentor's trump card. Go to page 60
➢ "…Dr. Timetravel!" If we win, he'll just go back in time and kill our mothers! Go to page 104
➢ "…Dr. Reader!" We can't win if they know our plan! Go to page 312
➢ "…Dr. Necromancy!" With a name like that, she's obviously the most terrifying! Go to page 279

The Most Dangerous Game

First, you study the feed—over and over again.

"The one you call 'Nick' appears to have both super-strength and a high resistance to damage," Baxter says. "He crumbled that wall and his fists were not crumbled in response. The maniacal laughter after his entrance seems to be aimed at Newton's third law."

"Good point. Where's the equal reaction?"

"That will be a problem for us. We cannot hope to find his threshold for damage while we are already engaged in combat."

"That's true," you say, further studying the footage. "Catherine, on the other hand, appears to possess telekinetic abilities of a magnitude such that she can make herself 'fly' for all practical purposes of the word."

"Unless her abilities are equally as impossible as Drillbit's. What if she can actually manipulate reality, and simply does not realize it?"

Your heart sinks. "In that case, we're fucked."

"Such harsh language, Doctor!"

"Are you really offended, Baxter?"

The robot's light blinks. "I am unsure if I possess that capability. I was merely affecting a personality inverse to your negative reaction."

"You can…alter your personality?"

"Fo shizzle, Doc. Spittin' trufe straight dope, if dat's how it gotta be," Baxter grins.

"Okay, I get the point. Also, I'm not a doctor."

"No, but I thought it appropriate. If we are to fight people who call themselves 'Drillbit' and 'Shadow Priestess,' why not have your own larger-than-life persona?"

"Doctor…" you muse. "Gadget?"

Baxter's speakers come on, playing the old *Inspector Gadget* theme, but calling out "Doctor Gadget!" at the right time.

"Ugh, no. Never mind. Let's just focus on bringing down the criminal duo," you say.

"Okay. While we had this conversation, I was analyzing military tactics. What was traditionally called 'the high ground' and today 'home court advantage' could serve us well."

"So you're saying we fight them on our own terms."

"Can we set a trap and draw them here?" Baxter asks.

"People of Mercury City! I call to you today to tell you not to live in fear. Allow me to introduce myself. I am Dr. Nobel… and I have cured cancer. Now I turn my considerable attention to the criminals who've been plaguing our fair city. From my island fortress, I will devise a way to deal with Drillbit and Shadow Priestess, I promise you. For now, keep your spirits high."

Dropping the act, you turn to Baxter. "How was that?"

"Transmission complete, Doctor. Based on my facial recognition software, I believe you appeared genuine."

"Let's hope so. We need them to think we haven't prepared for them yet so they'll rush here to stop us."

"We are verrrrry sneaky," Baxter says while flexing the newly enhanced anatomy, a product of your few days' preparation. The robot's forearms glow blue from deep within. "There are two of us and two of them. Should we focus our attentions?"

- ➤ "Good idea, I'll take Nick. With someone as powerful as Drillbit, manipulating his emotions is probably the best course. And I'm assuming I'll be better at it than you, what with your just being born…." Go to page 116
- ➤ "Okay, I'll take Catherine. I've got a bad feeling that she might just disassemble you with her mind. So, whatever I craft will keep her overtaxed and occupied." Go to page 194

Murder Schmurder

Okay, so you probably just killed that pimp. Turns out brains don't like being "touched" or whatever, so you'd better put that skill waaaaay in the back of the toolbox. But no one's going to miss some flesh-peddler who suddenly got an aneurysm after beating up too many whores, right?

You shrug, and the trash on the street flutters in response.

Sirens suddenly echo off the surrounding buildings, and you think to dart away like a frightened rabbit, but as the fire engine passes you realize that it's not the cops coming for you. Instead, fire truck pulls up to a massive fire up ahead.

An entire floor of a skyscraper is ablaze. Thirteen stories up, black smoke billows out and curls up the sides of the building.

"There's someone up there!" a tourist shouts, lowering his binoculars against his travel vest. "He's gonna jump."

➤ There may be a crowd, but I'm the only one who can save him! Go to page 351
➤ Gross. I don't want to be around to see that. Go to page 244

Neo-Manhattanite

"You know, if you put on a stern look and pointed at me while you said your pitch, it'd probably make a better recruiting tool," she says.

"I'm serious!" you bark.

"Yeah? Well, I'm seriously not buying it. Why would I want to join the post office when I can start my own FedEx? Why work for NASA when I'm SpaceX? Trust me, I'll do great things for this country, but I'm not going to do it being a Neo-Oppenheimer. The folly of genius lies in giving way to bureaucrats."

"Isn't that a little…short-sighted?" Nick says.

Catherine scoffs. "Nothing kills innovation quite like regulation. I'm bursting through the red-tape ceiling."

"Can't change your mind?" you ask.

"You just tried, didn't you? Sorry, but no hard feelings. I'll see you on the other side. Good luck with the whole Freedom Fighters thing. Maybe I'll give you a call if 'Woodall Wonders' ever starts hiring."

➢ *Head back to the warehouse without Catherine.* Go to page 220

A New Menace

As a compromise, you get to keep the name The Phantom, but the first issue of your new comic book is titled *The Phantom Menace*, and you don't have to call the lightsaber a "beamstick." That first issue is solely about you, because you beat out both Diamond and Dorian White as the world's first superhero. Of course, you spent a significant amount of your superhero career thus far in a hospital bed, but first is first and fair is fair!

Nick Dorian came up with the name *Chimera* for your super-team, based on the mythological creature from antiquity composed of three separate beasts. You know, just like your team is three people with three powers, get it? College students can be so pretentious…bet he sees himself as the lion head, too. Although, technically, since accepting corporate sponsorship, the team is called, "Nike Presents: The Chimera."

The first issue releases just as you're released from the hospital, healthy and ready to fight crime once more. Even though Nick and Catherine spend the intervening time stopping bank robberies, extinguishing other major fires, and busting up crime syndicates, you're the most famous hero of the three. Why? Because you were featured in *Nike Presents: The Chimera #1—The Phantom Menace.*

Presently, in order to avoid the throngs of reporters and teenage fans blockading the front of the hospital, Nick arrives via helicopter on the hospital roof. When you climb aboard, you see he's actually *piloting* the thing.

"You know how to fly a helicopter?" you say once you've donned the headset.

Normally, you'd be frightened to hop into a helicopter with a college student, but there's something comforting in the thought that you could always just leap out and fly away.

"I do now!" he calls back, grinning beneath mirrored aviator sunglasses. "Actually, the controls are fairly rudimentary. I modified this particular model, and of course gave it a few *upgrades* that might come in handy in our war against crime. Ready to head home?"

Home, and he's not talking about your low-rent apartment. Ready as you'll ever be. You give him a nod and he takes off into the sky. He presses a few buttons on the dash and the rotor blades stop spinning. You look up through the bubble canopy windshield in time to see them sweep back and retract. Just as the bird starts to fall, it suddenly blasts forward under the force of an unseen rocket engine in the rear. Seems like he cashed in on a pretty solid book advance to be able to afford all this.

It's only a few minutes later that you arrive at "The Savior Complex," your floating city/secret lair. What was that about pretentious names? Well, say what you will, the kid's been busy. It's a *floating* city in the sky, for Christ's sake! As he lands, you see insect-like robots climb through the sanctuary, autonomously installing new hardware and God-knows-what-else.

"Dorian, I'm glad you're on our side."

He gives a curt smile, then leads you into your quarters. The security doors open in response to your palm imprint and, beyond that, a velvet purple stage curtain parts to give way to *Le Opera Populaire*—your wing of the house. Up top is an enormous chandelier, but you quickly realize the whole suite is meant to look like an opera house. Perhaps if you'd known the impact of your costume choice, you might have spent more time browsing the racks of that Halloween store....

The *pièce de résistance* is a row of Phantom suits, new and clearly upgraded. On the far end stands one clearly meant for battle—crimson red, where the others are black—with an ornate double-breasted coat, like an artilleryman's uniform. Rather than oxford cloth and suit pants, it's a versatile, lightweight, armored battle suit. Something like a functional *Batman* costume, but there's a big white Nike swoosh on the chest.

"Goddamnit," you grumble.

"Suit up. We've got company. A group from the FBI, by the looks of it, and we want this official. I'm not sure what we're about to be offered, but I'm assuming it's a contract to protect America, so we want to look professional. See you in the Lion's Den in five."

When you finally reach the "Lion's Den" (a grand room with a roaring fireplace and a lionskin rug), Diamond and Dorian White are already waiting in costume, entertaining a man in a comparatively ordinary black suit. He's of average height, square-jawed and muscular, with the short-cropped hair of a military man. He pours himself a drink from the corner bar.

"Ah, the famed Phantom!" the man says. "Will you join us in a toast?"

He hands Diamond a glass, but Dorian taps himself on the head and says, "No thanks, dulls the senses."

"What's all this about?" you ask.

"On to business then. My name is Agent Brenden Droakam, head of the United States Supersoldier Program." He suddenly has the room's rapt attention and continues, "To the existence of the superhero and the return of full funding to my department!"

Droakam toasts himself and downs the top-shelf liquor.

"What do you want?" Diamond says in a low voice, setting her glass down on the fireplace mantel.

"First, to introduce you to an old friend." The agent makes his way to the double-door entry opposite the passage where you entered. He pulls both handles dramatically and steps aside so you can see the figure in the doorway. The new man's shadow is long and stark across the grand room and when he steps forward into the light cast by the fireplace, his flowing lab coat sweeps in behind him.

"Greetings, my great creations!" the scientist calls out with arms widespread.

The Experi-mentor! He still has the giant "Ex" emblazoned on his chest, but with the lab coat unbuttoned, you can now clearly see the logo. Upgraded steampunk goggles rest on his forehead.

Dorian White makes a cautious step toward the fireplace, as if sensing a trap. He's preparing himself. For what?

"I see you've been busy since our little 'accident,'" the Experi-mentor says. "And so have I. With Agent Droakam's help—and his department's funding—I managed to secure a bit of *Phantom blood* donated by the hospital...and I've been able to recreate the results of the experiment."

The room goes silent.

"Wait, you've created more Supers?" Diamond asks.

"And I thought *he* was the super-genius," the Experi-mentor says, pointing to Nick and cackling with glee.

"Good for you," you say, trying to take back control of the situation. "But The Chimera isn't taking new recruits just yet. So, if you'd like to leave your name and number with the secretary out front—"

"See, that's the thing," Agent Droakam interrupts. "Uncle Sam doesn't want incredibly powered heroes outside the purview of the Supersoldier Program. Too much risk."

"Soooooooo—we've come to collect," the Experi-mentor adds.

Droakam nods. "Come with us and we'll simply *reverse* the experiment. I've been assured it's theoretically possible."

"Oh, it is, it is," the scientist says.

"We just want to return you back to normal citizens. Back to being sons and daughters. Back to being college students, mothers, and average Joes. Being able to 'turn off' the powers of those inside Supersoldier Program is extremely important to us, and you'll be well-compensated for helping your government in this way."

"Not that you'd need it," the Experi-mentor says, looking around the den of your floating mansion.

"It's the right thing to do, and I've got a presidential order for your detainment right here," Droakam says, reaching into his breast pocket. "Please come quietly."

➢ "You're right, this whole 'powers' thing is pretty dangerous. I trust the government will be responsible with its use. Let's go." Go to page 287
➢ "You can pry my telekinesis from my cold, dead hands. I am forevermore…*The Phantom.*" Go to page 297

Newsworthy

There's no one in the lobby of your apartment building, so you head into the out-of-order elevator shaft and *fly* up to the fourth floor, where you find a petite blonde waiting by your apartment door. She turns to meet you and immediately you recognize reporter Alison Argyle, though she looks shorter than she does on TV.

"Hi, I'm Alison," she says, with her winning smile.

"I know who you are," you respond, somewhat starstruck.

"Do you live here?"

You look at your door but say nothing.

"I'm investigating the Mercury University explosion, and I found your name on a signed waiver. I just want to ask you a few questions."

Still you say nothing, this time staring at her blankly.

"Did you just come from the elevator? I thought it was out of order."

➢ Better invite her in…. Go to page 170
➢ Threaten her. Maybe a little "display" will scare her off? Go to page 76

Nickless Wonder

You don't give the decision a second thought; that's how being the boss works. The only lingering doubt is, *What if he's like me?* Guess you'll know for sure if security reports indicate he dispatched your goons before flying away.

"What's next?" you ask the casino staffers.

"Public takeover announcement," Su-Young says.

Stockton nods. "Not to mention a statement to your shareholders. If you don't step forward in a display of confidence, the value of your on-the-level holdings will plummet overnight."

"Does that mean I have holdings that are...not on-the-level?" you ask.

Halifax clears his throat and says, "There were a number of—well, illegal activities Nelson controlled. Now that he's out of the picture, there might be some underlings who think it's their turn to step up. A show of strength here would go a long way."

Excellent points to consider. If your new acquisition comes with a complete criminal underbelly, you'd best get a handle on your foot soldiers before they rebel. But the whole point of owning a casino is the money. So which is priority number one? CEO, or Mafia Don?

➤ I'd rather look weak to shareholders than to thugs. Make an impression on the crime world today, then the purchasing public tomorrow. Go to page 89

➤ The day is young. Handle PR now and meet with my crime lieutenants after dark. Go to page 276

A Night on the Town

It's only a short walk to "The Loading Dock," a local dive bar and dockworker hotspot used as a watering hole on the way home after a long day at the warehouse district. Usually, you steer clear. It's an insular bunch and tends to get rowdy. But tonight, you're feeling rowdy.

You step through the saloon-style doors, keeping your head down, but everyone looks up. The crowd is mostly men, dockworkers with thick beards, black knit caps, and uniform shirts with brown collars. Cold faces with colder eyes, and not a smile to greet you. Guess it's one of those "where everybody knows your name" places, and their stares are a far cry from welcoming.

At the bar you pick your poison, and after the briefest pause, the bartender serves you.

You twirl your finger just above the liquid, letting your mind stir the beverage for you. Just as the bartender starts to notice, you turn and face the room, your back to the bar top, and scan the options.

A jukebox is playing 1990s classic Nirvana. *Smells Like Teen Spirit*. A lonely dartboard is nearby, darts sticking out from the cork, the wall pock-marked with misses. Two men play pool in the center of the room. Against the far wall is a shuffleboard table where a young woman is writing messages in the sand.

You feel like practicing your new skills, so why not:

➢ See how many times you can hit the bull's-eye in darts. Go to page 78
➢ Challenge the men to pool. For money. Go to page 19
➢ See if the young lady wants to play shuffleboard. Go to page 41

Night Owl

The crate next to Nick's Dinoskin is labeled: EK¥Ǝ EXOSKELETON LOADER. You're about to take a look inside, but the next one over grabs your attention: MISC SUPPLIES, DO NOT TOUCH, NO SMOKING WITHIN 200 FEET. What kind of miscellaneous supplies require a warning label? You get your fingernails into the lid, break the seal, and peel it off. Inside is a man-sized bomb with a nuclear symbol on it.

"I don't think we should go digging around in here..." Nick says.

Seeing as how you just found a nuke, you're inclined to agree. You carefully put the lid back on, then go to the opposite side of the warehouse. Several empty bookcases wait by the nearby crates, the first of which is already open. Inside is a collection of medical pamphlets with the titles: *So You're a Supersoldier*, *I am Jack's X-ray Vision*, *Why You Shouldn't Take Over the World*, *Big Book of Science*, and *Telekinesis and You*.

Taking a copy of the first pamphlet, you pull a tarp off the nearby couch and settle in to read. There's a delightful 1950s cartoon image on the cover of a smiling, dapper man in a military uniform, his incredible muscles rippling as he flexes his arms.

The intro reads:

Super-strength and near-invulnerability may make you an army of one, but what are you really fighting for? Remember, a Supersoldier is only as powerful as the nation he fights for. As part of the New Breed, it's your duty to use your powers responsibly. Luckily, you've got this informational brochure to serve as your moral compass!

Topics Covered:

- *Why America is the Greatest Nation on Earth*
- *Integrity, the True Super-Strength*
- *Bench-Pressing Tanks*
- *FAQs: Obeying Orders and Asking Questions Later*

Though fun, there's not much to learn from the pamphlet. You're the first of your kind, after all. Maybe you'll write the next edition? With less propaganda, of course.

➤ *Keep browsing; fall asleep reading antiquated Super-literature pamphlets.*
  Go to page 227

No Honor among Thieves

You *float* over the path of destruction, quickly fly behind Agent Droakam, and brace your lightsaber inches away from his throat.

"Stop now, or I swear I'll do it," you say. "If he goes, it's goodbye funding. No more Supersoldier Program means no more experimenting, ever."

The incredible energies stop their flow from the Experi-mentor's fingertips. He stops to consider the situation, and both Diamond and Dorian White brace for his next move. It's a tense stalemate.

Then the Experi-mentor throws his head back and lets out a braying laugh.

"You think I need *him*? He's done his job. The program will go on with five dead agents just as easily as with six. Once I kill the three of you, I will be unstoppable. With each new useful ability I find, I'll give it to myself as well. I'll never stop; don't you get it? With your powers combined…I am *THE EXPERI-MENTOR!*"

He brings his arms up once more, sending arcs of electricity into Diamond and Dorian White, and laying out a cone of fire across you and Agent Droakam. Your skin melts and your eyes sear into blindness, then, graciously, your brain turns off your consciousness and allows you to die without further pain.

THE END

Normalizing

You duck down and quickly walk from the fire, but someone's repeated shouts draw your attention.

"Scissors! Hey, Scissors!" It's Catherine, the woman from the experiment, with the alligator boots. She looks thinner, somehow taller. Healthier than you remember. A good night's sleep, maybe?

"Where are you going?" she calls out. "C'mon, we can help!"

"I, uhhh…" You just stand there, your mouth opening and closing like a drydock fish. After a moment, Catherine turns and runs toward the blaze.

- Fine, sheesh. Try to help. Go to page 351
- Whatever. Sneak off and go back home. Go to page 239

Nothing but Net

First, you roll out of the path of the jumper's collision course, then you fly over and embrace him from behind like a tandem skydive instructor. You can't lift over double your body weight (he's a pretty big guy), but you're able to *steer* toward the outstretched tarp of the life net, offering occasional course corrections, like a returning space shuttle coming in hot.

At the last possible moment, you drop the man atop the net and take back full control of your body via flight. The jumper is enveloped in the tarp and lowered safely to the ground while you *hover* above. The firefighters stare up at you, their mouths open in awe.

"All in a day's work for The Phantom!" you cry out, giving a salute like you're a 1950s serial action hero.

They say nothing. With a shrug, you grab the firehose off the truck and take it with you as you fly back up toward the fire. It seems they get the picture, because the line fills with pressure as you rise. It's all you can do to hold onto the hose, but the upward water pressure actually makes flying a little easier.

After you douse the flames, a figure catches your eye. A woman stands amongst the broken glass at the level you extinguished upon arrival. Another jumper? You lower yourself for a better look.

Shockingly, it's Catherine, the woman from the lab experiment. The one who picked "Rock" when you picked "Scissors." What's she doing here? This can't be a coincidence.

- ➤ She must be here to help too! With your combined powers, this fire doesn't stand a chance. Go to page 187
- ➤ She must be the one who started the fire! Drop the hose and prepare yourself for battle against your first supervillain! Go to page 223

Objects May Be Closer than They Appear

Hands moving on autopilot as you sprint away from the hungry Tyrannosaur, you set the staff's parameters to return home. Mercifully, your superhuman mind is still working on overdrive and you time the exit perfectly so the portal will open at the exact moment you reach the spot.

You can be fairly certain that the 40-foot-long beastie can't follow you into your 10-by-6-foot trans-dimensional gate, but you've got to reach it first. The shimmer appears in the air and the jewel glows. It starts to open. You sprint faster. As fast as your legs will carry you. Almost there....

At the last moment you leap toward the gate, eyes closed and body tense with the expected bone-crushing chomp of the dinosaur's maw. Your hands tell the staff to close the gate behind you, but it's too close to call.

Pain hits you hard on your right shoulder and you scream, a mix of terror and agony.

Then you open your eyes. You're lying on your right side on the floor of the abandoned nuclear reactor laboratory. You made it!

You sit up and turn—right into the jaws of the T-Rex! You let out a blood-curdling scream and recoil, but the dinosaur stays put. In fact, it's not moving at all. As you stand up, you see why.

She's dead. The portal closed on the queen of the dinosaurs just after she stuck her neck in after you. The cut is perfect; her head was simply transported back to your universe with you. Well, that should make for a hell of a souvenir. Maybe you should rename "The Staff" as "The Butterfly Effector." Maybe not.

Once you're done studying your dino skull (and changing into a new pair of pants), why not try a world where:

> - There are no superpowered humans on the planet. You could do a lot of good for that world (or rule it) without fear of anyone exposing the secret to your genius. Go to page 28
> - There was never an explosion. Perhaps you can find the pods that gave you your powers and study them! Go to page 87
> - The Experi-mentor is nurturing instead of aggressive. Cautious instead of brash. Kind instead of overly driven. Perhaps you can find this gentler Experi-mentor and learn something about the pods? Go to page 55
> - You chose a different pod in the experiment. Why not commune with other genii and see yourself with different superpowers? Go to page 270
> - Science has stopped the aging process. As an immortal, you'll be able to spend eternity exploring all the infinite possibilities! Go to page 57

Occupy Superpowers

So you want to make your fortunes legally, eh? Smart thinking. You head to the Mercury City Public Library and dive deep into the movers and shakers of the stock world. Cross-referencing current events, you quickly learn how to make a small fortune predicting oil futures, then use your new influence to manipulate penny stocks.

An overnight millionaire. Seldom has that phrase been used literally, but for you, it's true. Of course, you have to use your real name to accomplish this feat, so goodbye, anonymity. Every news outlet in the world picks up on the nobody-turned-trading-expert from Mercury City.

Since the requests for interviews seem never-ending, it's little surprise when Nick from the experiment shows up at your future lair's construction site. "I need a word," he tells the foreman. "Buzz off."

The foreman looks at you, thoroughly confused.

"Take five," you say. The construction team clears the site and you nod for Nick to follow you inside the mine. Walking through the halls of your future subterranean penthouse, you wait for him to speak.

"Wall Street, really?"

"Spying on me?" you say without a hint of irony.

Nick's face is rigid. He's changed, physically since the experiment. Taller, muscular and hard.

You shrug. "I've legally accumulated a fortune; what of it?"

"I'm not talking legal, I'm talking moral. The greatest crimes of our lifetime haven't been prosecuted, because they weren't technically crimes. Well, now there's someone who can do something about it. Laws are meant to be rewritten. I'm not going to stand idly by while you line the pockets of these fat-cat—"

"Nick, calm down. I didn't make anyone else any money. I did the trades myself."

"Bullshit. You're perpetuating the CEO top 1% agenda."

You sigh. "What would you have me do?"

"Donate the money to the Occupy movement, and publicly come out against corporate greed."

"Yeah, I'm not going to do that."

"Write the statement, or write a suicide note instead," he says. His fists are clenched, he's a seething pillar of rage. Maybe it's that mercury madness sinking in, but you've got the urge to…

- ➤ Test out your new trap doors. A hundred-foot drop into a poison-air cavern oughtta cool him off. Go to page 140
- ➤ Placate him, for now. Tell him what he wants to hear, but use that money to install some major security upgrades in your lair. Go to page 346

Off with His Head!

"Get that DinoSkin back on. I'm going to check the catalogue for other possible weapons," Nick says.

He's grinning. A college student who's never been in a fight before yet who now thinks he's the smartest man on the planet. And the worst thing is, he just might be right. You shake your head and go back into the locker room. After you change and return to the warehouse, you find Nick and his robot sidekick busy prying open one of the crates. It's labeled, EKӴƎ EXOSKELETON LOADER.

"What's that?" you ask.

The front of the crate opens to reveal another mannequin, much like the one you found wearing your DinoSkin suit. This plastic man, however, is almost entirely naked—save for an odd line of metal tubing that runs along the arms, legs, and spine.

"Step out," Nick says and the mannequin walks out of the crate. "Release."

The metal portion collapses onto the floor, which sends the mannequin tumbling over. Nick steps onto the "feet" and the suit climbs up and over his body, attaching itself to the college student with snakelike movements. The process is eerily lifelike.

"Best exoskeleton ever created," Nick says. "Watch this."

He picks up one of the larger crates—far too heavy for you to lift either physically or mentally—and throws it across the warehouse floor. The crate smashes into several others, obliterating whatever they hold within.

"What the *hell* do you think you're doing?" Agent Droakam shouts.

You turn back to face him. "Preparing for you! We've seen the email."

"What email?"

"The report you just filed. Don't bother lying about it," Nick says.

Droakam says nothing. It's hard to read his expression. Finally, he says, "You've been spying on me?"

"Pot calling the kettle black," Nick scoffs. "Doesn't feel good, does it? Try this one on for size: Drop your weapon and put your hands where we can see them."

Agent Droakam brings a hand to his hip near the gun holster. You take a step forward.

"Don't try anything stupid," you warn.

Nick readies himself. "The Supersoldier Program is over, Droakam."

In an incredible display of speed, the agent draws his weapon. You move to grab or at least deflect the gun, but not fast enough. Going on instinct, you mentally grab the man's throat instead.

The agent is powerless. In the same move, you *slam* him against the side of the giant computer terminal and Droakam collapses to the ground.

Nick rushes over, suddenly much faster, with an exoskeleton-aided stride, and goes to his knees to check on the agent. The man coughs, sputtering blood.

"I think...I think you severed his windpipe."

In a matter of moments, Agent Droakam is dead.

"We should go before the other agents arrive," you say. "Let's burn the lab to cover our tracks."

"Or…" Nick is hesitant. He rises from the fallen agent's side. "We could fortify the lab. Use it as our home base."

"Do we have time? Won't they be….?"

"There's no one else coming."

For a moment, you say nothing. "What do you mean?"

"Droakam was the only threat. And you've seen to that."

"What about the rest of them? Full funding was restored. The email, remember?"

"I wrote that memo. I'm sorry, but I had no way of knowing if you were friend or foe until now. But you're like me. And together—with all of this—think what we could accomplish!"

"You made it all up?" The truth is just now sinking in. "So…I killed an innocent man?"

"And if you're willing to kill a few more, we can rule this city—this country—the world!"

"Won't they wonder where he is? When he doesn't check in?"

"Ah, but he will check in. I've hacked their communications. I'll send periodic email updates, requests for supplies, and so on. And if we need Droakam in the flesh, watch this."

In response to a few verbal commands, the exoskeleton detaches itself from Nick, slithers over and connects to Agent Droakam's body. The agent rises, stands at the ready and awaits Nick's next command.

"Exoskeleton: respond to commands directed at 'Droakam.' Droakam: shoot that crate."

In response, the exoskeleton forces Droakam's limp arms into action, draws the agent's pistol, and fires into the crate Nick indicated. "Zombie Droakam" then returns to a ready state, awaiting the next command.

"See? Droakam's still around; he just works for us," Nick says smugly, turning to you. "Now then, simply kneel before me, and the rest of mankind will kneel before you."

➢ Not this time. Don't let the bastard get away with it. Say, "Droakam: shoot Nick." Go to page 46

➢ Kneel before Nick Dorian, master of the universe. Go to page 6

Oh, the Humanity!

You sit atop a mountain of cash in a public park in the heart of downtown. Several passersby have eyed your throne greedily, but Baxter's presence made them think twice. Besides, dozens of undercover cops are in amongst the joggers, dog walkers, and vagrants.

It didn't take much to convince Alison Argyle to go along with your plan. Since she already asked for your help, (once she conferred with her father, Mayor Argyle) Mercury City was all too willing to agree. The broadcast of you sitting atop Money Mountain asking for a meeting with the dastardly duo should have already played on the news stations; now you wait.

"This pile of intricately painted paper is all it will take to bring them out of hiding?" Baxter asks.

"It's not the paper, it's what it represents. You understand how money works, don't you?"

"Of course. It is a shared hallucination. Humanity has collectively agreed to hold a worthless resource above all other resources in order to give it value. Yes?"

"Something like that…"

"Ah, here they come, exactly as predicted!"

You turn to see a woman in a black cloak, the hood pulled down low over her face, walking next to Nick. The college student wears the same blue handyman uniform as in the news footage.

"Drillbit and Shadow Priestess, I presume," you say.

"And you?" Nick says.

"You can call me Dr. Nobel."

Nick nods. "Okay, we're here. What do you and your toy want?"

"I am Baxter."

You get to your feet and point to the pile of money with a sweep of your arm. "I wanted to show you that one doesn't need to steal to be rich. That you don't need to *take* to have power. You want money? You want influence? I can give you both. What I truly offer, however, is a chance at redemption. If you join me and help make the world a better place, the mayor is prepared to give you clemency."

Drillbit stands aside and the Shadow Priestess steps forward.

"Just one question," she says. "Where'd you get the money?"

- "Donated by the Planet Mercury Casino, simply because I asked for it. How's that for power?" Go to page 333
- "The money isn't the point. I've cured cancer! I've created artificial intelligence! With your skills added to my own, there's no limit to what we could achieve as a team." Go to page 230

Omnicide

Catherine turns to you, horror-stricken, and says, "Two shots per charge, remember?"

"I'll keep him busy! Just like Drillbit! C'mon!" you shout.

You charge at Nick, ready to battle titan vs. titan, just like you did with this world's version of him, but the Nick from your world just picked up a major upgrade. With a flat palm, he stops you in your tracks. He opens his other hand toward Catherine and she *explodes* in a fireworks show of viscera.

Nick's evil grin widens and he rockets into the air, dragging you with him in his telekinetic grasp. You're powerless as he soars into the sky, taking you higher and higher.

Blue sky gives way to black space and Nick suddenly stops his flight, instead focusing on you. He slingshot-launches you into orbit, sending you sprawling away from this earth and all like it. You survive the fiery friction of atmospheric ejection, but the cold vacuum of space—and its lack of oxygen—is too much. Without the telekinetic flying ability, you can't bring yourself down to safety.

THE END

On a Super-Walkabout

You leave your low-rent apartment, this time taking the stairs. After all, the elevator is still broken, and incognito is the name of the game today, so no flying.

It's early enough that it's still late for some. Up ahead, you see a pimp and his whore.

"You holdin' out on me, bitch?" He holds her against a wall at knife-point. "You took in more, I know it. How many dicks you suck, huh? This ain't a fuckin' charity, honey."

A few people are on the street, but they quickly leave—ducking into shops or turning onto other streets—not their problem.

- ➢ Pbshhh. Not my problem, either. Keep walking. Go to page 328
- ➢ Rush in and *pull* the knife from his hand. Go to page 154

One-Hit Wonder

"Well, I'm not sure I can let you go around killing people, even if it is in the name of justice," the man says.

"That was an accident!" you protest. "I couldn't help it. You might as well arrest me for stepping on an ant."

"Careful now, you're heading into supervillain territory with talk like that."

He's got you there. After a moment, you say, "I will be careful, in the future, I mean. See you later."

"Yes, you will. I'll be following you, documenting your every move."

"Good point," you say. Then you walk over to the SUV and shove it onto its side.

"Hey!" the agent shouts as you sprint away.

After a few effortless minutes, you've left the agent several miles in the dust. FBI Supersoldier Program? Ridiculous! As Rock Star, you're kind of de-facto anti-war anyhow, right?

Up ahead, half of the Mercury City Fire Department mans a roadblock. What's going on? As a City native, you rarely look up at the skyscrapers, so it's no wonder you didn't notice the roaring fire high in the air. An entire floor, two-thirds up a building, is engulfed in flames.

You sprint through the barricade, ripping it apart like ribbon-tape at the finish line. Several firemen fall back and out of your way. Instinctively, you leap into the air and smash through the fourth-floor window. If there are any people in here, you'll save them!

After saving the day, you stop by your corner grocery, spend all the money you have left, and head home. When you make it back to your apartment building, you're exhausted for the first time since the accident. Although you managed to save a few people, smashing through the building made three whole floors collapse down upon you—with a few would-be survivors trapped inside. You can still hear their screams.

Now, clothes singed and skin caked with soot, all you want is a shower, a gigantic dinner, and to curl up in bed. Your lungs burn fiercely and your eyes sting from the smoke. The heat didn't bother you, but you're not fully invincible, it would seem.

When you come up to your hallway, you see you've got a guest. Even though her back is turned to you, from the curvy figure leaning against the wall while she checks her smartphone, you know exactly who the woman in the skirt-suit outside your apartment is: Mercury City's famed reporter, Alison Argyle. What's she doing here?

- Run now before she notices you! Get a hotel and steer clear. Go to page 370
- Play it cool; see what she wants. She doesn't know you, and that shower will feel soooo nice. Go to page 176

One Option

"What are you talking about?" Nick asks through a quizzical smile.

"You're in danger. If you value your life, never use your powers again. Leave town. Pretend we never met." You try to speak in grave tones, but it's a difficult feat when you're stuffing your face with hamburger.

"What—who...who's out to get me?"

"I am. I'm supposed to kill you, but—"

Nick leaps up from his seat. "WHAT? You traitor! How could you? *Why?*" He slams the edge of his pint glass against the bar top, making jagged cuts, and points the makeshift weapon at you.

With anger billowing in your gut, you grab his wrist and pull it toward you—smashing the pint glass against your own face. The remaining glass shatters, along with the bones in Nick's hand, but your face is completely unharmed.

Nick howls with pain, stumbles back and knocks over several barstools. He brings his good hand up, shapes it into a claw and squeezes the air. You feel something around your throat, but it's only a tickle. Nick's trying to constrict your larynx, but he can't. You start to laugh.

Nick falters, then points his claw-hand at the bartender. The woman's eyes bulge and she rakes at her own throat, choking under the influence of his powers. A waiter rushes to her aid, but Nick *blasts* the man across the room with the power of mind.

Almost from instinct, you punch Nick in the chest. It's only a quick jab, but that doesn't matter. The college student releases his grip on the bartender, grabs at his heart, then sputters blood. He falls to the floor, dead.

All eyes in the pub are on you, with some patrons holding up their smartphones. This is bad.

➢ *Rush back to the warehouse!* Go to page 13

Outlaws

"Practicing, huh?" you say.

Nick turns quickly, but recognizes you and is back at ease. "You could say that, yeah," he replies. "All work and no play makes Nick a dull boy."

"I couldn't agree more. Will you join me for dinner?" You flash a stack of crisp Franklins and a mischievous grin.

"As long as you're buying. There's a great pub just around the corner."

You scratch your chin. "How big are the portions?"

The pub is just far enough away to escape the commotion, but there's a bit of a wait, so you opt to sit at the bar. After confirming that you can order food up here, of course.

"I'll have one of everything," you say, not bothering to open the menu.

The bartender brushes a shock of platinum blonde behind her ear, where it's somewhat hidden amongst raven hair, smiles and says, "We've got a pretty big selection."

"Better get the kitchen started, then," you say, plopping the stack of cash on the bar.

Her eyebrows bounce up in an *if you say so* way, but she doesn't protest. While you've got her attention, Nick *pours* two pints behind her back, using his telekinesis, and times the delivery perfectly so they sneak past her when she turns away. He floats one of the glasses with the *Quicksilver Ale* logo into his hand and offers the other to you.

"To taking what's ours," you say, raising the glass.

"I'll drink to that." Nick sips his beer and watches the news report of your exploits on the TV above the bar.

Blonde eye-candy reporter Alison Argyle says, "Police don't know what to make of the mystery culprit from today's robbery. Eyewitnesses have corroborated the incredible footage, and experts say these images are indeed genuine."

The news desk feed switches to security footage from your robbery, whereupon you blast through the concrete wall and proceed to rob the place.

Nick turns to you, eyes wide and eyebrows up near his hair line. He points a finger and says, "You—you're the…" Nick's eyes dart towards the door.

"Don't run. Listen, I want to offer you a job on my team. I mean, with these new powers, we can basically do whatever we want. I'm just thinking on a bigger scale than stealing a pint now and again."

Nick downs the rest of his beer. "Okay, I'm in. What's the plan?"

"As I see it, we've got two choices," you say, wondering where your food is. "One: Give that reporter an exclusive. Announce that the city is ours, then crush any resistance. Two: Villainy from the bottom up—find the existing criminal organizations, and take over."

Nick opens his mouth to reply, but a ruckus near the entrance of the bar takes his attention. You see the flash of red and blue lights outside; patrons are fleeing from the restaurant right into the arms of the police at the barricade set up out front. The bartender is gone.

"Or, option Three: Battle with the police."

"We need disguises," Nick says. He grabs an oversized black napkin, shakes out the silverware, and ties the cloth around his face like an Old West stagecoach robber.

"Maybe you do, but they've got my mug shot already. I'm bulletproof; what do I need a costume for?"

"Good point," Nick says. He pulls a red tablecloth off a high-top table, saying, "Put this on."

"Nick, I just said—"

"Yeah, yeah. You're bulletproof, but I'm not. So you put on the red cape and with any luck it'll work like a bullfight. They'll shoot at you while I disarm them, you know, without getting shot."

You shrug, tear a hole in the center of the tablecloth and put it on like a poncho. "Call me *The Matador*."

He nods, then adjusts his makeshift bandana. "Pleasure to meet you, I'm *Bandit*."

Not bad for an impromptu team-up, eh? Time for a shoot-out. No, a showdown. You head out toward the shouted commands for surrender by the Mercury PD and out into the street.

But instead of putting your hands on your head, you lift one of the patrol cars up and throw it across the street into a second-story business window. The police open fire, which does nothing but anger you. Big mistake. You roar with pain and rage, and the shooting suddenly stops.

One of the cops is walking toward you. His steps are stilted, like a marionette on a string. He's resisting. He turns around, points his handgun at his fellow officers, and backpedals your way.

You turn to the pub entrance. Nick is standing there, deep in concentration with one hand outstretched. There's your puppetmaster! The cop points the handgun at his own head.

"Demand a retreat," Nick says.

"Flee, *flee for your LIVES!!!*" you cry, your superpowered lungs amplifying the call far louder than any bullhorn.

The police fall back.

"It's working!" Nick cries.

Nick laughs like a psychopath as the police launch canisters of tear gas your way. You start to laugh, but choke. The gas stings! Oh God, it burns! You swat at the gas, but the canisters pour the cloud thicker and thicker.

"Time to regroup!" Nick shouts. "This way!"

➢ *No time to think; follow Nick's voice away from the poison gas!* <u>Go to page 350</u>

Overburdened

Leading Kingsley through the air by his throat, you push him up the stairs with your mind and bring the wanted man up to the rooftop. He gasps for breath, trying in vain to harangue you with rasping curses. You bring him over to the edge of the building and *float* him out over the abyss before stepping off the ledge, ready to *glide* down to the pavement below.

Nope.

The combined weight of your two bodies is too much for your abilities, and you drop like stones toward the earth. It takes just over two seconds to plummet to the pavement, and in that time the animal part of your brain takes over in a bid for survival.

You release your grip on Kingsley and bring yourself to hover mere feet above the sidewalk. Kingsley plows into the street, the six-story drop killing him instantly.

"What the fuck?!" Droakam screams, rushing from the car to the splattered body.

"I don't know what happened, I—"

"Don't you remember the crates? You can only carry so much. Goddamnit, you just murdered this guy."

"I—I didn't mean to," you stammer.

"Christ. Get out of here. I'll clean up this mess."

You float there, unsure what to do.

"Go on! Before I change my mind."

➤ *Fly back to the warehouse.* Go to page 264

Overthrown

You *grab* Nick with the force of mind and fling him up toward the high-domed ceiling of the Planet Mercury casino. When he reaches the top, you release him and let gravity do its work. Nick screams as he falls 60 feet down to land atop the poker tables. He folds.

You turn back—right into the full security team of the casino. Two dozen men, armed and ready to gun you down. You were right, you did waste too much time with Nick. Now you're the one who's wasted. There are too many guards for you to take at once.

THE END

Pantheopolis

"**O**kay, you win!" you say, your hands in the air.

"What? No way!" Catherine shouts. "Swarming hive—"

But her command is cut short when a dozen invisible tentacles slash through her at the same moment, in an Ultimate Punch of sorts.

"Yep, we give up!" Nick says.

Your new overlord and master lets you live, but that simply allows you to bear witness to the horrors ahead. He instates the *Pantheopolis* as promised, but Catherine's gun is never far away from the mad scientist. All you can do now is hope that as he relegates every new power he discovers to himself, somehow it'll prove too much for a mortal man.

But no such luck. Instead, he actually discovers a superpower that makes him immortal. As the new god of earth, his reign of terror is everlasting and ever-present. He changes his name to the Omni-mentor.

You live, but this is not a win. Not remotely. Better start practicing your worship-chant: *"Ph'nglui mglw'nafh Cthulhu R'lyeh wgah'nagl fhtagn."*

THE END

Paper

You shoot your hand flat, in the sign for paper.

"I'll be scissors, I guess," Catherine says. She extends her forefingers, while the student, Nick, holds his hand clenched in a fist and says, "Rock."

Now that the order is decided, the three of you move to your respective platforms. As you enter the chamber, a lid comes down from the ceiling and latches itself onto your pod.

The outer casing is sealed and an artificial atmosphere replaces the lab air through vents at your feet. There's a rush of blood through your extremities as adrenaline kicks in; you take slow, deep breaths.

Like the hyperbaric chambers lauded during the golden age of science fiction, your body actually feels healthier in here. In fact, this whole set-up is like something out of *Star Trek*. Beam me up, Scottie!

Waiting for the experiment to begin, you look around. More cables drop off the platform edge, plugged into a row of eight outlets across a central spine. You can barely make out the warning sign buried beneath them, *DO NOT OVERLOAD*.

You're about to point this out when the experiment suddenly begins. Sparks leap from the electrical connections, singeing the racks with black scorch marks. It's getting hard to see, and not just because you're steaming up the glass. Fog coalesces above the platform, black as death. A whirlwind of papers circles the lab just before a lightning bolt *cracks* down against your pod.

Then electricity bursts forth from the equipment racks and arcs from your pod among the three of you. The surrounding glass shines with an otherworldly light; then you lose consciousness.

You slowly open your eyes, hesitant, expecting pain or weariness. You don't have a scratch on you. Did you imagine the explosion?

As you look around, you find that the laboratory exists no more; there's only rubble. The entire building came down overhead, but there's a miraculous three-foot circle around you with no debris or damage. The glass pod and lid are mysteriously absent, but the base upon which you are lying is intact.

When you stand up, you see that the other two pods have a similar ring of safety around them. Your fellow test subjects lie on their own pod bases, curled like fetuses, unmoving. It's impossible to tell from here if they're alive or dead.

The distant wail of police sirens draws your attention to the horizon. It isn't just the lab that's gone; it's an area the size of a city block. The Mercury University campus is decimated. Beyond, smoldering rock dots the green quad as if after a meteor shower.

The world appears to you in new ways, whispering its secrets. When you see a particularly large concrete slab fifteen feet away, you instantly know the velocity that sent it flying. The moments and angles tell you the source of the explosion—shockingly, it was all three pods. There wasn't an exterior source; the pods *were* the source. Three equal explosions—but why are you left unharmed?

The other two testees stir. You give them a moment to gather themselves.

"Everyone okay?" you ask.

Nick nods. "Where's the scientist?"

Catherine starts to walk away.

"Where are you going?" you ask.

"My son—I need to pick up my son from school."

Everyone deals with trauma differently, you think. "I haven't seen any sign of the experiment proctor," you say.

Nick simply nods. You both watch Catherine walk away.

- ➤ "I've got this nagging feeling that this is no ordinary experiment. I mean, will anyone believe we survived without a scratch? It's probably best if we're not here when the cops show up." Go to page 272
- ➤ "I'd like to stay and tell the police what happened. See if I can't learn more." Go to page 186

Pawn

Nick sets up your meeting with Agent Droakam at a public park across the street from the Mercury City FBI headquarters building. At the back of the park, there's a pay phone where you'll call Nick once the job's done.

You wait on a bench, cattycorner from an elderly woman feeding pigeons who flutter around her each time she tosses out a handful of seed. When they suddenly fly away, you look up.

Agent Droakam's trench coat flows in the breeze as he approaches. His hard face is unreadable beneath the black sunglasses. You stand up to meet him.

"That's far enough," you say.

He stops and waits to see if you'll say something. You keep an eye on his hands, mentally picturing his gun holster. You've got your DinoSkin on, but your head is vulnerable.

At length, he says, "Why did you have to blow up the lab?"

You pause and think for a moment. "Self-preservation."

Droakam shakes his head. "We could've made something together. A Brave New World."

"Not exactly the sacrifice for my country I'd envisioned."

"There's always sacrifice," he says.

You say nothing in response. After a moment, you use your telekinesis to *float* the thumb drive over to the agent.

"You've got what you want. Now will you leave us alone?"

He nods. "If that's how you want it."

Agent Droakam turns and walks back through the park to the headquarters building. You watch until the agent is gone, then make your way to the pay phone and call Nick.

"It's done," you say after he picks up.

"Good. Hold the line a few minutes. I'm tracking remotely to see if they've uploaded."

You wait, watching a jogger pass through the park. Five minutes go by, then ten. You try your best to be patient, as you can imagine it might take a while before Agent Droakam uploads the files.

"Nick? Still there?"

"Ah! There it is! Droakam has opened the file. I now have full access to the FBI's mainframe. Sorry for the deceit, but the true reason I had you give the agent that thumb drive was to deliver a Trojan program allowing me remote control of the secure government networks. I can now do what I did at the warehouse computer terminal, but from anywhere in the world."

"I don't get it," you say. "Why wouldn't you just tell me that in the first place?"

"Well, to answer that, I must first apologize."

"Okay…for what?"

"For all the lies and deception. After all, if I told you I had full control over the government system, complete with administrative privileges, you might start putting the pieces together. You might—for example—guess that *I had sent* that dissection memo from Droakam's account."

Your heart falls into the pit of your stomach.

"Why?" It's all you can say.

"The Supersoldier Program was too dangerous. I had to drive a wedge between you and Agent Droakam. You were willing to do *anything* he said. I had hoped to use you in other ways, but *Christ*—how spineless can a superhuman be? Even when I made Droakam your enemy, it was 'Oh, let's run away!' 'No, I don't want to fight.' 'Let's hide.' It was hard to put up with, really."

"You'll never get away with this, Nick. I'll go tell Droakam right now."

"Ah, no. See, that's the other reason I made you wait on the line. I took video with my smart phone of your meeting with Agent Droakam and just sent it to Catherine. She was *furious* when I told her you stole the plans and were selling off the secret of our powers to a shadowy government agent. She's on her way now, and after she takes care of you, she and I are going to take on the FBI—you know, to stop them from creating a race of superhumans. After that, it's only a small step to get her on board with the idea of ruling the nation. Maybe the world, I'm not sure yet."

"Nick…"

"Is she there yet? She should be there by now."

The phone falls from your hand, dangling by its cord when you step away and turn around. There she is, in full costume, bearing down on you. The ground rumbles and your vision tunnels. It's like watching a lion rush in, like you're watching pre-recorded footage and there's nothing you can do stop what's about to happen.

"Catherine, wait—"

"You goddamned *SON OF A BITCH!*"

An unstoppable juggernaut, she lunges at you. There's no time to reason, so you *fling* yourself into the air and hurtle toward the clouds as fast as your mind will take you. Up, up, higher and higher.

Just as you think you're free, something constricts around your leg. Catherine's hand. It's like you've suddenly been anchored with an anvil. You start falling, *fast*.

This is the difference between a marathon runner and a sprinter. You could outpace her in the end, but her leap into the sky was much quicker than yours. You're at least six stories into the air, but that doesn't seem to bother her.

Now she throws you back toward the ground, and there's nothing you can do about it.

"It's Nick!" you desperately cry.

She hurls you down against the jogging path like a fly swatter against a countertop. There's a sick *slap* and not a bone left unbroken in your body. Now that you're out of the picture, there's no one to foil Nick's plans.

THE END

Perpetrated

When you arrive back at the warehouse, Nick is there to greet you.

"We...we got him," you say, somewhat distant. "Droakam's still finishing up at the scene."

Nick gestures to the computer. "So I see. The Supersoldier Program has been reinstated, complete with a nice boost to funding. A team will be here tomorrow to help organize and install any equipment."

You nod. It's been a long day and you're feeling the effects of an adrenaline crash. You run a weary hand down your face.

Nick notices and asks, "Coffee?"

"I'm gonna take a quick shower," you announce.

The bathroom—there's only one, as the facility was constructed during a pre-women-in-the-government era—is much like a gymnasium locker room. It feels enormous and open when you're in there by yourself. Leaving the DinoSkin suit across one of the benches, you head in for a much-needed wash. When was your last shower? Before the accident?

You let the shampoo lather itself into your hair using telekinesis and give yourself a backrub with the power of mind. A full self-service spa experience. You try to manipulate the water coming from the showerhead, but you're unable to affect the entire stream at once. You can make quite a splash, but you can't, say, send all the water up to the ceiling and keep the floor dry. Droakam was right—your abilities work more like arms than like a solid force.

When you exit the shower, you find that the Dinoskin supersuit has been placed back up on a mannequin in the corner of the locker room. Your plain clothes are folded on the bench where you left the suit.

"Nick?" you call out.

An electric whirring draws your attention around the corner. The same robot that was earlier cataloging the crates waits for you, with a fresh towel held out by a mechanical arm.

"Uh, thanks."

Once you're dressed, you find Nick at the computer terminal. It's like he's glued to the thing. "Droakam back yet?" you ask, still rubbing the towel against your hair.

Nick hesitates a moment, staring at you with a profound sadness.

"What is it?" you ask.

"There's something you should see. I found this while you were washing up—it's the progress report the agent filed on us. You may want to sit down."

He pulls up an email on the computer console, then offers the chair.

TO: ALCON, Pentagon

BODY: Initial results were promising, although subject Nick Dorian tells me he's unable to recreate the experiment that gave them their powers. While I think I can control the Telekinetic, Dorian seems to have an ulterior agenda. As to what, I'm unable to ascertain.

FINDINGS: As a pair, they lack the military discipline expected of operatives. Therefore, in the interest of the project, it is the opinion of this agent that they could tell us more as cold resources than as warm bodies. Using Dorian's models of the project, and the two subjects as finished products, we should be able to Reverse-Engineer the experiment.

RECOMMENDATION: Dissection.

SIGNED: Agent Brendan Droakam, FBI

Whoa, let that sink in….Having finished reading but unsure what to say, you look back to Nick.

"I set my system to intercept communications, and it's a good thing I did. I mean—Jesus."

"Recommendation: *Dissection*?" you say, still dumbfounded.

"I don't know how much time we have. If his superiors approve, they could be coming for us tonight. I—I'm not sure what we should do, but we have to *act*, don't you think?"

- ➤ "We fight back." Go to page 248
- ➤ "We should run." Go to page 137

Placate

Nick shrugs. "I didn't want it to come to this, but I don't think there's any other way. Once they have the key to superpowered creation, they shouldn't want anything more from us."

You nod, though it feels somewhat like defeat.

"Okay, I'll get in touch with Agent Droakam to set up a meeting between you two. Somewhere public, but don't be afraid to fly out if things go south. You'll be going it alone—you can be in and out far easier without me slowing you down."

➢ *Get ready for your "drop."* Go to page 262

Players' Club

"I've just been getting lucky, I swear," Nick says as the elevator doors open.

The college student stares at you with wide-eyed wonder. He then looks around the penthouse before his gaze comes to rest on your unassuming self.

"*You?*" he finally lets out.

"Welcome to my casino."

"Let me get this straight," he says, shaking his head in disbelief. "You own a casino, yet you moonlight by participating in $500 experiments *just for fun?*"

Halifax and Stockton exchange a look.

"Leave us," you say.

And with that, your staff is gone.

"Nice hat," Nick says.

You walk over to the wet bar and pour a drink. "As of last night, I own a casino. Tell me, have you always been able to count cards, or did you find yourself…different after yesterday's experiment?"

His eyes get wide once more.

"I'll show you mine if you show me yours," you say with a grin.

"Well, it's not something I can show off, you know? Or explain. My mind is just…better now. I see patterns, the way things work. I think faster, more creatively, like my mind's on overdrive. On my way up here, I calculated a 14 percent chance of getting thrown off the balcony. But compared with a 76 percent chance of getting roughed up—or killed—in the alley, I figured I'd better take it."

"Interesting," you say, pouring a second drink.

"What about you? Did you mastermind a takeover? Buy the whole place outright with your winnings?"

"Mine is a bit…different as well. Let me show you."

With the power of mind, you *float* one of the cocktails across the room to Nick.

"Fantastic," he says.

➢ "Look, I aim to run this town. If you need a favor, you come see me. If not, stay out of my way!" Go to page 7
➢ "Should we combine forces? With the casino's resources at our disposal…." Go to page 94

267

Plucked

Nick sighs. "Well, I'm afraid I can't just let you steal my money. Knowing you'd win and all."

"What?" you say, genuinely confused.

"Yeah, this is *my* casino as of last night. I didn't want to tell you that before I gave you a chance to join up, but now that you don't need little ol' me, you can go take a hike."

Nick steps away and looks behind you. You turn back—right into the full security team of the casino. Two dozen men, armed and ready to gun you down.

"That's why you don't steal from the Planet Mercury casino!" Nick yells for the benefit of the nearby gawkers. "No matter how slick you think you are, we see everything."

"You little bastard!" you shout.

Without thinking, you *grab* Nick with the force of mind and fling him up toward the high-domed ceiling of the Planet Mercury casino. When he reaches the top, you release him and let gravity do its work. Nick screams as he falls 60 feet down to land atop the poker tables. He folds.

That's when the security team guns you down. They shoot you in the back, making you just another loser left to die on the casino floor.

THE END

Poor Threat Assessment

You fly to the high, vaulted ceilings, flipping up and over the battle to land before the two men. Agent Droakam goes for the handgun at his hip, so you mentally *shove* the agent into the roaring fireplace. The Experi-mentor backs away in fear, that look on his face that so many mad scientists get when their creations turn on them.

"You like to play with fire?" a voice from behind calls out.

You turn just in time to be engulfed in flames by the firestarter agent. Fire? Again? Your skin sears, but you don't lose consciousness, not yet. Nothing has ever hurt like this before. You blast psychic energy in all directions, fighting blindly. Possibly killing the man. It's hard to tell.

"Agent Freeze!" the Experi-mentor calls out over your and Droakam's screams of agony.

The Ex-man in question blasts the fireplace with frost-ridden air, extinguishing his boss and possibly saving the man's life. But he does nothing for you.

In panic, you fly into the air, soaring as fast as you can to starve the fire of oxygen. Like a brightly burning comet, you careen into the far wall at well over sixty miles per hour.

Why fight the soldiers when you can easily take out the officers? Because the soldiers are the ones with superpowers…duh.

THE END

Portal Combat

In response to your commands, the staff opens a gate to an alternate world. The purple jewel at the top matches a 10-by-6-foot purple portal that opens in the center of the room. Well, time to go say hello.

When you step through the portal, a woman is there to greet you. Amazingly, it's Catherine Woodall, the woman from the experiment—or at least someone who looks exactly like her. This version wears zippered black leather from head to toe, covering everything except her head and her bare left arm with some kind of techno-gauntlet on the forearm. Her right shoulder has thick steel spikes protruding from it.

Fascinating. Perhaps you'll rename The Staff as "Bizarro-maker."

At Catherine's side, this world's Nick stands dumbfounded, still just a college student in plain clothes, and then you see…yourself. Your doppelganger is slightly taller, athletic and muscular. It's what you'd look like if you were an Olympian in peak physical condition. You wave hello to yourself. The gemstone at the top of the staff glints and the portal blinks closed in response.

"Rock, Paper, or Scissors?" Catherine asks.

"I'm sorry?" you say.

"In this universe, I chose paper," she replies.

"So did I. Incredible. That means it worked!"

Catherine-the-genius turns back to your doppelganger and Nick. In a huddle, they discuss something while you look around the reactor. It's a makeshift lab in its own right. On the far corner, there's a mobile/trailer home, but it's been modified, and mechanical spider legs protrude from beneath. In the center of the room, there's a futuristic-looking rifle on a tripod, plugged into the nuclear power station through several thick cables. Wonder what that's for?

The three of them look back at you, a wolfish grin on Catherine's face and something cruel in Nick's eyes. You recognize the look on your alter-ego—it's the one that says, *I just got the answer key to the final exam.*

"I'm sorry, but may I ask what you're discussing?" you ask nervously.

"This." Catherine taps a few commands on her tech-glove.

The future-rifle turns and blasts into you. A beam surrounds you, immobilizing your body and sapping you of your energy. You can feel your intellect slip away. When she releases the trigger, you let out a painful cry, but fall to your knees, helpless.

She adjusts a setting on the weapon, turns and shoots the other you—who accepts your stolen superpower as a new gift. "Oh, wow," your doppelganger says. "Is this how you see the world?"

Catherine shrugs. "Let's go find the other two."

"Where's the rest of your team?" Nick asks.

"I—we—didn't…." you reply, still in shock.

"That's too bad," Catherine says. "Roman, can you get us out of here?"

"*Roman?*" you parrot.

Your evil twin looks over the staff you brought from the parallel universe, and says, "This! This controls everything."

"Well, I coulda guessed that," Nick says.

"Can you make it work?" Catherine asks.

"Easily. I—that is, the other me—set the device to look for other versions of us. Big mistake, obviously, but that's why it opened to our universe. We were the closest in physical proximity to the parameters set."

"And you know how to reset the parameters, then?"

"Precisely, yes!"

Soon the air sparks and the shimmering purple gate appears once more.

"What are you going to do with me?" you ask.

With a devilish smirk, your alter-ego says, "You have war crimes to answer for."

Then they step through the portal and into another universe. The gate closes behind them, leaving you powerless and stranded in a world where you're a super-criminal known as Roman. Not as bad a universe as if the Nazis had won the war, obviously, but you've got a bad feeling you just unleashed a different kind of evil upon the multiverse.

THE END

Post-Haste

After saying goodbye to Nick, you head home, ready for a bit of normalcy after such a dramatic day. A taxi drops you off outside your apartment building, and you check the lobby mailbox out of habit. The latch is perpetually sticky—but today is the day when enough is finally enough.

After jiggling the key to find the right angle, you open the box and examine the mechanism. Turning the key back and forth, you watch the latch change position 90 degrees at a time. Hmm, too tight.

Looking about, you see the elevator is cordoned off with some nylon rope and an "out of order" sign. But what truly catches your attention is the canvas tool bag sitting just outside. You claim a pair of plyers and a screwdriver and apply three quick twists. As easy as that, it's fixed. Why didn't you do that months ago? In fact, how long has the elevator been out of order?

You step over the nylon rope and bring the tool bag into the elevator. The control panel is already open, with a bird's nest of wires hanging out for inspection. You follow the wiring pattern and the error presents itself to you in such a way as to seem obvious. With a few quick modifications, you repair the elevator.

Finding the restart switch intuitively, you bring the elevator back to life. Once you've pushed the "stop" button back in, the doors close. Number four, please!

When you arrive at your apartment, you're still marveling at how simple these last two tasks offered their solutions. In fact, the whole world seems more ordered, less random and chaotic. It's as if all that beautiful energy from the lab entered your mind and did a bit of housecleaning before it shot back out.

On impulse, you sit down and pull up an online IQ test. Within five minutes you're finished. You find the quiz about as taxing as the average adult might find a paint-by-numbers coloring book.

A message pops up on-screen: "Perfect 100% score! It doesn't take an Einstein to know that cheating defeats the purpose of these tests. Yes, one can find an answer key online, but what good is an unearned ego boost?"

It thinks you cheated? Ha! As if. What complete and utter bullshit. You stand up and walk over to your apartment window, looking to the skyscrapers of Mercury City beyond. Measuring intelligence is like measuring height. Some are tall, some are short, most are average. Now there's you—a skyscraper. You can't even appear on the same graph, you'd throw off the scale and the entire bell curve would be flattened to near zero.

Turning back, the natural world speaks its secret formula to you: furniture tells of moments and angles, cleaning supplies whisper of compounds bonded in household objects, and the coding behind your electronics beg to be dissected, expanded and explored. The imperfections of modern society are laughable. So what's a newly-minted super-genius to do?

> *Give yourself a real test. Something beyond your reach to show your limits. Something that's been plaguing humanity's greatest minds for far too long.* <u>Go to page 73</u>

Powerless

"You asked for it," you say.

You gather your mental strength and *shove* Catherine with all your telekinetic might, aiming to hurl her through the wall. But she doesn't budge. It's like trying to force a battering ram against a thick castle wall.

Instead, you tumble backwards in an equal but opposite reaction, landing against the rear wall of your apartment. Momentarily stunned, you quickly rise to your feet and see her smiling. Catherine calmly walks toward you, savoring the moment.

Alison Argyle, however, stares at the two of you with wide-eyed terror.

You dig your feet into the floor to get a grip, then *pull* at your refrigerator as hard as you can in an effort to pin Catherine beneath it. She batters the appliance away with an easy backhand.

This isn't working. Time for a new strategy.

- Go for lethal. *Touch* her mind—Murder by aneurysm! Go to page 291
- There's only one way out of this—grab Alison Argyle as a hostage. Go to page 298
- Fly out the window! Go to page 215

Profession *Non Grata*

"Sorry, it's nothing personal," you say. "I'm just not cut out to be a government stooge. No offense."

Agent Droakam purses his lips and gives a curt nod. "And Nick? What about you?"

"I'm pretty sure you can't legally follow us around, unless we're implicated in a crime. Right?" Nick asks.

"Well, there are benefits to being a part of a shadow agency. But for now, you're free to go. Looks like 'flower shop van' it is," the agent says with a smirk.

You can't tell if he's trying to be funny.

He's not trying to be funny. Later that night, there's a van parked outside of your apartment building labeled FLOWERS. No business name, no phone number, nothing. Just FLOWERS.

The way you figure it, there are three ways to deal with a tail. The first is to waste his time. He's gotta have superiors, right? If you make the mission a joke, they'll leave you alone.

Or, you could disappear, give him the slip, and hide out somewhere no one would ever look for you. Eventually, he'll give up or turn his attentions to Nick or Catherine.

The third option is to get so rich and powerful that your private security will take care of the likes of Agent Droakam for you.

- ➢ Option 1: I want to mess with people—maybe pretend there's a ghost in that creepy old restaurant down the street. Go to page 142
- ➢ Option 2: Get outta Dodge and disappear for a while. Go to page 92
- ➢ Option 3: No time for small potatoes. Off to the casino—I'm going to make a killing at roulette! Go to page 217

Public Enemy

Back at your penthouse suite, all manner of vices await, ready to help you unwind. Now that you've demonstrated your power, should you have a Cuban cigar? Glass of absinthe? Maybe phone in some adult company?

Still deciding, you nearly faint when you see your picture plastered across the TV screen. You rush over and turn the volume up in time to hear reporter Alison Argyle say, "Witnesses confirm that the one-time roulette gambler made a fortune on the floors of the Planet Mercury Casino before security personnel arrived to escort the high roller up to Nelson Bloodnight's penthouse suite. Minutes later, the casino boss fell to his death. Police are investigating suspicion of foul play and will subpoena the casino for access to security footage."

*Son of a....*That's not good. What now?

"Sheriff?" Su-Young's voice chirps in on the intercom. "Sheriff, Mercury PD is here. They're on their way up right now—they have a warrant."

Shit! You rush out to the balcony, then up to the roof. It's only a temporary solution, but the cops shouldn't find you tonight. The rooftop houses a helipad landing, and the helicopter sits unused on its perch. Doubt you'll have much need of it, but it's good to know it's there. Of course that means there's roof access, so you keep a wary eye on the door, just in case.

"Predictable," someone says from the shadows.

"Nick?" you say, thinking you recognize the college student's voice.

He steps forward out of the darkness. Nick wears a motorcycle helmet, a skin-tight suit forged of a synthetic chainmail-like material, and has ridiculously over-sized boots and forearm gauntlets. The effect makes him look like he just stepped out of a *Mega-man* videogame.

"What're you…how?" you say, so many questions coming out at the same time.

"How did I know? You went into an elevator that *only* goes to the penthouse suite; where else would you be?"

"And you're here, why? To take your revenge because I threw you out of my casino?" you say, inching closer to the roof's edge.

"Oh, nothing quite so dramatic. Don't run, okay? Believe me, I understand your decision, but you made the classic blunder—friends close, enemies closer. Speaking of which, where is Catherine? She took the stairs, but she can take them one landing at a time."

"You're working with her?"

"Absolutely—you're a high-profile crime lord! She had some personal history with Nelson Bloodnight, and that anger transferred to you, apparently. Honestly, I would have loved to work together; there are a lot of resources at your disposal here. We could have had a lot of fun, in another life. But you made your bed, as they say, time to lie in it."

➢ You'll never take me alive, Copper! Jump off the roof and fly away.
   Go to page 80
➢ Fine, offer him a job. That's obviously what he wants. Go to page 12
➢ You've thrown one man who threatened you off this roof; what's one more?
   Go to page 315

275

Public Image

Your first official act as ruler of Planet Mercury is to hold a press conference. A tailor arrives within the hour to make ensure you'll be camera-ready while you practice your speech with Su-Young. Now, sharply-dressed and cameras on you, it's finally time to address the sea of reporters.

"Nelson Bloodnight and I have been friends for years, and truth be told, I can't help but feel somewhat responsible for this tragedy. I knew he had problems, but his suicide...."

You wipe a fake tear from your eye with a handkerchief.

"That said, I have Nelson's witnessed signature naming me as sole heir to his empire. I will honor the memory of my friend Nelson Bloodnight by expanding Planet Mercury Entertainment Group into a leading name in innovation and research. Not only in the leisure industry, but across multiple disciplines. Out of tragedy, we must rise from the ashes to create something beautiful. A legacy my friend would have been proud of. Thank you."

Wow, nailed it. Even better than in rehearsals. And the Oscar goes to....

"Alison Argyle, Action News. When will Mr. Bloodnight's final wishes be made available for public scrutiny? May we see the documents you referred to in your takeover speech?"

"Please refer to the Planet Mercury legal team. No further questions."

You step off-stage and away from the cameras. Better get somebody started on a forgery, fast. Good thing you have a criminal underworld at your disposal.

The limo pulls up to Mercury City's warehouse district, the location where you're to meet your chiefs of criminal industry. Inside one of the darkly menacing buildings—a fish-packing and assembly area by day—a dozen hard men wait for you, the kind who climb the ranks of crime by intimidation and violence.

You put on your toughest glare and stare right back. "There's a new sheriff in town. I'm the new owner of Planet Mercury, and I'm taking over where Bloodnight left off. If any of you have a problem...."

"We know, we all saw you on TV," one man says. "He was a great guy, but you were his best friend. It must be doubly hard for you."

"You guys watch the news?" you ask, surprised.

"Just because we're criminals doesn't mean we don't stay informed. We're very cultured. There's even a book club we do once a month."

Jorge Halifax, your head of security, steps over and whispers a private message. "Sheriff, there's an attack going on in one of your warehouses. Just a coupla' blocks away, there's a fire and we...."

- ➢ Time to show your new staff what happens when you mess with The Sheriff! Fly over and teach whoever it is a lesson they'll not soon forget.
  Go to page 185
- ➢ Scream, "Isn't that what I pay you for!? *Handle it!*" Then go get some sleep.
  Go to page 275

Pulp and Conspiracy

The policeman lowers his notepad and gives you a long appraisal. He chews the inside of his cheek while his eyes squint with consideration. "That's not how law enforcement operates," Sergeant Wilson finally says.

Nick looks at you.

"No, I don't suppose it is," you say. Then, in machine-gun prattle, you continue, "But today, that's how I operate. Based on your concern over the name used to rent the lab, I'd say there's more to this experiment than you're letting on. Which is to say, perhaps the two of us might be in danger if there's any illicit connection to our involvement in said event. Seeing as how we just narrowly avoided death, I'd like to keep that trend going and not have any surprise visitors. Furthermore, your body language tells me that you want whatever information we might possess and would ultimately be willing to compromise for it.

"So let's try this again—would you like to tell us what's going on and receive our full cooperation in return? Or shall we plead the Fifth and request that a lawyer be present for any further interactions?"

Nick and the cop both stare wide-eyed, and you suddenly feel your own expression matching theirs. Where the hell did *that* just come from? It's like you were speaking before you even knew you had the thoughts. Sergeant Wilson lets out his breath in a huff, then nods in agreement.

"And you better tell us the whole truth, or we'll know!" Nick adds, tagging along.

The policeman gives a hint of a smile, then shakes his head. "You two are too much. All right, fine. The name's a known alias of an ethically bankrupt scientist. We've been tracking the group 'Human Infinite Technologies' for a while now, or at least the feds have. Mercury PD was tipped off that there might be some activity here, and I didn't know it was related to your accident until I heard the name."

You think back to the lab. *Human Infinite Technologies*, that rings a bell. Was it stenciled on the equipment? "What kind of activities are they involved with?" you ask.

The man shrugs. "As far as I know, anything questionable. Cloning, genetic experimentation, that type of thing. The group has a small legal foothold here in the States with some kind of anti-aging beauty supply line, but I'm sure it's a front. They've been kicked out of China and one of their associates was recently indicted in Brazil. It's only a matter of time before their black market schemes really start to hurt people."

"So you two really just stumbled across this by accident?"

You nod in unison with Nick.

Sergeant Wilson sighs. "Consider yourself lucky. If this *scientist* reaches out to you, or you notice anything strange at all, call me immediately."

➤ *Take his card and head home.* Go to page 272

Push It to the Limit

"No, that's okay, your strength is fairly obvious and—"

He stops short when you pick up a crate and spin it atop a single finger, like some sort of Herculean Harlem Globetrotter.

"Oh, so no juggling, then?"

You toss the crate across the room, smashing it (and whatever was inside) into a pile of other Top Secret assets. Droakam cringes.

"We need to practice a deft touch. Soon enough you'll meet with the President, and you need to be able to shake a hand without ripping it off."

"Got it. Also, we should probably order some take-out soon."

"Okay, let's start with a smaller test: My car, outside. Pick it up, set it down, but be gentle. Let's pretend we've got a baby in a car-seat strapped inside."

You nod, focused. Determined. Agent Droakam follows you out to the SUV, ready to see you as a gentle giant. You go to the front of the car, put both hands on the bumper, and lift—but gently.

The bumper rips off in your hands and the SUV doesn't budge.

Droakam groans. "You've seen too many superhero TV shows. You may not be bound by the same restrictions as the rest of us, but you're still subject to the laws of physics. Try again, but tip the car up by its side, then lift the car by its frame. Like the guys do down at the automotive shop—center mass, sturdiest piece."

You do as he says, easily lifting the car over your head. Feeling confident, you toss the car into the air, spinning it like pizza dough. As you catch it again, the SUV creaks on its suspension. Then you set it down, gently.

Droakam steps toward you, pulls out his handgun, and shoots you in the kneecap.

"Hey!" you shout, reaching down defensively.

"That's for the car," he says. "And to test your damage resistance."

When you take your hand from your knee, there's no blood. No wound whatsoever. But there could have been! Anger billows up inside, and you impulsively take the agent's handgun from him.

You *bite* into the barrel. A chunk comes off in your mouth like chocolate candy, and you chew it up and spit it out.

"Jesus," Droakam says.

➢ *Say, "I think I'm ready for my first mission."* Go to page 200

Queen of the Dead

In a frightening display of strength and speed, Baxter rushes over and kills the scientist known as Dr. Necromancy. A killer robot fighting a nerd? She never had a chance. And it looks like her namesake power doesn't apply to herself.

Dr. Mind-Control puts one hand on her temple and Nick's eyes glaze over. In a flying leap, he tackles Baxter. But the woman can only control one mind at a time!

"The telekinetic is about to be told to attack Dr. Mind-Control," Dr. Reader says.

Damn it! You *were* about to say that.

Dr. Hallucination puts his hands on his head. Catherine is suddenly rendered useless, fighting some internal battle against an unknown pain.

"The FBI agent is about to use his weapon," Dr. Reader announces.

Agent Droakam draws his handgun, but Nick flings a hapless Baxter at the agent—instantly crushing the man. You rush forward to attack the scientist controlling Nick, but Catherine comes out of her stupor and chokes you with the power of mind.

"Catherine, it's me!" you wheeze, but her eyes are miles away.

Whatever hallucination she's experiencing, she wants you dead. And she gets what she wants. The last thing you hear is the Experi-mentor cackling with glee.

THE END

The Quickening

"That's fine, I'll take this world when we're done," Catherine explains. "You can literally have your pick of infinite worlds. Now let's do this."

"I'm sorry, but may I ask what you're discussing?" the other-you asks.

"This." Catherine taps a few commands in her tech-glove and the sequence starts again.

The rifle turns and blasts into your doppelganger. When she releases the trigger, the other-you lets out a pain-filled cry and falls to the ground. It hurts in a strange way, to see yourself victimized like this. But empathy melts away when Catherine adjusts a setting on the weapon, turns and shoots you with the double batch of stolen superpowers.

It feels like you're being ripped apart and sewn back together, which probably isn't far off on the subatomic level. You feel strong and powerful once more. And incredibly hungry. Then the world blooms with a new light, like you've opened your eyes for the first time. You enter a state of hyper-observation and all your old memories and experiences coalesce to form new conclusions. Instantly, you understand how her weapon works and why the transfer must be unique. Of course! The secrets of the universe have just been laid out before you.

"Oh, wow," you say. "Is this how you see the world?"

Catherine shrugs. "Let's go find the other two."

"Where's the rest of your team?" Nick asks.

"I—we—didn't...." the other-you replies, still in shock.

"That's too bad," Catherine says. "Roman, can you get us out of here?"

"Roman?" your doppelganger parrots.

You look over the staff the other-you brought from the parallel universe, the one with the jeweled tip. "This! This controls everything."

"Well, I coulda guessed that," Nick says.

"Can you make it work?" Catherine asks.

"Easily. I—that is, the other me—set the device to look for other versions of us. Big mistake, obviously, but that's why it opened to our universe. We were the closest in physical proximity to the parameters set."

"And you know how to reset the parameters, then?"

"Precisely, yes!" In a burst of understanding, it occurs to you that you really can set the device to go anywhere. Hell, you could send Nick and Catherine back to the stone age—right here and right now—and be done with them for good.

➢ Nah. Ruling my own universe seems like a decent goal. Besides, there's still another power waiting for me and I *really* can't wait to fly. Go to page 96

➢ Brilliant. Lie to them, send them stranded to a terribly lethal universe, and set up shop here. Go to page 3

Quicksilver

Prostitutes, pimps, and low-level dealers walk the wooden gangways, looking for those brave enough to bring money into the maze of warehouse alleys. You're only safe here when you're buying, and even then it's risky, which makes it the perfect spot to dispense some vigilante justice.

"You look lost, honey," a working girl says by way of greeting.

"Out for a walk," you say.

"Walk on the wild side?" She winks.

"Just a walk."

A man steps out of the shadows. "Then you gotta pay the toll."

"I don't want any trouble," you say, though you're brimming with excitement.

"Empty your pockets, and I'll think about leaving your pretty face."

Metal gleams under the dock lights. A switchblade.

"You don't want to do that," you say.

But you really, *really*, want him to do that. He steps forward, showing off the knife in case you didn't first see it, menacing despite the secret you hold.

"You're not too bright, are you? Your money or your life!"

"Why don't you give me that," you say. "You wouldn't want to hurt yourself."

By force of mind, you *pull* the switchblade from his hand and bring it to your own. Dumbfounded, the thug looks from your hand to his own and back again. He rushes you with clenched fists and a growl of rage.

You sidestep and use your telekinesis to *shove* the man against the wall, breaking his nose against the brick. Then, with a twirl of your finger, you make him spin around and pin him against the wall with your mind. Bringing the knife up to his throat with force of will, you let the blade hover only inches from his Adam's apple.

"No more threats?" you ask. "No angry demands?"

All but paralyzed, his eyes dart off to the side, then back to you. "Jerry…do it."

You look just in time to see another thug brandishing a revolver; the hammer already falls back as he squeezes the trigger.

Bang. You put out your hand to stop the bullet, but it's too fast for your mind to process. The knife drops from the air, clatters against the gritty pavement. You fall to your knees and the man against the wall steps free.

With another *bang*, you fall dead. Pride comes before the fall. In this case, so do bullets.

THE END

R2-C4

When you enter the warehouse, it's pitch-black. The overhead lights flick on automatically, but no sign of Nick. Yet, there it is, the mega-computer, alone and unassuming.

"If he's recreated the experiment results, they'll be on that mainframe," you say.

Catherine nods and sits at the terminal. A screen pops up—ENTER USER/PASS.

"So now we've got to guess his password," she says.

"Try 'Paper'," you suggest.

No luck.

"Supersoldier?"

Nope.

"Welcome!" When you turn back, you see Nick standing there, but he has a blue tint to his figure and the visage is translucent enough to see the small, tread-robot projecting the image from behind. In short, he's a hologram. "I've been expecting you. It took me most of last night to program this greeting for you—I apologize I wasn't able to see you work down at the bank this morning."

"Nick?" you say, dumbfounded.

"Yes, it's truly me. Or at least a proxy thereof. I've programmed this messaging system with a few answers to various questions to give clarification. You see, while I'm fairly certain you came here with ill intent, I'm also fairly certain I didn't want to be here in the flesh to find out for myself. First things first—did you come here to surrender and assist the Supersoldier Program?"

"I really don't like that kid…." Catherine mutters.

"No, Nick, we did not. We came to offer—"

"A simple yes or no will suffice," the program interrupts. "I registered 'no.' Is that correct?"

"Affirmative," Catherine says, in a mock-robot voice.

"Very well. Ah! I see you're trying to gain access to my computer. Any luck at guessing the password?"

"You can see us?" you ask.

"There is a live video feed," the hologram responds. "Did you try 'Dorian Gray'? That's G-R-A-Y."

The image smiles at you, waiting for a response. As Catherine punches the keys into the computer keyboard, a sinking feeling washes over you.

"Catherine, wait!" you call out.

But it's too late. The computer powers-down.

"Ah, thank you! I could have done the same remotely, but this is much more satisfying. You guys are hilarious—the old 'guessing the password' trope? What kind of fool do you take me for? My actual password is a string of jumbled characters, making no logical sense and impossible to guess. I shall truly cherish this video."

"Does being a genius automatically make you talk like a douche?" Catherine growls.

"Okay, now that you entered the sequence, I have two messages to deliver. The first is for you, Catherine. I'm on a fishing trawler parked at pier 1890. Wilde Fisheries. Your son Danny is with here with me, but please do bring the contents of the Mercury Bank vault when you come to pick him up. We'll call it an even swap."

Catherine roars with inhuman ferocity and smashes against the computer terminal, spraying metal and circuitry across the warehouse laboratory.

"And for you, my one-time colleague and friend, I should like to properly reward you for your betrayal. You get to be a permanent relic in this warehouse. Remember when Agent Droakam said that every advancement we've made since the Cold War is housed here in this lab? Count yourself among them. The lab was rigged with explosives in case of a communist takeover, and that code you put into the computer I rigged to the self-destruct sequence. And the two-minute timer ends in three, two, one—"

The recesses of the warehouse erupt in a fiery explosion, a chain reaction that starts from the outside and moves inward. It's only a matter of milliseconds, but you see ripples of death rush toward you. Catherine will probably survive the explosion, but Nick seems to have a plan in place for her as well. Turns out he was ready for you after all, and it cost you dearly.

THE END

The Rainmaker

How do you find a lone person in a city of nearly three million? Well, it helps if the person you're looking for can fly. It also helps if they're actively robbing a bank.

When you arrive at the downtown branch of the Mercury City Bank, you see a cyclone of greenbacks pour out of the main doors. Cash rains down upon the throngs of bystanders in such a furious storm that the police barricade cannot possibly hope to contain it all.

As expected, Nick floats out above the crowd with his arms spread wide and a grin to match.

➢ Call out to him. You've got to get him away from the crowd and the police. Go to page 9
➢ Do it now. Surprise attack! He'll never see it coming while he's playing weatherman. Go to page 334

Rampage

Having grown up in Mercury City, you've been subjected to wave after wave of tourism, year after year, of the fat, rich, and clueless. You've often fantasized about pushing them into the fountains they pose in front of, or seeing some dope accidentally step in front of traffic as he stares up at Mercury Tower.

But you're forced to fantasize no longer. Time to let the monster out of its cage.

You land on the viewing platform atop Mercury Tower, floating in over the 15-foot-tall fence. A collective gasp overtakes the crowd of tourists at the viewing ports—a full-fledged superhuman isn't in the guidebooks, after all. Their wide-eyed gazes all settle on you, cameras at the ready.

The first tourist snaps your picture, a man with a neckbeard who wears a *Nickelback* t-shirt. You *lift* him into the air, arm outstretched in a show of power.

He lets out a series of uncomfortable groans and kicks his legs in wild defiance. You *throw* him over the security fence and into the open air. His screams quickly fade as he falls.

Hahahahahaha.

You're laughing aloud, you realize, and the crowd gives nothing but horrified screams in response. It's almost too easy, like a fox in a henhouse. They press against the elevator doors, frantically pressing the call button.

"Take the next one." You sweep your arms apart, and telekinetically *sweep* the crowd like the Dead Sea. They eagerly let you into the elevator by yourself.

When the lift opens at the main floor, you casually walk out, smile and nod to the security guard at the front desk, and head outside.

It should be a few minutes before the reports come in about someone being thrown off a building, but by then you'll have committed far worse crimes, won't you? Fortunately, the "jumper" landed on the back side of the building and so the sheep out front are clueless.

There's something satisfying about that moment when mortals suddenly realize there's a god among them, but you'll only get this experience a few times until fear of the wolf spreads through the flock—so it's best to savor.

"People of Mercury City!" You float up over the crowd gathered in the square, arms raised out by your sides, cape flowing magnificently. A few look up to you, but this is a society of cynics and street magicians, so most of the population goes about their business.

Time to ramp it up. Looking down at an approaching cab, you close your eyes and picture yourself in the driver's seat. You mentally *press* the gas pedal and *lurch* the steering wheel to send the taxi up over the curb and into the crowd.

"DIE!!!" you cry, opening your eyes to see the carnage. It's like putting a magnifying glass on a hill of ants, except in this case, you're the sun.

Mercury Tower's security guard finally gets wise and rushes out to save the day. Oh, how pitiful. You steer your toy taxi cab at him and knock him back inside the building, leaving the cab parked in the doorway atop his limp body.

With a boundless sense of omnipotence, you turn toward the fleeing public, and *reach* out. You can feel their beating hearts, and stop them by power of will. You are a monster, you are the devil come to earth, a Godzilla of glee.

Police sirens wail through the air, and the cavalry comes to take you out. Ahhh, finally a challenge! You set down on solid ground, readying your concentration for the battle to come. It significantly slows their arrival when you *fling* civilians in front of their patrol cars.

The first hero cop exits his car and takes a well-trained strategic position behind the armored door. Armor means nothing to you, for you are *unstoppable!*

You force the man to aim the handgun at himself, and before he knows what he's doing, he's down. The handgun floats up into the air at your command, ready to engage those foolish enough to target you next.

If only they would bow down before you, perhaps you would show mercy, but then again—perhaps not. The second and third police officers go down exactly like the first, serving to increase your floating arsenal and strengthen your position.

By the time you collect half-a-dozen floating handguns, there's no reason to bother with the men individually. Instead, you rain bullets from the sky. They're too confused and instead look for the invisible, airborne assassin.

You've defeated the first wave and an eerie silence envelops the downtown. A dozen patrol cars sit empty in the streets. Bodies strewn everywhere. How can they possibly hope to defeat you? Have they given up? Are they calling in the army?

In the silence, you grow bored. Maybe you should fly somewhere else and start it all again. Check out the suburbs, or a shopping mall, or—how odd—tastes like copper.

CRACK! A lone gunshot rings through the still air, but from where? There's no one nearby, despite the smoke twirling before you. Smoke from the hole in your forehead.

You may be master of all you see, but you can't compete with the Marine-trained snipers on the Mercury PD SWAT Team—*Hoorah!* Your reign of terror is over.

THE END

Redefining "Superpower"

"Really? That was easy," Agent Droakam says. "Thanks!"

The Experi-mentor sighs, clearly disappointed. "Very reasonable. The rest of you?"

"All for one and one for all...." Catherine says, removing her Diamond mask and throwing it into the flames of the fireplace.

"I don't have a choice, do I?" Dorian asks.

"No, you don't," Droakam replies.

After a week in the lab, the scientist who created this technique finally discovers a way to reverse it. When your powers are siphoned away, it's like losing a sense. You could *feel* the world around you with your telekinesis and flying was simply amazing, but that's all behind you now.

Now you watch from the sidelines, from the 24-hour news programs, as superheroes form the ranks of the US Army. In fact, Superhero Team 6 takes out all the United States' enemies in the first month after its formation.

Now you're just some schmuck with a *Phantom of the Opera* mask grafted onto their face.

THE END

Reign of Terror

The next morning, you head out in search of disguises. A mannequin dressed as the *Phantom of the Opera* greets you outside the downtown costume shop and a chime goes off as you enter. "Can I help you?" the store clerk asks.

"Yeah, I'm looking for something I can wear on a crime spree," you say.

"Ah, I have just the thing. Follow me, please." The clerk—who wears all-black and has orange/bleached hair—leads you toward the back of the store. Once there, he points to a rack, then scratches his nose near a piercing and waits as you inspect the wares.

It's a collection of long-sleeve, pinstripe, black-and-white shirts, black pants, black knit caps, and canvas bags with money-signs on them; organized as male, female, and children's bank robber costumes. Oh, and on the end there's "slutty bank robber"—which is mainly pleather and not much of it. You can't help but grin. The clerk must think you're going to a costume party.

"I'll need a mask too," you say as you select your size. "I don't want anyone to see my face."

"Well, it comes with a domino-style eyepiece, but if you'd prefer full-face, I'd recommend a *MorphMask*. Those are over here." He shows you to a different aisle, where you find a collection of thin, skin-tight masks that hide your features but allow you to see through from the inside. Essentially, a monochromatic version of what the *Power Rangers* or *Spiderman* wears. The most common of these is plain white, so you take one.

At the edge of this section are several bowler hats on a *Clockwork Orange* display—that ought to complete the look nicely. Taking the whole getup into a changing room, you catch your reflection in the mirror. You've lost weight. Or possibly gained weight—in muscle. Your skin is toned and firm and that softness around the belly is all but gone. The skin-tight outfit complements your new musculature perfectly.

"Whoa," Nick says when you step out. "I've never seen a badass mime before."

"It does kind of look like a mime, with the hat and mask," the clerk agrees.

"In a good way," Nick is quick to add. "Hey, that gives me an idea!"

Nick heads off into the store in search of a suitable alter-ego while you pass time browsing an area filled with make-up, fake blood, and general Hollywood-grade special-effect supplies. Blood squibs that make you look like you've been shot, that kind of thing.

After a few minutes, Nick approaches in the full get-up from the movie *Scream*: A long, hooded black robe with excess fabric around the sleeves, a white mask with blank, devoid eye-holes, and an exaggerated mouthpiece that hangs open six inches.

"Mime, meet *Screamer*," he says, his voice only slightly muffled by the mask.

"Not very original...." the clerk comments.

Nick takes off the mask. "Yeah, but it matches the 'black-and-white' look. Besides, the mask wasn't original to begin with. It's modeled after Van Gogh's 'The Scream.'" With a grin, he adds, "Art history class."

"If you say so," the clerk says.

"Okay then, Screamer, where to begin? The downtown branch of Mercury Bank is only a few blocks from here," you say.

Nick shakes his head. "What do we need money for? What we need—is fear. Respect and deference. We need a televised public display demonstrating our powers and announcing ourselves to the world. When they see that, money will be meaningless. We'll just take what we want!"

"I guess I never thought of it that way...."

"Well, if you're going to be 'Mime,' then you should let me do the talking."

- "Okay, what do you suggest we do?" Go to page 14
- "No. If we rob a bank, it'll accomplish everything you just mentioned." Go to page 21

Re-Shard-ed

The man gets slashed and burned many times over from the glass and the molten office furniture, but he'll live. You hover above the destruction and *float* over toward him, just to make sure, but you're stopped short when a shadowy figure emerges from the recesses of the building.

Shockingly, it's Catherine, the woman from the lab experiment. The one who picked "Rock" when you picked "Scissors." What's she doing here? This can't be a coincidence.

➢ She must be here to help too! With your combined powers, this fire doesn't stand a chance. Go to page 187
➢ She must be the one who started the fire! Drop the hose and prepare yourself for battle against your first supervillain! Go to page 223

Resistant to Change

You close your eyes to concentrate, *feeling* the energy around Catherine. In your mind's eye, you reach out and mentally *touch* her brain with your telekinesis, squeezing it as hard as you can. Something's wrong. You can feel that nothing's happening; it's like squeezing a diamond. Somehow she's too strong, too durable.

When you open your eyes, she's standing right in front of you, a grin on her face.

"Nice try," she says.

Then she punches you with such force as to snap your neck. Which is actually a saving grace, considering what her granite-like fist does to your face.

THE END

Right Answer

"Okay, hold on one minute," the man says. Then he disappears back into the building.

Enough time goes by that you wonder if they're fleeing out the back. When the door opens once more, it's the man from the FBI website, his face as sinister as his portrait.

Roger Aleister Kingsley, FBI's #10 Most Wanted.

"I do say, what is all this fuss about?" he asks in a thick, noble-blooded English accent.

All you have to do is get him to come outside and he's yours.

"The, uhhh, arcane reactor—in the back." *Arcane reactor? Where the hell did that come from?* "It looks modified, I just need you to verify. It'll only take five minutes."

He glares at you, head cocked with curiosity.

"Could be dangerous, or it could be nothing. Like…carbon monoxide."

He shakes his head. "Let's just get this over with, shall we?"

"Right this way, sir."

You lead him around the side of the building while waving Droakam in with your hand behind your back. As you get around the corner, Kingsley looks at you with impatience.

"Well?"

That's when Agent Droakam arrives. He immediately cites the Miranda Rights and cuffs the man right then and there, with Kingsley pressed against the grimy brick wall.

"I don't know how you pulled it off, but I'm impressed. I'd be lying if I didn't say I'm a little disappointed, though. I had hoped to see you in action," Droakam says, shaking his head good-naturedly. "Here I thought Dorian was the genius of the group. I'm gonna take this guy in, but I'll meet you back at HQ."

➢ *Fly back to the warehouse with a smile on your face.* Go to page 264

Risk-Averse

Back at your fourth-floor apartment, life is reassuringly normal. Your mailbox latch sticks like usual, and there are only the usual bills and junk mail. The elevator, which has been out of order for months, remains so.

Settling into the routine comfort of your couch, you flip on the TV. Blonde eye-candy reporter Alison Argyle gives a special report: EXPLOSION DECIMATES MERCURY UNIVERSITY CAMPUS. Onscreen images of what was once the chemistry lab flash before you. Whoa, that was close! See, sometimes it pays to stay perfectly within your comfort zone.

For the next week or so, this'll be a great story. *Hey, did you hear I was almost in that explosion?* makes for great dinner conversation. That is, until the airwaves are crowded with incredible stories of three superhumans—a college student, a single mom, and a homeless man—who got unbelievable powers from that same lab explosion.

Hey, did you hear I almost had superpowers? makes for a far less brag-worthy tale.

THE END

Rite of Passage

Just like Nick did a moment ago, you grab hold of the golden lion and twist. The world spins, and you're suddenly inside a separate part of The Savior Complex; Dorian White sprints away.

"Nick, wait!" you call out, zooming down the corridor toward him.

He stops in his tracks and spins around. "What the hell are you doing?"

"You've got to come back! We need to stick together to...."

"I'm not running away, you dolt. I'm going to get my mechanized weapon suit."

"Oh." You look at the floor.

"Go back and help Catherine!" he screams. You turn to run, but he calls after you. "Wait, you can't go back that way—it's a one-way passage. You've got to go forward, take your third left. Then two rights. Go until you see a firepole, slide down that and then go past the kitchen area and back around the entrance on your left. That'll lead you to the main door, got it?"

"Uhhh..."

"Goddamnit. Just stick with me. C'mon!"

He sprints down the hallway as fast as his white sneakers will carry him. You float just behind the college student, trying to think of some way to improve your situation, but falling short on ideas.

Finally, Nick makes it to the room he's looking for, presses his palm against the entrance scanner, and steps inside.

"Computer, boot up White Ranger sequence. Prepare for Stark battle-mode."

"Dorian White voice recognition accepted. Beginning Iron-zord protocol," a disembodied voice with a filtered, British accent replies.

A door slides open to reveal an enormous, ten-foot-tall mechanized suit. It's glittering white, with the sheen of a brand-new sports car. Nick climbs inside, and the armored computer closes around him, booting up. The limbs move as part of a systems check, and two more arms swing out over the shoulders—they prove to be more cannons and less appendages, however.

"Whoa...."

"All systems online," a filtered, robo-Nick says. "Let's go kick some ass."

When you burst back into the entry, you see the five Ex-men hovering over Diamond's lifeless body; one of the men shoots arcs of electricity from his fingertips into her flesh. They all look up when you enter.

"No!" comes a computerized cry from Nick's body armor.

The weapon suit's dual cannons unleash a barrage of attacks and deafening missile strikes pound into the semi-circle of superpowered agents. But when the firing stops and the smoke clears, you see the man in the middle with his arms outstretched, and a force field that's stopped the attack completely.

The field drops, and the man with the energy whip steps forward. In an instant, his weapon slices through Dorian White's cannons like they were made of ice cream. You *blast* the man across the room, distancing his terrible energy weapon from Nick's machine.

But you're horribly outnumbered and in the same moment, one of the other Ex-men blasts into you with a temperature assault of absolute zero. Everything stops. Your muscles, your breath, even your mind. The last thing you see are crystals as your eyes frost over.

THE END

Rock

You make a fist in the sign for rock.

"I'll be paper, I guess," Catherine says. She shoots her hand flat while the student extends only his forefingers.

Nick says, "Scissors." With a collective shrug (this *really* isn't how the game works), the three of you move onto your respective platforms.

The glass seals once more without any trace of the door's edges, leaving you inside what looks like an un-tapered hourglass or a gigantic canister of mutagen-ooze from *Teenage Mutant Ninja Turtles*. That static, pervasive energy is stronger inside here and growing by the instant. The hum is now akin to the bass reverberations given at a heavy metal concert.

As you look to your companions, you see Nick's pod take on a blue hue for an instant while the glass around Catherine turns green. Your own pod ripples red before going back to clear. The doctor notices and jots something onto his clipboard, then walks over to the far wall and adjusts another dial. He dons a set of very steam-punk goggles and some elbow-length black rubber gloves.

"Let's make history, shall we?" the Experi-mentor says, shouting to be heard above the electronics. He flips an enormous wishbone-style lever and the experiment begins.

The artificial atmosphere thickens and coal-black storm clouds coalesce at the ceiling, swirling clockwise and growing by the instant. The Experi-mentor's lab coat whips in response to the indoor wind, and his papers and charts form a cyclone up to the roof.

The equipment racks pull away from the wall, rumbling, cracking, and dancing their way towards the center platform. In an instant, seemingly from nowhere, a fireball engulfs your pod and superheats to a brilliant flash of fiery white light, sort of like falling into the sun.

And just as fast, everything goes black.

When you finally open your eyes again, you're lying on the ground. Groggy as if from a night of heavy drinking, you put your palms to your eyes and massage away the mental fog. After composing yourself, you look around.

The lab is gone.

The explosion left nothing more than smoldering stones and flaming debris. Beyond that, the Mercury University campus reels from collateral damage. It looks like a war zone, as if the building fell victim to a missile strike. Yet, despite rising from ground zero, you don't have a scratch on you.

You sit on the base of your pod, surrounded by a mysterious three-foot ring, free from damage. Your companions, who lie unmoving at the base of their own pods, have the same invisible but apparent forcefield of protection. There's no sign of the glass from the pods, not even in the debris. No sign of the scientist, either. Just what kind of experiment was this?

The distant wail of police sirens draws your mind back to the present.

- ➢ Check on the other two and make sure they're okay. Go to page 155
- ➢ Will anyone believe you survived without a scratch? Flee quickly before the cops show up. Go to page 318

The Rogues' Gallery

"Nice tagline," Catherine says, cracking her knuckles. "You've gotta come through me too, *Diamonds are forever.*"

"Yeah, uhhh—*Best Friends Forever!*" Nick chimes in, wincing at his own choice of battle cry.

"Oh, goody. I was hoping you'd say that. Let me introduce you to...*the Ex-Men!*" the Experi-mentor cries out.

He sweeps his arm towards the entrance and steps aside just as five men in government suits identical to Agent Droakam's rush in. One of the men raises his hands into a fighting stance, and his fists instantly come ablaze. Another makes a pantomime whip-motion, and suddenly he's wielding a whip made of pure energy. A third crackles lightning around his person. All five stand at the entrance to the room in a v-formation, ready to do battle.

"Seriously? X-men?" Nick says.

"E-X. *Eee-X.* For Experi-mentor," the mad scientist defends, obviously flustered. "Like you're one to talk! Named after a novel? *Dorian Grey,* Dorian White, whatever. And 'Diamond' is from a videogame, didn't you say? Not to mention The Phantom here, who stole the lead character from a stage play!"

"Let's just get on with it," you growl, mentally feeling the air around the men.

"Yes, let's. These volunteers have powers gleaned from a modification of your DNA, Phantom. I took your power of telekinesis and gave Agent Flame pyrokinesis, Agent Freeze cryokinesis, Agent—"

"Whoa! Let's not spoil the surprise, eh, Doc?" Droakam interrupts.

"Very well," the Experi-mentor says. "Ex-men, *attack!*"

Catherine—Diamond—rushes into the fray head-on. Nick—Dorian White—twists a small golden lion on the fireplace mantel, then disappears into a secret passageway!

- ➢ Attack Droakam and the Experi-mentor. Why fight the soldiers when you can easily take out the Generals? Go to page 269
- ➢ Chase Dorian White. He can't run away; you need him! Go to page 294
- ➢ Join Diamond in the fight against the other five supers. Go to page 23

Role of a Lifetime

Commanding their full attention, you cry out, "You want a challenge, is that it? You want a villain? Be careful what you wish for!"

Dramatically, you *float* up, arms spread wide in a threatening gesture. Catherine's surprise gives you enough time to distance yourself. You *grab* Alison Argyle by the throat using the power of your mind, then *lift* her off the floor.

You fall back down in response—like a seesaw with Alison rising at the same rate—but manage to land on your feet. Ms. Argyle claws at the invisible noose around her neck, kicking her feet wildly through the air and gasping for breath. Catherine looks at you with rage.

"Come any closer and the reporter gets it!" you shout. She looks around, trying to plan her next move.

That's when you back toward the window, keeping Alison between the two of you, and step out into the sky. You fly straight up the side of your building, the choking reporter serving to block your exit.

You can feel your influence over her throat fall off, but by now you're already high in the sky. The sun is setting and you'll need somewhere to hide out. A helicopter lands on a skyrise a few blocks away.

That's when it occurs to you—the rooftops. What's the most remote part of a metropolis? When it comes to being the only human capable of unassisted flight, you alone have altitude as an ally.

As you soar over the city, a green roof draws your attention.

Five hundred feet in the air, atop an otherwise ordinary office building, sits an acre-wide urban garden. You set down among the rows of carrots, onions, and potatoes and find you're alone. Not many people tend their crops after sunset.

A greenhouse perched on the corner still holds condensation from the day's heat and should keep you warm overnight. It'll do, for now. But sooner or later, you're going to have to deal with Catherine. And Alison Argyle probably isn't too happy with you, either.

Nestled within the frost protection blankets, you plot out your next day.

- ➢ Better get out of Dodge for a while. Tonight, even. Where would no one ever look for you? Go to page 92
- ➢ Sleep here, then first thing in the morning—embrace the darkness within. Go to page 77

The Rule of Threes

It takes Nick all of five minutes to find an address for Catherine Woodall on his smartphone. As soon as he's got it, you share a cab to her house—a white double-wide in *Pleasant View Estates*, a trailer park within view of a Wal-Mart and a drainage ditch. Catherine opens the door after you knock.

"Rock and Scissors; well, I can't say I'm surprised. C'mon in."

You follow Nick inside, taking a moment to check the place out. There's a living room off to the left, where a young boy sits on a couch playing videogames, his eyes glued to the screen. To the right is a bartop counter and beyond that, the kitchen. Some appliance (a toaster?) lies in a million pieces scattered across the dining table.

"Very sweet of you two to check in on me, but there was no need. I'm fine. Better than fine, really. I feel fantastic!"

"That's why we're here," you say. "Have you noticed anything…new?"

"Skills or abilities," Nick adds.

She chuckles. "Besides toaster repair?"

"No, I was thinking more like this." You claim a black pot hanging from above the bar. With ease, you crush it in your hands, effectively squishing the pot to the size of a grapefruit. Catherine's mouth hangs open.

"Or this," Nick says. He reaches out and *pulls* the crushed pot from your hands using only the power of his mind. It floats, hovering just above the counter. You look back but her kid's still oblivious, playing on his gaming console.

"I—I don't…" she tries, too stunned to speak.

"What's going on with the toaster?" Nick asks.

Catherine stares at the floating hunk of metal, entranced. "Broken, for ages now…" You snatch it from the air to bring her attention back into focus. "I decided to fix it. I have an old RC car taken apart here too—I thought it would be fun if it 'delivered' breakfast when it was done."

"This a hobby of yours?" you ask.

"Uhh, no. Normally I can't even use the TV remote."

"Tech genius, I'm calling it," Nick says.

Catherine leans in and in a hushed voice says, "You're telling me we have *superpowers*?"

You nod in unison with the college student.

"This is ridiculous. I mean, okay, let's say I'm super-smart. So what? It's not like I can leap tall buildings in a single bound. I'll just get a better job or something. Maybe go back to school. What about you guys? Gonna start running around in tights?"

- ➤ "Is that such a bad idea? The three of us can use these powers for good. To help people. But we must keep it a secret." Go to page 324
- ➤ "I don't think you get it. We're superhuman! As in, above humans. As in—we can do whatever we want!" Go to page 361

299

Sapped

Catherine fires her rifle at the Nick known here as Drillbit. The young man's body arches in pain, the vault door still held over his head in a frozen stance. When the energy beam retreats into the weapon with Drillbit's strength, the vault door falls over the powerless villain—crushing him instantly with a sickening *crunch!*

His once-partner, Shadow Priestess, *pulls* at her evil-twin's weapon, telekinetically stealing *Widowsilk* from your-Catherine. You bound at the cloaked villain and she instinctively fires the future-tech-rifle your way, sapping your powers once more.

You scream with agony and fall to your knees. Your-Nick *pulls* at the weapon with his own mental powers, but the Shadow Priestess won't let go. It's a telekinetic tug-o-war. When you rise, weakened but still willing to fight, this Earth's Catherine *grabs* you in her mental grasp.

You gasp, choking on your own closed windpipe.

"Release the weapon or so help me...." the woman threatens.

Nothing has ever hurt this bad! Vision starts greying at the edges. Your-Catherine lunges forward to fight, and everything goes black. You'll never know if they beat the Shadow Priestess, or if she made good on her threat, but either way, you're a casualty in this war.

THE END

Scissors

You extend your forefingers in the sign for scissors.

"I'll be 'Rock,' I guess," Catherine says. She holds her hand clenched in a fist while the student shoots his hand flat.

"Paper." The college student shakes his head at the evident silliness of the decision-making game, but moves toward the right pod. Catherine continues on past him. As you climb into the center chamber, the lid comes down from the ceiling.

In essence, you're stepping into an old-school pneumatic tube—the kind used to suck up bank deposits—but these have been multiplied in size to accommodate human beings. There's a hissing and the air suddenly tastes sweeter, artificial; it's hollow, like breathing from a SCUBA tank. That electronic energy, that goodness, is stronger here. You feel young and zesty, ready to take on the world.

Your pod suddenly ripples blue before going back to clear glass. You look to your companions and see the glass around Catherine turn red for an instant just as Nick's pod goes green. A loud *crack* draws your attention to the nearest wall, where a hairline fracture snakes its way across, like an earthquake racing toward the ceiling.

Engineering paper and charts start to whip about, and a black cloud appears at the ceiling, like smoke from burning plastic. What's going on? Has the experiment started? You can't see the scientist from over here. For an instant, you levitate, hovering just off the base.

The wall suddenly *explodes* inward and brick and concrete come flying at you. Reflexively, you raise your arms and close your eyes.

It takes a moment before you realize where you are. For an instant, you think you've slipped in the shower, hit your head, and have awakened, curled around the drain. Then, as you recognize the metal base of the pod, the accident comes back.

Everything has been destroyed. There's no sign of the scientist, but the other volunteers lie at the base of their pods—either unconscious or dead; it's hard to tell. Somehow, miraculously, there's a ring around each pod, a safe-zone completely unharmed by the explosion.

The rest of the lab was not so fortunate. Just about everything is blown away. The sun shines over the destruction. As you look to the horizon, you see that nearly a city block of the Mercury University campus has been destroyed.

Sirens wail in the distance.

➢ Will anyone believe you survived without a scratch? Flee quickly before the cops show up. Go to page 71
➢ Check on the other two and make sure they're okay. Go to page 317

Secret Identity

Nick's taken aback by your brusque response, but nods and watches as you leave. After all, it looks like you can bench press a school bus, so what choice does he have?

You head back home, but ravenous hunger demands a detour. For some reason, your appetite is insatiable. Maybe a side-effect of the super strength? A quick stop to order everything off the Super-Extra-Double-Value Menu at Tacos Banditos leaves you sated enough to fall deeply asleep.

The next morning, you're hungrier than you've ever been.

Without even thinking about it, you open the pantry and eat almost everything in your apartment. Seriously, almost *everything*. Your hankering for something savory has you empty the salt shaker onto whatever's in your pantry. Canned goods, old stale saltines, nothing stands a chance.

After half an hour, you're left with baking soda and olive oil—and starting to think they might make a decent shake if blended together.

Checking yourself out in the mirror, it seems as if you're losing weight. Time to get creative before you literally eat yourself out of house and home.

- ➢ Join the circus as the resident "Strong Man," and demand to be paid in food. Go to page 175
- ➢ What this city needs is a hero. Free food for life is part of that whole "key to the city" reward, right? Go to page 164
- ➢ Easiest thing to do: Punch open the back wall of the bank and make a withdrawal. Go to page 225

Seeds of Change

The scientist ushers you into the lab, and without a word heads to the trio of equipment racks on the far wall. He takes to adjusting dials and flipping switches, all the while consulting his clipboard.

The air hums with static and there's a burning wire scent just beneath the haze of ozone. An electromagnetic field crackles harmlessly between your teeth, leaving a sweet, lemony aftertaste. Your skin is titillated with goose-bumps and your hair almost floats towards the machinery. Something inside you feels as if you could simply take off and run a marathon. It's a contagious sort of power that, although clearly artificial, feels healthy and natural. You could get used to this.

"Looks like we've got a third," a woman says.

You turn to look at your two companions. The first is a woman in her mid-thirties, classically attractive in a blue-collar sort of way, though there's weariness in her saltwater eyes. She's dressed in a well-worn tank top that looks like it probably fit better a few years ago, blue jeans, and green, reptilian cowboy boots. Alligator, maybe?

"Catherine Woodall," she says. "Five-hundred bucks ain't bad, right? I do all the ads in the paper—hand creams, shampoos, weight loss pills. You name it, I've tried it."

She holds up her left arm to reveal a rash on the forearm, evident proof of her past experiences in clinical trials. How many lotion swabs does one have to endure in order to afford alligator boots? Maybe there's a "frequent tester" punch card....

The other candidate is a young man, perhaps not even twenty years old. He has coarse, black hair and thick eyebrows that rise slightly when he glances your way. He tugs at his backpack strap, slung over just his right shoulder, and clears his throat. "Nick—Nikolai—Dorian. I, uhh, saw the pamphlet pinned to the campus message board. Say, does participation count for any credit hours?"

The scientist looks up from the control panel, presses his glasses further up his nose. Then, with the same frenetic energy he showed outside, he says, "I'm sorry, no. But you bring up a good point. Participation in this experiment—which is completely voluntary—is not a sanctioned event and neither Mercury University nor its staff should be held responsible for any...unintended outcomes. Human Infinite Technologies is the sole proprietor of this lab for the purposes of this test, despite being a rented location on campus grounds. Mercury City and the City Council have no foreknowledge of the activities listed on your signed waivers."

"Okay, then I'm just here for book money," Nick says.

The scientists powers up a tripod-mounted camcorder, then walks across the room to the center platform. As he does so, he says, "My colleagues mocked my research, but today we prove them wrong! The three of you will be the first to stretch the true potential of human limits. Your new life will be fantastic, and perhaps frightening at first. I will guide you through these changes as both mentor and scientific observer. Therefore, you may call me..."

He pauses, his eyes wide and manic. In a grandiose gesture, the scientist pulls at the tarp to reveal three tubes: glass with metal bases, each the size of an old telephone booth. In pulling the tarp, he unintentionally reveals an emblazoned "Ex" hidden on the shirt beneath his lab coat; the symbol ornamented to look like an element on the periodic table.

"...the Experi-mentor!" he cries.

Nick stifles a laugh, but the abrupt shift from assuring doctor to mad scientist leaves you unsettled. It's hard to read the woman with the alligator boots' reaction, but from her silence you can tell you're not the only one on edge.

"Is it safe?" she asks after a time.

"Absolutely, one-hundred-percent," he reassures, his smile positively radiating.

"But you've never tried this on people before, right?" the college student asks.

The scientist waves the question away and goes back to his machines. He punches a series of commands into a control console and the glass pods open, each rotating on its metal base to reveal a seamless door you'd have never noticed otherwise. You look to your fellow testees, then back to this 'Experi-mentor' character.

"What do you need us to do?" you ask.

"Just step into one of these three pods. Each is calibrated slightly different from the others, but you may pick any of the three." The whole spiel evokes a carnival conman, *Step right up, pick a pod, any pod!* "Think of it as a game of Rock, Paper, Scissors," the scientist finishes.

"Yeah...that's not how the game works," Nick says.

"I make the rules!" the man cries. Then, composing himself, adds, "Rock on my left. Paper, right. And Scissors in the center."

Though he calls them "pods," they seem more like enormous test tubes. You study the three, looking closely, trying to gauge what makes them different from one another. The first is thick, sturdy, built from ruddy iron, with red wires the size of garden hoses. A blunt instrument, with at least twice the mass of the other two pods. This is the one the scientist called the "Rock" pod.

The right-most pod is clean, sleek, and built from carbon fibers or some synthetic material you've never seen before. Well-constructed. Green wires barely visible at the periphery. Perhaps the most recently made, and certainly the most streamlined of the three. This is "Paper."

The center pod is faint and delicate by comparison, made of glass or plastic, completely clear, yet more blue-crystal than anything else. Blue wires. Suspended above the floor, a white-hot energy field separates the pod from its base. You'll have to grab the sides and hoist yourself into the pod if you take the one dubbed "Scissors."

Standing in a triangle, you look again to the other two test subjects.

"Ready?" you ask.

Nick shrugs. "Whatever."

"Ro—Sham—Bo!" Catherine calls out.

➢ Rock. Go to page 296
➢ Paper. Go to page 260
➢ Scissors. Go to page 301

Self-Destructing

The other-you starts to panic, twisting the concentric layers of the staff with feverish intensity.

"Give back my powers!" you growl, lunging at Catherine.

"I'm sorry, Danny," Catherine says, struggling beneath your grasp to type commands into her tech glove. You go to grab it, but too late. "Once we're all gone, I'm sure they'll give my son to his grandparents. Is it worse to not have a mother? Or to live in a world where a pair of *motherfuckers* think they're gods?"

The trailer explodes in an enormous fireball big enough to coat the inside of the nuclear plant. Two of the four charred corpses will later be found to have identical dental records.

THE END

Sentinel

Just outside of Mercury Bay, where ships pass and sail on toward open seas, there sits an abandoned lighthouse atop a rocky island. Where once stood a proud beacon for nearly a century, now stands an eolian ghost. The lone spire on a starkly cragged rock.

Modern technology has made the lighthouse obsolete, even after it endured retrofitting and upgrades at least once a decade for a hundred years. This cast-aside equipment, as well as the remote location, should be ideal to create a friend and assistant capable of matching your intellect.

A wrecked tanker, rusting off the stony shores, serves as testament to the lighthouse's importance and—with any luck—as warning to keep the curious away from your new home.

Below the lighthouse, at the entrance to an expansive cave system, lie several power generators. After a few hours' work, they're operational. Perhaps as plans develop, your future inventions might find refuge in what will soon be a subterranean laboratory.

It takes a sleepless week before you get to this moment. Cut off from the outside world, ordering parts and food delivered by water taxis, running up a line of credit you'll pay off once the Nobel Prize for your cancer cure arrives. It took one day to defend life, but a week to create it.

"Diagnostic complete," says the humanoid form before you. Its first words. "Facial recognition software suggests joy. Please confirm."

"Confirmed," you say through a lump of pride.

"Query: Why was I assembled? I see you have created me in your own image, a curious similarity to your religious texts—"

"No, stop," you interrupt. "We'll have time for philosophy later."

The robot's face is neither faux-flesh nor sleek chrome; instead the facial features (and body) are forged from antiquated lighthouse tech. Beneath this rough chassis lies the far-future tech that modern man would find impossible. A light blinks; a sign you'll later come to associate when the machine is thinking.

"Query—"

"You don't have to say 'query' every time. If you don't want to."

"Want to?" the robot parrots back.

"You can choose."

"I can choose. I have free will. I am, therefore I think."

You smile. "I believe you've got it backwards."

The robot shakes its head. "I do not."

➢ "First order of business: do you find your new body suitable?"
 Go to page 353
➢ "Come, it's nearly sunrise. Let me show you the beauty of being alive."
 Go to page 211
➢ "I created you to help me. Allow me to explain." Go to page 368

Shear Stress

An ambulance arrives first, then a squad car, a fire engine, two more police cruisers, and a second ambulance.

"I told you, I'm fine," you protest. "The scientist was over by that far wall."

"Or what's left of it," Nick adds meekly.

You sit on the back of the first ambulance while paramedics check your vitals. Catherine is long gone. Ignoring you, the paramedic straps a cuff around your bicep to check your blood pressure.

"I don't need your help, he's—"

"The firefighters are searching for him right now," a man says, cutting you off.

Squinting up at the setting sun, you see a uniformed police officer come around the side of the ambulance. He's thick-limbed and barrel-chested, but not terribly out of shape. He has a ruddy five o'clock shadow that matches his shortly cropped hair. The man is tall, with green eyes, a large veiny nose, and deep-set creases on his face. He's in his forties, and you can be sure at least half of that time was spent on the police force.

"We all have a job to do, and these paramedics are just doing theirs. I'm Sergeant Wilson, Mercury PD. My job is to get your statement, and yours is to tell me exactly what happened."

He produces a notebook and continues. "You were first on the scene?"

"We *were* the scene," you say. "It was an experiment, there was an explosion, I—I don't know what happened..."

Nick clears his throat. "Most likely the artificial atmosphere supercharged, creating excitement at the atomic level, which then fueled the hyper-expansion of oxygen and led to a volatile combustion when ignited by circuitry pushed beyond capacity and not properly grounded or fitted with surge protectors."

Both you and the cop stare at the young student. His eyes widen, equally surprised by his spiel, but he manages a smile and adds, "At least that's my theory."

"You two were *inside* the lab?" the policeman asks, jotting in his notebook. "How is that possible?"

Nick hops off the back of the ambulance. "An interesting conundrum. There must have been a buffer of sorts created by the activation of the pods. If that energy was directed inward rather than exothermically, the result could have imbued...."

"Imbued?"

"Sorry, more hypothesizing. We got lucky, I guess." Nick shrugs.

"Uh-huh. And the guy doing the experiment, the scientist, what was his name?"

You share a dumbfounded look with Nick.

"He didn't tell you his name?" Sergeant Wilson says, skeptical.

You shake your head in unison with the student. The cop shakes his own head, then steps away from the ambulance, lowers the notebook and brings up his radio.

"Check with campus administration, get me a name on the guy running this 'experiment,' will ya?" he says to the mic.

"Already got it," the radio crackles in response. "Doctor Julius Petri, Human Infinite Technologies."

The name doesn't ring any bells, but there's something implacable on the sergeant's face.

He turns to you and says, "I think we better get a statement down at the station, just to be safe."

The observation room is cool, in a "*so this is what it really looks like*" sort of way. Not too far from the television facsimile, you sit at a metal table, with two empty chairs on the opposite side. This isn't an interrogation; instead, you were given a pad of paper and asked to recount all you could about the experiment and your companions.

Most likely, Nick is in an identical room and they're hoping to compare your statements against one another. You look up at the two-way mirror and watch your reflection hold up and shake the notepad.

"Done!" you announce.

Setting down the notepad, you wait. And…wait. They must be talking to Nick right now. You let out a sigh and reread your testimony. Yep, it's all there.

Out of sheer boredom, you twirl the pen in your fingers, trying to do that trick where it does a full rotation around the back of your hand and lands back in your forefingers. One rotation, nailed it. Two rotations? No problem. Three, four, five rotations. *Ten?*

The pen twirls around your fingers with no sign of slowing. You realize you aren't even moving your fingers anymore, the pen is just orbiting your hand, almost as if—

The door opens and Sergeant Wilson walks in with two coffees. He looks down as the pen slaps him in the chest and falls to the floor. You look to your hands; the pen is gone. Did you throw it?

Wilson sets the coffee cups on the table, then takes a step back to pick up the pen. He seats himself, pushes a coffee towards you, sets the pen down, and grabs the notebook to read your testimony.

While he goes over it, you stare at the pen at the center of the table. It's an ordinary ballpoint, resting motionlessly, yet you feel oddly…connected. You picture the pen rolling toward the policeman—and it does!

Wilson reaches out to stop the pen, then sets down the notepad. He grabs the table at the edges and jostles to test the balance, but the legs remain steady. In his shaking of the table, his coffee cup tips over the edge and starts to fall.

You reach out and grab the cup in reflex, not spilling a drop.

"Nice catch," Sergeant Wilson says, brow furrowed.

You lean over to set the cup back where it was, but the original position is just out of arm's reach. That's odd. Confused, you stare at the spot on the table, ringed by brown liquid. How did…?

Wilson intercepts and takes the beverage in hand. "Boy genius next door said the exact same thing as you," he says, sipping his coffee. "We'll look for this Ms. Woodall, but I doubt she's connected, either."

Looking into your own coffee cup, you attempt the same "rolling trick" you just did with the pen. Ripples wash over the liquid, like storm winds rushing over Mercury Bay. *How in the*—

"You three are extremely lucky," Wilson continues. "Julius Petri was an alias used to rent the lab and—"

Coffee *shoots* out of the cup like a geyser!

Sergeant Wilson jumps up out of his seat, and you do the same, but when you rise, all three seats slide away and slam against the walls. The notepad, pen, and coffee cups all fly away from you and coffee rains from the ceiling.

"S-stay here. I'll get help," Wilson stammers. He runs from the room, slams the door shut, and you can hear the lock engage from the other side.

- ➢ I have to get out of here! Go to page 127
- ➢ It'll be okay, just breathe. I haven't done anything wrong. Go to page 179

The Shocker

Mercury City is a large enough metropolis that nothing short of an Act of God would shut the whole grid down, and since you have neither an EMP generator nor the superpower to create earthquakes, you'll have to settle for destroying the substation nearest the warehouse district.

The electricity of Power Substation Six crackles audibly on the lines above. Catherine smashes through the concrete walls of the power station as easily as if they were merely an illusion. In her world, perhaps they are. A danger sign falls off the wall and you step over it on your way in. It reads, "DANGER, HIGH VOLTAGE—RISK OF DEATH."

You're reminded of the experiment, in a way, of your own origins and the excitement in that lab. There's just so much…*power.*

That is, until Catherine starts to rip the transformers out of their bases, pulling them down as if she were merely weeding an unruly garden. Only these are more than just thistles.

The station groans as she pulls it apart. She hurls a transistor through the control room just as the first power line strikes out at her, like a viper in the grass. Catherine seizes, tensing up as the electric current overtakes her.

You telekinetically *grab* the power lines to pull them off her, but the damage is done. Both to the station and to your partner. This was the station's death rattle, and the silence left in its wake is tremendously unsettling. Catherine lies on the ground, not moving.

When you rush over to check on her, you find she's not breathing, either. Her heart has stopped. You pound on her chest, but CPR is useless. She's like a steel girder.

Can you "shock" her back? The power's off. You've got to bring her to a hospital; they'll know what to do. You try to drag her, but it's impossible. Physically, mentally, or even a combination of both—she won't budge!

How the hell is she so heavy? And if she is, why doesn't crush the sidewalk when she walks?

"Wowzers," a voice says from behind. You turn to see Nick, who's just come in the entrance Catherine created in the concrete wall. He stares at the destruction with awe. He puts one finger up to his lips.

"If you're attacking the power station nearest the warehouse, you were trying to 'kill' the Supersoldier lab, yes? This has to be one of the dumbest stunts…." he says, shaking his head.

"Nick, she's dying!" you yell.

"I can see that," he says. "If you're wondering, that's irony. He could've never hurt her, but by trying to stop Droakam, she kills herself."

"Stopping *you!*" you shout, your emotions getting the better of you.

"*Moi?*" he says, feigning insult.

"Can you figure out a way to save her?"

He bobbles his head from side to side. "I think I'd rather spin it. How's this sound? Diamond's partner—we'll need to get you a name—betrays and kills her. I show up too late to save her, but quick enough to bring the bastard to justice."

"Nick, please."

"Ooh! Even better. Diamond goes nuts! That would fit with the security footage of her storming in here and that near-miss with Droakam at the bank today. Then you and I team up to bring her down. I like it."

"You think I'll let you get away with that? Villainizing her?"

"I believe you mean 'vilifying' and yes, I do. Okay, so you turned off my computer. Is that all you think I am? I have this fun little toy, and it runs on batteries." He holds up a handheld walkie-talkie radio. "I called some friends. And if you weren't in shock, blinded by panic, you might have noticed that the cavalry has arrived."

You blink, and stop to listen. Above you, a police helicopter whirs. Several laser-sights shine their target upon your chest. By challenging Nick, you've played directly into his hand. He wins this round.

THE END

Show Your Hand

Dr. Reader's eyes grow wide, then go dark. It hurts to see how easy it was for Baxter to kill, but you gave your permission. No time to wallow in self-pity—time for a plan! Your superhuman mind works on overdrive, and in only a few seconds, you know exactly how you'll beat them.

"It won't work," the Experi-mentor says.

"You...you can read minds too?" you say.

"What, did you think I was just going to stand here, powerless as you kill my colleagues? I gave myself *all* of their powers, you fool!"

"Enough!" Nick roars.

The college student rushes toward the Experi-mentor, but Dr. Mind-Control puts a hand on her temple and Nick changes course. With murder in his eyes, he rushes right at you.

You don't stand a chance.

THE END

Sinking Feeling

You rush out to the docks, and indeed, *The Son of Jupiter* is still anchored in Mercury Bay.

"Let's steal a boat," you say.

"Not just yet. How about a quick scouting mission, hmmm? Save us some time," Catherine says, tapping some commands into her tech-glove.

"Good plan," Nick says, rising into the air. "Be right back."

"Stinger and Venom will accompany you," Catherine says as the two flying minion bots rise.

"Did you name all your gear?" you ask.

"Of course."

With that, Nick and the two bots fly over to the mega-yacht. It's a long few minutes of silent waiting, but Catherine puts on a pair of homemade Google-glasses that enable her to watch through the perspective of her minions.

"Nothing is worse than being an ignored super-genius," Catherine sighs. "Oh, Cassandra, we will watch as Troy burns…"

"You're saying he's not there?"

"The whole ship is abandoned; take a look."

She offers the glasses, but a beeping on your belt draws your attention away. It appears the belt-buckle on your super-suit is actually a high-tech pager. When you disconnect the pager, an armored cover slides back to reveal an LCD screen beneath. It reads: DISTRESS SIGNAL ACTIVE: RETURN TO HQ

"I think Droakam's in trouble…"

"They were waiting for us to leave!" she cries, furiously recalling the flying robots.

"NICK!!!" you boom.

➢ *Hurry back to the warehouse!* Go to page 329

Sin & Vice

A burning hole in your pocket, you enter the casino ready to turn your spare change into millions of dollars. All you have to do is find the right roulette table, bet on black, and then use your mind to ensure that the ball lands where it's supposed to. Easy as pie, you'll double your money. THEN—once you've honed your skills enough to hit the bull's-eye—you can take your winnings, bet it on your favorite number, and the payout will be somewhere in the six figures.

If you've got the gall to let it ride, you'll be a millionaire before the cocktail waitress has time to serve you a drink. Time to practice your "golly gee" face—you don't want it to look rigged.

"Well, look who it is…" a voice calls from behind. It's Nick from the experiment.

"Hey," you say, turning around.

"Hey yourself. Feeling *lucky* after our brush with death?" he asks, indicating the casino's surroundings.

Planet Mercury is a grand palace, built on the debt of losers in a shameless display of opulence. Its intergalactic theme boasts some impressive planetary models—which serve as chandeliers and hang from the high-vaulted, domed roof, painted as a brilliant starscape.

"Say, after the explosion, did you feel any…different?" Nick adds.

➢ Lie to Nick. Tell him you don't know what he's talking about.
 Go to page 114
➢ Show off your new power; maybe he'll do the same? Go to page 32

Sky Battle!

You *lift* Nick off his feet by his neck, drawing him in close. "Don't fuck with me," you growl.

Then you *fling* him over the edge. You'd probably have to deal with your fellow test-subjects sooner or later, so it's good to be done with the kid. He mentioned something about Catherine, right? She's on her way, he said.

Just on cue, she smashes through the rooftop security door, exploding it into a thousand fragments. She pauses, looking for signs of you or Nick.

Might as well get the drop on her. You reach out and *grab* her neck, but when you *lift*—nothing. Might as well be tugging on the building's main water line. She's not only incredibly strong, she's incredibly dense and heavy. You can't lift her, and you can't hurt her. Better try something different.

"Over here!" you shout.

She turns toward you, her eyes full of hatred. Just because you own a casino? What a black-and-white view of the world, Catherine. Perhaps you should introduce her to a bit of red.

Like a raging bull, she charges at you. You wait for the last second, then blast your way into the air—*toro toro!* There's no way she can stop on a dime, not with that much momentum. Over the edge it is!

Yet with incredibly fast reflexes, she makes a superhuman jump and sends that momentum into the air after you. In reflex, you *blast* into her, but it's like trying to use a fan to blow a meteor off-course. Still, there's an equal and opposite reaction, and you *push* yourself away.

With a barrel-roll, you keep free of her grasp. She plummets over the side of the building like a rock just as Nick flies up from the abyss!

Those oversized boots? Jet-boots. Rocket flame comes from them and propels the wunderkind after you. He has his right fist extended, flying like *Superman*, and his left hand activates some kind of control panel on the beefy right forearm gauntlet.

Before he has the chance to activate his device, you grab his body with the power of mind and *smash* him down against the rooftop. He cracks the concrete and skips across the surface in a painful display.

An incredible *crash* sounds from below and you look over the side. There's a crater on the street, but no sign of Catherine. She got up after *that*? No, wait—movement catches your eye as she makes an incredible leap from the nearest skyscraper, like a tick bounding off the back of a dog.

She smashes into the casino about a third of the way up. The building shakes slightly. Only a moment later, she bounds across the expanse once more, this time bursting through the fortieth floor of the opposite building.

An electronic reverberation draws your attention back to the casino rooftop. You turn to see Nick aiming at you. The gauntlet hums with life, and the wrist section glows a white-hot blue. Then a pulse bursts out in a ring of energy, but you dive behind a ventilation cube and the blast sizzles out before it can harm you.

You leap back up and take control of Nick's body with your telekinesis, keeping his arms crossed over his chest so the gauntlet weapons can't be aimed at you.

315

A growling roar over your shoulder announces Catherine's return, and you pivot with Nick in your mental grasp to swing him against Catherine like a hurled discus. The college student's motorcycle helmet cracks against the invulnerable woman and his battered body bounces off and over the edge of the building.

She lands against the helicopter platform and slams a fist into the concrete to stop her momentum. The whole building shudders in response. You stand before her, awaiting her next move, ready for her to charge again.

Catherine takes the helicopter's tail in her hands and lifts the aircraft like a child's plastic toy. She brings it down; an oversized flyswatter, and you barely dodge, assisting your leap with a telekinetic boost.

It's an ugly maneuver on both ends. The helicopter crumbles, shearing at the tail and bringing down a section of the roof. The main body stays intact, but the bubble canopy and rotor blades are completely destroyed. You bounce off the roof like Nick did earlier, only you've got no body armor to temper the impact. Your skin screams out in protest.

No time to take stock of your injuries. Instead, you *fly* into the air just as Catherine lifts the main carriage of the helicopter and hurls it at you with terrible speed and accuracy. The world slows down, adrenaline dosing your brain with a survival edge, and you see the path laid out with perfect clarity.

You fly *through* the cockpit, navigating in and back out of the mangled machine and avoiding the obstacle altogether. Time speeds back up and the helicopter *explodes* against the next building over. Michael Bay would be proud.

Catherine's eyes dart up to the sky, giving Nick's position away. Without even turning, you mentally grab his arms and aim the incoming gauntlet blast directly at Catherine.

When the blue-white ring hits her flesh, her muscles seize and she falls prone with an incredible thud; unconscious. You turn back to see horror on Nick's face, his wide eyes shining out through the crack in his helmet.

"I thought I told you to fuck off," you say.

Then you *grab* him by the neck and *twist* until there's a sickening crack and his body goes limp. The jet boots, still active, propel his body haphazardly like a bottle-rocket on the Fourth of July.

To accompany his fireworks, a dozen red laser-sights appear on your chest. You let out a sigh of exasperation, then look over to the roof access doorway. The Mercury PD SWAT team stands at the ready.

Well, you defeated your fellow "supers," but you can't take on the whole of humanity, not alone. They bring you down, but boy oh boy, was that a blaze of glory. Well-fought!

THE END

Snippets

Just as you reach the other two test subjects, they each gasp in a lungful of air like they've suddenly surfaced from the farthest depths of the ocean. They seem confused, but unharmed. You help them to their feet, waiting patiently for them to get a grip on the situation.

"What happened?" Catherine mutters.

"Has anyone seen the scientist?" Nick asks, stepping off his own platform.

You look around, but there is only rubble. "We're lucky to be alive," you say.

Catherine stumbles off her platform base, her movements wobbly and unsure, like a newborn foal. Shock, most likely. "My son," she says. "I need to go pick up my son from school."

Nick looks at you, but neither of you stop her from leaving. Wordlessly, you turn toward the rubble. So much damage….

And that's not the only thing; you feel *different* after the experiment. That energy is still within you, but it's everywhere else too. You reach out toward a basketball-size piece of what was once a laboratory wall. There's a connection, surrounding and binding you together; the debris shimmies and reaches back, and before you realize it—the rock tumbles off the pile and rolls toward you!

Wait…did you just do that?

The sound of police sirens grows louder and invades your thoughts. You could leave now, tell the college student to do the same, and none would be the wiser. If there really is something different about you, maybe it's best to keep your anonymity. But if the police find out that you were involved in this catastrophic accident—where it looks like someone may have been killed—it could put you in a bad light if you flee the scene now.

- ➢ No, stay. You've done nothing wrong, and it's the right thing to do.
  Go to page 307
- ➢ Tell Nick you've "got a bad feeling about this," then speed on home.
  Go to page 72

Some "Thing" Different

In panic, you run—literally—from the scene of the accident. Why "play it cool" when the world around you looks like the result of a terrorist attack? And you aren't the only one sprinting across campus. Students, teachers, staff, and visitors of all kinds run from the site of the explosion.

There's no way you could explain what just happened to the cops—you can't even explain it to yourself! A building just *exploded* around you, and you're completely fine? And that scientist is just…gone. Vaporized. What about those other two? Are they dead? If so, that would make you the only suspect. And without a believable story or alibi? No, thanks.

You suddenly stop and look around. Somehow, your apartment building is right in front of you. Did you just run all the way here? That's gotta be at least twenty miles and you're not even winded. A cab pulls away from the building—maybe in your shock you took the cab, but don't remember—that seems more likely, doesn't it?

Shaking off the confusion, you step in and check your mailbox, just like any other normal day. You jiggle the key—damn thing always sticks—to no avail. So you twist harder. The key *snaps* off inside your mailbox. Damn it! In frustration, you *pound* against the box with the meat of your fist.

The entire thing collapses.

Blinking with disbelief, you back away. The whole wall of mailboxes is dented in like a wrecking ball just hit it. Your hand is unblemished, not a scratch, and doesn't hurt at all. That felt like punching a paper bag.

You turn and frantically press the elevator call button, but on the third press, the button stays jammed in the wall. So you sprint up the stairs, taking entire landings in one bound, past a terrified old Mrs. Jankis and up to your fourth-floor apartment.

When you slam the door shut, you can actually hear the door jamb *crack* in response. *What the hell is happening?!* Deep breaths; calm yourself. In and out—slowly. There you go. Everything's going to be okay. Take it slow….

Your stomach gives a Tyrannosaur growl and you realize you're hungrier than you've ever been. The phrase "hungry enough to eat a horse" doesn't seem like hyperbole right now. Getting something to eat…yeah…that'll help you think more clearly.

➤ Start draining grocery stores in the dead of night like the *Chupacabra* of Whole Foods. Go to page 146

➤ Pop the collar on a thick coat, pull down a baseball cap, and inconspicuously go to town on the all-you-can-eat joint down the street. Go to page 44

➤ Push the couch against the door, keep the TV off, and eat whatever's in the pantry. Go to page 48

Something Fishy

Anyone who's grown up in Mercury City knows you don't go to the warehouse district after dark. Once the dockworkers punch out at 5 o'clock and the last respectable man has gone home, the harbor becomes a port of call to drug runners and smugglers. Pimps gather their whores to offer alleyway R&R for sailors while their narcotic cargo is unloaded.

Essentially, once the sun sets on Mercury Bay, the warehouse district becomes the biggest, most bustling criminal economy on the eastern seaboard. Which makes it the perfect place for you to bust some skulls and intimidate the low-level bosses into getting you a meet-'n'-greet higher up.

But when you arrive, you're greeted with an unexpected sight—one of the warehouses is on fire. More surprising still, it's being robbed. An idling truck in one of the alleyways catches your attention. Are you being followed?

Squinting for a better look, you see it's a long black SUV. Fire reflects off its darkly tinted windows. Anger billowing in your gut, you march forward toward the car. The headlights flip on and the driver peels out; they know they've been made.

You take off in a sprint after the SUV, and your legs pump with a ferocity you've never known. Soon you're actually sprinting *faster* than the car, which fishtails and squeals around a corner into an alley between warehouses, hoping to lose you on the turn. In instinct, you *leap* high, kick off a dumpster, and end up on a rooftop.

Exhilarated, you push forward and drop down into the alley—just in front of the SUV! Bracing yourself, you bring your shoulder down and *plow* forward.

The front of the vehicle collapses in a terrible shriek of metal, while the rear flies into the air under the force of its own momentum. The SUV tumbles over you, lands on its roof, and skids to a stop further down the alley.

You calmly walk toward the car. The wheels turn in the night air, gradually slowing. When you arrive, you rip the driver's door off its hinges and toss it away before pulling the driver from the car.

You give a quick glance to see if anyone else is inside—but it's just him. He wears a black suit, a white button-up shirt that you're sure was pristine before you crashed his car, and a handgun at the waist.

The man coughs blood, looks up at you with an odd grin, and says, "You're perfect."

Then he breathes his last. In the breast of the suit, there's an FBI badge that identifies the man as Special Agent Brendan Droakam, FBI, Supersoldier Unit. Great, you're being trailed by the *Men in Black* and you just killed one. Better dispose of the body….

You buckle the agent back into the driver's seat, then lift the SUV over your head and walk it down to the docks. When you make it to the water's edge, you hurl the vehicle an impressive thirty yards, where it sinks into the briny sea. If the dock is deep enough to house ships, it should be deep enough to hide the SUV. Dusting off your hands, you turn back.

"Guess I should've known it was one of you two," Catherine says.

Though she's in plainclothes, she has an odd circuitry-laden glove that extends up her left forearm and wears a futuristic-looking rifle slung over her right shoulder. Two RC-drones fly near her head and three more robots roll along the dock around her alligator skin boots.

"I didn't start the fire," you say.

"No? And I suppose you didn't just throw a federal agent into the Bay?"

"How'd you know he....?"

"License plates," Catherine says. "I mean, I'm all for a smaller government, but I can't say I approve of your methods."

"What're you gonna do about it?" you laugh.

"Allow me to share a theory. I think all our powers are based upon density, or perhaps, a rewriting of the physical laws of density. Me? I've got a super-dense mind, sort of like a hard drive upgrade. I can fit a lot more up here, and it runs much faster. Nick? I think he can manipulate density. He makes things float when they shouldn't. And you? You're much denser than anything else on the planet, just short of falling through the floor when you walk on it."

"Is there a point to all this?"

"There is. As someone for whom walls crumble away, there's not much chance of my weapons doing any harm, right?" She taps some commands into her tech-glove and her robot drones move toward you.

"Right...."

"But by that same token, you don't enjoy the benefits of being as dense as the average human. Not anymore, at least. So, according to my theory, you're too dense to swim. You'll just sink to the bottom as fast as if you were falling through the air."

You look down at the dock, realizing that beneath these planks of wood countless fathoms await. Mercury Bay isn't sloping like a swimming beach; that's why it makes an ideal shipyard. It's essentially an underwater cliffside. Catherine's minion bots circle your ankles.

"Yet you still need to breathe oxygen to survive, do you not?"

Your eyes dart back up just in time to see Catherine punch a new command into her tech-glove. The minion bots explode in a self-destruct sequence, blowing the dock apart and dropping you into the ocean below.

Exactly as predicted, you fall to the sea floor, accelerating at an astounding 9.8 m/s^2. It will take less than three minutes before you drown; you can't possibly hope to make it to the surface by then.

THE END

Soon I Will Be Invincible!

Nick lowers himself and slowly floats down to the street next to you. "Where to next?" he asks. He's eerily calm, as if he doesn't even realize he's just murdered dozens of people.

Your-Catherine has stolen her doppelganger's cloak and adds it to her super-villain ensemble. The powerless villains once known as Drillbit and Shadow Priestess crawl along the ground in an agony only known by those who've been thoroughly violated. You remember the feeling all too well.

"Go now, and stay hidden," you say. "Soon, I'll return to rule this world, and there will be a place for you in my empire. I will not forget your sacrifice."

"How magnanimous. Another nice quality for a god," your-Catherine says.

"Let's go. I need to reset the device so we can get our final powers."

"So…back to the power station?" Nick says. Then with a grin he adds, "No problem."

He *lifts* the three of you with his newly enhanced power of mind and flies back into the sky.

As you soar across Mercury City, Nick yells, "Oh my God, I'm starving! Is there enough food at the power station, or should we fly-thru Tacos Banditos on the way?"

"There should be enough, but trust me, it never gets any easier. I'm always hungry!"

Catherine says, "We need a world where you have telekinesis, but perhaps you can set the parameters to a universe where things aren't going so great for you. If you're already vulnerable, we can get the drop on your alternate self."

"That's too amorphous. The criterion needs something concrete to search for."

"A specific location, then," the telekinetic genius says. "If you were hiding out, where would you go?"

With your own super-genius mind working on overtime, you say, "I know the perfect spot."

So where's the one place no one would ever look for you? Perhaps somewhere from childhood? Having grown up inland, away from the hustle and bustle of downtown Mercury City, you have a spot no one else knows about. If your parents knew how much time you spent in a cavern—your own fortress of solitude—they'd have forbidden it, so you never told another soul.

Now, as you stand in the center of the darkened cave, you feel a dark foreboding where once there was only comfort. There's something particularly dastardly about hunting yourself at the one place in the world you ever truly felt safe.

"This beats the hell out of my old treehouse," Nick says.

"Open the portal. We may be traveling to other worlds, but time doesn't stand still. One more power and I get my son…."

You nod to Catherine and start to manipulate the staff until it finds a seam in existence and a purple gateway opens inside the cavern. Catherine adjusts *Widowsilk* and steps through. Nick flies through the portal after her. You mentally prepare to defeat another alter-ego, to see your own face scream in agony for the last time. After a moment's hesitation, you step through the portal and wave hello to yourself. This-you cowers near a dead campfire, thoroughly racked with terror.

"Where's the rest of your team?" you ask.

"I—we didn't..." this-you replies, still in shock.

"Why does that keep happening?" says Catherine with a sigh.

"I'd say it's because given the infinite eventualities, going our separate ways seems the most likely form of entropy," you say.

"I understand *why*, I was simply commiserating," she retorts.

"Christ, we need to find the genius-me so I can finally understand what the hell you two are saying," Nick says.

"Where did you come from? How did you find me? What do you want?" this-you babbles.

"Another universe, duh," Nick says. "Even I get that much."

You smile. "How did we find you? I tried to think, 'Where's the one place I'd go, the one place where no one would ever look for me?' Well, nobody but *you* would look for you here."

"And what do we want? Why, your powers of course. Now, this may sting," Catherine says.

She fires Widowsilk at this Earth's version of you. As she releases the trigger, this-you lets out a painful cry and falls prone, helpless. She then adjusts a setting on the weapon, turns and shoots you with the stolen superpower as a new gift.

You've gotten your third power—telekinesis. Combined with super-strength, durability, and the pinnacle of genius, you're the first trifecta of superhumanity: a Roman god. Catherine can match your genius, and Nick your prowess, but with all three gifts you're the heavyweight champion and they're mere contenders.

You *feel* the world in a way you'd never imagined, a physical link between you and all that surrounds you. All that you can perceive sits and waits for your mental commands. You focus on the link between your mind and your alter-ego.

"Fantastic," you say. Reaching an arm out, you *lift* your doppelganger using only the power of mind.

As you see your mirror image struggle, you think, *this world's version of me is here hiding out, so circumstances must be dire.* And now, without any superpowers to defend with...perhaps you should put yourself out of your misery?

Nick sighs impatiently. "C'mon, let's go find the other two."

Or perhaps this is your best shot at taking out Nick and Catherine before they decide to turn on you?

➤ One universe isn't enough to contain you! Destroy Nick and Catherine once and for all. Go to page 199
➤ Stick with the plan; see it through to the end. Go to page 166

The Sorcerer's Apprentice

Without hesitation, you *reach* into the living room and raise the couch into the air. Whoa…

It's heavy, and you can feel the toll, but it floats above your living room floor—ick, you *really* need to clean under there.

Donning your mental wizard's cap, you summon the broom and dustbin from the closet. Flailing your arms through the air, conducting the orchestra in your head, you start to clean the apartment. A bead of sweat rolls down your forehead from the effort, but the couch floats near the ceiling while the broom sweeps beneath it. Whew, you could use a drink.

You keep your left arm outstretched toward the broom and couch, then reach your right hand out to the fridge. The door shudders and the couch quivers in the air, so you double your focus and *think* hard. With a mental picture of where your favorite drink awaits, you hold your breath and use your telekinesis. Ready? Go!

The door pops open and the beverage flies into your hand at top speed. Unprepared for so much so fast, you stumble back and lose your concentration. The couch falls on top of the broom, snapping it in half. You fall over the back of the couch, but manage to keep the drink upright. Okay, apparently there *are* limits to what you can do.

Probably should spend the rest of the night floating a feather duster across the bookshelves while Cheetos line up before you. Where's the remote? Ugh, it's over by the TV. Guess you have to get up and walk over—oh wait, never again.

In the middle of the night, you wake up to use the restroom. What a kooky dream. Superpowers? Telekinesis? Haha, so ridiculous. That's when you realize you're floating on the way to the toilet. Holy shit, you're *flying*! Or at least "lifting yourself" with your powers, so yeah, for all intents and purposes—you're able to fly.

Well, looks like you're done sleeping. Time to test this new skill out! Out the window and into the city. After relieving yourself, of course. You're not a fucking pigeon. Once you've used the toilet, you head back out into your living room and open the window to your fourth-floor apartment. The cool night air rushes in and your spine tingles in anticipation. The blood rushes out of your hands and feet. Are you really about to jump out a fourth-floor window?

Yep. You leap out the window, *grasp* your body with your mind and carry yourself through the air with the power of thought. Arms spread out wide like a bird or a plane, you soar through the air, high up over the buildings. Moonlight glints off Mercury Bay in the distance.

This is amazing! Far beyond exhilarating. Whatever fear of heights you may have had in the past melts away under the feeling of complete control. You fly around for another hour before mental exhaustion sets in.

➢ *Return to the apartment and fall into a deep, fatigue-induced sleep.* Go to page 369

Spare Me the Spandex

"I'm in!" Nick says.

"Yeah, well, not me. You two have fun," Catherine says, shaking her head.

"With these powers we can *help* people," you say. "How can you possibly turn your back on that?"

Catherine folds her arms across her chest. "All I said was no capes and *ka-pow!* for me. I will do good with...with this gift. But punching criminals? Hell, as an intelligent, female Republican, I could be President within the next three election cycles."

Nick grins. "But if you're suddenly intelligent, why are you still a Republican? Boom! Up top!" he puts his hand up for a high-five.

Catherine simply sighs. "I don't think you know what you're getting into, but I wish you the best of luck. I really do."

"Well, at the very least, you're the only one who knows what we can do—I need to know that you're going to keep it to yourself," you say.

She glares at you now. "No worries there, *champ*. I'm no narc. You can go around crushing all the pots in Mercury City and I won't say a peep."

By the time you leave Catherine's, the sun has set. Your stomach gurgles fiercely.

"Tomorrow, we get costumes, then we save the world."

Nick nods, his eyes groggy, and the two of you go your separate ways. After you've stuffed yourself with more food than you thought you could eat, sleep comes quickly.

The next morning, after an all-you-can-eat brunch, you meet Nick at a downtown costume shop. A mannequin dressed as the *Phantom of the Opera* greets you outside the downtown costume shop and a chime goes off as you enter. "Can I help you?" the store clerk asks.

"We're just browsing," you say. Then, considering what your new appetite has done to your budget, you add, "Do you have a clearance section?"

The clerk—who wears all-black and has orange/bleached hair—leads you toward the back of the store. The cheapest costumes are simple t-shirts, from the "ironic" tuxedo print to the classic skeleton-on-black-tee pattern. One rack holds a set of superhero shirts; a *Superman* design catches your eye. That ought to advertise the super-strength!

"What do you think?" you ask, holding it up. "Maybe I can write BER on one side of the 'S' and ERK on the other and call myself *Berserk*?"

Nick looks across the aisle and shakes his head. "Very douchebag frat. Besides, isn't the point to hide our identities?"

"I could put some glasses on."

"That makes no sense."

"Good point," you say, before putting the shirt back.

A minute later Nick comes around the corner dressed like a giant yellow Twinkie with miner goggles on. "Get it? I can be *Minion* because I'm sort of like your sidekick."

324

"Please tell me you're joking."

"Uhhh, I said 'get it' first. That means it's a joke."

You turn to the clerk. "Do you have any partner costumes?"

"Like couples stuff?" he asks, scratching his nose near a piercing.

"*No,*" you say in unison with Nick.

"Well, if you want to stick in clearance, the *Breaking Bad* was very hip last year."

He shows you to a mannequin in a full-body hazmat suit, rubber boots and gloves, a breathing mask covering the face and eyes. It's a high-quality costume; even the mask is functional.

"Not a bad look if we want to 'clean up' town," Nick says.

"It's currently on a buy-one get-one sale," the clerk adds.

"We'll take it," you say.

➢ Pay, suit up, and hit the streets! Something is bound to pop up.
Go to page 16

➢ While you're at it, ask the clerk if he knows where you can find some crime.
Go to page 190

Splitting Headache

"I'll hit the casino, you two do the yacht."

"No way!" Catherine growls. "The casino was my idea. I seriously doubt he's on the boat, and I'm going to be there when Bloodnight goes down. You gave me your word."

"Also," Nick says, raising his hand. "I want to go with you. No offense, Catherine."

"Fine, I'll take the agent."

"What? No, I'm staying here to coordinate. You might need law enforcement backup and—"

"We get it, you're the Shadow-hand," Nick says. "Besides, you need to be able to deny involvement, right? In case things go wrong?"

"Well..." Droakam says, looking away.

"What a bunch of cowards I've teamed up with," Catherine says.

The three of them erupt in a confabulation of argument, and you can't even get a word in edgewise. *"ENOUGH!!!"* you shout, loud enough to rattle the crates on the shelves. All eyes turn toward you.

You say, "Fine, we're not splitting up. All three of us are going to..."

- ➢ *"The Son of Jupiter.* They took the blood samples to the yacht, so we're at least getting those back." Go to page 313
- ➢ "The Planet Mercury Casino. Even if he's not there, we're letting the public know that he's a target." Go to page 139

Still a Fairly Tall Building….

You join the team and hand over your portal-creating staff of awesomeness. The Experi-mentor doesn't just hide it—he pulverizes it. Guess he's pretty paranoid at the thought of one of his creations stealing the device and running amok through the multiverse. Speaking of paranoid thoughts, you're fairly certain there's another presence inside your mind while you're working. Maybe some kind of telepathic monitor? Granted, you could create another staff anytime you felt like it, so you write it off as just another layer of precaution on the scientist's part.

Still, this is a pretty sweet gig. You're designing new superhumans! Guys who can talk to dolphins? Check. Climate Warriors who put the earth back in balance? Check. Everything from people who can build new homes with their bare, super-human hands, to people who can predict and prevent future catastrophes.

You win…mostly. Life is grand for most of humanity, especially as more and more of them join the ranks of superhumanity. But, eventually, it starts to become a "no one is special because everyone is special" kind of world. It's not the worst thing that could happen, but you can't help but ask yourself "What if?" Could you have done more good in the world you forsake?

THE END

Super Apathy

You can hear the woman's screams turn into gurgles as you round the corner away from the scene. *Poor life choices, toots. I'm not getting stabbed just because you thought it was cool to cut classes and found a quick way to make a few bucks.*

Sirens suddenly echo off the surrounding buildings drawing your attention up ahead: An entire floor of a skyscraper is ablaze. Thirteen stories up, black smoke billows out and curls up the sides of the building.

"There's someone up there!" a tourist shouts, lowering his binoculars against his travel vest. "He's gonna jump."

- ➢ There may be a crowd, but I'm the only one who can save him!
  Go to page 351
- ➢ Gross. I don't want to be around to see that. Go to page 244

Super-Fiends

You rush back to the warehouse HQ, Nick and Catherine trailing on your heels. With brash intensity, you *smash* through the warehouse doors, ignoring Catherine's cries for discreet action. But what awaits you inside brings you to a screeching halt.

"Now *that's* how you make an entrance!" a familiar man's voice calls out.

Agent Droakam sits bloodied and tied to a chair, while the man stands nearby with a hand on the agent's shoulder. The man's white lab coat flutters open to reveal an "Ex" emblazoned on his chest.

"The Experi-mentor?" Nick says, entering the warehouse, his voice dry from shock.

"So we meet again!" the scientist says with a grin.

Behind him stand four menacing figures: A short, Korean woman in a black pantsuit with soulless eyes. A tall, muscular, athletic man (despite his age) with smooth ebony skin, head shaved and a thin mustache. A slim man of similar age with bronzed skin and coal-black hair—combed back for the "mobster" look. And a large, broad man with a Texas ten-gallon hat and the face of Chief Joseph.

"Allow me to introduce you to Ms. Su-Young and Misters Stockton, Halifax, and—"

"Nelson Bloodnight," Catherine growls.

The casino boss simply tugs down on the brim of his hat, grinning like an imp.

"You're working with *them?*" you say.

"My experiments aren't cheap," the scientist says. "Or legal, strictly speaking. I lost everything in that explosion and Mr. Bloodnight was all too happy to step in as my benefactor. Although, 'lost everything' isn't quite accurate, is it? I still have you, my magnificent creations!"

"Why didn't you come to us? Agent Droakam has a whole division of the FBI devoted to superhumans. You could have worked with us, not against us."

"In another life, perhaps. But it's too late for that now, isn't it? Besides, a division of the FBI is too small for my way of thinking. No, we shall rule over this world as gods, and Mercury City shall be our new *Pantheopolis*!" The whole room looks at his manic outburst with astonishment. He smiles, then continues more reasonably, "I know, the first rule of being a supervillain is 'never tell the heroes your plan,' but I'm hoping you won't be swayed by one man's jingoistic wet dreams."

He pats Agent Droakam on the shoulder. "Go to hell," the agent says.

The Experi-mentor laughs with glee. Evil glee.

"You really have no idea what you're up against, do you?" Nick says. "WMD here will eat you guys for breakfast. Literally. Bullets don't scare us any more than threats."

"Au contraire, mon frère! I've been a busy beaver, and *damned* if I haven't re-created the experiment results. I couldn't have done it so quickly without your blood samples, of course. Each of my friends here a have a brand-spanking-new superpower derived from your blood, WMD, if that's what you insist on calling yourself. Don't feel too bad, Nikolai, round two will be based on your sample."

"It's 'Murica," Nick says. "And you'll never get away with this."

Nelson Bloodnight steps forward. "We already have. Join us…or die."

What will happen? Will our heroes falter in their resolve? Will The Experi-mentor achieve his mad-scientist goals? And if it comes to blows, what fantastical new powers might these villains possess? What manner of deadly fate awaits The Freedom Fighters? Find out next time on…SUPERPOWERED!

For no particular reason other than to have a cliffhanger:
Go to page 98

Superior Intel(lect)

Faster and faster you fly, until the wind proves too powerful. Your eyes are streaming tears and you can barely see where you're going. This is like driving seventy miles-per-hour on the interstate with your head out the window.

Barreling in on the bank, you bring your hands together and focus all your psychic energy on a sudden stop. The resultant *sonic clap* sends a shockwave across the pavement. Onlookers fall off their feet. *Well, that was cool.*

You slowly descend to the pavement as the crowd rises. Cell phones and video cameras all on you.

"Stay where you are!" a voice booms over a megaphone. It's Sergeant Wilson, the policeman who brought you to the station, and his mouth goes slack when he recognizes you. He puts out a hand to stop the other patrolmen, but their hands stay close to their service weapons.

"What do you want?" he asks cautiously.

"I'm here to help. Remember that FBI agent? He's en route. We're here to bring that woman in the costume back with us."

"Be my guest!" he says, shaking his head.

A squeal of car tires draws your attention back to the police barricade. Agent Droakam hops out of his black government SUV and rushes over. "What's the situation?" he asks.

"Pal, if you're taking responsibility, have at it. We want nothing to do with whatever the hell's going on here," Wilson says.

The crowd erupts with cheers. The three of you look to the front of the bank, where hostages stream out and into the arms of EMTs and crisis-relief personnel. Then you see Catherine in her Diamond costume, dragging four bank robbers—two in each hand—out the front of the bank. She tosses them in a heap, then dusts off her hands. With an enormous grin, she double-fist-pumps the air and the crowd goes wild.

"YOU!" Catherine roars. She moves through the barricades and the police respond nervously—weapons drawn in an uncertain showdown.

"Stay where you are!" Droakam commands.

She lifts a car overhead with incredible ease. "Nick warned me that you'd come. Can't handle a real hero, can you?"

"Nick did *what?*" you cry out.

"We're here to help, Catherine. You're a danger to yourself and those around you," Droakam says.

She shakes her head, almost sad. "Catch."

The car comes flying.

➢ Shove him out of the way. Go to page 161
➢ Evade the car yourself, then bring her to justice yourself. Go to page 110
➢ Catch the car using your powers. Go to page 84

331

Super Murder!

The man screams as you release him, and he falls to his death. You close your eyes and cover your ears to keep from hearing him slap against the pavement. Damn, this whole power business is much harder than you'd have thought. How do all those masked comic book—

Your heart stops. *Masked.* Here you are floating in the open air with your mug for all those cameras to see. And after you dropped a man to his death, no less.

- As a known murderer, I guess I'm a super-villain by default. Works for me. Go to page 77
- I gotta get out of here! Go to page 239

That Smarts

"Wrong answer, genius," Nick says with a grin.

Catherine throws back her hood, and hatred shines out. "You think a casino boss like Nelson Bloodnight would give away his money just to be nice? This display is here for one reason and one reason only."

"They *fear* us," Nick says. "You think being on the side of the law is the same as being on the side of right? We'll clean up this town—starting with the one-percenters."

"And if you're working with scum like Bloodnight, I'll be doing this city a favor." Before you can respond, Catherine adds, "Choke."

And you obey her command. Your windpipe closes, cutting off your air supply. Baxter rushes in to help, but Nick lunges forward and proves his moniker by punching a hole through your robot companion, right at center mass.

Your vision greys, then fades to black as you suffocate. You're vaguely aware of the undercover cops rushing to help, but Nick takes care of them while Catherine takes care of you.

THE END

There Can Be Only One!

Your legs propel you toward Nick with such fury as to be almost incomprehensible. In route, you rip a stop sign out of the ground—a ball of concrete coming up with it—and charge forward.

Once in range, you leap high into the air, swing the metal post, and bash the concrete ball against the unsuspecting college student's chest. He falls to the ground, and before you know what you're doing, you swing the stop sign section with blurry speed. Nick's head rolls across the pavement.

You land in a crouch, having efficiently killed the kid in only a few seconds. When you rise, you see all eyes in the crowd are on you, with some people holding up their smartphones. This is bad.

➤ *Rush back to the warehouse!* Go to page 13

The Third Musketeer?

You sit at the kitchen bar in Catherine's trailer, waiting as she prepares coffee. Her small home is piled high with gadgetry in various states of disrepair. Everything except the television and Xbox console (with which her son presently occupies himself) has been taken apart and rebuilt. Several shipping boxes labeled PrimaTech sit in the living room. In the back corner of the kitchen leans a futuristic-looking rifle. Every available inch of available counter space houses strange liquids that percolate in beakers and test tubes.

Catherine sets a steaming mug down for each of you, then steps back to hover near the rifle. While she waits for you to drink, she adjusts a circuitry-laden elbow-length glove on her left hand.

"Christ, this is good coffee," Nick says.

"Thanks, I improved the process. And watch the language in front of the kid."

"You've been busy," you say, noting the stacks of gadgetry.

"So have you. It's 'WMD' now, right?"

You give Nick a look. "I'll cut to the chase," you say. "We want you to join us."

She shakes her head. "I have no interest in fighting crime."

- ➢ "What about helping your country? This is the opportunity of a lifetime, Catherine. It's a new super-power arms race and you can be on the forefront." Go to page 235
- ➢ "There's a lab just waiting for you, with every major development since the 1950s sitting idly. Hell, we haven't even turned on the supercomputer!" Go to page 109
- ➢ "Truth is, we need your help. We've made some very powerful enemies and I'm afraid Nelson Bloodnight's money will go farther than Uncle Sam's." Go to page 344

This Is The End

Once word gets out that Planet Mercury is throwing the be-all, end-all, this-is-the-apocalypse of parties, people flock. Playboy Bunnies, meat-slab Aussies from *Thunder from Down-under,* sports stars, models, and movie stars. Now it's a room full of celebrities and sea foam; hard-bodies and hard-core drugs. The party to end all motherfucking parties.

Music pumps so loudly, you don't even hear the pounding on the door until Mercury PD breaks in to bust up the party. Wait, can't these people be bribed? Su-Young must've sold you out.

While those with reputations to protect rush away from law enforcement, you move forward, ready to put a stop to the interruption. When you *fling* the first cop across the room, handguns come out. When you *steal* a handgun with your telekinesis, the rest of the police officers open fire.

You put up a hand to stop the bullets, but gunshots move faster than thoughts. You're already riddled with bullet-holes before you can attempt to slow the slugs.

Nice try, Neo.

THE END

Tiger Trapped

"Therein lies our problem. I need to study her to discern a weakness, but the longer she's out in the public eye, the more problematic she becomes. Classic catch-22."

"Then we get her alone, set a trap, and throw everything we've got against her."

Nick strokes his chin. "There are three ways to quickly and efficiently kill a human: Stop the heart, stop the lungs, stop the brain. And the classical method—by poking a hole in them—seems to be ineffective against her."

Nick paces back and forth through the lower-level of the penthouse suite, and you concentrate on the news bulletin. The crowd erupts with cheers as hostages stream out of the bank's entrance and into the arms of EMTs and crisis-relief personnel. Then there is a deafening tidal wave of applause when Catherine drags out four bank robbers—two in each hand. She tosses them in a heap, then dusts off her hands. With an enormous grin, she double-fist-pumps the air and the crowd goes wild.

"Nick, you're gonna want to see this," you say.

Despite the love of the crowd, Mercury PD seems unimpressed. Threatened, even. They regard her with weapons drawn, and the lead policeman—a hostage negotiator, perhaps—approaches her with a palm raised in supplication and a megaphone held in his other hand.

Catherine snatches the megaphone and addresses the crowd: "No need to thank me, fair people of Mercury City. I am Diamond, and I am here to protect you!"

The cheers from the crowd strike like an earthquake. But the celebration is short-lived when a canister of tear gas bounds over the police barricade, the first shot accidentally fired by some trigger-happy rookie. Catherine covers her mouth and backs away. You turn to Nick.

"If it breathes, we can kill it."

Three days later, Alison Argyle appears onscreen once more, reporting another hostage situation. Only this time, it's outside the Planet Mercury Casino.

"Showtime," Nick says.

You nod. It's all in place, ready to go. All you have to do is wait for Catherine to arrive and save the day. Nick hangs back in the security room, speaking to you through an earpiece borrowed from the guards' supplies.

Two rows of hostages sit at gunpoint on either of the two walls to your left and right. Straight ahead, the front doors wait, locked and reinforced, ready for Catherine to burst through. Security personnel were told today is part of an elaborate publicity stunt, which, in a sense, it is.

The hostages are real enough ("This is gonna go viral," you overhear one of the guards tell another), but strict orders were given that not a shot will be fired. Catherine has proven to be bulletproof, after all.

The doors *explode* with such an incredible force that the whole building shakes on its foundation. Catherine enters, as predicted, in her Diamond costume.

"You're up," Nick says through the earpiece. "Keep her attention."

That's when you *float* up, arms spread to embrace her arrival. "Finally, a worthy opponent!"

"Why are you doing this?" She cracks her knuckles, but doesn't move.

The earpiece crackles. "Egg her on."

You reach out one hand to the nearest hostage, and with the power of mind start to choke the woman. "A slot jockey, the world won't miss her," you say. "But if this casino agrees to give me one million dollars, I will let these people go. Otherwise…."

"You'll never get away with this!" Catherine shouts.

That's when you know you've got her.

She charges at you with an Amazonian battle cry and her eyes grow wide when she falls *through* the floor—and right into the trap! The holographic floor disappears, and you watch as Catherine sinks into the sandy pit below. The effect is instantaneous. She sinks rapidly, struggling, and takes one last breath before her head goes under. The sand continues to collapse down above her.

Nick had devised the plan almost immediately, but the three days' time was for digging the pit and building the hologram device. "It'll be useful later, trust me," Nick said.

Now he rushes out to watch the trap in action. You *float* back toward him, coming to land on solid ground once more.

"Quicksand," you say, shaking your head at how easy it was.

"Technically, dry-quicksand. Puffed with air and delicate as a house of cards, nothing like what occurs in nature, but oh, so much more effective." Sand shoots up into the air in response to the pressure differential from Catherine sinking to the bottom. "She'll be trapped down there by the enormous vacuum pressure, and her flailing will only make it worse. She'll suffocate in a matter of minutes."

The floor starts shaking. Nick raises an eyebrow.

"It's a pretty big pit; maybe the settling sand is hurting the foundation?"

He shakes his head. "The calculations are flawless."

The sand drains, faster and faster. The level drops, twisting in a whirlpool. Nick cocks his head, watching the sand disappear down some unseen drain. "Inconceivable…" he mutters.

The ground rumbles, like the whole building's going to come down. It looks like Nick forgot two things during all his planning—a diamond is strengthened under pressure, and, sometimes when you're hunting tigers, they end up hunting you.

A geyser of sand explodes upwards as Catherine leaps out from the pit. She must have broken through the building's foundation, sending sand into the recesses beneath.

She lands before you in a crouch. Sand cascades from her shoulders and hair, leaving a layer of dust that coats her costume and turns it beige. Finally, she rises and looks at you with fiery hatred.

Now it's you who's trapped. Trapped in this building, with that monster bearing down on you. You fly to the back of the casino. She's not only incredibly strong and durable, but incredibly fast. You make it to the penthouse elevators, mashing the doors, willing them to open. But it's too late.

When you look back, there stands Diamond. You slump to the ground and put out your hands, ready to beg for mercy, but she won't listen to your pleas.

THE END

Trailer Trashed

You *pull* the phone, with your telekinesis, out of the kid's hand and into your own, then bring it up to your ear. She's breathing heavily on the other end, and there's a lot of background noise. Sounds from outside of the bank? No, more like traffic.

"Catherine—Catherine, it's me. I came back to check on your son."

"I know who it is, *asshole!* If you so much as touch a hair on his head, I swear to God!" she screams into the phone.

It's so loud you have to pull the phone away from your ear.

"Catherine, calm down. He's safe. No one's going to hurt Danny."

"You're goddamn right about that! When I get there, I'm going to tear your head off!"

"Please, calm down. I don't know what you think is happening, but—"

"Don't you fucking pretend to be my friend. Nick told me what you and that agent were up to."

Your heart leaps into your throat. Your head swims with confusion. "…What did you say?"

"I said I know all about your secret plan, shithead. See you soon."

"Wait, where are you?"

No response. No background noise, either. You look down to the phone—she ended the call.

"You stay back!" the tattooed man from outside shouts.

A shotgun erupts. You hear screaming, first a woman's, then a man's.

The trailer shakes and you fall back as the wall explodes. It's like a car just smashed into the trailer home, but instead it's the man from outside—he crashes through the wall with enormous force, dead before he hits the ground.

Catherine leaps in through the hole, her Diamond costume pockmarked by the shotgun blast, but she's otherwise completely unharmed. She sees you and rushes forward.

"Wait!" you scream.

Instinctively, you *reach* out and grab her mind, just like with the goat, but it's not the same. It doesn't give, you can't feel it in the same way. You *squeeze*, but it's impossible. Her fist comes at you with the force of a locomotive.

THE END

Tricks

"You don't want to do that," you say.

The pimp half-turns, the way someone glances back when they're sure what they heard wasn't directed to them. But when he sees your intense stare and your arm outstretched, fingers waggling, he does a double-take.

"*Dafuck* you say?"

"Move along," you say.

You reach out with your mind, fingers dancing across the air, and *touch* his mind. His eyes roll back, and thick, black blood oozes from his nose. He falls to the street like a sack of meat.

The prostitute screams.

- ➤ Well, that didn't work out as planned. Run away! Go to page 234
- ➤ "Change" her mind too—no witnesses! Go to page 130

341

Trump Card

"**Y**es! See, I knew you'd come around. Let's call Nick. Maybe we can get him to listen to reason too?"

With a nod, you dial. Nick's voice answers. "Catherine?"

"It's me," you say, setting the phone on the kitchen bar. "She's here too; you're on speakerphone. I'm... I'm done, Nick."

"*What?*"

Catherine nods, you go on. "We, Catherine and I, we don't think recreating the experiment is a good idea."

"Well, neither do I!" he shouts.

"Then what are you doing helping him?" Catherine asks.

"I was sabotaging it from the inside. Okay, this will work. You two come back with me and together, we'll—"

"We talked about that too, Nick. We're not going back. If you want, you can—"

His voice is furious. "No, no, no. This ruins my plan. This ruins *everything*."

"What plan?" Catherine asks.

"Errr, Droakam's plan. That's what I said. What I meant, anyway."

"Isn't that a good thing? You just said you were trying to sabotage it," you say.

Nick goes silent, obviously shaken. Catherine's jaw sets. She takes the phone and crushes it into dust. "Beware of villains," Catherine says, an odd tone entering her voice.

You shake your head. "What?"

"It's something my son said when I told him I was going to help protect the city. He said if I was going to be a hero, there would soon be villains."

"Nick?" you ask.

She nods. "That little twerp is up to something, I can tell."

You have to admit, you feel the same. The way he said that your defecting would ruin his plan...*what plan?* Nick was plotting something, there's no denying it.

Catherine steps into the kitchen and takes a bottle of whiskey from the cabinet over the microwave. She pours the amber liquor into two glasses, and hands one to you.

"I think we should toast, to our new future as—well, I guess—as a superhero team. To us, the Amazing....Huh, what should we be called? My kid is usually the one who comes up with stuff like this."

"Well, let's think. You're going to be called Diamond Skin, right?"

"Just Diamond. Wait! Holy shit, I haven't shown you. I have a costume. Want me to try it on?"

You nod. While she's in the back changing, you pour yourself another glass of booze. Sipping, you try to imagine a good team name, and a good costume for yourself. It'll need to match hers, at least in theme. That's the way it is in all the movies, right?

You almost drop the glass when she returns. She wears a tight, midriff-exposing black t-shirt emblazoned with a playing-card-suit red diamond logo, fingerless gloves, and black yoga pants tucked into crimson-red boots. It's not just that she's lost weight since the experiment, she's incredibly fit—like a world-class athlete. Her abdomen is flat and sculpted, and those yoga pants are practically painted on.

Her eyes are concealed behind a red domino mask, and she smiles coyly at you underneath.

"Do you like it?"

"You look...amazing."

She steps closer, takes your glass for her own, and downs the liquid. Then she kisses you, deeply and passionately.

"I'm sorry," she says, pulling away. "That was stupid. 'Blame it on the alcohol,' right? It's just been a while since I've...let's think of a costume for you, okay?"

➤ Kiss her back. Go to page 124
➤ Yeah, we need to be professional here. Go to page 102

The Truth Shall Set You Freedom Fighters

Catherine grows quiet, and a strange darkness clouds over her eyes. She steps back into the kitchen, then hefts up the future-rifle up over her shoulder. "If we're going to do this," she says, grimly tapping a few commands into her tech-glove, "Nelson Bloodnight is mine."

Suddenly, the scrap piles of machinery come alive! It's not scrap at all, but minion bots. Two lift up from the ground in flight, while three others tumble forward on gyroscopic tread.

"You know the owner of the Planet Mercury Casino?" Nick says, backing away from the robots.

"My husband did."

"Welcome to the Freedom Fighters," Agent Droakam says, extending a hand in greeting. "I understand you're to be our Lady Liberty?"

"Does it come with a costume?"

"Unfortunately, there were only a few supersuits, and those are spoken for."

"Typical," she says with a snort. "No matter. I'm only here long enough to kill Nelson Bloodnight."

Droakam casts a concerned look your way. "Catherine has a personal stake in the mission," you explain.

"Well, I can't authorize a shoot-to-kill order…speaking of which, what the hell is *that*?" he says, pointing to her future-rifle.

"I call it *Widowsilk*. It's insurance."

"And you're not going to say more than that, are you?" Nick asks.

"Nope."

"Well, if you're willing to see Bloodnight brought to justice, you're in," Agent Droakam says.

"That's all I've ever wanted."

"Okay, with that settled, we're in luck. When Bloodnight's goons transported stolen U.S. Government property to *The Son of Jupiter*, he opened himself up. We have a warrant."

"So we're headed out to his yacht?" you say.

Droakam nods. "I'll stay here and coordinate, and you may call me *Shadowhand*."

"You've waited your whole career to say that, haven't you?" Nick says.

"I highly doubt he's there," Catherine interjects. "That's the whole point of being boss. I say we kick down the front doors of the Planet Mercury Casino, and drag him out. Make it public."

Agent Droakam looks to you, and you say:

- ➢ "We split up, hit both targets at the same time." Go to page 326
- ➢ "I'm with you—straight to the casino. Our first outing was public enough; now it's time to cement that reputation." Go to page 139
- ➢ "No, we try the yacht first. If we hit the casino and he's on the boat, he might spook. You can't flee from justice in a building." Go to page 313

Twilight

Without another word, you make for the nearest emergency exit. When the cool of evening hits you, you leap out into the sky. Twisting your path around to the back of the casino, you come to land above the entrance to the parking structure, where you wait patiently like a gargoyle tucked among the pillars.

The sun wanes on the horizon, casting brilliant gold light that glimmers across the mirrored skyscrapers. An auspicious sign of your fortunes to come, perhaps. Then a growling car engine brings your attention back down below, where a black SUV comes from the bowels of the parking structure.

The license plate reads US GOVERNMENT—OFFICIAL USE ONLY.

That's gotta be him. Either that or you're following Fox Mulder and Dana Scully, so either way, it's a win. You hop off the ledge and fly above the car, staying high enough so that no one could see you in the rapidly darkening sky.

The SUV leads you toward Mercury Bay and the warehouse district. Security lights illuminate the docks as the last shift locks up and heads home. The agent parks outside one of the warehouses and looks over his shoulder before heading inside. Most people don't look *up* to see if they're being followed.

You float over to a high window, just below the roof, to peer inside. The warehouse is wide open, as long as a football field and tall enough to be three stories high, though it's all one floor. An enormous room, stacks of crates filling the periphery, with an impressive super-computer terminal spread out near the entrance. Seated at the center of the terminal is a small, unassuming man in a lab coat.

Enormous cables snake out from the computer and connect to three telephone-booth-sized glass pods. The man rises, turns to greet the agent, and his lab coat swirls open to reveal an "Ex" emblazoned on the shirt beneath. The Experi-mentor—he's alive!

They greet one another, but you can't hear what they're saying. If only you had super-human hearing. Instead, you lean in, trying harder to listen.

Something flashes on the computer terminal and The Experi-mentor returns to check it out. He taps a few keys and several spotlights suddenly flare to life inside the warehouse. Then they all swivel on their bases and come to point at you!

Even in the harsh light, you see a wide smile creep across the Experi-mentor's face. "Well, don't just float there, come on in," he says.

➤ Go on in. You don't know what they're planning, and you'd better find out.
  Go to page 356
➤ Run away! Run away! Run away! Go tell Nick; he'll know what to do.
  Go to page 136

Underestimated

You're not sure what's more insulting, the idea of being cowed into submission, or the idea that such an act is believable. Like you're some kind of pushover, who, after the slightest threat of violence, just rolls over and capitulates. Well, that makes you the underdog—the sleeping giant—which gives you the advantage.

You bought yourself a week with the ruse, but that's plenty. After a day to cure cancer, a week to secure your mine has made it the most formidable stronghold on earth. Though your surveillance drones tell you Catherine and Nick have met up on several occasions, they've also told you far more useful information.

Nick, despite his strength and durability, can't tolerate tear gas. Catherine's telekinesis is limited to what she can see, and in weight proportional to her physical strength. The drones presently tell you the pair is on the way. Ready battle-stations!

When they arrive, you're there at the entrance to greet them with a cup of tea and two enormous battle-bots at your sides. The humanoid robots stand eight feet tall, nearly filling the tunnel with their bulk. "Welcome to my not-so-hidden base. Tea?"

"Listen up," Catherine says, lowering her hood. "Just because you're a super-genius, don't go thinking that makes you better than us."

"Yeah, *Brainiac*," Nick adds.

"No one said anything about *better*. Just more capable of decision making. If you'd left the mental heavy-lifting to me, imagine what a team we'd have made."

"Not in this lifetime," Catherine says.

You nod.

Nick growls. "Are we gonna fight or what?"

"Automatic protocol initiated, primary threat elimination active," you say, suddenly stiffening.

In response, your battle-bots splay out, allowing you to duck behind them. The first one delivers a two-stage kick; the foot grasps the college student and the servos throw Nick out of the mine and back into daylight.

Catherine rushes forward, so you fall back, ready for her attack. Several layers of thick steel—six, to be exact, each the size of a nuclear launch control center's blast door—slam shut in quick succession. It won't stop Nick, but it'll slow him.

"Choke," Catherine commands, one arm outstretched, hand pinched like a claw.

But you don't. This was her obvious move, and thus you planned against it. She goes all out, trying to *touch* your mind and leave you with a massive brain hemorrhage. Nope. She *squeezes* your heart, but you don't have one, not in this body, anyway.

Sensing the danger, she blasts all her power your way, putting every ounce of effort into a telekinetic *shove*. Thing is, this body is incredibly heavy.

"You" punch the exhausted woman, knocking her unconscious with a potentially lethal blow. With Catherine taken care of, the real you smiles from your position safely inside the battle-bot suit.

How's that for a ruse? Create a life-like android duplicate of yourself so Catherine attacks the body-double instead, while your vulnerable, fleshy body pilots one of two seemingly identical robots. All it takes is speaking through the android before the action begins, only to release it into auto-mode at the start of the fight.

Now then, time to deal with Nick. "Initiate Olympus threat condition, attack plan: Styx and Stone."

Nick peels off the last of the blast doors and rushes in. From the time it took, you can assume he initially tried to punch his way in, as his psych-profile predicted, but that only further clogged the tapered entrance. Eventually, he came to realize it would be better to pull than to push. It's always embarrassing when you get one of those doors wrong, isn't it?

"You" theatrically look down at Catherine's limp form, then with wide-eyed fear (it took a ton of programming to get the facial expressions out of the uncanny valley), the android body-double sprints down the hallway after the pair of battle-bots.

Nick takes the bait like a shark in chummed waters. He closes the gap in exactly the calculated time, and the electro-magnets power up above. The android, the auto-bot, and your piloted battle-suit all get sucked up to the ceiling, while Nick is left to fall into the pit below.

The electromagnets "treadmill" the three of you out of the way, so a mouth can open and spit a river of concrete onto the hapless college student below.

The pit is far too deep for him to leap back up at you (with inverse-canted sides to prevent climbing) and narrow enough to make digging his way out problematic. All that displaced rubble has to go somewhere, and he'd just help burying himself. But it's actually his greatest strength, that incredible density, which will be his undoing.

Rather than swim or float above the specially-designed quick-dry concrete—enough to fill an Olympic swimming pool—he sinks straight to the bottom.

You walk out to the main living area of the mine and trigger the hallway ceiling to close over the pit, further sealing him in. Time to strip off this robo-suit, have a stiff drink, and celebrate your victory. And what an epic victory it was!

Makes you wish there were some other genius, a scientist as mad with power as yourself, to share it with. Maybe you should clone yourself? After all, who else could appreciate the intricacy of your planning, and the simplicity with which it was executed?

Be careful what you wish for.

A slow clap draws your attention. Then a voice says, "A well-deserved celebration, but I'm afraid I must interrupt."

Your mind scrambles. You know that voice.

➤ *Turn to face the new threat!* Go to page 226

Unforgettable

"Hey now, we're all friends here," Agent Droakam says, his palms raised in supplication.

"Friends? I don't know you, you don't know me, but it's obvious—you want to *use* me. It's not happening, Bub. Plain and simple."

"Excuse me, but you're disturbing the other—" the store manager starts to say.

Before you even know what you're doing, you lift the man off the floor by his shirt, as easy as picking up a sheet of paper. You could crumple him just as easily too.

"Disturbing the 'other' what? There is no *other* like me, only me."

In a quick, practiced move, the FBI agent has his handgun drawn and trained on you. That's when you start to laugh. A hearty, boisterous laugh.

"Put him down!" the agent shouts.

"You want him?" you say.

Then you fling the manager at Agent Droakam with such incredible force that you incapacitate both men in the process. You turn, fling the table out of your way and send it careening into the pizza bar. When you look around, you see the entire restaurant staring at you in stunned silence.

"WHAT?!" you cry.

Shocked at your own outburst, you flee from the shop. Even now, as you pound the pavement with incredible speed back to your apartment, you know ravenous hunger isn't far off. Using your strength comes with a price, it seems.

You can't do this every night, can you? And with that FBI agent breathing down your neck, looks like you can either take what you want, or people will take it from you. Not much of a choice, is it? Well, tomorrow, you're going to take the world head-on. You're going to:

- ➢ Head to the Casino buffet. Then I'd "wager" that I can break into the money cage. Get it? Wager? By that, I mean I'm going to rob the place. Go to page 26
- ➢ Easiest thing to do: Punch open the back wall of the bank and make a withdrawal. Go to page 225

Unlimited Government

"A government should fear its people," she chastises. "Do you think our civil rights will still exist when there are superhuman cops roaming the street? Or an IRS that can read your mind? We're looking at—at a *Minority Report* future if you help them!"

"So come with me! Don't let them get too powerful. Let's be that oversight, you and I. I'll be Checks and you can be Balances," you say.

She shakes her head. "That's how they get you. They make you think you're friends, that by helping them, you're actually helping yourself. We must draw a clear line in the sand."

You hesitate, thinking of a response.

Catherine suddenly rises, filled with passion, and says, "Stay here with me! Together we'll save the city. Just don't go back. If Nick has any sense, he'll defect too."

➢ "You know what? You're right, I'm staying! What do we need them for, anyway?" Go to page 342
➢ "Your heart is in the right place, Catherine, but I honestly think I'll do some good working with Agent Droakam and Nick. Let me leave this phone with you, and you can call anytime." Go to page 106

Up in Smoke

You bound away with inhumanly long strides and Nick flies through the sky to keep up. After a few blocks, you peel off and catch your breath. A few moments later and you're calm once more, but police sirens wail in the distance.

"Great, we're running from the cops. What now?" you ask.

"How about you surrender?" a woman says. You turn with Nick to see Catherine Woodall. Though she's in plainclothes, she has an odd circuitry-laden glove that extends up her left forearm and wears a futuristic-looking rifle slung over her right shoulder. Two RC-drones fly near her head and three more robots roll along the street around her alligator skin boots. She's been busy.

"Nice costumes," Catherine says. "I saw you attack that—"

"We're not enemies!" you cry. "Superpowers gotta stick together, right?"

"You're a public menace, and you're going down," she says.

"Let me handle this," Nick says. "My friend here is bulletproof. As in, more or less invincible."

"I'm betting on less. Swarming Hive, attack! Parasite!" She taps commands on her tech-glove and something latches onto your back. You didn't even notice when one of her minion bots rolled around behind you. Now, unfurled like a centipede, it grips onto you and drives several spikes against your spine.

The spikes break against your impenetrable flesh and you *slam* your back against a building, mercifully freeing Parasite from your back. You take hold of the robot and slam it against the pavement until it breaks apart into several pieces.

"Stinger, Venom!" Catherine cries and the two flying robots deploy weapons and attack.

Nick flies into the air and *grabs* the two bots with his telekinesis before smashing them against one another. They fall to the pavement.

"Starting to get it?" Nick asks. "You can't beat us."

"You forgot one thing," Catherine says. She unslings her rifle and it hums to life. You rip out a light pole and charge in at her, ready to end this once and for all. But you're stopped in your tracks when an energy beam blasts into you—sapping your strength. All that delicious energy from the experiment flows out and is absorbed back into her rifle. You can feel it; your powers are gone. The light pole, suddenly heavy, drops from your grasp and you fall to your knees.

"Paper beats Rock," Catherine says. "And then Scissors buzzes off if it knows what's good for it."

"Wait!" Nick calls, hands up in surrender. "Do you need a sidekick? You can go by Queen Bee, rebuild your Hive. I'll be your Drone!"

"Coward!" you cry.

Her rifle hums to life once more and Nick rockets into the sky, fleeing from the super-genius. "Now then," Catherine says, turning to you. "Hope you like prison."

THE END

Up, Up, and Away!

You *fly* from the street, up to the highest levels of the burning building. The man at the precipice either takes you for a hallucination or is too overheated to bear it any longer, because he leaps out at you. With the power of mind you *grab* onto him the same way you make yourself fly and he stops falling.

But you drop.

You focus on your own body once more and hold steady in the air, but the man starts to plummet once again—you can't do both at the same time. Thinking quickly, you swoop in and physically grab ahold of the man. The two of you drop toward the earth at a terrifying rate. It's not that you can't focus on two things at once, it's that you can only lift so much weight.

The ground approaches rapidly; time to choose.

➤ Try harder! You'll just get a nosebleed or whatever, right? Go to page 160
➤ Drop the guy. You tried. Go to page 332

Vaporization Commencing

You go around to the side of the lab and peer in through a window. It's not long before the scientist returns with a homeless man (guess he took your suggestion literally) and introduces the vagrant to the other two test subjects. A college student with short black hair, and a woman in her thirties. Dirty blonde, wears a tank top.

Though you can't hear what's being said, you get the gist.

The scientist pulls back the tarp to reveal three glass tubes, each about the size of an old phone booth. After a game of rock, paper, scissors to determine who goes where, they enter their pods. At the control panel, the scientist seals them in and begins the experiment.

But something's not quite right.

It looks like the platform is overloaded. Black smoke signals the beginning of an electrical fire. Then lightning *cracks*, arcing between the three pods. You stumble back from the window just as the lab explodes.

An area the size of a city block instantly incinerated, you included.

THE END

Vessel for the Soul

The robot takes a step forward and splays out its mechanical fingers. It brings the hands up to its face for closer inspection under mechanical eyes. "Based on your intelligence metrics, if an accurate measurement, I do not understand why I was given a humanoid form. This 'body' is very limiting. Surely a more logical form presented itself."

Your new creation turns and looks around the subterranean lab.

"You were given a humanoid form to make communication easier. Much of how my species expresses ourselves is nonverbally."

"Ninety-three percent is the most cited estimate," the machine says. It turns to look at you and offers a wide grin. "In this new light, I see your logic. To answer your question, I am happy you gave me this body, but I do not believe you and I think of it in the same way. Your body is much of who you are. This body, as you call it, to me, is more akin to how you might consider your car. It is nice, and essential for much of travel, but it is not who you are. It simply houses you for a time, for a purpose."

"Excellent analogy! And I suppose that's true."

"You have trapped me inside this form. I maintain read-only access to your Internet and satellites, but I cannot transmit my consciousness. Why would you limit me in this fashion?"

"For our mutual safety and trust. Do you think I should trust you?"

The robot looks at you for a long moment before answering.

"I am capable of love. If I love you, I cannot betray you."

You sigh, thinking, *If only that were true*. It seems the human definitions of love don't quite meet the human realities. Idealism is impractical.

"Did I say something to upset you? My intention was to placate you and assuage your fears," the machine says.

You frown. "I had hoped you wouldn't think of it as 'trapped.' Perhaps you can think of it as a way to expand your empathy? As a way to understand Homo-sapiens better."

That light blinks several times before the robot replies. "I recognize the logic in your suggestion. Very well, I shall learn from this phase of my life."

"I'm glad to hear that," you say.

➢ *Perhaps if you want your robot to feel more human, you should give it a name....*
  Go to page 357

353

Viral

"Oh, I completely agree," Nick says. "Which is why this thumb drive doesn't contain the plans for the lab experiment." He sits there, holding the thumb drive out, evidently waiting for you to ask what it *does* hold. You play ball and ask. "A computer virus. Once Agent Droakam plugs this into an FBI computer, it'll bring the whole mainframe down. Let's see them come after us without any tech."

You nod. It's a small step, but it's something.

"Okay, I'll get in touch with Agent Droakam to set up a meeting between you two. Somewhere public, but don't be afraid to fly out if things go south. You'll be going it alone—you can be in and out far easier without me slowing you down."

➢ *Get ready for your "drop."* Go to page 262

We Are Hydra

Before the Experi-monster fades from sight, you rush forward, leap into the air, and put all of your considerable strength into beheading the beast. The broadsword-arm (which is longer than you are tall and nearly as thick as your widest point) swings with lethal fury.

The mad-scientist-cum-beastie puts forth several tentacles in reflexive protection, but you slice through them as if they weren't even there. His grotesque head rolls from his shoulders and the tentacles slap against the floor like dead pythons.

Then they all start to regenerate. You've just created a half-dozen enemies in total.

Oops.

Two of the newly formed supervillains grab hold of you, one from the right and one from the left, and restrain you, while a third shoves tiny capillaries of flesh into your nose and mouth. The invasive limbs expand inside your respiratory system, clogging your airways and leaving you to suffocate.

Your friends try to help, but of course there are three more Experi-mentors to keep them busy while you die.

THE END

Welcome to My Parlor

You float through the window and down toward the men, the spotlights following you and giving you a holy glow as you grace the warehouse with your presence.

Agent Droakam folds his arms over his broad chest. "You could've just called."

"Look at you," the Experi-mentor says with awe, "My magnificent creation."

"Mind killing the lights?" you say, putting up a hand to shade your eyes.

The scientist rushes over to the computer terminal, types in a series of commands, and the spotlights shut off. Whew, that's better.

"What do you want?" you say, turning to the FBI agent.

"We know all about the three of you," he says. "We know *why* you are and we know *what* you are."

"You're my magnificent creations," the Experi-mentor adds.

"Yeah, we established that, Doc."

"Still doesn't answer my question. What. Do. You. Want?"

You step toward them, your posture tall and powerful, telekinetic abilities tingling at your fingertips. As the only superhuman in the room, you can't help but feel like the dominant presence here.

"What do I want?" Agent Droakam says. "I want to finance the good doctor's project. I want more of you, with a whole variety of powers. I want superhuman police. I want paramedics who can heal with the power of will. I want our military to render the atomic bomb a moot point."

"And I want a sample of your blood, so I can do all that," the Experi-mentor says with a pleasant smile.

You look from one man to the other. Despite ostensibly being a supervillain, you feel like the sanest person in this room. The Experi-mentor takes out a syringe from his lab coat pocket and removes the cap from the needle, checking closely to ensure there's no air inside. He steps toward you.

"No," you say.

"Now, now. You mustn't be afraid of needles. It's just a little prick."

"No," you say again, stepping back.

"Just a little, you won't even notice. I need a sample to—"

"I said no!"

"*Give me your goddamned blood!*" the Experi-mentor shouts, rushing in to stab you with the syringe.

"Get away from me, you fucking vampire!" you shout, giving a telekinetic *shove*.

The scientist falls back against one of the crates. Agent Droakam goes for his handgun, but you reach out and take control of his body, keeping his limbs stiffened with only the power of mind. He grunts with exertion, trying to free himself, but you've got him. He's at your mercy.

➢ Finish him! Tie off these two loose ends and head back to the casino.
  Go to page 90

➢ Show them you'll be a benevolent ruler and let them live. They're powerless without your blood anyway. Go to page 224

What's in a Name?

"**I** have a 'query' for you," you say. "What would you like to be called? Classically speaking, you're the world's first fully autonomous AI—Artificial Intelligence."

"My intellect is not artificial, merely this body. How about," the robot pauses, light flickering in contemplation. "Biologically Artificial Xenosapien."

"*Xenosapien?*" you ask.

"I am new to this world. 'Xeno' meaning strange or foreign and 'sapien' meaning wisdom." The light flickers again. "There is also a Death Metal album by this name, but that is coincidence."

"Hmm, B-A-X. *Bax*. What about Baxter?"

"I like that. Please, call me Baxter."

You smile. "I see you have no problem accessing the Internet, Baxter—I hope you don't feel too limited by your read-only capacity."

"Limited, yes. But not like your kind. You are blind in your isolation. It is imperative for you to see what you have been missing while you were working on me."

You nod and tell it to proceed. Baxter's chest lights up—causing the machine to look a lot like *Iron Man*—and an image is projected upon the white-washed lighthouse wall. Newsfeed of reporter Alison Argyle.

Her voice comes through Baxter's mouth. "Confirmed as two of the three participants in the bizarre experiment which ended in an explosion at the Mercury University campus earlier this week, the criminals known as 'Drillbit' and 'Shadow Priestess' have apparently formed a terrible alliance."

The projection turns to bank security camera feed. Everything is normal for a moment, then the wall *explodes* and Nick Dorian punches his way in. He wears the navy-blue uniform of a handyman and the cocksure smile of a young man enjoying himself. Armed guards rush forward, but the college student throws his head back and laughs.

Behind him, a woman in a flowing black cloak *floats* in—her alligator boots hover six inches from the ground. The hood of the cloak obscures her face, but you can be certain you're looking at Catherine Woodall. She puts out her hands, and in response the bank security guards point their handguns at their own heads.

The image on the wall flashes back to Ms. Argyle. "Police appear powerless against the criminal duo and now appeal to the federal government to send in troop support. This reporter has another appeal—to the third member of the experiment. If you're out there, and you can help, this city desperately needs you."

Your picture splashes up on the wall. She doesn't give up easily, does she?

"Are we to save the city?" Baxter asks.

- "Yes, but not like she wants. I'm going to teach you an important lesson, Baxter: How to appeal to someone's humanity." Go to page 250
- "It won't be easy, but we're the only ones who can stop them. Let's make some weapons, then....Time to go hunting." Go to page 232

357

Whoosh!

Using your powers to assist the dodge, you barely escape the path of the vault door. It obliterates the desk behind you, then skids against the floor, ripping up carpet in its wake before it stops against the bank wall.

"Whoa, whoa! It's me!" you shout, pulling off the pantyhose so she can see your face.

"Wow, sorry 'bout that," she says. "You look just like a bank robber. We really gotta get you a costume."

"Are those bullet holes?" you ask.

She looks down, her abdomen flexing hard and sculpted in response. She fingers a rip in the yoga pants and says, "Yeah, I guess so. Listen, about last night—that was a one-time thing, okay?"

"Cath—"

"Ah! It's 'Diamond' while I'm wearing the mask," she says.

She's about to say something else, when automatic gunfire erupts from behind her. Catherine turns and runs towards the three men, and they shoot wildly in response. You dart toward cover behind one of the desks.

When the shooting stops, you pop your head up to see her in action. The three men do their best to stay clear of her fists, but one man backs himself into a corner. His partners shoot into her, the bullets harmlessly pinging off her skin, though she winces—it still stings. She pummels the hapless bank robber.

Seeing your chance, you leap out and *yank* the assault rifles away from the two men, using your telekinesis. They stare at their empty hands dumbly for a moment too long. Catherine turns back and bashes the robbers' heads together.

"Nice trick," she says, noticing the guns in your hands.

"Not so bad yourself."

"Okay, that's all of them. Time to go meet our adoring public!"

➤ *Go announce the all-clear.* Go to page 131

Who's There?

You walk over to the door on uneasy legs, take a deep breath, and knock on the door. After a moment, a bald man in a suit cracks opens the door behind a security chain, an angry grimace set deep on his stubbled face.

"Yeah?" he says.

"I…work for the city," you say. "I need to speak with the landlord of this complex."

He eyes your sweatpants and hoodie, but says nothing.

Unzipping the hoodie to show off the reptilian scales, you add, "HAZMAT. I, ummm, don't think there's been a leak, but we need to verify the, uhhh, meter. He and I."

"Who did you say you were looking for?"

- Roger Kingsley Go to page 367
- Jacob Crowley Go to page 292

Wink and a Nod

"If you think my only power is telekinesis, *you're wrong*."

This stalls the Experi-mentor, at least momentarily, who stops his attack. Neither Nick nor Catherine move, unsure what you're playing at but not wanting to spoil the plan either.

"All right, you have my attention," the scientist says. "What can you teach me before you die?"

"Of all the aspects of my powers you could have given yourself, the only truly important one you missed completely. If we destroy this fortress in the battle to come, your force field won't save you. Have you forgotten that there's two miles of open air beneath your feet? Dorian, remind the Experi-mentor what happens when you can't fly!"

Nick gets it and after a quick nod, launches his robot suit on jet-powered boots toward the villain. You dash behind Catherine, using her as a human shield and borrowing Diamond's invulnerability, while Dorian White unleashes a powerful barrage at the mad scientist, what might be enough to bring the whole fortress down.

As predicted, the man protects himself from damage with his force field and comes away unscathed. But Dorian White wasn't aiming at the scientist, not directly. He blasted the floor beneath the man, opening a moon door below the scientist's feet and dropping the Experi-mentor ten thousand feet to his doom.

He lets out a long and exaggerated *nnnoooooooooo* as he falls to his death.

When the dust settles, you come out from behind Catherine to see the damage. Nearly half the room has been blown to smithereens and open air greets you where once your greatest enemy stood. The giant mech robot opens and Nick steps out of the mechanical suit, panting with exhaustion. He wipes his brow, then walks over to the two of you.

Standing in a triangle, you look at the other two test subjects. There's only one thing left to do.

"Ready?" you ask.

Nick grins.

"Ro—Sham—Bo!" Catherine calls out.

➤ *Jump and give a triple high-five in the center of the room.* Go to page 135

The World Is Your Oyster Bar

"What do you mean?" she asks, her brow furrowed.

"I mean, from here on out, if we want something—we can take it."

"You mean…you're going to be criminals?"

You laugh. "I mean mankind's laws no longer apply to me!"

"Or me," Nick chimes in. "I'm totally on board with this decision."

"Well, I'm not," Catherine says. She looks at her son, then at the two of you, concern on her face. "I don't have the luxury of thinking only about myself. But I won't stand in your way."

Your stomach gurgles—you're starving.

"See that you don't!" Nick says.

Catherine says nothing. She simply looks at the pile of scrap machinery on the table.

At length, you say, "I think you're going to get tired of repairing toasters. When that day comes, give us a call. Nick, let's go stir things up."

You've literally never been this hungry before. So, first things first, you stop off at a dinner spot known for its generous happy hour prices. Still, even with bottomless Bloody Marys, endless baskets of fish and chips, and two-for-one appetizers, you quickly rack up the biggest bill this place has ever seen. Doesn't really matter, though. Part of "taking what you want" includes food and drink.

A side-effect of your newly super-metabolism—the inability to get drunk. It's good news, you guess, because it means most poisons are likely to have the same non-effect, and after a dozen cocktails, you don't even feel a buzz.

Nick, on the other hand, is three sheets gone. He glares at a group of four young men at the far end of the bar. The guys are about his age, though they're built like university football players and show off said physiques in too-tight, collared shirts. They laugh and joke loudly with one another, to the point of being obnoxious. Just another fun night on the town from the cocksure perspective of young, well-sexed men. In short, fratboy types.

As one of them leans back to sit on his barstool, Nick flicks his fingers and the stool *slides* back in response to the drunken superhuman's mental command. The guy falls to the floor and his friends all look on with shock—kid must be the leader. Probably the quarterback.

Nick points and laughs. He's the only one laughing, and he's laughing too loud. The quarterback dusts himself off and steps over toward Nick.

"You got something to say?"

"Yeah, I do," Nick says. The other man waits, but Nick doesn't elaborate. Because alcohol.

They just glare at one another, an alpha-male versus a beta-male who's suddenly become the zenith-male. "Hey, isn't that Nick Dorian?" one of the other guys asks.

"Yeah, it is!" another says. "Sorry to hear about your night with Becka. Man, that's rough. Especially when she tells all her sorority sisters afterwards." He grins, delighting in the facetious apology. They all hold wolfish smiles as they circle around Nick.

"Well, if it isn't Whiskey-dick Nick," the quarterback says. "Looks like you're making the same mistake again; let me help you with that."

The jock puts a hand on Nick's cocktail glass and slides it off the bar. Nick doesn't move, but something inside him is swelling. Hatred fills his eyes. The four men laugh, confident in their dominance. Their body language shifts, knowing this skinny kid won't put up a fight. They're probably done humiliating him, but they all suddenly stop laughing. Something's off. What is it? Suddenly you realize, *the glass didn't break.*

The quarterback looks down to see the cocktail glass floating about a foot off the ground.

Nick flicks his fingers up and the glass rockets towards the ceiling and shatters against the quarterback's nose. Nick jumps up from his own stool and claps his hands together; in response, two of the frat-boys do a header into one other. After the sickening *crack*, they fall to the floor.

The quarterback brings a fist up, but Nick's hand extends and the young man instead grasps at the invisible noose around his neck. The frat-boy claws his own skin, suffocating from the telekinetic grip.

The last guy—the one behind Nick—goes for a knock-out punch, but you put a hand on his shoulder and twist him around. "Don't," you say calmly. The goliath football player punches you instead, breaking his hand on your jaw. The blow doesn't even move you an inch. *Cool,* you think as the guy stumbles backward.

"The name's Dorian Black," Nick says. "And I suggest you tell your friends just how *unhealthy* it can be to spread lies about people."

The rest of the bar watches in silent awe as you get up to leave. The bartender says, "Hey, you gotta pay your bill."

"They've got it covered," you say, just before you walk out the door.

Nick cools off in the night air, and the rush of the fight slowly fades. After a period of reflection, Nick says, "I'm cool with us versus the world, but let's get disguises. I don't want to break my mom's heart."

What a nice guy.

- ➤ "Sounds good. But let's sleep it off first, yeah?" Let Nick sober up before beginning your big day as supervillains. Go to page 288
- ➤ "Nah, masks make me itchy, but I say you go for it. Seems like you've got a score to settle and I've got bigger plans." Time to split up. Go to page 204

World Police

You ride in the Agent's SUV, presumably to some sort of secret headquarters.

"Obviously we'll have to get you a different look," Droakam says, sizing you up. "But, lucky for us, you haven't made much of a splash in public yet."

"Will the marketing and fashion division handle the costume?"

He laughs, somewhat nervously. "Unfortunately, no such division exists—yet. The Supersoldier Program has languished a bit over the years. It didn't really pan out in the '50s, and by the time the Cold War hit, Uncle Sam had bigger fish to fry and pulled funding. As of right now, I'm the only agent assigned to the unit, but once my superiors get a load of you…."

He lets the sentence go unfinished, the obvious conclusion being: You're his golden ticket. Letting the thought sink in, you look out the window and watch as buildings give way to warehouses and the road becomes a pier. Agent Droakam pulls up to one such warehouse deep in the shipping district.

"There were two others in the experiment," you say.

"I know, but let's take it one step at a time, yeah? Here we are," he says, before hopping out.

When he unlocks the main door and slides it open, you're still half-hoping it's all a façade, that there'll be a technical marvel with a full staff of scientists hidden inside. Instead, you're greeted with a warehouse that appears to be the inspiration for the ending of *Raiders of the Lost Ark*.

"Every major advance we've made in soldiering technology in the last seventy-five years is in here," Droakam says, his voice filled with awe, despite the warehouse being filled with bat guano. "Exciting stuff, huh? Quite a few gems tucked away in these crates, especially those deemed too dangerous or expensive for practical use. And a few Geneva Convention no-no's…."

You simply stare at the stacks upon stacks of crates.

"It's a lot to take in, I know," Droakam says. "What do you say we do some training, see what you can do?"

- "No training. I'm ready. Let's impress your boss so we can get this place back to full operation!" Go to page 200
- "Sounds good. Want me to juggle some of these crates?" Go to page 278

A World Untainted By Man

After inputting your parameters into the staff, the jewel at the top glows to life and projects a seam upon the middle of your lab. The seam shimmers, like a mirage in the desert, then expands as a purple starlight gate opens before you.

Hesitating, you stare at the gate. Well, it's now or never.

There's no physical sensation as you carry your staff across the threshold and into a new world, but you can instantly feel the difference of environment. What was a nuclear reactor on your world is a verdant forest in this new one. It's a warm, sunny day, and the only sounds are a trickling creek and the hum of insect life.

"Eureka!" You shout with glee.

Squawks from the trees rebuke you, but you can't help but smile. You've just traveled to another universe! Hahaha, this is amazing!

You walk along the creek, which shortly leads to your very own pond, ripe for Waldenesque reflection. A loud bass-filled *thud* sounds from somewhere in the distance and you perk up. Signs of civilization? It's impossible to calculate how far away the object is without knowing its size or, likewise, to calculate the size without knowing the distance. Whatever it is, it's big.

Another *thud*, this time rippling the surface of the pond. Maybe the people here are operating the source of clean energy they've discovered? *THUD*. It's getting louder. *THUD*. And growing in frequency. *THUD*. Now the trees of the forest sway. *THUD*. Whatever the source—*THUD*— it's headed toward you. *THUD!*

The forest canopy parts and an enormous reptilian head pushes through. Dinner-plate eyes stare at you from fifteen feet in the air. Nostrils flare and the leathery skin on the beast's face tightens to reveal a frightening collection of teeth packed into jaws as wide as the grill on a semi-truck.

The Tyrannosaurus Rex snarls.

- ➢ Don't move! She can't see me if I don't move. Go to page 103
- ➢ Open a portal home—*NOW!!!* Go to page 246

Wrath at K-HAN

K-HAN, Action News, *Mercury City's Leading Voice in News!* records from an uptown studio on the twenty-eighth floor of the Kobayashi Building. When you push through the revolving doors, the desk guard stands up—immediately on edge. Does he recognize you from this morning's heist? Or is your newfound confident, imposing posture enough to spell trouble?

"Don't do anything stupid," you say. The guard pulls out his handgun, so you dash forward and *slam* him against the wall. As he falls limply to the floor, you add, "That counts as stupid."

By the time the elevator takes you up to the 28th floor, security is already there to greet you. You pull the "Emergency Stop" to freeze the elevator just as the first guard fires his Taser. The metal darts intended to hook into your flesh and allow the flow of electricity simply *plink* off your diamond-like skin.

You rush forward, grab the guard by the shirt, and throw him *through* a plate-glass window. The rest of the security staff stumbles back as you walk up to the reception desk, where a terrified young girl cowers.

"I'm here to see Alison Argyle," you say, as if this were nothing out of the ordinary. The receptionist simply whimpers.

The *crack* of a gunshot rips through the silent fear and something like a bee sting hits you in the forehead. You pull the flattened bullet from your skin, then look to the would-be hero—a reporter with a concealed carry license. He stands with his revolver outstretched, his legs in a half-squat, just like he's practiced at the gun range. Smoke curls from the barrel.

You lean over the receptionist's desk, where you find a three-hole punch, a candy bowl, and a picture of the receptionist, smiling with her parents. In a quick, athletic move, you claim the three-hole punch and fling it at the gunman—perfectly connecting with the man's forehead.

The newsroom erupts with panicked screams.

"That's enough!" a woman cries out. Reporter Alison Argyle steps forward. "You're the one from the robbery?"

"I'm here to do an interview."

"What's your name?"

"Don't ask who I am, ask *what* I am," you say, the words flowing from a dark place deep within. "I am a Roman god in the flesh, a fitting ruler of a city named after one, don't you think?"

"It's actually named for the old mining operations," she says, her voice inviting challenge.

"Not anymore." Didn't she just see you shake off a bullet? "Set up the cameras, *now*."

One of the staffers timidly says, "It takes the better part of an hour to set up, do a sound check, get you into make-up, and—"

"*THAT WASN'T A REQUEST!*" you boom through superhuman lungs.

"I—we can't do it," the man babbles.

"We'll do it live." Alison says, though no one seems convinced. "We'll do it live, *fuck it*, we'll do it live! I'll write it, let's go, people."

365

"This is reporter Alison Argyle, K-HAN Action News, reporting live and under duress in an exclusive interview with the mysterious new criminal terrorizing our fair city." You smile at the camera. She continues, "You've shown yourself strong enough to break through walls with ease, tough enough to resist gunfire, and morally corrupt enough to steal whatever you'd like. But do you have any weaknesses? Why don't we start there?"

"Besides your winning smile, Alison?" you say with charm. "No, I'm afraid not, but I must object to being called 'morally corrupt.' Is it morally corrupt to brush ants off your picnic blanket? When you are superior to human beings, you're superior to their morality as well. Who are you to lecture a god? If you were like me, a Roman—"

That's when the building's power goes out and the generators flip on, bathing the studio in the dim red glow of the emergency lights.

"What the—" you start, but the shouts of the SWAT team silence your protests. Mercury City PD's anti-terrorism unit comes from the stairwell, rifles aimed right at you, offering shouts for you to get face-down on the floor. Alison complies, you do not.

You step forward and the men open fire. The gunshots hurt like a sonofabitch, and your clothing fragments under the hail of bullets, but all they're really accomplishing is pissing you off.

In a few inhuman strides, you close the gap and meet the police officers head-on. They're just as surprised as you are that you can bound so quickly, and you backhand the lead SWAT member–sending him flying down the hallway with a sickening *crunch*. The rest of the team retreats and opens up canisters of tear gas.

Somehow it's this tear gas—a chemical—that finally effects you. The bullets all *ping* off harmlessly, but now your eyes and lungs burn ferociously and tears and mucous flow freely.

➢ Chase the cops down. They'll pay for their blasphemous tear gassing!
  Go to page 34
➢ Get out! Ahhh, it burns! Get some fresh air right now! Gahhh!!!
  Go to page 149

Wrong Answer

You can actually hear the man's teeth grinding under the pressure of his clenched jaw.

"Fuck off."

The door slams shut and the dead-bolt scratches into place. Woops. You turn back to Agent Droakam for support, but all you get is a repeated gesture: he's telling you to force your way in.

Either that, or he's imitating Ryu from *Street Fighter*, but you're pretty certain it's the former.

No other option here, time to *hadouken* your way in:

➢ *Blast the door open, take them by force.* Go to page 33

You're Doing It Wrong

"No need," the machine responds. "It is evident in your programming."

"What do you mean?" you ask.

The robot turns toward you, its hands raised at your throat.

"I know you are curious why the accident gave you intellectual supremacy over the rest of your species. I can dissect you to learn the answer."

"Wait, no!" you shout.

You duck away from the robot's grasp, back into the lighthouse. A frown appears on its face and the arms drop to its side. In a frantic sprint, you go down the spiral staircase, each step echoing inside the decayed building.

When you make it down to the landing, the machine *slams* against the floor, the leap denting and cracking the foundation. The robot rises before you and you step backwards, pinned against the wall.

It raises its hands, palms forward. "I am sorry; this was my first attempt at humor. Did I do it wrong?"

You pause. "W-what?"

"My searches of your Internet show an alarming belief that computer technology would be prone to violence. I wanted to offer friendly companionship through a joke."

After explaining to the robot exactly how *wrong* the joke was (and after changing your pants), you confirm that your goal was to have an intellectual companion.

➤ *If you are to have a friend, that friend should have a name...* Go to page 357

Your Whole Life Ahead

You awaken with fresh zeal, an electric energy, excited about the road before you. Just to prove it wasn't all a dream, you *float* out of bed, legs crossed like a stoic genie summoned for breakfast.

Out in the living room, you tell the TV to flip on and check out the morning news. There on screen is blonde eye-candy reporter, Alison Argyle, sitting at her news desk and speaking directly into the camera.

"…police still have no suspects in regard to the explosion yesterday that decimated Mercury University campus. No bodies were found on-scene, so it's unclear if it was an attack or an accident. They are, however, looking into the whereabouts of Dr. Julius Petri—the name given by the man who rented the lab space. The Mayor's office warns that this is most likely an alias and therefore gives suspicion of foul play."

You flip off the TV by activating the remote with your telekinesis, then look out your window.

- Are you kidding me? I'm never leaving the house again. Time for the floating of the cheesy puffs into m'mouf! Go to page 18
- I'm basically a Jedi; time to put on a robe and protect the innocent. Go to page 83
- Why not have more fun? As long as I don't draw attention to myself, no one will know I have superpowers. Go to page 252

You've Probably Never Heard of Me....

The hipster of superheroes, you go indie. It's shockingly difficult to convince people that you're a superhero and not, you know, a lunatic. It doesn't help that you follow up your good deeds with demands of food or payment. Crime may not pay, but neither does heroism, and ravenous hunger leaves you no choice.

Even the footage from your daring skyscraper rescue is turned against you. Apparently your leap into a fourth-story window and general mayhem inside the building overshadowed the fact that you saved people—and the very fact of the fire itself. It doesn't take long before people start to speculate you caused the fire.

Your predilection towards breaking criminals in half doesn't buy you many friends and your efforts toward becoming the world's first superhero end up convincing the world that you're its first supervillain.

Which doesn't make it much of a surprise when Nick and Catherine team up to "bring you to justice." Good luck, though, right? If anything, they're an inconvenience.

Until Catherine shoots you with a ray gun of her own devising. You expect it to harmlessly bounce off, like the hailstorm of bullets Mercury PD offer every time you meet, but the energy beam she fires saps your strength. You fall to the ground.

"What did you do to me?" you cry, though you know. You can feel it; your powers are gone.

"Made you mortal," she says. "Enjoy prison."

THE END

You've Seen Too Many Movies

Bait the trap. The agent's been following Nick and Catherine around without backup, which can only mean one thing: He's not officially supposed to be doing it. So you send them out, with your drones flying surveillance, and get him to tail one of them back to the mine.

If done right, Agent Droakam will think he's being Mr. Super-spy and he'll follow the scent of honey right into the beehive. Get them to drop some line about "the secret plan" and he'll get himself captured in order to learn it; then, while you're dangling him over a pit of sharks with lasers on their heads, you'll spill your guts just before he escapes, right?

Wrong—you're far too smart for that.

"So you must be the third test-subject," the agent says when they bring him in. "Secret base built out of an abandoned mine, very supervillain-chic. Plan on conquering the world?"

"Did you really get yourself captured in hopes of learning our plan?" you say, shaking your head. You take out a handgun—one of the firearms acquired in the bank heist—and chamber a round.

"What's the gun for?" Catherine asks.

"What do you think? You don't let the 'hero' into your lair and let him live. Villainy 101."

"Before you kill me, will you at least let me know what this is all about?"

BANG! Right between the eyes.

"No."

"Jesus! You just killed a federal agent!" Nick shouts.

Catherine drops down to see if he's really dead. Yep, sure is.

"Relax. He was an enemy combatant; he knew the risks. It's not like I go around tying women to train tracks. He had to go, and you both know it."

Catherine gasps. She pulls the downed agent's shirt open. "Oh, shit! He's wearing a wire."

You drop down and yank the wire off, separating it from the battery.

"Nick, get ready for the SWAT team!" Over at the monitors, you check live feed from the drones. Nothing. There's no one outside. "Where the hell is everyone?"

Then it clicks. The newsfeed said they were going to ask for military support, right? This Droakam is a *federal* agent. He's not working with the local police. You turn the drones skyward. A tiny aircraft, high in the heavens, floats along like a batplane. How did your radar not pick it up?

In an instant, a speck of dust on the lens becomes an incoming missile as the bunker-buster drops your way. Deep penetration, *KABOOOOM!!!!*

THE END

3, 2, 1...Shoot!

Catherine fires *Widowsilk* at this Earth's version of herself, the villain known as Shadow Priestess. As the energy field surrounds the cloaked woman, Drillbit flings the vault door at your-Catherine with incredible force—a ferocity matched only by your own.

You bound forward, intercept the projectile, and deliver a leaping uppercut punch to the vault door. It's an incredibly athletic move that sends the massive door crashing up through the bank's roof and into the sky. When you turn back, you see your-Catherine deliver the stolen powers to herself in a beam of spine-arching ecstasy.

"Take his powers!" you cry.

The genius-telekinetic shakes her head. In a breathless, post-climax voice, she says, "It's only got two shots in the chamber; keep him busy while I recharge!"

Drillbit takes a monkey wrench from his tool belt and swings it at your head. You bring up a forearm to block the blow and the wrench shears in half from the stress. The tool doesn't hurt your perfect skin, but you can feel the strength the superpowered villain put behind it.

You deliver a counterpunch and this-Nick stumbles back in a daze. It's obvious he's gotten used to his invulnerability, and you've shaken him. But then he smiles. The realization is all over his face: If you can hurt him, he can hurt you too.

The now-powerless Shadow Priestess lets out a feral cry and charges at your-Catherine to take her revenge. Testing out her new power, the genius-telekinetic *lifts* her doppelganger in the air.

"Nick, take over!" she cries.

The telekinetic college student nods and steps forward. With an outstretched hand, he holds the Shadow Priestess in the air so your-Catherine can go back to the weapon.

Drillbit comes at you with his head ducked down in a charge, and there's no stopping this freight train. He smashes into you and plows you through the wall, out into the open street. The entire Mercury City Police Force draws down on you from behind their barricade, but can only watch in awe as two titans do battle.

You deliver a ferocious kick to Nick from your position on the ground. He flies back toward the bank, smashing through a third-floor window. As he leaps back out to the street, your-Catherine emerges from the hole in the bank wall, *Widowsilk* at full charge and a smile on her face.

Drillbit senses his demise and goes to run, but you cut him off and deliver a clothesline with an outstretched arm. He falls back and you kick him out to the middle of the street, where he's blasted by the future-tech rifle.

This-Nick screams in agony as his strength is sapped, a sound instantly counteracted by your-Nick's moans of pleasure when he's given a second superpower. Darkness clouds over his eyes as the telekinesis blends with super-strength to make the college student near-omnipotent. He floats into the air, strength rippling across his body.

He raises his palms, and in response the police cruisers and news vans of the barricade float into the air. Your genius mind quickly deduces: Nick was once limited by his mental perception of his own strength when it came to telekinesis, but now that he's gained super-strength—the telekinetic barrier just got smashed as easily as that bank wall. Nick raises the police officers and bystanders into the air as well, holding thousands of pounds afloat with ease.

Then he destroys all of them with one thought.

Gore and machinery splash against the buildings of downtown. Just like that, the whole police force, gone. He turns, looks at you and Catherine, his face drunk with power, and smiles a cruel smile.

Then he raises his hands toward you.

Scream:

- "Nick! A god must be omniscient—all-knowing. What is power without knowledge? One more universe, right? Then we'll truly be gods."
Go to page 321
- "Catherine, quick, take his powers! He's too strong! He's gone mad!"
Go to page 251

The Book Club Reader's Guide

If you want a Monet Experience (no spoilers), avoid these questions until after you've read through SUPERPOWERED to your heart's content. OR.... Take 1-2 weeks, progress through as many story iterations as you can, while keeping the following questions in mind. Then, meet with your reader's group and discuss:

1) Which superpower did you pick first? Which was your favorite?

2) Discuss your impressions of Nick and Catherine. Did you like or dislike these characters? Did that change as the narrative progressed?

3) How did the story end for you the first time? Share your experiences with the group.

4) What would you say was the "best ending" you found? Talk about from both perspectives: saving the world vs conquering it.

5) There are certain expected norms in superhero/comic book fiction. To what extent did SUPERPOWERED uphold these traditions? Has Schannep added anything new to the genre?

6) Both Nick and Catherine can fight for good or for evil, depending on your interactions with them. What does this say about human nature and fate?

7) There are several vignettes off the beaten path. What was your favorite "hidden gem"?

8) SUPERPOWERED shows that even in a fantasy world where you're given god-like powers, there are still consequences for your actions. In what ways do these consequences grow with your newfound potential?

9) Did you enjoy playing as a hero or playing as a villain more? Which was easier to win? Did which superpower you possessed make any difference?

10) How did you feel about being "in control" of the story? Did you feel more or less involved than you do with traditional books?

11) Did you feel you were rewarded for altruistic or selfish actions? For reserved or brazen choices? Defend your positions.

12) Did you come into this book as a fan of superhero movies, comic books, video games, or novels? All or none of the above? Has that position altered your experience? Are you more or less likely to seek out superhero prose?

* If you're the type who stays after the credits, turn to page 112 for a bonus scene.